PRAISE FOR *BL*

"Bryan Gruley's *Bleak Harbor* is an ele...... ...., ...
with twists and surprises. Gruley's plot races along, powered by
characters—big and small—who truly crackle. A masterful follow-up
to his Starvation Lake trilogy."

—Gillian Flynn, #1 *New York Times* bestselling author of *Gone Girl*

"The best book Gruley has ever written and unlike any other crime
book I've ever read."

—Steve Hamilton, two-time Edgar Award–winning author of
Exit Strategy

"Bryan Gruley creates a fascinating calamity of flawed characters, each
hiding secrets in the haunting town of Bleak Harbor. His portrayal
of an autistic boy's kidnapping, and the subsequent efforts to find
and rescue him, gradually and brilliantly exposes the decidedly dark
underbelly of both the town and all those living in it. I dare you to put
the book down. I couldn't."

—Robert Dugoni, #1 *Wall Street Journal* bestselling author

"The myth of the happy family! Bryan Gruley dives deep into twisted
psyches, well-hidden secrets, and dark, explosive desires. Welcome to
Bleak Harbor. Be afraid."

— Tess Gerritsen, *New York Times* bestselling author

"Vivid, spellbinding, and laced with tension, *Bleak Harbor*'s
labyrinthine mystery is packed with characters so real you want to buy
them a beer—or hide under your bed to pray they don't come for you.
If you're not reading Bryan Gruley, you're missing out."

—Marcus Sakey, bestselling author of *AFTERLIFE* and the
Brilliance trilogy

BLEAK
HARBOR

OTHER TITLES BY BRYAN GRULEY

THE STARVATION LAKE TRILOGY

Starvation Lake
The Hanging Tree
The Skeleton Box

NONFICTION

Paper Losses

BLEAK HARBOR

BRYAN GRULEY

THOMAS & MERCER

Published by Thomas & Mercer, Seattle
www.apub.com

Amazon, the Amazon logo, and Thomas & Mercer are trademarks of Amazon.com, Inc., or its affiliates.

ISBN-13: 9781503904682 (hardcover)
ISBN-10: 1503904687 (hardcover)

ISBN-13: 9781503904675 (paperback)
ISBN-10: 1503904679 (paperback)

Cover design by Shasti O'Leary Soudant

Printed in the United States of America

First edition

For Joel, Miles, and Sawyer

PROLOGUE

"You won't hurt the boy?"

"Not if I don't have to."

"Do not hurt him."

"How 'bout his mother?"

"I didn't hear that."

"Heh. I'll take the kid for a milkshake. Least that's what I'll tell him."

"He's a troubled young man."

"Dude, he's fifteen. You weren't fucked up at fifteen?"

"He'll be sixteen soon. That could be our deadline."

"Serious?"

"Things appear to be headed in that direction."

"Which things?"

"Again, none of your business. You need to worry about getting him to the safe place. He won't throw a fit or something?"

"The kid's got issues, but he ain't crazy."

"You've been in touch with him?"

"I told you, him and I are good. And there ain't no neighbors. Bank took the one place, and nobody's ever at the other one."

"Should we go over the details once more?"

"I got mine. What about you? The bitch is gonna call the cops."

"Once they realize the boy's really gone, of course they'll contact the police. Remember, though, he ran away before. They called the police, and it was embarrassing for everyone."

"That was then."

"It's the Bleak Harbor Police. By the time they get a clue, the boy will be in the safe place, and you will be long gone with your money."

"Better be."

"Plus, there's the festival in town. The cops will be busy."

"Who the hell has a dragonfly festival anyway?"

"Remember: do not contact me. Just wait. Don't change a thing about your life. Keep working where you work."

"I'll be glad to get the hell out of there."

"Not until the job is done."

"Don't even think about trying to pin it on me."

"That would be foolish for everyone involved."

"Don't forget it."

"Trust me—my client is a much bigger fish than you."

"Your client better just have my money ready."

"The initial payment was transferred fourteen minutes ago. The rest will be tendered when the job is complete."

"Tendered?"

"You will have it."

"A hundo now, two and a half later."

"As agreed upon."

"And your boss, whoever the hell he is, gets to be the hero."

"Not your concern. Now, you may find it tempting—"

"Is this client screwing my ex, by chance?"

"—to take the down payment and run. That would be a bad idea."

"Don't worry."

"Just as we can help you disappear, we can find you. You saw the photos from North Dakota."

"Seen 'em. Nice dogs. Pits or rotts? I'm a rott guy myself."

"Those people thought they were home free with a semi full of catalytic converters. They were mistaken."

"I seen worse. My boss ain't no shrinking violet, you know."

"Once you have the boy, use the disposable, and text the number I'm about to give you. Do you have something to write with?"

"Putting it in the phone right now . . . got it."

"Did you write it down?"

"It's in the phone, man."

"Write it down, please, then delete it from the phone."

"All right, Jesus, hold on . . . OK. Written down."

"Send one letter: *Y* for yes, you have him. *X* for no."

"Yo."

"After that, wait for us to contact you. My signal could come at any moment. When this is done, we will never speak again."

"Fuckin' A. Fine by me."

THURSDAY

1

Danny sits at the end of the dock, watching.

The dragonfly appears to his left, skimming a flat line one foot above the glassine surface of the bay.

It skitters up as if on a wire and takes the first mosquito without slowing. Danny pictures the cruelly efficient jaws and serrated teeth tearing the prey into a gooey black mash while the dragonfly plots the geometric path to its next target.

"Pretty pretty pretty dragonflies . . . pretty pretty." Danny sings softly into the sunshine, the lilting ditty his mother made up when he was a little boy. He stops and listens. He knows he was singing a little off-key. He closes his eyes.

And smiles, feels the sun warm on his cheeks.

He adds the mosquito to the running tally in his head: 694 since Saturday morning, heading for a record by sundown Friday.

Which will be Danny's sixteenth birthday.

"Sweet sixteen," his mother told him.

"What's so sweet about it?"

"It's just a saying, honey. You're sweet every day."

No, Danny thought then. *I don't think I want to be sweet.*

The dragonfly vanishes into the cloudless blue to his right. It will soon be back for more. Danny dips a toe into the bay and kicks up some water, watches the scatter of beads settle back into the bay, many becoming one again.

Down the pebbled-sand shoreline that winds around to downtown Bleak Harbor, the upper arc of a Ferris wheel juts above the shops and bars along Blossom Street. Danny imagines the smells of hamburger grease and powdered sugar, the impatient shrieks of children, the contorted faces of clowns and drunks. The Twenty-Eighth Annual Southwestern Michigan Dragonfly Festival begins tomorrow.

Twenty-eight years ago, Danny thinks, *the Cubs should have won the World Series.*

The festival was what first interested him in Anisoptera, the dragonfly, when he and his mother came from Chicago to visit her parents. He sometimes wonders whether any of the people attending the festival actually know what the dragonfly is about, how its flitting beauty, wings aglint in sun, masks the bloodless killer within. Probably not.

He shifts his gaze across the bay to the Joseph E. Bleak Public Library, between city hall and a parking lot that will be crammed all weekend with cars and trucks and SUVs bearing out-of-state license plates. Danny was at the library yesterday and other days before that, stationed at a microfilm machine, reading local history. He'd taken a liking to the library since moving to Bleak Harbor.

Zelda, the librarian, always helped him when the microfilm roller got stuck, as it often did. And Danny would watch as she fiddled with the machine, fixated on how Zelda had put on her makeup that day, whether she had smeared her red lipstick or layered her mascara so thick that it clotted. She had recently separated from her husband, and Danny had noticed that since then, her mascara was usually not right, and some days she skipped it altogether.

Sometimes he would imagine Zelda at her vanity mirror, calling out orders to her four children—Gregory, Helen, Ronald, Alex; names Danny knew because he'd asked her—as she did her makeup, noticing a fresh gray strand in her blonde waves, making a face at it. She never made a face when Danny asked for help. He was used to people making faces at him. But Zelda's smile was patient and true. "It's no trouble,

Daniel; that's why I'm here," she would say. He liked the way she said "Daniel."

When he was leaving the library yesterday, he stopped at the desk where Zelda was sorting returned books. She didn't notice him at first, and he just waited and watched until she looked up and saw him. "Oh, I'm so sorry, Daniel," she said. "How long have you been standing there?"

"I'm fine."

"Is the machine giving you trouble again?"

Danny shook his head and said, "I just wanted to say something, Mrs. Loiselle."

"All righty," she said, "and what is that?"

"You are a very beautiful woman."

She blushed, and for a second, Danny thought she might cry. "Oh, my," she said, "you're such a nice boy."

"I don't know. Thank you for your help. I hope to see you again."

———

Pete didn't know how much time Danny spent at the library because he wasn't home a lot during the day. Today, though, he had stopped at the cottage to check on him. Danny was out on the dock.

"I gotta go to this meeting, or your mother will have my nuts," he told Danny. Of course Pete didn't want to go. He wanted to spend the afternoon praying customers would come to his medical marijuana shop downtown. But Danny's mother was ninety-seven miles away in Chicago and wouldn't be home till after five o'clock.

"Dulcy's at the shop in case you need something and you can't reach me," Pete said. "Coverage sucks inside city hall."

"How is Dulcy?" Danny asked.

"She needs to work on her English. And her punctuality. Why? You got the hots for her?"

Pete thought that was funny. That's how he was.

"She's nice."

"Nice and late, every morning."

"Maybe she's not a morning person."

"Unfortunately, some of our clients are morning people. You gonna pack the cooler?"

"Yes. For fishing. When will you be home?"

"Sixish. Gotta stop back at the dope den after the meeting."

No, Danny thought. *You gotta stop at the bar.*

"The cooler will be ready," he said.

"You feeling up to it?"

"I feel fine. The sun's been good today."

"OK. Pack a whole six-pack. I'm gonna need it."

———

Danny stands and walks back toward the house. He likes the sting of the nailheads in the sunbaked planks on the bottoms of his feet.

Stepping off the dock, he crosses the sand to the deck attached to the cottage. He finds his cell phone on the picnic table next to his book. He turns the phone on and taps in his password.

There's a new text message:

milkshakes at 5 al right >?

Danny doesn't really like milkshakes. But he answers:

K have to be back before 6.

The reply comes immediately.

c u soon

2

Carey fights the tears until she hits the Skyway Bridge into northwest Indiana. She catches a glimpse of downtown Chicago in her side-view mirror. A flash of sunlight off a window high on one of the skyscrapers looses the sobs. They shake her so hard that she almost jerks her car off the road. She closes her eyes, feels the soggy burn of her tears, tries to wrest herself out of the nightmare.

She picks up her phone and rereads the text, wishing it would disappear:

we know about v day

The blurt of a horn startles her. She glances up and sees the trucker's frown as his semi pulls up on her right. She looks at the phone in her hand and realizes she's been gliding along below the speed limit in the left lane of Interstate 94 East.

"Sorry, sorry," she says, thinking, *I am such a wimp.*

The trucker slows and holds steady alongside her, staring from behind mirrored glasses. *He doesn't know*, Carey thinks. *Don't be ridiculous.* She waves him on and flicks her blinker and eases into the right lane. The trucker pulls away, shaking his head.

Bitch, she tells the rearview mirror. She sets her phone aside, picks it up again immediately, glances in her rearview, sees nobody close, starts typing with her right thumb while steering with her left:

talk to my lawyer

The phone pings with a response:

better get one ms peters

Fuck you, she thinks. *Fuck me. Fuck everybody.*
Everybody but Danny.

Carey is in over her head. She knows this as clearly as she knows the distances from the Loop to exit 21 at Interstate 94, from there to the Michigan border, from the blue **WELCOME TO MICHIGAN** sign spanning the highway to the sandy bluffs along the big lake and the little cottage in Bleak Harbor where Danny waits. She knows it as clearly as she knows how much she loathes making this drive.

She takes a breath. Everything will be all right, she tells herself. One way or another, she will gain the freedom to put her life where she wants it, away from her husband and Chicago and Michigan and everything but her son. She isn't about to give up this time. She isn't about to settle again.

She flips the sun visor down. The snapshot paper clipped there was taken five years ago, when Danny was ten. He's wearing his auburn hair the way Carey loves it, long and curly down the sides of his narrow face, his saucer eyes the green of Lake Michigan on a crystal summer morning. He is standing beneath an enormous silver sculpture in Chicago's Loop, an ice-cream sandwich melting in one hand as he gazes up at the countless reflections of himself in the sculpture's shiny skin, all the ice-cream sandwiches dripping in the heat.

And he's grinning. The photograph is too small to see the thin gap in Danny's front teeth or the pale freckles on his cheeks, but Carey imagines them and allows herself a fleeting smile. She loves this picture.

She sees herself in Danny's face, his eyes, his curls. He's happy. She wants to be happy. She wants to be happy with him again.

She tries to remember, as she does whenever she's feeling down or overwhelmed—a lot, of late—how hard he squeezed her this morning when he hugged her goodbye. Then she recalls—she'd almost forgotten—that he whispered in her ear, "Be happy, Mommy. OK?" She just laughed and shook her head. She wishes now that she had squeezed him right back and said, "You too, my beautiful boy."

Or was that yesterday? Or last week? Between her commute and working and nights falling asleep on the sofa watching shows about couples buying homes in exotic foreign cities, Carey loses track of time.

People tell her how beautiful Danny is. Because he *is* beautiful, as beautiful a boy as Carey could have hoped for. But also, she thinks, they say so as some nebulous means of solace, as if his looks are a trade-off for the things about her son that they will never understand, as if it is a tragedy that Danny is so lovely a boy at the same time that he is so unattainable to them. Carey has taught herself to tune them all out, even the various doctors with their various, supposedly well-intentioned labels—autism, apraxia, on the spectrum, pervasive developmental disorder, high functioning and low. None of them matter anymore.

Tomorrow, she will have Danny to herself. She will work from home and make him his CoCo Wheats with maple bacon on the side. She will tell her husband to go to his pot shop and stay there, busy or not. She and Danny will walk the beach to the channel and count the boats chugging out to Lake Michigan, maybe stop for a cold pop at the little shop at the channel's mouth.

Back home, they'll sit in the adirondacks on the deck and pass the book back and forth, reciting Danny's favorite poem. They'll recall again how Carey mistook the palm in the poem's opening line for a hand instead of the tree it is. Carey will raise an open palm and point at it and shake her head, and she and her son will laugh again.

And Danny will point past his mother across the bay, past the drowsing sloops and catamarans, the festive tavern decks, beyond to the stolid pink mansion looming above it all, judging the town from one side, Lake Michigan from the other. Once Carey called it "the wedge of space," mangling a line in Danny's favorite poem, "because," she said, "that's it—there's nothing in the world after that, nothing but the big damn lake."

It made Danny laugh. "The wedge of space," he said. "Yes. Between town and the lake."

Her phone beeps in her hand. She starts to look at the text, changes her mind, sticks the phone in a cup holder.

There was a time when even her short absences from home were intolerable for the boy, even if Pete was with him. Carey would return to glass shattered across the kitchen floor, smears of peanut butter and grape jam spelling obscenities on the walls, Pete rushing to clean up, Danny adept at timing his tantrums so that Pete would have to share the blame.

Where were you? Carey would demand of Pete when she thought they were out of Danny's earshot. Pete would shrug and make an excuse about a business call he had to take or a fishing reel he had to rig. *No*, Carey would say, *no excuses*, Pete wincing at the submerged pique surfacing in her voice, averting his eyes, apologizing partly because he was sorry but mostly to make her stop.

Then they would not speak for a day, maybe two or three. Sometimes Danny himself would go quiet, withholding even one-word replies, and Carey would wonder if it was because she had been gone or because he'd overheard the words she'd hurled at Pete or if it was just Danny being Danny, retreating into himself.

She picks up the phone, reads the text, wishes she had never gotten involved with the feds:

u have until end of the week. then i'll be at your door. v day
betwn us——for now.

She remembers how cold it was on February 14, how the Chicago
wind clawed at her cheeks after she left Randall Pressman's building to
hail a cab just after midnight.

He had taken her to Alinea to celebrate her promotion to executive
assistant, finance, at Pressman Logistics. Randall Pressman didn't believe
in glorified titles; his four executive assistants, all women under the age
of forty, were the most important and best-paid people at his company
except, of course, for himself. The chef had come by their private table
to shake Pressman's hand with both of his, explaining the unexplainable
food. After dinner, Carey had vowed to go back to her studio rental
alone, but there was Dom Perignon on ice and red roses in the back of
the limo, and Pressman, without asking her, had the driver take them
to his building on the Chicago River.

Forty-five minutes later, she had fucked her boss.

Now, as she eases back into the left lane and pushes the speed
higher, she hears his contented moan as he rolled off of her, sees his flat-
ted palms smoothing the mat of wiry white on his chest. She remembers
how she wrapped herself in a blanket and went to the floor-to-ceiling
windows, staring into the reflection of her porcelain skin, her wide eyes
set off by the angular sculpt of her cheekbones, the things that made
men like Pressman want her. She looked through the reflection to see
steam swirling out of the stacks atop a steel-and-glass tower across the
river and wished she could fling herself down the seventeen floors into
the water, all the way to the cold black bottom.

That night had been a slip on her part. A bad one. A terrible one.
Though she had to admit, in retrospect, it was one she'd made all but
inevitable. She'd let herself get caught up in the client dinners, the Gold
Coast pied-à-terre Pressman had insisted on having the company lease

for her. So she didn't have to worry about the commute, he'd said, and she'd let herself believe it. She'd let herself be taken in by the idea that she was valuable, even indispensable, to Pressman Logistics. In fact she was good at her job. But there was only one indispensable employee at that company.

His palms, she thinks, *oh God, dear God*, his sandpaper palms pressing on her shoulders as he groaned his climax. She shudders with disgust. He was old enough to have said that maybe one day they could have a "nooner," a word Carey once heard her philandering late father use. She flips the visor back up and rolls her window down, welcoming the rush of wind.

"I'm sorry," she says, to no one.

She picks up her phone and punches 1. She hears Danny's end ringing, hoping he will answer, knowing he probably will not. The voice mail comes on after five rings. "This isn't exactly Danny," his voice says, followed by silence, then a beep.

She wishes Danny's reply said something about leaving a message, something welcoming to those few who reached out to him. He seems steadier these days yet still absents himself from—she struggles for the word, reluctant to land on it—from life. She ends the call, hits 2. The phone rings on without going to voice mail. Pete isn't answering, no surprise. She hopes he isn't out on the deck with a cooler of beer but in the city council meeting she asked him to attend in her place. Pete certainly would not enjoy the meeting, but it was the least he could do while she was driving back and forth from Chicago to Bleak Harbor two or three times a week.

Another call comes in, one she was half expecting and dreading at the same time. "Carey Peters," she says.

"Why so formal?" The caller chuckles.

"You think this is funny?"

"No."

"You have till tomorrow," she says. "After that, I hand the stuff over, and you deal with the feds."

"You're not really going to go through with this."

"I am, and I will."

Pressman goes silent for a few seconds. Then, "Think about it, babe. Some of those documents have your name on them too. You're in this as deep as anyone."

"No, I'm not. And do not call me babe."

"You're going to blow up a bunch of lives, including your own."

I have every intention of blowing up my life, Carey thinks, *just not the way you assume*. "You can keep that from happening, Randall."

"Come on. This is extortion, plain and simple. What if I go to the police?"

"Go ahead."

Pressman gets quiet again, then says, "So this is really just about that one night."

No, Carey thinks but does not say. She can't hold that frozen Valentine's Day against Pressman entirely. He didn't rape her. Not literally. But he responded to her subsequent declinations and refusals by moving her from the office adjoining his to a smaller one on the floor below and supplanting her with a younger woman, his new executive assistant for transportation. He hinted that he might need Carey to move to one of the company's satellite offices, in Cleveland or, worse, Duluth.

He was too smart and too cowardly to simply fire her and face the publicity of yet another sexual harassment claim from yet another younger subordinate. Instead, he'd make sure that Carey's job slowly turned to shit.

Lucky for her, Pressman had gotten sloppy as his net worth grew and his stature in the business pantheon climbed: cover of *Fortune* magazine, Executive Club honoree, *Crain's Chicago Business* CEO of the Year. He'd gotten too busy, too worshipped, too much in demand.

Although he'd moved Carey's office, he had neglected to change the passwords he'd given her to attend to certain sensitive business activities. She'd spent two long nights in the tiny office beneath his using those passwords to fill her email inbox with company documents she wasn't supposed to have. She couldn't read all of them—some had been stamped in an Asian script—but she suspected, if she didn't outright know, that they showed Pressman Logistics wasn't always transporting legal cargo.

She had briefly considered giving the documents to the man who's been texting her, at the risk of losing her job and her benefits. Instead, she had determined that the documents she possessed were worth $10 million. She'd picked the number out of an article she'd read in *Us* magazine about what a famous and talentless actor had been paid for a two-minute cameo in a vampire flick. With $10 million, she and Danny could live off the interest for the rest of their lives. She wouldn't have to work. She could focus on being her son's best mother.

And $10 million would be a pittance to Pressman. It was less than half the bonus he had paid himself the year before. She really wasn't being greedy. Extortionate, yes, criminal, yes, but not greedy.

"How many times do I have to say I'm sorry?" Pressman says. "Can't you—we—just let it go?"

"You obviously couldn't. Anyway, this isn't about that anymore. It's about freedom, for both of us. You can afford it. And I'll disappear. Think of it as severance."

Carey hears the guttural whoosh of a boat passing on Pressman's end of the call. She pictures him on the veranda of his condo, sipping a martini. She lowers the phone, looks at the texts again. How the hell did this guy know about Valentine's Day?

"Sweetie," Pressman says, "the limp-dick feds have been trying to nail me for years. It will never happen."

Being called sweetie doesn't rankle Carey as much as her growing suspicion that Pressman can detect how desperate she is. It's precisely that cynical sense of the way things really work that makes men like Randall Pressman so rich and powerful. Carey had learned that from her father. How could she have forgotten?

Ten million, she thinks now. *Too much*. She should have demanded one or two million, no more, and Pressman would have paid her in fifties and hundreds to make her go away. Ten million drew some line he would not cross, not with a woman, not with a woman who worked for him, not with a woman he'd had between his sheets.

What had she been thinking?

She knows what she'd been thinking. She'd been thinking about that night, about how ashamed and furious she'd felt.

She tries now to summon some of that revulsion to steel her nerve. "Stop with the bullshit, Randall," she says. "Get me the money, or you and your company will be screwed."

"Carey, rich guys don't go to jail. You know that. You read the *Wall Street Journal.* Little guys go to jail. And little girls."

"Fuck you."

"What do you think the jury's going to think when they hear the star witness slept with the defendant?"

"They're going to put you in jail."

"No. Think about this, Carey. You're in over your head here. You know you are. But you have time. You don't have to burn this bridge. Call me tomorrow if you want—"

She ends the call and flips the phone onto the passenger seat. "Go to fucking hell." The phone bounces off the seat onto the floor. She starts to reach for it, decides not to, mutters, "Damn it."

The phone zizzes. A text. Maybe Danny. Again she stretches out her right arm, but the phone is out of reach. She takes a deep breath. Everything will work out, she tells herself. In the morning, she will call Pressman and tell him, *All right, you win, one million.* Or maybe two million. Two million will get him off the hook and her and Danny out of the country. He'll go for that. He'd be stupid not to. Two million will be enough.

She looks at the odometer. Sixty-nine miles to Danny. She steps on the gas and lurches into the left lane, thinking, *Two million, just two million, and everything is going to be fine.*

3

Pete feels the phone vibrate in his shorts pocket. Usually, on a July afternoon like this one, clear and blue with a breeze wafting off the lake, swirling down the channel and across the bay, he likes the buzzing sensation against his thigh, its comforting reminder that the world outside Boz's Bayfront Bar and Grill demands his attention and he can choose whether to grant it.

He yanks the phone out. Carey's calling. He'd rather not speak to his wife just yet, so he silences the phone and takes a sip from his vodka and tonic. He'll be seeing her soon enough. He did his duty, went to the city council meeting as she insisted. He can tell her all about it, what there is to tell, after he takes Danny fishing.

"So, Petey," Boz says. "Fun downtown?"

Boz leans his forearms on the bar. He grins, and tomato cheeks squeeze his eyes nearly shut beneath a cotton-white flattop. Boz is an ex–Chicago cop who took early retirement after a bullet splintered his left femur. He bought a plot of land, razed a defunct orphanage, and built a shack of knotty pine and four-chair tables with a wall of windows and screens opening on to a porch set on the beach. Pete appreciated Boz spelling *Grill* without an *e*, unlike the fancy joints on the downtown promenade across the bay. No ampersand either.

"Fun's not quite the word," Pete says. "Got there early and still couldn't get a seat. Found a nice wall to lean on, though."

Boz takes a drink from the plastic sport bottle filled with his early-evening rum. "The old lady show up?"

"No, never. Just her lawyers. A dozen or so, sitting up front, watching the circus."

"Buncha clowns, all right. They oughta sell peanuts."

———

The circus revolved around a peculiar proposition made months before by Serenity Meredith Maas Bleak, Pete's mother-in-law and Carey's mother.

Serenity was reputed to be the richest person in Bleak Harbor, perhaps in all of western Michigan, heiress to the fortune handed down through the descendants of Joseph Estes Bleak, the pointy-nosed New Englander who'd come to a shore of dune and swamp on Lake Michigan, dredged a channel, carved out a bay, and erected a harbor that birthed a shipping yard, a timber mill, a daily newspaper, and a burg of sturdy churches and families. The early Bleaks went so far as to build a massive steelworks across the Indiana border.

The timber mill was long gone; the steelworks shut; the tugs and barges replaced by sailboats and twin-screw cruisers; the downtown a flowery haven of cobblestone streets dotted with boutiques and galleries, overpriced restaurants, shops selling flip-flops for a hundred dollars a pair, even a bookstore. The cobblestone, made from a synthetic version of concrete, had been laid only in the past decade over the old, chipped, authentic stuff.

"Quaint," the travel catalogues inevitably called Bleak Harbor. "The Southampton of the Midwest." It was "renovated" and "refreshed" and a place where many of those sturdy families no longer could afford to live. Once a home, now a summer way station for people who wanted little to do with each other unless alcohol was handy, and plenty of it.

The main remnants of the city's past were the local newspaper, the *Bleak Harbor Light*, and Serenity herself, widow of Jack Bleak, who had died of a heart attack last Thanksgiving. Serenity hadn't been seen in public since being diagnosed with terminal cancer not long after her husband's passing. Local gossips speculated the cancer was cervical, the consequence of her late husband's playing around. Others thought it had to be liver cancer from Serenity's years of quiet, disciplined drinking. Nobody—not even Carey—really knew.

In a one-page statement released by her lawyers, Serenity had offered the city, the township, and the surrounding county, upon her death, her entire estate, rumored to be worth $200 million to $300 million. But there was a catch that was tripping up the politicians. As Serenity undoubtedly had expected.

———

"You gotta hand it to her," Pete says. "It's kinda like she gets to watch her own funeral, all these guys fighting over her money."

Boz nods. "She loves to mess with people. Like when I was trying to get my liquor license. I ever tell you that story?"

"Fifty or sixty times."

"Yeah, yeah. If only I could pull up and get the hell out of here."

"Any bites yet?"

"Nah, you know, I don't wanna just give it away."

"Smart."

"So tell me—why does Carey give a damn about those meetings? She ain't getting any of that money. She and the old lady don't even talk, do they?"

"Not much. But it's family. I do as I'm told."

Jack Bleak's will left Carey and her brother, Bleak Harbor mayor Jonah Bleak, nothing but a few acres of duneland set so far back from the shore as to be worthless. Serenity's lawyers are contesting even that paucity.

The rift between Serenity and her children dates back so far that nobody can recall its specific origins, except that Serenity didn't feel her kids defended her amply enough against the many slights and embarrassments her wayward husband inflicted upon her. Pete never understood exactly what she'd expected Carey and her brother to do. Their father was an asshole. They had to live with it too.

The year-round residents of Bleak Harbor are well aware, via the grapevine, that Carey and Jonah have been zeroed out of the family estate. Because of the locals' barely disguised feelings of pity and schadenfreude, Carey defiantly attends every public meeting concerning the disposition of the estate, when she isn't stuck working in Chicago. Pete suspects she goes partly to demonstrate that her pride is intact but also in search of something even she isn't sure of, some idea that she did what she could to close the chasm between her and her parents, especially after it turned out that Danny was not the perfect grandson they believed was their right.

Boz grunts. "You know, those numb nuts are already spending her money. The township ordered a Humvee last week."

"Today the council was talking about getting surveillance cameras."

"Keeping up with the Joneses."

"And, of course, a helicopter. Gotta have a helicopter."

"Shitbags. What in God's name for?"

"Emergencies."

"Like some asswipe at the festival gets drunk and falls down?"

"Or maybe they get high."

"Noooo," Boz says, mugging. "How is business anyway?"

Pete looks into his drink, shakes his head. "That shop in New Buffalo is killing me."

"New Buffalo sucks anyway. What's going on?"

Pete glances around the bar. Though he's been in the medical marijuana business for almost a year, he still isn't quite used to the idea that it's legal. "Their stuff's good," he says. "Maybe a little too good. Not that anybody uses it just to get high."

"No way." Boz points at his bad leg. "Totally therapeutic."

"And they're selling it for pennies."

"Undercutting you? Hey, man, that's what I do to the bars here." He waves at the row of taps on the bar. "Three bucks for a Schlitz pint—can't beat it, baby."

"Yeah, well, their stuff's more like Heineken. Anyway, I've been working with a new supplier."

"Local guy?"

Pete immediately wishes he hadn't brought it up. He squints toward one of the TVs mounted over the back bar. "Cubs up? I can't see the tube down there."

Boz ambles over and peers at the screen. "They were ahead 6–1. Now it's 6–5, and the Giants got the bases loaded, nobody out in the eighth."

"That's what my Cubbies do."

"Another cocktail? You know, you can't fly home on one wing."

Truth is, Pete wouldn't mind another drink and another and another. But then Carey would know he'd had another shitty day at the pot shop.

"A light one," he says. "Going fishing in a while here."

———

Pete couldn't tell whether Danny was genuinely happy that they were going fishing that night. He had left his shop downtown around three, putting Dulcy in charge so he could check on Danny before going to the city council meeting. He'd found his stepson standing on the dock, hands folded into the curls atop his head, gazing into the water. The boy's laptop was open on a picnic table on the deck.

"Ready to go out tonight?" Pete said.

Danny didn't move at first, as if he hadn't heard; then he slowly turned around, hands still on his head, and said, "I will have the cooler and the bait ready."

"Good," Pete said. "Going to that meeting. Back around six. I love you."

Again, Danny didn't seem to hear. Then, as Pete was going through the glass double doors to the house, he heard Danny say, "Peter."

It was a little joke. Pete's real name was Andrew Michael Peters. "Pete" was the nickname almost everyone called him. Pete stopped and turned around. "Yeah?"

Danny was looking right at him. "I love you," he said. Not *I love you too*, like he was answering Pete. Just *I love you*. He didn't say it often, but Pete sure appreciated it when he did.

"I love you too, pal."

Danny appeared to consider that for a moment. Then he said, "That's good. Do you love my mom, Peter?"

"Do I love your mom?" Pete laughed. "Of course."

"That's also good. Do you think my mom loves you?"

Pete cocked his head. "Come on, pal. Why wouldn't she?"

Danny turned away then. "Look," he said, pointing. "That one has taken sixteen mosquitoes since noon."

Pete looked, grateful for the distraction. He couldn't find the dragonfly Danny saw.

"Wow," he said anyway. "That a record?"

Danny didn't respond. But conversations with Danny often ended abruptly. Pete didn't take offense.

"OK," Pete said. "We'll get us a pile of fish later."

They fished two or three evenings a week in summer, anchoring in the deep middle of the bay or, when the water wasn't too rough, out on the lake a quarter mile from the seawalls flanking the channel. Pete would plunk his line on the port side, Danny on the starboard. Sometimes they caught enough for dinner, sometimes not a single fish. It didn't seem to make a difference to the boy. He threw back everything he caught anyway.

In the past year, Danny had gotten this thing about perch. Pete figured it had something to do with the baby perch that swam beneath the dock where Danny spent much of his summer afternoons. He was mesmerized by those damn little fish. Sometimes he'd ease into the bay and stand as still as he could, legs apart, staring down into the water. Once Pete asked him what he was doing. Danny kept staring. Pete waited.

"I want them to swim through," Danny said.

"Through your legs?"

Danny nodded. "They're afraid."

"Afraid of what?"

"Afraid of everything."

Pete smiled. "How can a little tiny fish be afraid of anything but a big fish?"

"They're all alone. Where are their parents?"

"Out there, I hope," Pete said, pointing toward the lake. "Waiting for us to catch them."

But now, when they were out fishing, Danny didn't like hooking perch at all. He'd read that the lake perch, a docile species that simply submitted once a hook was set in its mouth, might not survive the ascent to the boat if it was more than sixty or seventy feet. It could drown. So Danny would be tossing a dead fish back into the lake. It was impossible to avoid, of course, but it bothered him anyway. "Drowning fish," he'd say. "Not optimal."

Still, Danny went out with him. Pete liked to think it was because the boy liked spending time together. Just before dark, the two of them would reel in their lines and sit in silence watching the sunset, a quivering ball of orange and scarlet plunging the day into the water. *Listen,*

Danny would say, and they'd both smile, waiting for an imaginary hiss of steam, hearing only the cries of gulls. *Maybe next time*, Danny would say.

———

Pete takes a swallow from his second vodka tonic. He sees his phone on the bar, decides not to check it again until he's outside. He glances at his watch. If he walks into the house in fifteen minutes, he and Danny can be out on the dock untying the boat when Carey arrives home from Chicago. They can wave goodbye from the water. He can tell her about the meeting later, before bed, hoping she's too tired to ask about the pot shop. She might even be asleep by the time he and Danny get back.

"Closing early tonight?"

"Festival's on—deck closes at six," Boz says. He's never liked the festival, partly because it lures customers away, partly because he loathes anything involving "foreigners," as he refers to out-of-towners. Even though he's from out of town. Every year at festival time, Boz shuts his porch before nightfall and draws the shades so neither he nor his regulars can see the fool goings-on across the bay.

"I'll be out on the lake with Danny," Pete says.

"How's he doing?"

"Good. He's a good kid. Most of the time," Pete says.

"Hey, he's a teenager. Hormones."

That too, Pete thinks. The truth is, he doesn't always feel worthy of his stepson. Sometimes he wonders if Danny sees him less as a stepdad than a lovable fuckup of an older brother.

Boz nods toward the bay. "Saw him out on the beach just today."

The phone on the wall behind the bar starts ringing.

"Yeah? He talk to you?"

"A little—hang on." Boz twists to grab the phone. "Boz's Bar and—whoa, slow down there. OK, hold on."

Boz presses the receiver against his Hawaiian shirt and mouths the word *wifey*. Carey is calling Boz's landline because Pete didn't answer his cell. Jesus.

"Gimme," Pete says. He takes another swig of his drink as Boz passes him the phone. The cord isn't long enough, so Pete has to step up on the footrail and lean across the bar.

"Hey," he says. "You're early."

"You're not."

"I went to your—the meeting. Did you have a good day?"

"Fine. What happened at the meeting?"

"Not much. A lot of talk. No actual votes."

"Did Jonah make it?"

"He was wielding the mayor's gavel."

"How long have you been at the bar?"

"Just got here."

"And?"

"And I'm just leaving."

"Right."

Pete hears something thud on the great-room table at home, probably Carey's purse.

"Did you let her go?" Carey says.

"Did I what?"

"Dulcy. You said you were going to fire her."

"Tomorrow. I had to go to the meeting, and I couldn't just close up. That's a good part of the day."

"Uh-huh. Is Danny with you?"

"No. He's there."

"I don't see him."

"When I left for the meeting, he was out on the dock in one of his trances. Is his laptop out there?"

"Hold on. Yes. On the picnic table. Open."

"Good thing it didn't rain. What about the cooler? That ready?"

"Your precious cooler is here on the snack bar."

"So he's ready for fishing. Maybe he went for a walk."

"Why couldn't you have just come straight home?"

"I stopped for one," Pete says. He tries to bend away from Boz, who is pretending not to eavesdrop, but the phone cord won't stretch that far. "I went to the meeting. I could've taken Danny, but that might not have turned out so good."

He hears her sigh. He tells himself Carey means well. She's been under a lot of stress. She doesn't love her job at Pressman Logistics, especially lately. She certainly doesn't love the commute. Sometimes he wonders what she does love, besides Danny.

Do you think my mom loves you? he hears Danny say.

"So you're coming home now?"

"Yep." He waves at Boz. "Just settling up."

Carey hangs up. Pete hands the phone over.

"Everything OK?" Boz says.

"Who knows?"

"Bring me some fillets."

———

Outside, Pete starts up the rise to the road that encircles the bay, then changes his mind and lopes down past Boz's patio, peering down the crescent of pebbled sand bending toward his house. *Danny's gotta be there somewhere*, he thinks. *He was going to have the bait and cooler ready.*

Pete's flip-flop straps dig into the gap between his toes as he trudges. Across the bay, off-key voices warble "Peaceful Easy Feeling." Pete turns to see the broad decks outside the bars and restaurants, the pastel blue and pink umbrellas, the shapes of people drinking and laughing in the early-evening sun. Few of them live there year-round. Most are from

Chicago or Detroit, two hundred miles to the east, even Indianapolis, a bit farther to the south, and spend summers in Bleak Harbor.

From here, Pete can see his cottage. The rear half is shielded by the supposedly soundproof fencing Carey insisted on installing after some trouble with Danny. The boat is still covered. Danny usually has the tarp folded on the dock by now.

A hundred yards from the house, Pete stops and checks his phone. No new messages, but he rereads the text he saw as he was leaving city hall:

hows the fam?

Something like rubber bands grips his belly. He feels angry, then helpless, then angrier still for feeling helpless. The text came from a phone number he doesn't recognize, an area code he's never heard of. He searched it online, came up with codes in Cuba and Canada.

hows the fam? the text says.

The fam's fine, motherfucker, Pete thinks. *Why don't you stick to business, leave me and my family the hell alone?*

He looks up from the phone and sees Carey standing on the deck in her business suit, silk scarf bunched at her neck, arms folded, eyes on Pete. Those big green eyes that swallowed him whole when he first saw her sitting on a packed Chicago city bus a decade ago.

"Aren't you going to offer me your seat?" he'd said then, grinning. Carey had looked at him like he was a panhandler with sewer breath.

"Excuse me?"

"Your seat. I'm standing here, and I'm way older than you."

It had taken her a minute, but she had smiled, a little, trying to hide it, and Pete had put up his hands like he hadn't really wanted the seat anyway, just as the bus lurched to a stop, pitching him backward over a massive woman in a wheelchair.

That's how he and Carey had gotten started, with him apologizing to the annoyed woman and Carey with a hand over her mouth as she tried not to laugh, saying, "I guess you got your seat."

She's not smiling or laughing now. Pete deletes the text before dropping the phone back into his pocket.

"Hey," he calls out, waving.

4

Carey watches Pete pause to mess with his phone. She counts as he stands there: three seconds, seven, eleven. *Come on*, she thinks. *Get your ass home.*

He pockets his phone and starts walking again, waving at her, calling out. She doesn't wave or shout back. His cargo shorts sag on his skinny waist. He needs a shave and a T-shirt without a hole in an armpit. She imagines him showing up at Pressman Logistics looking as he does, how the receptionist would assume he was a bicycle courier.

She takes out her phone, deletes the texts she read in the car, then remembers the one that swooped in when the phone was on the floor. She can't find it. She's sure she heard it come in, but there's nothing to see. Then, as she's holding the phone in one hand, a fresh text pops up, from a number she doesn't recognize. Working for a logistics company, Carey knows plenty of area codes by heart, but she can't recall what place this one might be attached to. She opens the text. It's blank. No words, no pictures, nothing. She closes and opens it again. Still there's only an empty window. Probably a wrong number.

Pete comes up the four steps to the deck. He's grinning that effortless grin and pushing back the unruly salt-and-pepper mane.

"How was the commute?" he says.

"Fine until I hit Michigan. Some idiot ran out of gas, so of course the state cops had to block an entire lane."

"That sucks." Pete leans down to kiss her cheek.

"I appreciate you going to the meeting, but I wish you'd come straight home," she says.

"Sorry."

"It's late in the day and—"

"I know, I know, sorry. Danny's not here yet?"

"No. And he didn't leave a note. He knows he's supposed to."

"Sometimes he forgets stuff."

"Selectively. Where was he when you left?"

"I told you, right out there." Pete motions toward the dock. A minnow bucket dangles from a piling into the water. "Maybe he's at the library."

"No. Library's closed for festival parking. I called his phone when I got home and heard it ringing out here."

"Huh. You check for his meds?"

When Danny disappeared two months ago, he'd taken his prescription drugs with him. It was at once a relief and a fright to Carey. He could last awhile on his own if he had his meds. Without them, there was no telling what he might do.

"Yes," she says. "They're on his nightstand."

"And his chair's there by the window where he waits for me. So it's all good. He would've taken the drugs and the phone if . . . you know. Like I said, he probably just went for a walk."

"He would've taken his phone."

"Not necessarily."

"He doesn't miss fishing, Pete. It's burned into his schedule like brushing his teeth at eight fifteen. If you say you're going and you don't go, he throws a fit—you know that."

It pains Carey to say that, because she isn't always on Danny's schedule anymore. Not like Pete with the fishing. Her overnights in Chicago have disrupted their daily time together. She has rationalized that she can't help it, they need her income until Pete gets the pot business going. But she hates herself for it anyway.

"Sorry," is all Pete says, and she hates herself for that too, that sorry is all he ever seems to say.

———

One afternoon a few weeks ago, she came home after being gone for two days and poured glasses of iced tea with orange slices and asked Danny to bring the Wallace Stevens collection out to the deck. He was in the kitchen assembling the cooler for fishing.

"Never mind," he said. "It's going to rain."

Carey looked through the glass doors facing the beach and saw the southwestern sky churning purple and gray. "So we'll bring the chairs under the eaves. Or we can sit at the table with the umbrella."

"Poems aren't good at that table," Danny said. He was fitting Pete's cans of Old Style into the cooler with the labels facing up, one can one way, the next the other.

"Honey."

"I told you, I'm not 'honey' anymore."

It raked at Carey's heart. He'd said it before, but without so much conviction. She couldn't help but call him honey. Honey was the color of his eyebrows and the hairs on his forearms.

"Danny, if it's going to rain, why are you packing the cooler?"

He looked up from the cooler and gave her one of those stares that made her feel as if he were looking into her skull, reading words streaming across the front of her brain.

"The rain's not going to last *that* long."

"So you don't want to read poems today."

"Maybe not."

"*Maybe* not?"

Danny used his fist to tap the cooler lid into place.

"Not."

Carey turned away and gulped the rest of her iced tea, letting the sorrow drip down with the drink. She knew not to press it. Instead she went to the liquor cabinet and refilled her glass with vodka and went out to the deck alone as the sky began to spit, letting the first drops prick her forehead and cheeks.

———

Now Pete is telling her that maybe Danny has just gotten a little off schedule, that he'll probably come strolling in any minute. His words float around her head as she turns away toward the bay.

The sun beams through a crooked break in the cumulus towering over the hills of trees and sand across the water. Her family's mansion perches atop the bluff that separates the heart of town from Lake Michigan. The people of Bleak Harbor who aren't Bleaks can access the lake only by taking a boat along the serpentine channel out of the bay, or a car to the public beaches beyond the channel, as if they aren't worthy of having the sand and surf at their feet.

One of the pink turrets on each of the mansion's four corners juts up through the green. Carey slept in a bedroom in that turret as a girl. She hears a mewling pop song floating across the bay, the clanking of sail cables against masts in the evening breeze.

"He's not going fishing tonight," she tells Pete.

"You're punishing him? Come on."

"Call it whatever you like." She goes to the picnic table and gathers up Danny's laptop and phone. "He has to learn he can't just leave us hanging like this. He knows what he's doing."

"Look, how's about I get you a drink? When he gets home, we'll have a talk with him."

"You just want to go fishing so you can get the hell out of here and not have to explain why you didn't fire Dulcy."

"For Christ's sake, Care."

She slides the glass door aside and steps into the house. She sets Danny's laptop and phone on the kitchen island and kicks her heels off. Seeing them askew on the hardwood floor, she sees them again on the floor of Randall Pressman's condo kitchen, where he first pressed her back against the counter and kissed her. Her stomach turns.

Danny, she thinks. *Just come home, honey, and everything will be all right.*

5

Malone stares into her bedroom wall mirror, tucking the royal-blue button-down into her navy trousers for the fourth or fifth time. She wants it smooth and tight all the way around her waist before she straps on her gun belt, but the tail keeps bagging out above her hips. It looks sloppy, unprofessional.

She's lost too much weight since she last wore the uniform, probably should have asked the department for a new one. Probably shouldn't have subsisted for a year on 7-Eleven coffee and Cheez-Its. The not sleeping, the sitting up watching *Friends* reruns, the listening to her house creak and groan. Maybe should have just quit.

"Whatever," she says, stepping away from the mirror. Nobody's listening. She has been alone in the house for fourteen months, two weeks, four days. The particular hour of her young daughter's death passed fifty-seven minutes ago, while Malone was sitting on her bed, trying not to stare at the photographs crowding her dresser and deciding whether to even put the police uniform on.

Her phone rings in the kitchen. Radovich again. The chief has been good about the whole thing, let her take the extra leave of absence, stopped at the house now and then to see how she was doing. She really did appreciate it, even if sometimes she ignored Radovich's calls or sat still and quiet in the bathroom when he knocked at her back door.

She wishes he'd waited just one more week to ask her to return. "Gotta get back on that horse," he'd said again and again. She knows what he meant, and he meant well. She also knows he needs every cop he can find for the Dragonfly Festival.

Already the RVs with the out-of-state license plates are lining up on the Blue Star Highway along the lake south of town, the drivers waiting in traffic with cocktails hidden between their legs. Already the downtown pubs have their **YOU CAN'T DRINK ALL DAY IF YOU DON'T START IN THE MORNING** banners up. Already the cruisers and speedboats from Chicago and Milwaukee and Traverse City are swarming the harbor.

She has the midnight shift, 11:00 p.m. to 7:00 a.m., though Radovich asked her to come in a few hours early to get reacclimated. She'd requested the night duty, though it's a toss-up as to whether it's worse patrolling in the sticky heat—tomorrow's supposed to hit ninety-four, with 99 percent humidity—or dealing with late-night out-of-towners who've spent nine hours in the beer tent. She just wants to get off work in time to make her dawn cemetery visit.

Her phone is ringing again. She goes to the kitchen, picks it up, hesitates, then finally says, "Chief?"

"How are you?"

"Fine."

Radovich has been chief since Malone was in high school. Maybe grade school. He's ready to retire but still has two of his seven kids to put through college. His cheeks look pinker and baggier now than they did a year ago.

"I hate to do this," the chief says. "But listen, do you mind coming in right away? I got a heckuva mess on my hands already. Goddamn festival. Tell me, Katya, who frigging cares about dragonflies anyway?"

She's staring at her Bleak Harbor Police hat resting upside down on the table. It brings back a memory of herself, sitting in her uncle Smitty's lap, wearing his Chicago police hat, which brings another memory, of Louisa dancing around in the shade of the beach gazebo on her seventh birthday, wearing Malone's police hat.

"Katya?"

"Sorry, Chief. Sure. Of course. I guess so."

"Crazy stuff's going on, and the festival hasn't even started yet. Somebody got into the bars' sound systems, and they're all playing the same song over and over, and nobody can stop it. Some frigging Eagles tune."

Malone doesn't care. She picks up her hat, lifts her car keys from a hook next to the fridge, closes her eyes. "Ten minutes," she says.

6

The sun is gone. Pete and Carey sit in the adirondacks overlooking their beach, Pete on his fourth Old Style; Carey, her second scotch rocks.

They haven't said a word in an hour.

The cooler sits at Pete's feet. He went through it hoping for a clue as to where his stepson might have gone. He found the two salami-and-cheese sandwiches, the pop and beer, the bag of pretzels neatly packed around the plastic container of worms. At the near end of the dock, a bait bucket is filled with fresh, wriggling minnows. Two fishing poles lean against a bench. Danny must have untangled the line that had knotted when he hooked a bullhead two nights before. The boy had done everything he always did to prepare for fishing.

Carey gets up from her chair and flings the last of her drink at the beach. A moist smear on her left cheek glistens in the moonlight. She sees her phone move on the deck, picks it up.

"Goddamn it," she says.

"What?"

"This is the third text I've gotten that has nothing in it. I keep thinking it might be Danny, and then I pick it up, and there's nothing there."

Pete feels his Adam's apple bounce up to the back of his mouth. He swallows. "Who are they from?"

"I have no idea."

She shows him her phone. He sees the number, the same odd area code as hows the fam?, and a shock of heat radiates from the base of his neck through his shoulders down into his arms. "Should I call the police?"

"They were useless last time, remember?"

"What else are we going to do? It's dark. Danny could get lost. He could get hit by a car. Lots of drunks—"

"Don't talk like that, Pete."

His phone beeps on his armrest. Carey leans in to see, pulling hair away from her face. "Is it Danny?"

"He doesn't have his phone, remember?" Pete snatches the phone up and holds it close to his face. He hopes Carey can't see the tremble he feels in his fingers. There's a new text:

alarmed?

"What is it?" Carey says.

"This—just this guy."

"What guy?"

Pete deletes the text with a swipe of his thumb. "Some typical rich Bleak Harbor jag-off. Thinks I'm a twenty-four-seven dope-vending machine. Got his card because he has a sore shoulder from riding his Jet Ski six hours a day." Pete stands, feels faint, briefly holds himself still. "Want anything while I'm up?"

Carey turns away. "I want my son."

———

In the kitchen dark, Pete stares into the open fridge.

alarmed?

It seems too pricey a word for the person he suspects is harassing him. Why not *afraid* or, better, *scared shitless*? Pete is those, for sure. He turns to the window on the back door, hoping Danny will be there, smiling in at him. There's only the faint amber glow of a streetlamp on the bay road.

"Shit shit shit," he whispers. He thrusts his head deeper into the fridge and sucks in the cold, trying to calm himself. His family might be in danger, and it could be his fault, a poor choice he made, one questionable judgment. He'd made it with good intentions, but that makes little difference now.

He straightens, willing his heart to beat slower. He pulls the freezer door open. Inside is a lavender-and-white box from Kate's Kakes holding the strawberry cream pie Pete picked up for Danny's birthday celebration. Staring at it helps to calm him down. He closes the freezer.

When this is over, he tells himself, when Danny comes home as if nothing happened, as if he just went for a stroll nobody should have worried about, then Pete will take Carey aside and tell her everything, tell her he went a little too far, took too big of a risk, and he'll never do it again—he'll shut the damn pot shop down if she wants, and they can go back to Chicago and figure things out.

It makes him feel better. He grabs a can of Old Style from the fridge, snaps the tab back, takes a long gulp standing in the fridge light. Wherever Danny is probably has nothing to do with this asshole on his phone. He takes another pull of beer. "OK," he says.

He goes back outside. Carey is standing at the deck railing, staring out at the water. Pete regards his wife silhouetted against the softening sky. The ringlets of hair on her shoulders sometimes remind him of Danny. He wants to wrap his arms around her, but he doesn't want to feel her twist away from him.

"What do you want to do?" he says. "Did you check his room?"

"I glanced in to make sure he wasn't there. But I haven't—no. I haven't really looked yet."

Pete steps close enough to touch her, without touching her. "I suppose he'd probably walk in when you were in there and be all pissed off."

"I don't care if he's pissed off. It's going on eleven. I'm pissed off."

"You don't think this is still about Paddle, do you?"

"I hope—oh Jesus."

"What?"

She's looking at her phone. "What the hell is this?"

"Danny?" Pete says.

Carey twists her phone around her neck for Pete to see. There's a new text, this one with a photograph. A hard-backed chair stands in a pool of shadow. On the seat is an object the color of dull silver. Maybe a roll of tape.

Pete hears his heart start to thump again. "A chair? Who's sending you pictures of a chair?"

She turns to face him now. Her eyes are filled with fright. It gives him a start. "How the hell do I know? What's that thing on the chair?"

Pete takes the phone, squints at it. "Can't tell. Maybe it's"—he starts to say *somebody's idea of a sick joke* but changes his mind—"some kind of hacker or something."

"Gimme." Carey takes her phone back. "What's going on around here?"

"Maybe we should call the police," Pete says. It comes out half-heartedly. The cops might ask questions he'd prefer they didn't.

"Wait," Carey says, pressing the phone into his chest. "Just wait." She rushes past him and into the house.

"Carey. What—I'm going to call."

"Just wait."

"What are you doing?"

"Where are my sneakers?"

"Care."

"Where are my goddamn sneakers?"

7

The last time Danny left, it was about Paddle.

In early April, Carey stood next to Danny beside the foam-padded table in Dr. Torrent's examination room, Paddle lying on his side, groggy with sedation. Pete watched from the other side of the table. It was their sixth or seventh visit to the vet's since Christmas, none of them routine.

Dr. Torrent explained that the cancer had moved to Paddle's liver. She said he was in constant pain, although he would never show it because dogs so craved approval. *Like boys*, Carey thought. Danny kept his eyes closed as Dr. Torrent spoke. Carey recalled how nice he'd been to the vet when she first started diagnosing Paddle's illness, trying to make eye contact and smile, as if he could charm her into a positive verdict.

Now she said she could fix Paddle, but only for a short while. "I'm afraid a cure is not a realistic possibility," she said. Danny leaned toward Paddle, and Carey stared at the back of his head, imagining his brain at work. He had told her recently that, by his rough calculation, the many doctors in his life were no more than 62 percent sure of anything they said. "Which leaves considerable room for error," he had said. Even when it became clear that their assessments were off, they never admitted they'd been wrong. "There are always 'unforeseen circumstances' or 'uncertainties,'" Danny had said. "How convenient those are."

Carey remembered bringing the little dachshund with the floppy ears home to their Chicago apartment on Danny's sixth birthday. Each morning, Danny would descend the stairs with Paddle in his arms, turn onto Madison Street, and walk exactly two hundred steps to the café, where he waved through the window at the pretty young women making lattes. Paddle would rear up on his hind legs, smudging his wet nose on the glass as Carey watched from the corner.

Likewise, in Bleak Harbor, the first thing Danny did each day was take Paddle for a walk on the beach, exactly two hundred steps out, returning in the footsteps he'd left in the sand or snow. Paddle would curl up on Danny's feet while he washed his face and brushed his teeth; then Danny would share three level tablespoons of his CoCo Wheats with the dog.

Carey had to admit to some envy at Paddle's seeming ability to translate with ease Danny's sometimes frustrated, sometimes frustrating efforts to make himself understood. With a nod or a look or a shift of his shoulder that meant little to his mother or stepfather, Danny could make Paddle jump into his lap or go scuttling off in search of one of his fuzz-worn tennis balls. Paddle seemed to know intuitively when Danny was ready to play and when Danny needed to be left alone. She wished her son could be so simpatico with another boy or girl.

Paddle had begun to have trouble walking in January, started dragging his hind legs in February. Danny had had to carry him on their morning walks, help him up and down the steps to the beach. "I like it," he'd said. "He keeps me warm." He'd cleaned up Paddle's diarrhea without a word, swabbed the dog's chafed butt with baby wipes he'd bought himself at Meijer. Carey bought Paddle a bright-red coat that made him look like the dog in the Grinch cartoon. That made Danny smile.

Now Dr. Torrent laid a hand on Paddle's hindquarters and said he had only weeks to live, "Unless, of course, you choose to graciously put him out of his suffering."

Carey saw Danny wince before opening his eyes. She moved toward him, but he raised a hand to ward her off.

"Paddle does not want to be graciously killed," Danny said. "We will take whatever time Paddle has left."

"I understand," Dr. Torrent said. "As I'm sure your parents do. But it isn't that simple. You see . . ."

Carey wasn't listening but watching Danny watching the vet. She knew he was staring at the beauty mark on Dr. Torrent's left cheek. He'd told her how fetching he found it, how it subtly and beautifully disrupted the symmetry of her face. "Is that the only reason you like it?" Carey had asked him then, suspecting there was something else, and when he didn't answer, she'd said, "Don't stare at it, Danny; it will make her uncomfortable," and her son's knowing smile, his eyes averted, answered her question.

Now Dr. Torrent asked Danny to step outside. "I just need a few moments to discuss this with your parents," she said.

"Do you have children?" Danny said.

He knew Dr. Torrent had three children. He had shown them to Carey on Facebook.

"Why, yes, I do," Dr. Torrent said. "Two sons and a daughter."

"Are they perfect?"

"Danny," Pete said, "this really isn't appropriate."

Carey looked at her son. "Danny," she said, "you're perfect."

Danny ignored them. "You live in Saint Joseph, right? With all the rich Whirlpool executives. Your husband is a rich Whirlpool executive."

"I think we should talk about your dog," Dr. Torrent said.

"Paddle. Your commute is approximately fourteen miles then. Maybe twenty or thirty minutes, depending on traffic?"

"OK, Danny, that's enough," Pete said.

"That's about right." Dr. Torrent tried on a patient smile. "Now—"

"So you never leave your three children alone for long."

"Jeez oh pete, Danny." Pete came around behind his stepson. "Come on—let's go."

As Pete gripped Danny's elbow, Carey saw Danny tense and worried for an instant that he might wheel around and take a swing at Pete. Instead Danny just yanked his arm away.

"It's my dog," he said. "I take care of him—you don't."

"Honey."

"I'm not 'honey.' I am fifteen."

He swiped Dr. Torrent's hand away from Paddle. She moved back, clutching the hand he'd touched. "Paddle," he said. "It's Danny. I'm here."

The dachshund lifted his head, one ear flapping over an eye. His hind legs shifted. His head dropped back to the table. The doctor started to say something, but Danny cut her off.

"Shut up."

"Danny," Carey said.

He looked at Pete, then Carey, then at the door. "She is no oncologist," he told the door. "She doesn't have a single oncology degree on the wall in her office."

"I'm sorry, son. I am certified—"

Danny turned to the vet. "You didn't do a biopsy?"

Dr. Torrent's eyebrows hitched up just enough to suggest the question surprised her. "It wasn't necessary."

"How so?"

Carey slid between them. "I'm sorry, Doctor," she said. "Danny, it's time to go."

"No, it's all right," the vet said. But Carey could hear the trill of annoyance in her voice, how it really wasn't all right. "Danny, the dysplasia—I'm sorry, that's like a change in—"

"I know what it is. Even a kid like me can use Google."

That stopped her for a second. Carey could see that she'd had enough of Danny and that that was perfectly fine with him. "Anyway," Dr. Torrent continued, "the dysplasia was so extreme that further tests weren't indicated. He—Paddle—has liver cancer; there's no doubt about that."

"But there's doubt about what's next, isn't there?"

Dr. Torrent shoved her hands into her smock pockets. "There is almost never certainty."

Danny stood looking at her for a long moment; then he bent and kissed Paddle on the head and left the room, brushing Carey's hand off his shoulder.

———

The next morning, Carey sat Danny down. Paddle was lying in Danny's bed, where he'd slept for one of the last times. She told Danny that, although there were things the vet could do to make Paddle more comfortable, they were not cheap. "Some things are meant to be," she said, knowing as the words left her mouth that they were bullshit and Danny would hate her for it.

Paddle's last vet appointment came three days later. Danny cradled the dachshund in his arms as Dr. Torrent gave him the shot. "Pads," Danny whispered, rocking back and forth as he wept. "Pads. Pads. Pads." The dog went limp. Carey and Pete gathered Danny into an embrace. "No," he said, wriggling free.

At home, he locked himself in his room. For three days, he refused to come out or eat or bathe. He emerged the fourth morning and brushed his teeth and ate his CoCo Wheats at the usual times. Carey and Pete thought he'd come around. That afternoon, he went for a walk. He didn't come home.

Pete was at dinner with one of his weed suppliers. He wasn't answering his phone. At ten o'clock, Carey called the police. The dispatcher told her to call back when her son had been missing for twenty-four hours.

"Tell you what," she replied, loathing what she was about to say, "in twenty-four seconds, I will be on the phone to Serenity Bleak. You sound young, so if you don't know who that is, ask the chief."

She had no desire to involve her mother, nor did she believe her mother would care to be involved. But within minutes, two bored-looking men, one quite a bit younger than the other, materialized at her door. The older one, in a police uniform, asked her a series of perfunctory questions about when she and Pete had last seen Danny, whether he used a phone, who else he might know nearby, Pete's place of work, hers. The other one, wearing a polo shirt, belly straining at his khakis, scribbled with a ballpoint in a small notebook. When the uniform finished, the pudgy one said, "Can I ask you something, ma'am?"

"You just did."

"Yes, ma'am. I'm sorry to ask this, but—"

Carey knew what was coming. "No, you're not."

"Excuse me?"

"What do you want?"

Fatso is out of his league, she thought.

"Uh, I just—you and Dan didn't—"

"Danny."

"Of course. You and Danny didn't have an argument or anything like that earlier today, did you?"

"Anything like what? Who are you, anyway? Where's your uniform?"

"I'm sorry, ma'am; I thought I said. Will Northwood. I'm a—"

The uniform interrupted. "Will's kind of a plainclothes guy, Ms. Bleak."

"Peters."

"Peters. Yes, apologies. We're short-staffed."

"What's your question, Will?" She pointed past them. "You want to know why we put that fence up? Is that it? Spit it out."

Carey had heard echoes of the vile rumors around town, the whispers of screams coming from the house. Danny's tantrums invariably involved screaming. His screams had gotten louder as puberty arrived, or so she believed. Sometimes she thought he amplified his shrieks to embarrass her. Then she felt guilty for thinking it.

He had thrown a fit a few weeks before in the frozen foods section at Meijer. It was ostensibly over Carey's refusal to buy chocolate chip mint ice cream that contained casein, something his doctors said contributed to autism. Danny had never made such a scene about ice cream before, so she assumed he was really reacting to Paddle's deteriorating condition. It was clear, she thought, that he wanted his flip out to be public and he wanted to draw his mother in. So she had stood and watched in arms-folded silence as he emptied a freezer case of its Popsicles, scattering them across the floor while other mothers furtively pulled out their phones. Later, Carey forced herself to watch some of the videos the bitches posted online.

"Sorry, ma'am. I'll take that as a no," Will told her.

"It is a no," Carey said. "He's a fifteen-year-old boy. He doesn't agree with every single thing his parents tell him."

"It's just routine, Ms. Peters," the uniform said. "Do you have any idea where your son might have gone?"

She didn't, at least not then. The uniform and the chubby guy left. Carey stood out on the deck watching cop flashers flicker across the bay, waiting for Pete to call, hoping to God her mother wouldn't find out. Her brother, Jonah, called, asking if he could help. Carey told him thanks, but it would be better if he stayed away for now. That's when her mother beeped in.

"Carey, is that you?"

"Mother." Carey imagined Serenity Bleak lying in bed with a TV remote in one hand, a half-full glass in the other, cubes clinking.

"What is the matter with that boy now?"

"His name is Danny."

"Tell me, dear, why am I seeing our family's good name on the eleven o'clock news?"

"Feel free to turn it off."

"Why is Daniel wandering around in the middle of the night? If you can't keep track of your son, then perhaps he needs to be somewhere professionals can."

"You're slurring your words, Mother."

"It will keep him safe from the world."

"That's a big help. Thank you."

"You are in denial, dear. You need to get out of denial."

"You are certainly an expert in that. Good night."

It was the first time Carey and Serenity had spoken in months, and they had not talked since.

Around midnight, Carey was out scanning the beach again when she recalled how Danny had once remarked that he didn't like seeing the old Helliker place next door shut up and abandoned, how he wished he could go in and open windows to let it breathe. "No," she said aloud. Then she walked down to the dock and looked back at the Helliker house.

Curtains were fluttering in two open windows.

Ten minutes later, she found Danny curled into a paint tarp in a corner of the house's basement, asleep. He looked like a little boy again as she knelt over him, holding her breath against the odor of turpentine. He came awake as if she had roused him in his own bed. "Oh," he said, then broke free of her embrace, bounded up the stairs, out of the Helliker house, and around the security fence into his own house, where he locked himself in his bedroom until morning.

Pete finally appeared just after 1:00 a.m., stoned, apologetic, insisting his phone had run out of power. Carey dragged him out to the end of the dock, where she hoped Danny couldn't hear her telling her husband that she could not do this alone now that he was fifteen and able to do enough on his own to get himself in real trouble. Pete, as always, had nothing to say but sorry, he would try to do better.

8

Carey jogs up the driveway toward the bay road, around the far end of the security fence, then back down the driveway next door through dandelions and quack grass jutting up through ruts in the asphalt.

She despises the fence even though, or maybe because, she's the one who insisted on having it built, to keep the neighbors from hearing Danny's tantrums. She hears Pete call out as he rounds the end of the fence: "Carey. What the hell? He won't be there again."

The Helliker house is empty. Streaks of tar-black mold mar the siding. Screens on the wraparound porch are shearing away from their frames. There are gouges in the shingled roof and shattered windows in the clapboard walls.

The house was probably built in the 1940s or '50s, like a lot of the houses on this side of the bay, weekend getaways for the steelworkers then employed at the Bleak plant across the border in Indiana and other blue-collar laborers. The bank had reclaimed the house after the owner, a Chevy plant manager named Helliker, lost his job and stopped making payments. In town, of course, the rich rabble delighted in tales of a fractious divorce and the Helliker children taking sides. That's how those rubberneckers were.

After Danny's earlier escape, Carey had paid a locksmith triple his usual fee to fashion her a key to the Helliker house's back door. Just in case. Now she locates the key where she hung it on a withered forsythia near the porch. She swings the screen door open, unlocks the inner door, steps inside, and throws the deadbolt to lock it behind her.

She steps into the kitchen, and her nostrils fill with the reek of mildewed blinds and drywall rot. She remembers coming here the night Danny last disappeared. She'd used a rock to break the door's window and gashed her thumb as she reached in to undo the lock. She recalls how panicked she'd felt, how angry, how guilty for feeling such anger toward her son.

She hears Pete twist the doorknob. He bangs on the repaired window. "Carey," he says. "Let me in."

"Why don't you go down to the bar?"

"Seriously?"

Her phone vibrates in her pocket. She pulls it out. There's a text from Pressman:

think about what youre doing, C. it's your family. u have time.

She starts to type a reply—*you are the one running out of time*—but stops herself, thinking she does in fact have time—let him sweat for now. She turns and unlocks the door. Pete pushes it open.

"What are you doing?" he says. "We're in this together."

Carey ignores him. Using her phone as a flashlight, she steps across bubbled linoleum through the kitchen into the living room. Sheets of particleboard cover windows facing the bay. Cable wires snake out from a wall where a television once was mounted. The indoor-outdoor carpet is furrowed with tracks of the oven and water heater the Hellikers hauled out hours before the sheriff showed up with the foreclosure notice.

Carey stops and listens, as she did the last time she was here, swearing she can hear something in the walls, chipmunks or cockroaches or mice.

"Danny?" she calls into the gloom. "Where are you, honey?"

"He's not gonna answer to 'honey.'"

"Just shut up."

"Please don't tell me to shut up," he says.

As Carey shines her way through the shadows, the realization buried in the back of her mind pushes forward like a light cutting through dark: her husband, however charming and well meaning and even, on occasion, intelligent, is essentially unnecessary.

Yes, he's good for the fishing with Danny, the jabbering about the Cubs. But she has had to reluctantly conclude that he'll never be much good at the real work of bringing up her special boy. Pete, alas, is too much a boy himself, a six-foot-five-inch boy of thirty-nine, and not a terribly special one.

"Why don't you go down the hall and check the bedrooms?" she says.

Pete is her mistake. He is, at the core, a decent man, a better one than any others she was with before or after Danny, certainly better than Danny's birth father, whom Carey hasn't seen in years. She'd said yes to Pete for reasons that seemed at the time like the right ones, or at least the most convenient ones. She knows he will be heartbroken when she finally leaves with his stepson. It will pain her too, to a point, but the ache will fade in time, and she will be left with a new life with Danny. She just needs the money and the space to start it.

"He's not in the bedrooms," Pete says. He emerges from a hallway into the living room, where Carey is closing a closet door. "Do you really think he'd come back here again?"

"Here," she says, angling her phone up so it illuminates the ceiling. "Pretty sure that's a ladder."

Pete aims his phone's glow upward. Two sheets of mottled plywood are nailed haphazardly around a pull-down door to an attic. He goes into the kitchen and returns with a chair, which he places beneath the hatch. "Hold this steady, OK?" Carey grips the chairback with both hands. Pete steps up and reaches over his head for the handle to the door. He pulls. Nothing happens.

"It's stuck."

"Pull harder. Here, let me."

Pete uses both hands this time. "Damn old cottages," he says just as the hatch door attached to a fold-up ladder tears away from the ceiling and comes crashing down. He keeps it from hitting him or Carey by swinging it out to his left as the chair keels out of Carey's grasp. Pete pitches onto the floor, landing on his elbows and knees in a cloud of drywall dust.

"Sonofabitch," he says, blinking white shreds from his eyes.

"You OK?"

"Shit." He looks up. "Whoa."

Carey twists around to see the ragged hole in the ceiling and another hole shorn in the roof above, a crescent moon shining in its middle. "Come on," she says.

She turns and goes to the basement door. She raps on it a few times, hoping Danny will hear.

"I'll go down," Pete says.

Carey tries the door. The knob turns, but the door seems trapped on the jamb. "Danny, it's OK," she shouts. "I'm here."

"Let me in there."

"Get away."

"Carey."

She steps back. "Just do it. I'll go down."

Pete tries the door. "Wood probably warped in the heat." He wraps both hands around the doorknob, leans back on his haunches, and pulls. The door groans, budging a quarter of an inch. Pete stands, muttering under his breath, squats, and pulls again. Just as the door jerks open, a high-pitched squeal begins blaring from somewhere in the house.

"What the hell?" Carey covers her ears.

"An alarm? What the shit for?"

Carey starts down the stairway, right hand on the railing, her lit phone shoved out in front of her. The dead air scrapes at the back of her throat. She hears a phone ringing beneath the squealing house alarm.

"Danny, are you down here?" she yells. "Danny! Honey!"

"Carey, we gotta get out of here."

She trips on the bottom stairstep and slams into the concrete floor, feeling skin on her kneecap shred. "Danny, where are you? Please."

Pete scrabbles past her. "Look right. I'll go left—hurry. I think I heard a police siren."

They bustle around the basement, throwing open closet doors, rummaging through a pile of blankets, looking behind a furnace the Hellikers didn't take. Danny is nowhere.

"He isn't here," Carey says. "Damn it."

"Should we just wait for the police?"

"That's all we need. Come on—let's get out of here."

She bounds up the stairs, Pete behind her. As they go out the door they entered through, she sees police lights in the sky over the bay road. "This way," she says, trotting toward the water through the weeds along the side of the house.

They make the beach and curl around the end of the fence, then back toward their house as the police cruiser headlights shine on the Hellikers' roof. Ducking down, they slink onto their deck and into the house. They slide the deck door closed, lock it, close the blinds, and stand in the living room, gasping.

"You're hurt," Pete says, nodding at the smear of blood on Carey's knee. He takes his phone out, the glow playing on his face.

"Was that your phone ringing in there?"

"Looks like." He hits a button and raises the phone to his ear, listening. "Holy Christ," he says. "Now what?"

"What?"

"Another fucking alarm. At the shop."

"What do you mean?"

"Got a voice mail from the alarm company saying there might be a break-in."

"Could be drunk kids."

"On the third floor?"

"Or maybe it's Danny."

Pete considers this. "Yeah. Maybe. I'll go."

"I'm coming."

"No. What if he comes back here?"

Carey hesitates. "All right. Then go. Hurry. Call me."

"What if the cops come over? What are you gonna tell them?"

"Fuck them. I'll figure it out."

Pete starts toward the garage.

"Not that way. That's where the cops are."

"Right. I'll run down the beach."

"Hurry, but don't run. You don't want people—"

"Yeah, yeah, right."

Pete slips out through the glass doors and crab scuttles across the deck to the sand. Carey watches him move down the beach silhouetted against the distant downtown lights, his scarecrow shoulder blades jutting in and out of shadow. She reaches down and presses a thumbnail into the scarlet goo on her knee. It stings. She wants it to.

9

Three cottages short of Boz's bar, Pete veers left and creeps up the grassy sand slope to the birch stand along the bay road, hoping no one will notice. He looks back and sees the cop lights flickering at the Helliker place. He calls the alarm company, supplies his code, tells the operator everything is fine, no need to send police to his shop. Once he's far enough past Boz's, he scrambles back down to the beach.

He's tired and a little drunk and trying to think. If somebody is trying to mess with his head, they're doing a splendid job. *Alarmed? Funny,* Pete thinks. *So you break into my pot shop? Fine, fine, get it over with.* He knows he cut a deal he shouldn't have. He thought he had good reasons, but the reasons evaporated when the other guy kept changing the deal. And not at all in Pete's favor.

So now what does he do?

He thinks about the alarm inside the Helliker place. It has to be a coincidence. At least he hopes so. This guy who's taunting him, trying to intimidate him, is obviously a reprobate—what the hell did Pete expect from a drug dealer anyway?

But is the guy smart enough to have triggered both alarms, the one at his shop and the one at the house, at the same time? And how could he have known Pete was in the Helliker place? Unless the guy's been watching him. Or maybe he read about Danny's previous running away in the *Light*. But even then, how could he know Danny would be gone on this particular night?

Unless.

He starts to run. As he nears town, he hears "Peaceful Easy Feeling" playing again from one of the harbor taverns. *Those people*, he thinks.

———

The redbrick office building stands a block up from the bay at the intersection of streets named for two of Joseph Estes Bleak's three daughters, Lily and Blossom. That Eagles song is still blaring from the beach down Lily. Some sadist must have a bucket of quarters.

Pete scans Blossom. The darkened galleries and boutiques and pottery shops—Strawman Drug, Casurella Fudge, Kate's Kakes, Bascolino's Soda & Sandwich—all slumber beneath striped awnings, the sidewalks washed in the milky glow of faux gas lamps. The cars parked on both sides of Blossom all seem to be convertibles, all red or black—BMWs, Mercedes, Porsches—except for one silver Jaguar.

A ladder left leaning against a lamp pole reminds Pete the town is preparing for the Dragonfly Festival. Danny loved the festival as a younger boy. He still loves dragonflies. The kid knew more about those bugs than anybody Pete knew, even the dude from the Bleak County Nature Center who had been one of Pete's customers until he decided the shop in New Buffalo had better, cheaper product.

Pete approaches the entrance to the redbrick building, four stories of glowing glass atrium wrapping from Blossom around to Lily, the windows speckled black with mosquitoes, moths, other bugs that give him the willies. He can feel the radiance on his face as he takes a plastic card from his wallet and presses it to a black plastic panel. He hears a beep, then a click. He pushes the door open.

He uses the card again to open the elevator, and again to tell the elevator to take him to three. He can't imagine how Danny could gain entrance to this digital fortress, but maybe, just maybe—but no, there's no one in the elevator lobby or the corridor to his office.

At the door to AMP Botanicals, Pete punches a six-number code into a keypad. He hears another click and steps inside, flicking on a light, closing the door behind him.

———

A year before, Pete lost his job trading corn and soybeans for O'Nally Bros. & Co. in Chicago. He'd done OK as a trader, at least for a while. Had a few big days, then got on a bad streak that just wouldn't stop. In retrospect, he had panicked. His employer couldn't afford panicky guys playing with millions of dollars.

After leaving O'Nally Bros., he had enough in severance pay and savings to pay for lawyers, licensing fees, the office lease, and a $20,000 vending machine that kept track of his weed inventory and how much in taxes and fees he owed various government authorities. He sublet the office from a retiring dentist and reopened it as a medical marijuana dispensary, offering smokable weed, edible brownies and cookies, and salves and oils infused with supposedly therapeutic cannabinoids.

He'd gotten the pot idea from a couple of trader buddies over drinks one late afternoon. Zeus and Byrd were talking about how easy it had to be to make money selling legal reefer. By then Pete knew he probably wasn't long for the trading business anyway. After his fourth whiskey and Coke, he'd started scratching numbers on a napkin. He couldn't read much of the smudged ink the next morning, but he thought he remembered enough. He got on Google and in a few hours had sort of a plan.

When he first broached the idea with Carey, she actually seemed tickled at the idea of Pete, a semiofficial member of the Bleak family, peddling pot to the puckered asses on the rich end of the bay in Bleak Harbor. Maybe she didn't think he was serious, because she wasn't too tickled five months later when he announced that he'd leased a cottage and an office in Bleak Harbor and was just waiting on a license to launch the business.

"You are joking," Carey said.

They were having coffee and cold cereal on a Friday morning in their Chicago condo. Danny had finished his CoCo Wheats and gone into his bedroom.

"No. I'm going out on my own. I took the initiative."

"'Initiative'? How about your job?"

"Quit." It was a lie, but an irrelevant one, as Pete saw it. "You know I've been bored shitless since they took me off the floor and put me in that cubicle."

"When exactly did you quit, Pete?"

"The other day."

"What day?"

"Last week, or actually the Friday before. I've been so busy getting this new adventure going that—"

"Exactly when did you plan on telling me about your little adventure?"

"I'm telling you now. I wanted to have a good plan in place. I took the initiative, babe."

"You took the initiative to move us to Michigan?"

"You can't sell pot legally in Illinois yet, but you can in Michigan. But you gotta live there to sell there."

Carey gave him one of those looks that made him want to leave the room. He held his ground, though, tried to fill the silence. "Come on."

"'Come on'? I honestly can't believe this, Pete."

"I really thought it would be a nice surprise. It'll be good for Danny. He loves the lake. He'll be closer to family."

"We are his family. My mother doesn't give a damn about Danny."

"Keep your voice down. Danny loves Jonah."

"What about his school?"

"There's an excellent school in Saugatuck. You're not—we're not happy with the school here anyway. You're always saying that. You hate your job. This is an opportunity for us, Carey."

"Pete, what do you know about selling marijuana?"

"What does anyone know? I've done tons of research. I've done my homework. Really, I'm gonna kill this. It's a huge business. There's so much pent-up demand. They'll be lined up."

"And you're the only one in the world who knows that?"

The rest of the conversation had not gone well. Nor had the next few months. Pete had tried to get Carey to quit Pressman Logistics and move full-time to Bleak Harbor, but she'd gotten the promotion she wanted, and she told Pete she wasn't going to let his initiative interfere with hers. She would commute once or twice a week. The pot shop was barely a mile from the cottage, and Pete would hire an employee or two so he'd be free to be with Danny. Just for a while. It would work itself out.

Pete hadn't liked keeping his pot-shop plan from his wife, hadn't been proud of it, but he'd convinced himself that she'd come around when the money started rolling in. How hard could it be? All the experts were forecasting a multibillion-dollar business, with twenty- and thirtysomethings wanting to get high and older folks yearning for something other than opioids to salve their aching knees and shoulders. Pete would no longer have to fret about uncontrollable bullshit like floods and droughts and currency fluctuations and idiot traders on the other side of the world screwing up the markets. Selling marijuana was no different from selling hot dogs, he kept telling himself. Just sell a lot of dogs for more than it cost to make them. Get rich.

———

Nothing looks amiss in the customer area of AMP Botanicals. The antique dentist's chair with its twin porcelain spittoons stands in one corner, the plastic palm tree in another, the leftover Georgia O'Keefe print on the wall between them, all untouched.

The glass display case is empty, as Dulcy left it after closing that evening. The vending machine behind the counter looks undisturbed. Pete uses a key to open it. Seeing all the different products lined up in their cellophane wraps and plastic vials produces, as it does most mornings when he slinks into the shop, a twinge in his belly that reminds him how little he knows about what he's doing.

This was not hot dogs. This was pH levels and proper temperatures; building a brand and interpreting web analytics; coddling cranky customers and suppliers; and endless ass-covering, mind-freezing paperwork for the regulators and politicians with their hands in Pete's pockets. And hiring people he could trust who could multiply six by twelve and get seventy-two.

He had a good staffer for a while, an ever-smiling guy named Hank who knew the ins and outs of the business after working it in California. But Hank had left, smiling, for the shop in New Buffalo. He'd said it was because it was closer to his home in Union Pier, but Pete figured Hank could see he was flailing. Pete then settled for hiring a young woman named Dulcy who'd recently moved from Detroit, had a head for computers, and showed a lot of enthusiasm for the job until she actually had to start showing up.

All those people who had helped Pete open the business and cashed his checks and clapped him on the back and told him to remember them when he made his first $10 million were gone now. He had no more money to give them. He was on his own.

All of the inventory appears to be in the vending machine. Nothing is stolen. Which, in a way, disappoints Pete. He wouldn't mind if there really was a break-in and the guy who's been harassing him just took everything—the reefer and edibles, the fingerprint-matching machine, the card readers, the throwback roach clips. Then Pete could file an insurance claim or even bankruptcy, what the hell, and be done with this mistake. That way he'd also feel more certain that this guy hadn't done anything to Danny, that Danny had simply run away and would come home in the morning looking for his CoCo Wheats, stirred evenly and constantly so that not a single lump bubbled up on the surface.

Christ, Pete thinks, *I don't even know the guy's real name.* All he knows is what he calls himself over the phone: Slim. He wishes he could turn back the clock, tell Slim, "Sorry, we can't do business, no hard feelings, just go away—I'll have to fail all by myself."

Too late for that.

"Buddy," Pete says aloud. "Danny. Where are you, man? Danny! Come on. Help me out here."

He moves along the wall toward the door to his back office. If there was a burglar, maybe he didn't want the weed; maybe he went looking in the office for cash. Though there wasn't much of that.

Pete taps another code into another keypad. Maybe somebody's waiting for him back there. Or maybe the alarm was bogus. As he pushes the door open, something to his left catches his eye. He skips back from the doorway and waits, listening, hearing nothing but the quickened thrum of his heart.

Wimp, he tells himself, *it's your goddamn office.*

He reaches around the jamb and hits a wall switch. The office floods with fluorescent light. It looks as he'd left it. His gray hoodie hangs from a hook next to the file cabinets, a pair of his running shoes curled on the floor beneath. His desk is its usual clutter of unpaid bills and pistachio shells. Everything's normal, except for his computer monitor.

The screen, which should be black, is flashing. That's what Pete glimpsed from the doorway. The screen turns blue and then red and then black, blue and then red and then black.

Pete walks over, sits, takes the mouse in hand. When the screen goes red, he thinks he sees something at the center of the view. He waits for the next red flash. He sees the same something, a little clearer, though he still can't make it out. He leans closer, waits, squints. There:

hereheis

The screen goes black again, then blue. Pete doesn't see any words on those screens. Then the red returns. Pete sees the word again. Not one word, he thinks, but three:

hereheis

"No."

The red screen reappears. For the hell of it, Pete left-clicks his mouse. The flashing stops. The red remains, the words a white smear at the middle of the screen. Pete looks at his phone. Should he call Carey? Or the cops? And tell them what? There's a funny screen on my computer? Somebody's fucking with me, and he might have done something with my stepson?

Now the red begins to bleed away from the center of the screen toward each side, like a theater curtain opening. The revealed backdrop is newsprint gray. An irregular black shape forms around the words. The words begin to blink inside the shape.

Pete left-clicks again. The words vanish. After a moment, the black begins to peel away from the bottom of the shape, revealing a color photograph.

Pete feels a sledgehammer in his chest.

"Jesus."

At the bottom of the unfolding photo appear two feet. One is bare. The other wears a green high-top sneaker. Duct tape secures each of the hairless shins to the legs of a chair. The roll of tape sits on the floor between the chair legs. It looks like the thing that was sitting on the empty chair in the picture on Carey's phone.

It takes about a minute for the photo to reveal itself in full. Pete hits the print command again and again. A few seconds after the photo is complete, the screen goes black. Then three words in two-inch-high letters appear in white at the center of the screen:

DO NOT TELL

Pete taps Carey's number into his phone. His hands are shaking so badly that he has to do it three times.

"Is he there?" Carey says.

"Oh God."

"Pete, what?"

"Somebody—"

The texts flit again through Pete's mind:

how's the fam?

alarmed?

"Pete, goddamn it."

He can't catch his breath.

"Somebody what? Pete?"

"Fuck. Oh Jesus, oh Jesus."

"What is it?"

"Somebody has Danny. Somebody has our boy."

FRIDAY

10

Danny sleeps.

The room is dark. The room is hot. The room is stuffy. He feels the scratch at his throat. He swallows.

He is standing on the beach. His toes touch the water. The dragonflies are bigger than gulls. They are blacker than crows. They hover and glide, skitter and dart. Their shadows darken the water.

Anax junius, Enallagma civile.

Predator in emerald, damsel of the swamp.

Tramea lacerata, Libellula vibrans.

Spotted black killer, sapphire king.

Danny hears his mother singing:

> They flit about the sunny sky
> Like flowers that can fly
> Pretty pretty pretty pretty
> Their wings are sparkly gossamer
> They wear diamonds on their eyes
> Pretty pretty pretty pretty
> Pretty dragonflies

The dragonflies want the fishes. The baby fishes. They swoop and dive. Their wings make a murmur of clicking. The dragonflies disappear into the water. Some are damselflies. *Argia apicalis, Nehalennia irene.* Nobody knows this. Danny knows it. They emerge from the water with their jaws full. Their terrible jaws, their knives for teeth. They crunch and slurp and dive again.

His mother's voice fades, and Danny hears the music. It's close but far away. People are singing along. They don't care about the dragonflies or damselflies or baby fishes. Danny tries to speak. His jaw will not work. He tries to reach out and stop the dragonflies. His arm will not move. A fog descends. Danny can't see anything. He hears the splash and crunch and slurp.

He turns to the house. It has moved away up the beach. It is shrinking. Then it's gone, splintering into the trees across the bay road, the trees becoming the Willis and Hancock and AON buildings of Chicago. He hears her again: *Some things are meant to be.* As if he didn't know, couldn't comprehend it.

Danny remembers.

He was drinking coffee on the deck. It was 8:34 that morning. He had brushed his teeth nineteen minutes before.

His mother hugged him from behind. She kissed him beneath an ear. She was running late. She had broken a nail. *The goddamn traffic. Tonight you are all mine*, she said. *I love you.*

Yes, Danny said.

He drank his coffee. He heard the kitchen door slam shut. He heard it open again. He heard his mother call out, *Please, Pete, don't forget the meeting.* He heard the door slam again. He put a finger to his neck. He put the finger to his lips. He tasted sweat mixed with lavender body wash.

He made the two sandwiches, salami and muenster. He creased the folds of the sandwich bags. He arranged the cans of Squirt and Old Style in the cooler. He packed the pretzels and the worms. He hung the minnow bucket from a chain into the water next to the dock. He leaned the poles there. He left the boat covered.

His mother called. He watched the phone ring five times. He thought of Paddle trotting on the beach, ears of charcoal and copper fluttering back along the sides of his head, limp hind leg tracing a squiggle through the sand.

He didn't want to talk with his mother then. She would be home in a while.

Danny's eyes are burning. The room is hot. His cheeks are damp. The room is dark. Danny knows he is crying. He knows where he is. He wonders if he will see his mother and Pete again.

11

"You don't ever call him Danny boy, do you?"

Bleak Harbor Police lieutenant Katya Malone directs the question to Danny's mother. Carey Bleak Peters is facing Malone across the oaken table in the Peters cottage on the southeast corner of the bay. A dimmed overhead lamp splays yellowish light, leaving the rest of the room in shadow. Sitting in the middle of the table is a tin Ernie Banks lunch box, its edges fringed with rust.

"We do not," Carey says. She's staring at the tabletop, the fingertips on her right hand idly tapping the side of a glass of melting ice. Her husband sits two chairs to her right.

"No," Pete says.

Malone doesn't want to look at her watch while she's interviewing two parents about their missing son. She guesses it's a little after eight. The husband called the station around seven thirty. Malone had just finished her shift and was planning to visit the Bleak Harbor Cemetery before going home.

Malone had taken the call. She could tell Peters was talking with his mouth close to the phone. In the background she had heard a woman shouting, "He said not to tell anyone. He'll hurt—" Then Peters had hung up.

Malone had skipped her cemetery visit for the first time since the February blizzard buried her car. After scanning the police report from Danny's previous disappearance, she had gone straight to the Peters place, where she was presented with two printouts: one a screenshot of Danny tied to a chair, another of an email sent to Carey Peters at 6:45 a.m.

The email came from jeb@jeb.com and was signed "Jeremiah." It rests on the table between the lunch box and Malone.

"You don't know anyone named Jeremiah?"

"Not that I can think of," Pete says.

Malone slides the lunch box to the right, clearing the space between her and Danny's mother. The woman looks tired. Malone thinks of a handwritten note pinned to a bulletin board in her kitchen. The note came in the weeks after Louisa's death, slipped inside a sympathy card, the envelope bearing a Chicago postmark. "I can't imagine," the inscription said. "I'm so sorry." It was signed "Carey Peters."

"You don't really think a kidnapper would sign a ransom note with his real name?" Carey says.

"I don't want to assume anything at this point, Ms. Peters. It could be that this person who claims to have your son is trying to implicate someone else."

"I have a distant cousin or two named Jeremiah. It's a Bleak thing."

"We'll definitely check them out. Could you please—"

"They've been dead for years."

"I see. What about this email name, 'jeb'?"

"Family initials. Every male Bleak has a 'J' first name, middle name Estes, after the patriarch, Joseph. Jonah Estes Bleak, Jonathan Estes Bleak, et cetera."

The husband interrupts: "What's this guy mean by our 'sins'?"

"It doesn't say *your* sins, Mr. Peters. It says, 'Everyone gotta pay for *their* sins.'"

He wraps himself in his arms. Carey gives him a sideways glance, not especially kind. Malone jots this in her notepad. She inches the printout closer, scans it for the tenth time:

To who It Better Concern—

I got yr Danny boy.

He is OK for now. if u know what I mean

5145000 dollars.

11:46 tonight

details coming

Get the cake or that's the last of Danny.

every one gotta pay for there sins.

Jeremiah

Malone does the math in her head. They have a little less than six-teen hours till 11:46 p.m. The email arrived at 6:45. There's also a 45 in the odd ransom amount. On a whim, she counts the words in the email: 45. Could the 6 in 11:46 be a typographical error?

Maybe these echoes have meaning, Malone thinks. Or maybe they're random. Most criminals aren't nearly as clever as the ones on television and in books. Prisons are packed with people who think they're smarter than they really are.

"Your son was home alone yesterday afternoon, yes?"

"Danny," Carey says. Again her eyes slide sideways at her husband. "He was here, yes."

"I was just downtown," Pete Peters says.

Just, Malone thinks. *Feeling some guilt?* "Was he left alone on a regular basis?"

"He wasn't *alone* alone, Officer. I was—"

"The answer is yes, he was alone," Carey says. "Danny was alone at times." A shadow crosses her face. "Oh Jesus."

"Ms. Peters?"

"Danny was born at 11:46 p.m. Sixteen years ago. Tonight."

"I see."

Pete says, "That can't be a coincidence."

"Maybe, maybe not," Malone says. She's thinking not, but she wants to get back to the boy. "Ms. Peters," she says, "you were saying Danny was alone sometimes."

Carey takes a breath, then says, "Yes, sometimes. His issue isn't functioning on his own; it's functioning with—functioning well with others."

"So he's fine alone."

"We're both here on weekends, and I try to work from home at least one day a week. Danny isn't lacking for companionship."

Malone wants to ask about his grandmother but hesitates. She's aware that the relationship between Carey and her mother is fraught. The last time the boy disappeared, Serenity Bleak's assistant called the chief to express Mrs. Bleak's concern, less with the boy's whereabouts than the publicity surrounding the incident. The assistant didn't mention the hundreds of millions of dollars Serenity Bleak was dangling. He didn't have to.

"There was nobody else here?" Malone says. "A nanny or someone who—"

"No," Pete says. "Nobody else."

"Until recently, he had a dog."

Malone hovers a hand over the lunch box. "Here."

"Yes, Paddle—the dog's ashes are in there."

Malone looked inside earlier, saw the clear plastic bag secured with a twist tie, the doughy contents.

"That's the dog's name?"

"Paddle, yes."

"And Danny was quite fond of him."

Again Carey shuts her eyes. She appears determined not to cry in front of Malone or even her husband. Malone knows the feeling.

"Danny loved Paddle," Pete says. "He doesn't have a lot of friends—"

"That's not his fault," Carey says.

"—and Paddle was sort of his best pal."

"Thank you. And you found this lunch box where, exactly?"

"On his bed."

"When you checked his room earlier."

"Yes."

"We had to put the dog down," Pete interrupts. "Paddle was old and sick and, you know, he could barely walk. It was a lousy day for all of us."

"Of course. Did Danny always keep Paddle's ashes on his bed?"

"No," Carey says. "I'm actually not sure where he had them. Maybe in his closet, or one of his desk drawers. I know he keeps a little baggie of them in his wallet. But otherwise, this lunch box was out of sight."

"What about the wallet? You don't have that, right?"

"No. He probably had it on him."

"I have to say," Carey says, "I was kind of glad when I saw the lunch box on the bed because I thought maybe Danny was ready to finally do something with the ashes."

"Get some closure," Pete adds.

"Did Paddle—when did you put him down?"

"Around the last time."

"The last time?"

"The last time Danny left."

Malone recalls the *Light* story about Danny's earlier disappearance. She remembers feeling the story was unkind to Carey Peters, but she can't recall precisely why. She wishes she had reread it before coming over.

"I see. Do you think the dog's death had anything to do with Danny's leaving then?"

"Maybe," Carey says. "Probably. Danny didn't say, really."

"Has anything—"

"No, he's been fine. He's been good lately."

"We go fishing a lot," Pete says. "We were supposed to go last night. You can see the cooler—it's right over there—the sandwiches—"

Pete, apparently choked up, looks away. Carey eases back into her chair without looking at him. They don't seem like the happiest couple. But then who is the happiest couple but for a few scant years? On top of the usual, natural distancings over time and space, Carey and Pete Peters have had some of their own complications: the commuting, the new business, and of course, whatever challenges Danny must present.

"Danny's surname is Peters; is that correct?"

"We had it legally changed," Carey says.

"For any particular reason, may I ask?"

"Well, I'm a Peters too. And it's just easier not being a Bleak in Bleak Harbor. We're not the most beloved clan."

"I see. And Danny is autistic; do I have that right?"

"They asked us last time, Officer. He hasn't been cured."

"I'm sorry, Ms. Peters. I'm just trying to get a clearer sense of how Danny behaves."

Carey sighs. "I'm sorry," she says. "Danny is on the spectrum, as they say. What that means depends on which doctor you talk to. What we know for sure is that he's very bright. He likes to read, especially history."

"He likes the library," Pete interjects.

"He goes there on his own?" Malone asks.

"Yes," Carey says. "It's a short walk along the shoreline."

"He likes fishing," Pete says, "he likes poems, he loves the Cubs, as you can see. He's very interested in dragonflies. He can stand out on the dock for hours watching them."

"That all sounds fairly"—Malone stops herself from saying *normal*—"ordinary. What are Danny's, I'm not sure how to say this—"

"Deficits?" Carey says. "Shortcomings?"

"All adolescents have those."

"Problems? Danny's problem is he's not in love with people in general. He has trouble being around people he doesn't know well."

"And even the ones he does, sometimes," Pete says.

"Unless," Carey says, "he sees some purpose in them, something he needs."

"For instance?" Malone says.

"That's his mind-blindness," Pete says.

"For instance, the librarians," Carey continues, without acknowledging what her husband said. "They help him when he's there, and he actually talks about them when he comes home, especially a Mrs. Loiselle. It's—" Carey stops to compose herself—"quite sweet, actually, *especially* in an adolescent."

"He isn't just living in a shell," Pete says. "He's actually come out of it some."

"What about school?"

Carey keeps her eyes on Malone. "He was in a good place in Chicago. He had an excellent one-on-one aide—"

"Excellent," Pete says.

"—until she lost her job to budget cuts—"

"Politicians."

"—and Danny just wasn't the same after that. We tried a different school, and then, of course, we came here, and it wasn't working out, he wasn't engaging, so we took him out in February, and he's been working on a GED course online and, like I said, going to the library."

"Is he in therapy of some sort?"

"Yes. Occupational therapy, some speech, though speech isn't the issue it once was."

"I'll say," Pete says.

"Mr. Peters, what was that word you used? Some kind of blindness?"

"Mind-blindness?"

"Yes. What did you mean by that?"

Carey speaks up. "A state of mind. Danny will focus on one thing or idea or person to the exclusion of all others."

"He lacks sympathy," Pete says.

"Empathy," Carey corrects him.

"I see. Is that typical for someone with autism?"

"Is it typical for cops to eat doughnuts every morning?"

"Excuse me?" *She's annoyed*, Malone thinks.

"There is no 'typical.'"

"OK. Sorry." Malone flips a page on her notepad. "Ms. Peters, can you tell me again where you were at approximately five o'clock yesterday afternoon?"

"I was driving back from Chicago. I was probably, I don't know, more than halfway here. Traffic was a mess."

"You still work for the logistics company?"

"Pressman Logistics."

"And you, Mr. Peters?"

"I was at the council meeting at city hall. Everybody noticed me because I spilled coffee on Mrs. Naughton. I left around five."

"So you were back here at, what, five fifteen?"

"No, he had to stop at Boz's," Carey says, eyeing her husband again.

"The bar up the beach? Is that right, Mr. Peters?"

"Call me Pete, please."

He's avoiding his wife's gaze.

"Pete. Did you stop at the bar?"

"I had a tough day."

"Did you close your shop, or was someone—"

"I have an employee who was taking care of things."

"And who is he, please?"

"It's a she. Dulcy—I think it's actually Dulcinea—Pérez."

"Does she know Danny?"

"A little," Pete says. "He saw her at the shop a couple of times; no biggie."

"And when you got home, nothing seemed out of place?"

"Danny wasn't here," Carey says.

"Is that unusual?"

"Not really," Pete says.

"Yes, it's unusual."

"He goes for walks sometimes late in the day."

"Not for twelve hours."

"To answer your question, Officer Malone, no, nothing was amiss. You can see the cooler over there."

"The boat was still covered," Carey says. "His phone was here. He always takes his phone wherever he goes. We insist on it."

"And you checked his room."

"Yes. Everything seemed normal."

Malone had made a cursory check of the house when she arrived. She had pulled on disposable gloves and followed Carey and Pete around. The cottage was cozy, simple, well kept: two bedrooms, two bathrooms, a kitchen, a great room that opened on to the beach deck and the boat dock. A low-ceilinged basement devoid of anything but a furnace and water heater. Malone had looked for signs of a disturbance as well as evidence that one had been tidied up. She'd seen neither.

Carey had hesitated before opening her son's bedroom door, saying, "He doesn't like us going in here." Malone's thirteen-year-old, Louisa, had been the same. Danny's room looked as undisturbed as the rest of the house. Half-full vials of prescription pills sat on Danny's nightstand. The parents said that probably wasn't a good sign.

"What about this, Officer?" Carey points at the screenshot printout in front of Malone. "See his cheekbone?"

In the photo, Danny is wearing most of what he had on when Carey left him that morning: gray cargo shorts, a faded purple Prairie Surfers T-shirt, one of his green high-tops. His right foot is bare. Danny's eyes are obscured by a blindfold that looks torn from a pillowcase. His arms are behind his back, presumably duct-taped like his feet. His head lolls to one side.

"I see. Our lab will take a closer look, make sure it isn't just—"

"It's a bruise," Carey insists. "He fought back, and they hit him."

"Or, forgive me, Ms. Peters, they made him up to make you think they hit him."

"To scare us," Pete says.

"That's the same chair that was in the picture I showed you on my phone," Carey says. "Don't you think? And the roll of duct tape."

"Very possible," Malone says. "Again, I don't want to presume anything. We'll be checking that number."

"Danny can hit, so it has to be a man," Carey says. She seems angry all of a sudden. "Women don't steal other women's children."

The lump that rises in Malone's throat surprises her. "Excuse me, Ms.—Carey. Can I just say something?"

Carey sits up. "Go ahead."

"You sent me a note. A very nice note, last year, when my daughter was—when she died."

Pete turns to his wife, puzzled. Carey leans forward, recognition gradually widening her eyes. "Oh. Yes. I was—I'm so sorry."

"That was very kind of you. Thank you. It came at a particularly good—well, not good, but you know."

"Of course. You're welcome."

"So," Malone says, "we will assume for now that whoever this is did strike Daniel."

"Danny, please."

"Danny, pardon me. Even so, the boy appears to have left the house willingly."

"So he probably knew the kidnapper," Pete offers.

"Possibly. It would be helpful for you to give us a list with contact information for any friends or family who might be able to help us."

"I'm sorry," Carey says. "Nobody in my family gives a shit about my son, except for my brother. I'm sure you know him."

"I've met Mayor Bleak. What about your mother, and . . . is there any chance this could have anything to do with her"—Malone reaches for a word—"her proposal?"

Serenity Meredith Maas Bleak had offered the local municipalities her estate if they met one seemingly simple condition: that the town, the township, and the county, after 140-odd years as the namesakes of Joseph Estes Bleak, rechristen themselves as Serenity Bay, Serenity Township, Serenity County.

It seemed like a no-brainer to Malone. Hardly anyone liked what the place was called anyway. But the no-brainer had become mired in tiny-*p* politics and threats of litigation as the fiefs bickered over who would collect how much of Serenity's booty before any of them would relinquish their sole leverage, endorsement of the new name.

That's where the diabolical final sentence of Serenity Bleak's New Year's Day proposal came in. It stated that, if Serenity died before the names were changed, her entire estate would be placed in a trust that would in turn be bequeathed to the towns of South Haven, Saugatuck, Grand Haven, Union Pier, and New Buffalo, all lakeside resorts that vied for tourist business with Bleak Harbor.

"What would that have to do with this?" Pete says.

"It's been on the national news. A lot more people know about your mother and her wealth than a few months ago."

"So it could be just some random stranger, somebody Danny doesn't even know?" Carey says.

"Possibly. Though without any sign of a struggle, probably unlikely. Excuse me, but can I ask why you didn't call when you first determined Danny wasn't here?"

"You guys won't look for missing persons until they've been gone for twenty-four hours," Pete says.

"Actually, no, that's TV."

"No, that's what you told us last time," Carey says.

"Plus, we were worried maybe Danny was pulling another of his disappearing acts, like last time."

"So you looked for him."

"Yes. We even went next door, like last time."

"You set that alarm off?"

"We were in the house then," Pete says. "Why would an alarm be on anyway?"

"The bank probably wants to keep kids out."

"Exactly how many child abductions have you been involved in, Officer?"

One too many, Malone thinks.

"Pete," Carey says. "What's the matter with you?"

"It's all right," Malone says. "Plenty of children get taken in custody disputes." She recalls now what that *Bleak Harbor Light* story insinuated, and the rumors of tensions—potentially physical ones—between Carey Peters and her son. Sitting here, looking at the woman, Malone finds the whispers hard to believe. She decides not to ask about that, for now. "Ms. Peters," she says instead, "you wouldn't have any issues with your ex, would you?"

Carey sits back in her chair, hair falling away from her face, and Malone notes how much she looks like her son, the big eyes, the cheekbones. With a bit of makeup, either could pose as the other.

"I don't have an ex," she says.

"The record from the previous incident indicates your husband is Danny's stepfather."

"Pete is my first and only husband."

"I see, but what about—"

"I haven't seen him in years."

"—Danny's birth father?"

"I have no idea where he is."

"His name, please?"

"Bledsoe," Pete says. He sits up straighter, seemingly buoyed by this turn in the questioning. "Jeff Bledsoe. Loser."

"Jeffrey?"

"Yes," Carey says.

"Oh, he could've done this," Pete says, nodding. "For sure."

"Is that with a *j* or *g*?"

"*J*," Carey says.

"R-e-y or e-r-y?"

"R-e-y."

"Middle initial?"

Carey thinks. "I don't remember. I'm not sure I ever knew."

"I ask because this email is from J-E-B-dot-com," Malone says. "Could be a coincidence. You don't know if his middle name started with an *e*?"

"I didn't really know him all that well, unfortunately."

"I'd say fortunately," Pete says.

"Do you know this Bledsoe person, Mr. Peters?"

"Just what my wife's told me."

"Have you ever met him?"

"No. No desire to either."

Malone looks at Carey. "Apologies for asking, ma'am, but was this a brief, shall we say—"

"One-night stand? No. A fling. A month or two."

"And this was when?"

"Danny will be sixteen tonight, so almost seventeen years ago. I was working in Detroit, just out of U of M."

"And how did you come to know this man?"

"He was a client."

"A client?"

"I was working at the Wayne County Department of Social Services in Detroit. I helped people kick drug habits."

"Jeffrey Bledsoe had a drug habit?"

"Habit's a nice word for it."

"What was his drug?"

"What wasn't?"

"I gather he didn't kick it."

"For a while he did. Then he didn't. I told him to go away. By then I was carrying Danny."

"So, forgive me, but to be clear, you had an affair with a known drug dealer."

Carey opens her palms on the table and looks into them as if the right words might be written there. "I was young," she says. "I was bored. I don't know. He was, you know, my project."

"Something a little wild."

She turns her palms back over, looks up at Malone. "Something like that."

"I wouldn't think your department would allow fraternizing with clients."

"Of course not. I got suspended, actually, because after I told him to get out of my life, he ratted me out. I took my son and got out, came back here for a while, then to Chicago, and then"—she gives her husband another look—"back here."

"Do you know where he is now?"

"I know he was in prison. I think he got out."

"Why do you say that?"

"He contacted me."

"He did. When?"

"Late last year."

"Really?" Pete says. Malone studies his face, now turned to his wife. He had not known until this moment.

Carey's face is in her hands now, her elbows propped on the table. "He emailed me at my office. I told him to go away or I'd call the police."

"What did he want?"

"I don't remember exactly. Something about him coming to Chicago or something. So I guess he was out of prison. I erased it from my mind. I don't like thinking about Jeffrey."

"You didn't tell me about this."

Carey answers from inside her hands. "I didn't need to. It was bullshit. Jeffrey loves to fuck with people."

"Do you still have the emails?" Malone says.

"I doubt it. We wipe our servers clean every month."

"He sent it to your company email? At Pressman Logistics?"

"Yes."

"Did you ever hear back from him?"

"A week or so later. He told me he could just show up at my work if he wanted, make trouble."

"And what did you do?"

"I blocked his email."

"You didn't take it seriously."

"No."

"Did he ever just show up?"

"Not that I know of."

"And you didn't go to the police."

"And tell them what? I got a nasty email?"

"Jesus," Pete says. He should be upset with his wife, but the way he slumps back in his chair suggests to Malone that he's somehow relieved. "So it could be this asshole who took Danny."

"You don't know where Bledsoe was, which facility? Jackson?"

Carey thinks about this. "I'm not sure, but I think I may have heard Muskegon."

"Not too far from here," Pete says. "Goddamn."

"We'll track him down." Malone picks up her phone, sends a text to a colleague outside the cottage.

Pete says, "Isn't that a weird number?"

"Which?"

"Five-point-one-four-five million. I mean, wouldn't it normally be five million or ten million, something round?"

"There's no normal in these situations, but I take your point."

"Well, we don't have it. Not even close. And whoever took Danny, if he knows us, has to know that."

"But this person might think you could get it."

"My mother's not about to come to the rescue, Officer."

Malone wants to say, *It's her grandson, for God's sake.* Instead she closes her notepad and sets two business cards on the table.

"We will do everything we can to find your son as quickly as possible," she says. "We'll contact the FBI and alert other departments nearby. If you think of anything, don't hesitate to call me. My cell number is on the card. If for some reason you can't reach me right away, call the station and have me paged. Do you have somewhere else to stay?"

"Why?" Carey says.

"I'm afraid this is now a crime scene."

Pete says, "Are we suspects or something?"

Malone waits a beat. "No."

"Do we have to leave this minute?" Carey says. "What if Danny comes home and we're not here?"

Malone considers, then says, "We'll be back. Please do your best not to disturb anything in the meantime. It'd be good now if I could have Danny's phone and any other electronics, tablets, computers, whatever."

Pete's phone bleats.

"Why?" Carey says.

"It could tell us things—"

"Like?"

Out of the corner of an eye, Malone sees Pete turn sheet white as he looks at his phone.

"Like whether somebody was communicating with him."

"I will go through it and tell you."

"Danny's devices are evidence, Ms. Peters. We need them."

Carey's phone starts to shimmy across the table, a call coming in. Malone watches her check the phone. She knits her eyebrows as if the call is from someone she doesn't recognize. Carey stands. "I'll drop everything at the station later," she says. "I want to take a look first. I won't change anything. I'm sure that you can understand, Officer Malone."

Malone thinks of the note in her kitchen again. She could get a search warrant, but it would take longer than having Carey just bring the stuff in. She gets up from her chair. She has a bad feeling about all of this—the picture of the kid, the mark on his face, the ex-convict. She hopes Bledsoe was in for something like drug possession, nothing violent.

"All right, but please drop it off by ten o'clock sharp," she tells Carey.

"Eleven," Carey says. "We've been up all night."

Malone nods reluctantly. "Eleven," she says. She picks up her hat and fits it onto her head. "Mr. Peters," she says, "would you mind walking me out?"

"Uh, sure," Pete says, standing. "But I gotta hit the john. Meet you out there."

12

Pete closes the kitchen door behind him so as not to alert the neighbors on the side opposite the Helliker cottage. They probably aren't there, but he doesn't want to chance them seeing. His phone is in his back pocket, so he's less likely to look again at the image that appeared on it a few minutes ago.

In the bathroom, he locked the door and sat on the closed toilet seat with his head in his hands, wishing he could stay there until Danny showed up and the cops went away and everything went back to normal. Standing outside, he feels like he does in the foggy middle between sleep and waking on a hungover morning. None of this can be real: the photographs, the ransom email, the taunting texts, the silvery walking-away footprints left by Malone in the dewy grass.

How could it feel real? Who could ever imagine these sorts of things happening before they actually did? The phone blasting you out of dead sleep in the pit of night, the marines like ghosts on your front porch, the doctor whose look of pained resignation devastates you before he utters a word. Nightmares, that's what every parent calls them. Pete is in one now.

He sees Malone standing next to her police cruiser, talking with a heavyset young man in street clothes. He's holding something in his hands that he moves out of sight when Pete approaches.

"Got nothing for Jeremiah," the young man is saying.

"And you tried Bledsoe?"

"Excuse me?" Pete says.

"I'm sorry, Mr. Peters—Pete—this is my colleague, Will Northwood. He'll be assisting with the investigation."

"Sorry for your trouble," Will says.

"Will likes anagrams. I asked him to try *Jeremiah*. I figured this guy, whoever he is, might think he's clever."

"I see." Pete notices another car, unmarked, parked on the shoulder across the street. "Have you been out here all this time?"

Will Northwood is studying him. It makes Pete feel uneasy. He wants to go back in the house. But then he'll have to show Carey the new picture on his phone.

"Just checking things out," Will says. He turns to Malone and points down the high fence between the Peters and Helliker houses. "Found a turtle shell, pretty big one, cracked like someone whacked it with a hammer. Some empty beer cans. Two loose boards in the fence, fifteen up from the beach."

"Maybe that storm a few weeks ago," Malone says.

"That was a wicked one. I walked through the house next door too. It's pretty much gutted. Found what looked like blood at the bottom of the basement stairs."

"That was my wife's," Pete says.

"Looked fresh."

"She fell."

"Dangerous in there, sir. I wouldn't try that again."

"Mr. Peters," Malone says. She looks more official, even intimidating, with her police hat pulled down just above her eyebrows. "Do you have something you want to tell us?"

The "Mr. Peters" again, the questions, the "something," catch him off guard. "What do you mean?"

"I understand how you might want to protect your wife."

"Protect her from what?"

Will says, "Why the soundproof fence?"

"For privacy," Pete says. "To keep out nosy people." He had never wanted the damn fence anyway. Two grand, and it already has two loose boards?

"OK, Will," Malone says, taking a step in front of him. "I had to ask, Mr. Peters. I'm sorry."

It seems genuine, but Pete is still leery of the fat guy with his arm behind his back. "What kind of cop wears a golf shirt on the job?"

"I'm not an officer, Mr. Peters."

"Will's our tech guy," Malone says. "He's going to help find your son."

"Carey wouldn't harm a hair on Danny's head. Why are we even talking about this? What about Bledsoe? Are you going to look for him?"

Will and Malone exchange glances. "He got out of Muskegon in December. Paroled for good behavior."

December, Pete thinks. Wet and cold. Carey was bitching more than usual about the commute.

"I see. How long was he in?"

"Almost six years."

Pete recalls that Bledsoe called Carey once not long after they were married seven years ago. He can't remember much but that she'd told him to go to hell. He wishes now that she'd said something about Bledsoe's more recent contact, just so he would've known, though he's not sure what difference it would have made.

"We'll know more soon," Malone says. "Will, can you show him the shoe?"

From behind his back Will produces a clear plastic bag. It contains a green high-top sneaker, right foot.

"Jesus," Pete says.

"This is your son's?"

"Looks like it. Where did you find it?"

"Out by the road. Size eight and a half."

"Is there any . . . ?" Pete can't finish.

"No blood that I can see. But we'll run some tests."

"But the fact that it came off—Danny must have resisted." Pete can't decide whether this is a good thing or bad.

"Found this too." Will shows Pete a smaller plastic bag containing a phone. "Found it in the grass beneath the windows on the side of the house. Ever see it before?"

"No. It doesn't look like one of ours."

"It's a burner—a disposable phone, one you buy with prepaid minutes and throw away when it's used up. Your boy wouldn't have had one, would he?"

"Not that—no. Why would he?"

"You're in the drug business, aren't you, Mr. Peters?"

"What's that got—I'm in the legal marijuana business."

"How's it going?"

"Fine."

"I read it's a money-printing business," Malone says.

"I'm just getting started. What's this got to do with anything?"

"From what little we know so far," Northwood says, "it sounds like Bledsoe may have been involved in the same business in Detroit."

"I don't know about him, but my business is perfectly legal."

"Yes," Malone says. "You'll be closed today, by the way. We'll be cordoning off your office as a crime scene."

Icy droplets of sweat prickle Pete's temples. Could these cops possibly know about the illicit dealer he's been buying from? What might they find in his office? He mentally scours his desk for any scribbled scraps or sticky notes that could get him in trouble.

Maybe he should just tell them. But what's he going to say? *Find a dude who calls himself Slim?* Pete has never laid eyes on the guy. What good would telling do anyway? It would just confuse things, he tells himself, might even put him in jail when Carey needs him most. Better to focus on the ex-convict, Danny's real father, Bledsoe.

"I better get back to Carey."

"Can I ask you something, Pete?" It's Will again. Pete wishes he would go away. "Why did you go to the bar yesterday? Why not just go straight home to your son?"

He pictures Boz's, the TVs leaning off the top of the back bar like they might pitch onto the floor, the queue of beer taps beneath the fake reindeer head with the blinking red nose on the knotty pine wall, a Christmas decoration that stayed up all year. "I just sat through two hours of bullshit at city hall and I wanted a drink. What's the big deal?"

"We didn't say it was a big deal," Malone says.

"Officer Malone said you seemed kind of relieved to hear Bledsoe's name."

"Relieved? I'm not relieved about any of this. Christ." Pete takes a backward step toward the house. "I'm glad there might be a suspect. Could that phone, that disposable thing, could that help?"

"You've never met him, have you?" Will asks.

"Who?"

"Bledsoe."

"No, I've never met him."

"Inside, you called him a loser," Malone says.

"He is a loser, based on what Carey has told me. Didn't you just say he's a drug dealer?"

"Incidentally, Pete," Malone says, "when we were inside, it looked like you got something on your phone that upset you."

Pete tries to keep his breathing steady as the image returns to him. He considers showing them. But he doesn't want to make the same mistake twice. It'll be bad enough showing it to Carey.

"Everything is upsetting, Officer. It was nothing. It just reminded me that yesterday, we were—everything was fine."

"OK. You said you had an employee keep your shop open while you were gone yesterday," Will says.

"Pérez?" Malone says.

"Yes, Dulcy, Dulcy Pérez."

Will says, "Got a cell number for her?"

Pete takes out his phone, reads out a number for Will, who punches it into his own phone.

"All right," Malone says. "Can you think of anyone besides this Bledsoe who'd have the slightest motivation to do this?"

"We will definitely think about it, Officer."

"Don't think long. We have about fifteen hours."

As Pete turns for the house, he sees the blinds on the kitchen door flutter. He thinks again of that reindeer nose blinking red on the wall at Boz's. There's a man standing in front of it, with a stark, bony face. Pete thinks of the bruise on Danny's cheek. He thinks of what he's about to show Carey. He tells himself he will make the call he does not want to make.

13

Carey squints through the blinds on the kitchen door.

It's hard to see through the morning haze. The young man in the polo shirt is showing Pete something inside a clear plastic bag—it looks, from afar, like a shoe—then another similar bag containing something Carey can't quite make out. She remembers this man. He came to the house and asked the upsetting questions the last time Danny vanished.

She had forgotten about sending that sympathy note to Officer Malone. It was more than a year ago, when she and Pete and Danny were still living in Chicago. Carey had read about the accident in an online news story her brother had sent. Perhaps Carey imagined it, but sitting across from her at the great-room table, Malone appeared much older than the woman Carey remembered from photographs the year before.

Even now, Carey isn't sure why she took a sheet of Pressman Logistics stationery and jotted a message on the back to the bereaved mother. She isn't one of those people who are constantly dashing off little missives about birthdays and baptisms and such. But maybe she felt a distant kinship because Malone was in Bleak Harbor and the death of her daughter had, in a way, isolated her from everyone else there. Carey knew that feeling.

She catches a glimpse of Pete's face as he turns to come back into the house. It's creased with guilt. She lets the blinds close, steps away from the door, waits. Pete enters the kitchen and shuts the door behind him. Carey's not surprised when he chokes out a sob.

"I'm sorry," he says. "I shouldn't have called them."

"Who?"

"The police." He covers his face with one hand and gives Carey his phone with the other. "Look."

Carey's legs go rubbery when she sees the image on the phone screen. It's framed like the earlier one of Danny tied to the chair. But now the chair is in pieces, the seat and back askew on the floor, a leg snapped off and thrown aside. In the background shadows, a green high-top sneaker is lying on its side, and farther back, she can see the heel of a hand. Tiny white letters are printed at the bottom of the screen:

u told

"Bastard," she says.

"I'm sorry."

Carey feels herself starting to hyperventilate. "Fuck it," she says. "Just fuck it, fuck this asshole. Did you show the cops?"

"No. Should I have?"

"Probably. I don't know. I know I said they're worthless, but how could we not call them?"

They were sitting in the great room, silent, just waiting, dawn nearing, when the kidnapper's email arrived. Carey had closed her eyes for one second, dozed off. She woke to Pete on the phone with the cops.

"How could this guy know we called, anyway?" Pete says.

"Maybe he heard it on a police scanner?"

"Or maybe he hacked our phones somehow. Carey. What are we going to do?"

"Pete, you have to settle down."

"Carey."

"Come here."

Pete steps into her embrace. She feels the trembling along the backs of his arms. Closing her eyes, she conjures a memory of Danny. He's two years old on the crowded beach at North Avenue in Chicago, a steamy Sunday in August. He's jumping up and down at the water's edge. The pebbles at his feet glisten like black diamonds. He's jumping and laughing, the sand squishing up between his toes, and Carey is jumping and laughing herself when Danny's soaked diaper undoes itself and tumbles off. Carey shrieks another laugh and hurries to grab him up, but Danny is already running away down the shore, his lightbulb butt bobbing between the beach walkers.

Carey draws away from Pete. She feels, all of a sudden, unexpectedly calm. The panic and fear that gripped her driving home yesterday and then later when she knew Danny was gone have, for now at least, leached away. Which is good, because if Pete is falling apart, she has to stay as composed as she can so someone is figuring out what to do next.

"Maybe those photos are staged, like the officer said," Pete says.

"It's possible. He can't—whoever this asshole is, he wants his money. He has to keep Danny safe."

She hopes this more than believes it.

"The police found a disposable phone outside. It's got to be the kidnapper's. Maybe they can trace it or something." He pauses. "They found a shoe too."

"I saw."

"One of Danny's high-tops, out by the road."

"So maybe he tried to resist."

"Maybe. They said Bledsoe got out of prison in December."

"All right."

"So maybe it's him. The police will find him. I'm sorry."

Enough with sorry, she thinks. "I left a message at Mother's."

"You don't think Serenity's going to help."

"I'll worry about her. You need to reach out to Oly."

Carey suspects that Pete was actually fired from O'Nally Bros. Yet he maintains a relationship with one of the brothers, Oly, so maybe he really did just quit because he was bored. Oly has at least as much money as Serenity Meredith Maas Bleak.

"What about the 'do not tell' thing?" Pete says.

"We can't just sit here. And the cops already know. We need to raise the money somehow in case they can't find him."

Carey's phone goes off.

"Oly doesn't use a cell, you know," Pete says. "That Serenity?"

Carey looks at her phone. It's the second call from a Bleak Harbor number, but not her mother's. Bledsoe? She doubts it—or wants to doubt it.

"No," she says. "I'm going into Danny's room. Get with Oly, please."

14

Everything in Danny's room looks to be in its place. The blue Cubs bedspread neatly folded beneath the pillows, the pillows stacked in their checkered blue-and-white covers, the Wallace Stevens anthology on the nightstand, four of Danny's five pairs of sneakers and sandals lined up at the foot of the bed, toes out. His green high-tops, always second from the left, are missing.

Danny doesn't like his parents going into his room when he isn't there. Carey finds this endearing, perhaps because it makes him seem like a normal fifteen-year-old.

At the window facing the bay, she sees sun bleeding around the edges of the drawn blinds. Most summer dawns, she likes to leave Pete in bed, pad barefoot out to the deck, and stand shivering in the last moments of dark to wait, first for the caress of warmth on the back of her neck, then for the glimmers of light skipping across the water.

Now the light reminds her that Danny has been gone for—she glances at her phone: 9:29—something like sixteen hours. She's been without him, and he without her, for longer than that many times in the past year, since Pete had them move to Bleak Harbor. She tells herself yet again that she couldn't help those absences. She wishes now, more than ever, that she could have them back. She wishes she were sitting with Danny on the tiny balcony of their Chicago condo, drinking tea and watching the sun rise through the skyline, the wind making it impossible to read the *Tribune*, Danny trying anyway, his eyes needle-points of focus as he halves and quarters the pages.

She feels tears coming, squeezes them back. *I will find you, honey.* She promises herself that when she does, she will take Danny away—whether she has the money or not, whether Pressman calls her bluff or not—she will take Danny away, alone, just the two of them, forever.

She reminds herself that Randall Pressman's Chicago number has also appeared on her phone twice in the past hour. Maybe he's feeling desperate. As she is. He could help her now. The ransom, five million bucks, is chump change to him. But she hesitates to call him back after what Pete showed her on his phone. What if someone really is listening in? At the same time, the thought of it, the wrecked chair, the hand in the shadows, infuriates her.

Hurt my boy, she thinks, *and I will hurt you.* And then decides if Pressman calls again, she will answer.

Danny's twin desks, spotless but for identical black blotters fitted with calendars, stand on facing walls. One wall is covered with posters of fish, the other with photographs and drawings of dragonflies that Danny made. He alternates between the desks, rolling from one to the other on his swivel chair, laptop propped on his knees. Carey and Pete have tried in vain to discern some pattern to his choice of desk on a given day; Danny has told them, shrugging as if it was obvious, that some days one desk works better than the other.

Carey pulls the chair over to the desk beneath the fish, where she set Danny's laptop and phone. She opens the laptop. As she waits for the password prompt, she notices something stuck in the groove between the keyboard and screen, at the very middle, as if Danny placed it there on purpose. She takes it out, holds it up in front of her face. It's a cherry stem. Danny doesn't even like cherries. She sets it aside.

She demanded Danny's password after his previous vanishing act, promising to use it only in an extreme emergency. He protested, but Carey wouldn't relent. He stalked into his room and emerged with his Wallace Stevens collection open to a dog-eared page at the back of the book. Carey knew the poem. She had read it hundreds of times, had listened to Danny recite it at least as many. He held the book up in front of her face. He had circled one word: *unhappy*. His password.

She types the seven strokes now for the first time since that night, feeling the savage swell of her emotions. Danny could be cruel that way. His anger, as sudden as it was fierce, frightened her sometimes. She had to remind herself that he wasn't always in control of himself, that he could be as much at the mercy of his unexpected compulsions as she was, that she couldn't blame him for being what—that is, who—he was.

As his doctors and her therapist had repeatedly told her, although his tantrums were usually aimed at her rather than Pete, they weren't always a direct response to something she had done or said or failed to do or say. They were merely Danny's way of purging his feelings without hurting himself. She should not fault herself. She should ignore anyone who did.

None of which made Carey feel any better when Danny flung himself and his fists and elbows and knees at her, screaming as if he, not she, were enduring the blows. Once in a while he would apologize. But first he would descend into his own quiet mourning for what he had done to his mother. At least that's what Carey imagined, what she hoped.

Once, after he bit her so hard on her forearm that she had to sponge droplets of blood from the kitchen hardwood, Danny locked himself in his room and refused to come out even to pick up the food Carey left for him outside his door.

After a day and a night, he appeared in the front room, where Carey and Pete were watching a movie.

"Look who's here," Pete said.

"Danny, honey," Carey said. Before she could get out of the recliner, Danny had crawled onto her lap as if he were six years younger. He hadn't done that in a long time.

"Mom," he said. He touched the bandage on her arm. "Mommy."

"It's OK."

He put his arms around her neck and buried his face in her shoulder. "No, no, no," Carey heard him saying, and it was all she could do to keep from crying. She gently rocked him, feeling his warm tears on her neck, telling him it was all right because it was, because Danny was the son she had made and she loved him more than anyone or anything in the world. He kept mumbling. Finally, Carey understood.

"Who is it?" Danny was saying. "Who is it?"

"Who is what, honey?" Carey said, and then in a terrible heart-breaking flash, she understood that he was asking about himself. "It's all right," she whispered into his ear. "It's going to be OK." Then her own tears came. Pete got off the sofa and came over, but Carey shook her head and held Danny tighter as her husband stepped back.

———

While the laptop starts, Carey lifts her eyes to the poster over the desk. A banner in gold atop a field of blue announces, **THE GREAT FISH OF THE GREAT LAKES**. Below it are pencil sketches of fish: bloaters and alewives, Chinook and coho, yellow perch and white, muskellunge, pike, smelt, burbot. They all look pretty much the same to Carey. Some are bigger or longer or skinnier than others, some a little grayer or greener. They're all swimming in the same direction, toward the left edge of the poster. They're all wearing the same faint, ironic grins. Sheep, not fish.

Carey reaches for Danny's mouse and tentatively inches it around, following the arrow-shaped cursor as it darts about the screen. She halts the white arrow in the middle. Her eyes stray to the edges of Danny's laptop, flecked with yellow and orange scraps of paper, the remains of torn-off two-word sticky notes he writes to himself in precise block lettering:

TROUT BOOK. MOM SCHEDULE. PADDLE TREATS. PETE CALL.

The rows of icons on the laptop screen are aligned as orderly as the dutiful poster fish. Carey wonders if she should have just handed the laptop and phone over to the cops, to someone who might actually know how to find what clues could be hidden within. Yet, clicking into Gmail, Carey knows she's not as curious as she is afraid. This computer is a window into her boy's mind. She doesn't know what it might reveal, and she's reluctant to have strangers, even police officers, see.

The email program opens. The expanse of white space inside the inbox saddens Carey. She knows Danny doesn't get many emails or texts or calls, because he has few friends. Really none she knows of. Most of the kids on this side of the bay are here on weekends only. Most are younger. Sometimes Carey hears them chortling like chipmunks as they build sandcastles, and she wishes Danny were still eight or nine so maybe he would join them. He's good at sandcastles when he's in a patient mood.

Sometimes Danny seems fine with it all, and Carey takes a chance on thinking he's feeling more comfortable with himself. Then he flies into one of his fits, and Carey has to ask herself again whether she has given him a real chance at a normal life.

No, she has to answer. By marrying Pete, she bought her son financial security, or what she thought would be security until Pete's trading went south and he had his preposterous, un-thought-through notion of becoming a marijuana magnate. Before Pete, it was all she could do as a human resources nobody at Pressman Logistics to get the rent paid and fill the fridge halfway after paying for Danny's schooling and therapy and medical bills.

The blast of a horn outside startles her. She pictures the tourists crowding the tour boat's gunwales, the brims of floppy hats and baseball caps shading their sunscreened foreheads. She takes the mouse in hand again and whispers, "Danny."

Three opened emails wait. One is harmless, from a Cubs fan site peddling T-shirts and caps. The other two make Carey sit back. "Oh God," she says. The sender of each is "bleeds0." *Jeffrey.* He probably thought the reference to blood was funny. Violence to him was an occupational hazard, an occasionally entertaining one.

When she'd met him, she was twenty-one years old, a recent graduate of the University of Michigan, pondering tattoos and a master's in social work, disgusted with her parents, planning to save the world or at least some shadowy corner of it along Detroit's gentrifying Cass Corridor. Who better to save than Bledsoe, a supposedly recovering addict who was taking banjo lessons at Wayne State and had pecs of quivering bronze?

Bledsoe was her rebellion, Pete her surrender.

She recalls Bledsoe's face the last time she saw him—Detroit, Indian Village, Danny's baby things in cardboard boxes. He stood behind a locked screen door.

"I ain't the daddy, am I?" he said.

"If only," she said. "Go away."

Do not hurt my boy, Carey's thinking now. *Just give me my boy, and we will disappear forever.*

How the hell would he know how to contact Danny anyway? She clicks on the earlier of the two emails. It arrived at 9:27 a.m. on April 8. The date is familiar, in a scary way. Carey scours her memory. A shiver runs up her forearms. April 8 was three days after Danny ran away and hid at the Helliker place.

She doesn't know whether she's more upset that Bledsoe contacted her son, or that Danny didn't tell her about it, or that Danny chose to save Bledsoe's email, not delete it. *Easy*, she tells herself. She closes her eyes, takes a breath, opens her eyes again.

The email subject line reads "YOU."

> Champ,
>
> This is your real daddy. Sorry about what's goin on. Glad u are OK.

Carey hates that word, *champ*. Jeffrey had used it to label any male he encountered, friend or stranger, unless it was *ace* or *bro*. Or *pussy*. That was another favorite, reserved for those whom Jeffrey felt either absolutely superior to or absolutely threatened by.

Men are so fucked up, Carey thinks.

The email went on:

> Here for u, my man. Hope u know that.

Fuck you, she thinks. She wonders what Jeffrey knew or knows about what happened the day Danny ran away. Maybe he just read what that bitch wrote for the *Light*. Or, as much as Carey doesn't want to think it, maybe Danny told him. Maybe he was so furious with her and Pete that he sought out his birth father.

Why, Danny?

She remembers Bledsoe sprawled on a chair in her cramped office in Detroit with its odor of baseboard mold and scalded coffee. He would show up at her office unannounced and grin and flash his fingers for the number of days he'd been clean and sober. Carey would nod and smile and get off whatever call she was on. He made it to seventy-seven days. Or so he said.

———

She banished him from her life on what was supposedly Sobriety Day 81. It wasn't just that he was lying to her about using again. It was what it did to him that night as they hunted for parking on a Corktown side street before a Tigers ball game.

Carey drove her Ford Fiesta with the shattered side-view mirror. Jeffrey sat in the passenger seat with his rottweiler, Pip, curled at his feet. He brought the dog whenever they were out in the city. "Nobody fucks with Pip," he liked to say. "He's been expertly trained." Carey didn't like Pip much, but she tolerated him and supposed he tolerated her too.

Jeffrey was uncharacteristically quiet as they trolled the neighborhood that evening. Carey almost asked if something was wrong but wasn't sure she wanted to hear the answer. He had recently picked up that surly voice he adopted whenever he was around certain people. He'd had it when Carey first met him at social services. It had slowly disappeared as he got sober.

She saw the spot on Plum Street first, but a Civic full of young men coming from the opposite direction swerved to block her. "Jerk," she yelled out her window as she slowed going past.

By then Jeffrey and Pip were out of her car. She watched them in the cracked kaleidoscope mirror on her left and hand rolled the window down, shouting, "Jesus, Jeff, leave it."

Bledsoe walked to the Civic, Pip snarling beside him. The kid had made the mistake of rolling his window down. "What the fuck, old man?" he said, his pals laughing. Bledsoe reached through the window and dragged the kid—he couldn't have been twenty-five—out by his hair. Doors flew open, and Pip vaulted into the back seat and sank his teeth into a gym-popped bicep. Carey froze, her foot planted on the brake, as the bicep guy screamed and the driver yelled, "Dude, what the fuck?" while Jeffrey yanked him across the potholed street and rammed his head into the backseat window of a Buick, then pulled the kid's head back, blood spurting, and slammed it into the driver's window.

The kid's other two pals pulled Bledsoe away—he was laughing now—but they didn't have time or the balls to retaliate. They were yelling at Carey to call 911 as she pulled the car forward and screamed at Jeffrey to get in, goddamn it, get in before the cops show up. "Pipster, now, boy," Bledsoe shouted, and the dog sprang out of the Civic and scrambled with his master into Carey's Ford.

She screeched her way down the street, fishtailing so the kids might not pick up the license plate. She smelled the blood spackling Bledsoe's hairless arms, heard the sickening wet click of Pip licking his jaws. "What the hell are you thinking?" she said, but Jeffrey just grinned and said, "Serves 'em right, driving a Japmobile—don't it, Pipster?"

For the next few days, she avoided her office and ignored his calls and emails until, a week later, she felt like she had to tell him she was pregnant. It was his child, after all. Maybe he'd come around if he knew he was a father. She was mistaken about that. Bledsoe told her she must have fucked around on him. She told him goodbye. He told her good riddance, whore.

———

Carey skips to the more recent email from Bledsoe. She's trying to ignore the creeping realization that she's in the middle of one of those pathetic kidnappings that aren't really kidnappings, or that people don't count as kidnappings because they involve an ex-husband or ex-wife using a child as a human shield. But this is Jeffrey, she tells herself. If he'd learned nothing in prison, if he'd only grown angrier, if he's using, there's no telling what he might do.

The email's subject line says "Re: YOU." Carey assumes it's part of a string connected to the first email. She wants to see how Danny responded. The email opens. All prior messages, including Jeffrey's first, have been deleted.

The email had come the night before Danny was taken. *Oh fuck fuck fuck*, she thinks. The time signature says 10:29 p.m. Danny's bedroom door would have been closed and locked, but he probably would have been awake.

The email says only:

Y not, Danny boy?

Carey reads it again, then a third time, then picks up the mouse and slams it back down.

"Goddamn you, Jeffrey, goddamn you."

She scrolls to see what else is in the email. There's nothing. She can't see what Danny said to prompt Bledsoe's response. He apparently rejected something Jeffrey had requested or suggested. But what? A call? A visit? Had he pissed Jeffrey off enough that he would come to take her son by force? If Danny was unwilling to see Jeffrey, why would he have gone with him without a fight? She remembers the shoe the cops found discarded outside. Maybe there was a fight.

She returns to the first message, rereads it, then clicks back to the more recent one. There had to be emails in between. Why did Danny save only the two? She slides the cursor to the Sent folder, thinking she might find the entire string there. But there are only a dozen or so sent emails, all to the Cubs fan site, nothing addressed to bleeds0. If there was a string, Danny erased it.

She reads again:

Y not, Danny boy?

Why not what?

She picks up Danny's phone, fumbles it to the floor—"Damn it"—bends over, picks it up, turns it on. It wants a password. Carey didn't have the heart to demand Danny's phone password after the way he reacted to giving her the one for the laptop. She tries the laptop password: *unhappy.* Incorrect. Tries again. Wrong.

Her own phone is ringing. It's Pressman. She starts to answer, then calls out, "Pete? Are you still out there?" Deciding he's gone, she lets the phone ring once more before picking up.

"Carey Peters," she says, trying to sound tough, afraid she doesn't.

"Working from home today?" Pressman says.

"What do you want?"

"Wow. Right to the point. All right. You know what I want. I want to work this thing out."

Carey looks around the room as if somebody might be listening. "My son," she says.

"Your son?"

"I'm not at work because of my son."

"What happened?"

She thinks, for a short moment, about ending the call, then says, "He's been taken."

"What do you mean, 'taken'?"

"Kidnapped. For ransom."

The phone goes silent. Finally Pressman says, "You're serious."

"Dead serious."

"You obviously don't know who?"

"He calls himself 'Jeremiah.' And no, we don't know, but he wants five million dollars, or Danny—"

She can't finish.

"Five million? Have you called the police?"

"They just left."

"Jesus. Do you—do they have any ideas?"

She isn't sure what to say. She knows what she needs. She knows what Pressman will want in return. That's the way it is. Unless her mother helps. Which she can't count on.

"Carey?"

She imagines Pressman sitting in his office at company headquarters, a gray, three-story brick building hunkered like a dead hippo on a brushy bank of the Chicago River. Pressman took an absurd pride in keeping his gritty business of trucks and container ships and boxcars in that decrepit building on the river. He said he liked to count his money on the cargo boats chugging by. He took equal satisfaction in having a drab third-floor office with a plain steel desk, the two cheap angle-iron chairs facing it, the threadbare sofa, the Kmart lamp, the single window with its slatted perspective on the river. One black-and-white photograph hung on a wall to the right of the desk. A man with Pressman's dimpled chin stood in grease-smeared coveralls, holding a wrench the size of a baseball bat in his thick arms. It was Pressman's father, who had worked in a plant in northern Indiana, where Pressman grew up. Carey knew the plant. Her family had once owned it.

"I have to have five-point-one-four-five million dollars by 11:46 tonight. Which means right away, Randall. Are you going to help?"

He doesn't respond immediately. Then: "Sorry if I find it a bit surprising that you'd ask me."

"You called me."

"Your mother's loaded. What about her?"

"She's loaded, all right."

"It's her grandson."

"Who she hasn't seen in months."

"How do I know this isn't just another shakedown, with a discounted price?"

Again Carey feels the urge to hang up the phone, forget Pressman, pray the Bleak Harbor cops get lucky. "You prick. You don't have a choice."

"I have a choice, Carey. I can choose to just hang up now."

He's bluffing. He wants to be rid of her, the documents she stole, the threat she poses.

"Go ahead."

"And we'll all just take our chances."

"Go to hell."

"Sure. You can hold the door for me." He sighs. "Look. You don't have any idea who might have the kid?"

"His name is Danny."

A fresh email pops up in Danny's inbox. The From field says jeb@jeb.com. Subject: Danny boy. Carey grabs the mouse, clicks the email open:

boy safe for 14 hrs 3 minnits.

that's all

She skims the rest quickly, her heart thrumming. This person somehow knows she's in Danny's computer? Does he know she's talking to Pressman? She scrolls down as far as she can. No new images of Danny, thank God.

"Danny. Yes. Sorry. You have no idea? Carey?"

She does, of course. But all Pressman needs to know is that she'll turn him over to the authorities if he doesn't pay the ransom. If Bledsoe really is the abductor, the cops will have to find him. If he's not, she'll have Pressman's money to pay whomever it is.

"I don't know," she says.

"All right. We can help each other here, Carey."

"Tell me how, Randall."

"OK. Can we just forget about everything up to this point? Wipe the slate clean? No more blackmail games?"

She's reading:

U will get instructions on cash soon

5mill 145 grand

"It's possible," she says.

"Do you have something to write with?"

She pulls open a desk drawer, finds a legal pad and a box of sharpened pencils. Danny prefers pencils to pens for drawing because he likes to erase his mistakes and start over clean.

"Got it," she says.

"Write this down."

She hears the beep of a new call coming in as Pressman gives her the address of a restaurant across the Indiana-Michigan border. "How soon can you get there?"

She's reading the rest of the email:

yr bitch mama could pay with tens and 20s or maybe hit up randy bossman (get it?) if u haven't already

nummnuts cops aint gonna find danny boy

Jeremiah

ps. what I hear u don't deserve a kid anyway

She sits back straight, thinks, *You fuck.*

Another beep comes. She leans back into the desk, swallows hard, tells Pressman, "Hold on," flips to the other call.

"Roland," she says.

"Miss Carey."

It's her mother's personal assistant. *Your bitch mama*, she thinks. She has known Roland Spitler her entire life. She imagines him in his seersucker and bow tie, sitting at his little rolltop desk down the hallway from her mother's bedroom, his face as pale as if he lived his life in a closet. Which, in a way, he does.

"Have you found Danny yet?"

"No. You haven't heard from him?"

"We have not. I'm sorry. This is frightful news, of course. Miss Serenity is beside herself."

"Please, Roland."

"You really need to have more faith in your mother."

"I would love to. But now I need to call you back. I'm on the line with the police."

"We hope to be in position to help."

Hope, she thinks. *In position.* She taps back to Pressman. "Why am I going to a Mexican restaurant?"

"So I can help you."

"Randall, I need five million one hundred—"

"You will have it if we need it. But first we're going to find this scumbag who took your—Danny. He had—has a computer, right? Can you bring it with you?"

"A laptop." She hesitates. "The cops took it."

"Gimme a second."

She thinks she can hear irritation in Pressman's voice. He puts Carey on hold. She hears a piano plinking Devo. Pressman comes back on. "Does Danny have a portable hard drive?"

"I'll have to look." Carey knows what a hard drive is because she never remembers to use hers. "Why?"

"You'll be meeting Quartz. He works for me."

"Who?"

"Quartz. Like the rock."

She knows the names of most of Pressman Logistics' 153 employees. She thinks she'd remember a "Quartz."

"He's on my personal budget," Pressman says. "You don't know him."

"Do I want to?"

"Remember those boxcars of catalytic converters that disappeared from the rail yard in Roselle? How we tracked them down and had the bad guys in jail in under twelve hours?"

She recalls that one of the bad guys wasn't fortunate enough to get to jail. "In North Dakota. I remember."

"That was Quartz. My hunting dog."

She hadn't expected this. She just wanted the money. "This isn't a train, Randall. If this Quartz screws up, my son—"

"We're going to find your son. And if we don't, I will pay. And you will do your part. Just get to Valparaiso. Bring the hard drive. And there'll be no more discussion of documents or talking to the feds."

Carey looks up at the dumb grinning fish. *Dear Lord*, she thinks, *how did I put myself in this position?*

"Fine. And you will never touch me again."

"All right."

"And I will have my job as long as I want it."

"So be it. Quartz is an acquired taste. But he'll help you."

"He better. Or all bets are off—do you understand?"

"Get going."

She reads the new email again: "randy bossman." *Real funny*, she thinks. This bastard, too, seems to know about her Valentine's Day mistake. Would the police now know? Would Pete? Or, worst of all, Danny?

Carey rereads the postscript. *The hell with it*, she thinks. *The hell with all these people and what they think they know about me and my son. I'm gonna get him back and get out of this place forever.*

She looks again at the "randy bossman" line. This one she wishes she could delete. Just that one. Just those words. What difference would it really make to the cops or anyone? The rest of the email is what matters, not this random bullshit taunt.

But of course there's no way to selectively obliterate that phrase. She'd have to erase the entire email. She could delete it all and then go to the trash file and delete it again. The police would never see it, Pete would never know, Danny would never know.

Do not tell, Jeremiah had ordered.

She shuts her eyes, puts her fingers on the keyboard. Hits the print command.

She pushes away and rolls across the room to the other desk. Danny's portable hard drive, a black box about the size of a wallet, is in a drawer with other electronic paraphernalia. She grabs it, slides over to Danny's printer, snatches up the printout of Jeremiah's email. She gets up and walks back to the other desk. She shuts the printout in the laptop and picks up Danny's phone.

On her own phone, she punches the speed-dial number for her brother.

"Carey," he answers. "I've been trying—"

"Jonah, shut up—sorry, I don't have time."

"What?"

"I want you—I need you to meet me at the fork north of town, by Billy's Bait. I have something you need to take to the police."

"Right now?"

"Three minutes."

Arms full, Carey is leaving Danny's bedroom when something to her left catches her eye. She turns and stumbles back, bumping the door shut as she expels a yelp of fright. She fumbles for the doorknob behind her, eases the door back open. Sunlight from the hallway creeps across the pencil drawings pushpinned to the wall.

There's one Carey hadn't noticed until now.

The dragonfly's silver-dollar eyes are dense with fine, crosshatched strokes. Inside its mouth she sees two more eyes, a smaller insect being crushed in the dragonfly's dark maw. "My God, Danny," she whispers. She steps out of the room and closes the door.

15

"What the fuck, Quartz? I thought Bledsoe—"

"No names," Quartz says. He's sitting in an angle-iron chair across from Pressman, who just got off the phone with Carey Bleak Peters. "You don't know who's listening."

"I thought you hadn't heard from him."

"I have not."

"He got the kid."

"Obviously. But he hasn't yet alerted me as he was clearly instructed." *Idiot probably didn't write the phone number down*, Quartz thinks.

"And you haven't heard from him otherwise?"

"We agreed we would not communicate, lest people make connections you don't want them to make."

"So he's just gone?"

"No. He's probably lying low. You know I will find him if it's necessary."

"Where the hell did he get that number? Five-point-one-four-five million? That's not what you told him, is it?"

"I told him the ransom would be what you and I agreed upon, a nice round one million dollars."

"So he just decides on his own to quintuple it? What does he think he's doing?"

Quartz shrugs. It's amusing to see the captain of industry sweat over a few million bucks. "It's possible he thinks he can shake us down. That might be a potential downside of hiring convicted felons for contract kidnappings."

"Fuck you, Quartz—"

"Names."

"—you said this guy would be fine."

Quartz doesn't know a great deal about Carey Bleak Peters's ex, but enough. Or so he thought.

Before Jeffrey Bledsoe went to prison, he had managed the boys, most of them no older than fourteen, who ran pot, coke, meth, and heroin for a Detroit entrepreneur named Vend. Bledsoe had supposedly professionalized the operation with sales metrics charted on Excel spreadsheets and quarterly bonuses bestowed on top performers, according to a *Detroit Free Press* clip. Bledsoe had also meted out discipline to those who failed to hit sales targets. Quartz hopes Bledsoe's time in prison had served to temper his more vicious impulses. He hopes, for the kid's sake, that Danny Peters did not put up any fight.

"My record is perfect so far," Quartz says. "But I'm actually not surprised. Now that he has the boy, he has more leverage. Or at least he thinks he does."

"You put the fear of God into him?"

"He knows."

Pressman swivels to face the single window in the office, shakes his head.

What a fool, Quartz thinks.

If Pressman hadn't insisted on banging Carey Bleak Peters, he wouldn't be sitting here now, wondering whether he might be indicted for conspiracy to commit kidnapping as well as whatever the feds would have on him if they saw those documents Carey stole.

If he hadn't taken Carey to his condo, he wouldn't have been confronted with her threat to blow the whistle on his less-than-legal activities, wouldn't have hired Bledsoe to kidnap Danny Peters so Pressman could swoop in to rescue the kid and save himself in the process.

Quartz knows Pressman sees things differently than most people. The rich and powerful always do. To Pressman, bedding Carey Peters, the milky lusciousness of her taut belly beneath him, was something to which he was entitled as her benefactor and, as the local gossip blogs noted, the most eligible bachelor in Chicago. The rest was bad luck and circumstance that he now has no choice but to deal with.

"Do you think she suspects our guy?" Pressman says.

"I couldn't tell from what I heard, but I doubt it. Far as I can tell, she and our guy haven't spoken more than once in years."

"Well, maybe they're speaking now. Maybe he cut his own deal with her. Maybe she knows we hired the guy. Christ, she'd have us by the balls."

Not quite "us," Quartz thinks. Pressman doesn't know it, but an FBI agent is hovering. Quartz's days as the rich guy's Mr. Fix-It are numbered. He just has to make or steal enough money to afford a pristine getaway.

"If you think that," he tells the back of Pressman's head, "then don't you also have to consider that he may have made an arrangement with her husband?"

"Peters? No way. The guy's a drip."

"A desperate drip, therefore unpredictable."

"His wife has no clue he's been buying illegal pot?"

"As far as I can tell, no."

It had been Quartz's job to figure out how to pull off the abduction. Hiring some random thug to grab the boy was too risky. It had to be someone Danny knew, so he was less likely to resist. A fifteen-year-old boy wouldn't necessarily be easy to subdue. And Quartz couldn't be sure how the kid's autism would affect things.

A little research led him to Bledsoe, who'd recently been released from prison and was living only an hour from Bleak Harbor. A phony email about local MILFs looking for one-nighters got Bledsoe to click on a link, and the malware Quartz had attached let him rummage around in Bledsoe's tawdry digital existence. At one point he estimated that Bledsoe spent almost all of his weekly diner paycheck on porn of both genders and all ages. Bledsoe's email account also was littered with scraps of evidence that he had another income stream, from his old boss in Detroit.

Quartz couldn't believe his luck when he discovered that Bledsoe, under some preposterous false identity, was selling illegal weed to Pete Peters. Credit to Bledsoe, he'd thought. Even after Quartz induced Peters to bite on a bogus email about low-interest loans and hacked into the wide-open computers at AMP Botanicals, he couldn't tell whether Peters actually knew with whom he was dealing. There were no direct emails between Peters and Bledsoe, but enough oblique references that Quartz was able to add things up. He had two conversations with Bledsoe, sent him a few texts from a disposable phone, and the snatch was on.

Yet Quartz prides himself on never being surprised. He certainly didn't expect trustworthiness from a criminal. But he thought $350,000 in cash and a safe exit to a distant country would secure Bledsoe's loyalty. Not to mention the threat of Pressman's personal gestapo coming after him.

And "Jeremiah"? What was that? When he tracks Bledsoe down, he'll ask him what he was thinking, if *thinking* is the word. He's been trying for hours to get back into Bledsoe's computer, to no avail. Bledsoe must have changed a password or installed some sort of defensive software. Quartz isn't sweating it. Bledsoe knows how bad it will be for him if he skates on Pressman.

Pressman spins back around to face Quartz. "You know we have to find that kid before the cops do."

"You can't be a hero if you don't deliver the kid, right?"

"How bad is this guy really?"

"He's a felon convicted of aggravated assault for putting an unconscious man's mouth on a parking block and kicking the back of his head repeatedly. I told you this. Somehow the man lived, or Bledsoe would still be in prison."

"He isn't some kind of perv, is he? He's not gonna, you know?"

Bledsoe's past treatment of his young charges isn't reassuring on this point—neither is the porn—but Quartz says, "It's his son. But we will find him. Before the cops. The boy's mother can't have much faith in them, or she wouldn't be meeting me. I'll size her up. She might know something she doesn't know she knows."

"Jesus, what the hell are we doing?"

"We're doing what you decided to do a month ago when you were soiling your pants over Carey Peters and whatever she has on you."

"Fuck me." Pressman slaps his palms flat on his desk. "All right. We just—you don't think her old lady will bail her out?"

"I can see why that makes you nervous. If you're not the savior, maybe Carey goes back to the blackmail plan."

"That cannot happen."

"Serenity and your honey haven't been on speaking terms in ages. And I don't think Grandma's seen the kid in at least a year, even though she lives ten minutes away by stretch limo."

"She dislikes her daughter that much? Because the kid's retarded?"

"He's not retarded. He's autistic." Quartz searches Pressman's face for a hint of empathy. Unsurprised to find none, he continues. "The boy's condition doesn't help matters. But she and her mother haven't gotten along for a long time."

"That is one fucked-up family."

"Aren't they all?"

Pressman looks at his phone. "Son of a bitch," he says. "We gotta get this into the outbox, Quartz. We have other bullshit to deal with. The goddamn gooks are trying to get between me and the Chinks."

"The Vietnamese and Chinese never did get along."

"Shouldn't you get going? You gotta beat her there."

Quartz stands. "I am your loyal hunting dog."

"Why Valpo anyway? You can't find a Mexican dive in Chicago?"

"Best fish tacos in the Midwest."

16

Michele Higgins slides the ficus away from the window so she can see the cottage across the bay.

For some reason the weekly cleaning guy keeps parking the tree where it blocks the window facing the water. Michele likes the distraction of the view during the long hours she spends putting out the online-only *Bleak Harbor Light*. But this morning in particular, she wants to be able to see the Peters cottage if and when Carey Bleak Peters finally answers her phone.

Michele lifts the window and wedges the frame open with the ancient pica pole her editors had once used to lay out her articles before everything went digital. She'd rather use the air-conditioning, but it shut down two days ago, and the repair guy has yet to appear. She returns to her desk for her tea and her phone, then goes back to the window and sets her foam cup on the sill. She taps Carey Peters's number into her phone but doesn't hit the call button just yet. She'll wait the eight minutes till ten thirty.

The morning is as still as midnight. Across the mirror of water, the Peters cottage sits on a creamy lick of beach curling into the channel that winds out to the big lake. Three green adirondack chairs and a picnic table with an unopened umbrella stand on a wooden deck a few feet above the beach. The deck stretches across the sand to a dock where a small, covered fishing boat is tethered.

Michele tried Carey Peters's number twice earlier. She called the first time after getting out of bed a little after eight, checking her phone, and seeing the astounding bcc from someone calling himself "Jeremiah." The email had also been sent to Carey Peters.

Michele, who had never seen an actual ransom note in thirty years as a cops-and-courts reporter, immediately figured it as a malicious prank. The internet was full of trolls who for spiteful kicks would send a phony ransom demand to the mother of an autistic boy. But Michele couldn't discount the email entirely. She called Carey Peters, who didn't answer.

Michele went back to bed. Couldn't sleep. What kept her up was that, after the initial shock of seeing it, the ransom email didn't really surprise her. Subconsciously, she'd been expecting something more to happen with Danny, or to him, since she'd written her story about his earlier disappearance. Part of her hoped the ransom really was a twisted hoax. Another part told her something bad was happening. After so many years of mucking around in the dark slime of Detroit, she was inclined to believe the latter.

It didn't help that the whole extended Bleak family was reality-show weird. Michele had been posting stories for months about "Serenity's Gift," what Michele saw as the bitter old bag's way of entertaining herself on her deathbed, dangling a windfall Michele didn't believe she had any intention of delivering. At public meetings of Bleak Harbor City Council, there was Carey Bleak Peters, the estranged daughter destined for not one dime of her family estate, taking notes, saying nothing. And there was her castrated older brother, Jonah, nodding and rapping his little gavel as mayor. They'd grown up wealthy in a mansion on a bay, and there they were, at the pathetic mercy of their mother's cynical bidding.

Now Michele sits at the window of the old Victorian that houses the *Light* newsroom. Her phone shows 10:30. She hits the call button.

Come on, she thinks. *Pick up*.

Carey Peters answers. "Who is this?"

"Ms. Peters?"

"Who is this?"

"Michele Higgins of the *Light*."

There's a pause. For a second Michele worries she'll hang up.

"Aren't you done tormenting my family?" Carey says. She hadn't liked the article Michele wrote about her son's April disappearance.

"I'm sorry you feel that way."

"Why are you calling me?"

Michele hears a car horn in the background, wonders if Carey is driving somewhere. "I understand there may be a situation with your son." Michele waits, finally says, "I got a disturbing email concerning your son, Ms. Peters. I wanted—"

"What are you talking about?"

"The email says your son has been kidnapped."

"You don't have any email. You're lying."

"I'm afraid I do."

"I'll get a lawyer. You can't write this."

Confirmation, Michele thinks. *Not 100 percent, but close.* "The email comes from someone calling himself Jeremiah. It isn't a prank?"

Again she waits for the phone to go dead. She's hoping Carey is considering whether Michele can help her. Though it's not her job to help the people she writes about, if there's a kidnapping and her reporting helps bring a kid home, that would be fine. But really it's just a great story, the thing journalists call the terrible tragedies that befall other people. Michele hasn't had a great story since the *Free Press* purged her and fifty-two of her coworkers two years ago. But she has learned over the years that a great story goes a long way toward making a girl forget her life hasn't turned out exactly as she had hoped.

"I don't trust a word you say," Carey says.

"Ms. Peters—"

"Leave my family alone."

She hangs up.

Michele drops her phone into her lap. She understands. She'd almost decided not to post the brief story she wrote about Danny Peters in April. A kid found unhurt after a few hours wasn't much news, after all. But she'd dutifully posted anyway:

Boy's Disappearance Gives Bleak Clan a Fright

By Michele Higgins

Fifteen-year-old Daniel Peters, youngest member of Bleak Harbor's founding clan, gave his family a scare Thursday night when he disappeared from home and couldn't be found for several hours.

"We were terrified," said his mother, Carey Bleak Peters, 37. She declined further comment, as did her husband, Andrew "Pete" Peters, 39, owner of AMP Botanicals, the new medical marijuana clinic in town. Roland Spitler, spokesman for Bleak family matriarch Serenity Meredith Maas Bleak, issued a one-sentence statement: "Ms. Bleak is both relieved and dismayed to hear of this development."

The young Bleak was found sometime after midnight, asleep in the basement of an abandoned house next door to his parents' home at 39878 South Bay Drive, said Bleak Harbor Police Chief Booker Radovich. "He was lucky he didn't get hurt in there," Radovich said. The boy has been diagnosed on the autism spectrum.

Radovich said the police consider the case closed. A separate investigation by the Bleak County Department of Social Services is continuing, he said.

The last, innocuous sentence was what got Michele into trouble with Danny's mother. Michele had heard that complaints had been lodged with social services about screams and other noises coming from the Peters house. A county source had confirmed that department staffers were looking into it. Plus, there was that security fence going up along both sides of the property. To a former Detroit cop reporter, it all reeked.

Maybe Michele wouldn't have included the sentence if she'd had an editor to press her for more details. But for the most part, it was just her, a computer, and her cell phone. Technically, she had a boss in Grand Rapids, a woman named Gatti, who chimed in about what to cover, especially during the festival. But almost everything Michele wrote went on the *Light* website as she'd typed it.

Carey Bleak hadn't bothered calling Michele to complain. She'd gone straight to Gatti, who ordered Michele to delete the sentence. Gatti had no desire to mess with the Bleaks. Michele had obeyed, but the damage was done.

The next day, she started watching the boy.

Each morning at ten o'clock sharp, Danny emerged onto his deck, barefoot in droopy shorts and a T-shirt, a laptop under one arm. He positioned the laptop just so on the picnic table.

He never went near the water in the morning. He sat tapping on his laptop, two-finger style, for two and a half hours, stood, went inside, and reemerged with lunch on a paper plate. After Michele started using the cheap binoculars she'd bought at Crova Hardware, she could see that the plate always held a sandwich, potato chips, and a cookie. Some days, the boy's stepfather joined Danny for lunch. Michele watched to see if and how much they talked. The boy seemed to dictate this. Some days he couldn't shut up. Others, he simply ate and looked at the bay while Pete Peters talked.

After eating, Danny would pat his lips clean with his napkin and roll it up in the plate. If it wasn't raining, sometimes even when it was, he walked out to the dock. Some days he sat and read a book. Michele couldn't make out the book's title, but it looked like the same book, the same green-and-black cover, every day. She wondered why he didn't finish it and read something new. He never seemed to even turn a page.

Some days he left the book behind and walked out to the end of the dock. He peered into the water as he shifted from one side of the dock to the other, or he gaped at the air around him, his head twitching back and forth, following something he apparently saw that Michele couldn't make out from afar. Other days Danny walked the beach. Sometimes that white-haired bartender hailed him.

Almost nobody came to see Danny besides his mother and stepfather. Once, though, Michele had seen a short, buxom woman emerge onto the deck late in the afternoon while Danny was out on the dock. The woman had a dark complexion and wore a blue sweatshirt emblazoned with the Detroit Tigers' big-*D* logo. She carried a package under one arm. She waved at Danny. He pointed at the house. The woman went inside. Danny stood where he was for a moment, looking around as if to be sure no one had seen. Then he went into the house. Michele never saw the woman again.

She was beyond feeling pity for children after seeing the rib cages of twelve-year-olds blown to bloody shreds by shotguns. But, looking at Danny, she felt something. He reminded her of her adolescence, how she had wriggled out of her parents' embraces, not understanding why she felt angry or whether she was upset with them or herself or merely the idea of being fifteen years old and wanting desperately to be on her own while knowing she needed these adults, these suddenly repulsive total strangers, for almost every single thing that kept her safe and warm and fed. She supposed Danny felt that too.

She takes her phone and foam cup back to her desk, dumps the rest of the tepid tea in the trash. She can already feel the day's heat like glue on the insides of her elbows. She wants to write something about what she knows, but she knows she doesn't know enough. She picks up her phone, dials.

"Police."

"Hey," she says to the dispatcher. "Michele Higgins."

"Good morning. We don't have any crowd counts yet—the festival doesn't officially start till noon—but let's just say, oh, ten million or so."

Dragonflies, Michele thinks. Why would anyone celebrate a spooky insect that flits this way and that on those skeletal wings? To her they seem more like lizards.

"At least," she says, acknowledging his joke. "That's not why I'm calling."

"There's something more important than the festival?"

"Who's around?"

"Uh, let's see, the chief, but he's on a call. Will, Malone—"

"Katya Malone? She's back?"

"Yeah."

"How's she doing?"

"Fine, far as I can see. But I'm not supposed to comment, you know."

"Don't worry. Can you have somebody call me?"

"I'll try."

Normally Michele would stroll down to the cop shop and wait around, but she's supposed to meet one of the festival organizers. Gatti, who arranged the meeting for Michele, has made it clear she wants the *Light* website full of updates on how fabulously the festival is going and photos of people in painted faces gobbling funnel cakes and guzzling beer.

She clicks her mouse to get her computer going, check the website before she goes. The thing's been balky lately. Michele hasn't called the tech guy in Kalamazoo yet because she doesn't want to admit that a week ago she fell for an emailed link offering cheap Vegas flights that turned out to be bogus. She hopes it's just a glitch. She hopes nobody has hacked her. Gatti would not be happy about that.

Michele looks at her phone: 10:44. The computer screen comes alive, though not in the normal way. It starts flashing—blue and then black, blue and then red and then black again. Michele taps the mouse on her desk. The flashing continues. "What the hell?" she says. Now she'll have to call the tech guys.

She shoves away, grabs her backpack, and glances a last time through the window at the Peters place before heading out.

17

Carey waits, knees beneath her chin, atop the picnic table facing the lake, a brown paper shopping bag at her feet.

She hears him coming, doesn't turn around because she's waiting for his arms. And then, there they are, embracing her shoulders. "Jonah," she says. "Thank you—thanks . . ."

She can't get it out.

"Carey, my God."

Her older brother slides onto the table next to her. She keeps crying. She feels a sob shake him, pushes in closer to his embrace. A minute passes, maybe two, before they separate and look out at the water.

They would come here when they were children and didn't want to hear their parents fighting. Bicycles carried them away from the mansion and the shoulder of Blue Star Highway to the small cut of thin grass and sand where the waves sloshed up over pebbles and driftwood. They would sit at this picnic table and tell each other that they would leave Bleak Harbor someday, never to return.

"I talked with the chief," Jonah says. "They're on this."

Carey just shrugs.

"Who could this be?" he says.

She shakes her head. "Somebody who thinks they can get at Mother's money?"

"The thought crossed my mind. Goddamn it." Jonah lays a hand on her knee, squeezes. "I understand why you wanted to come here, but now we have to get back to town."

She hands the brown bag to Jonah. "I need you to get this to Officer Malone," she says. "It's Danny's laptop and . . ." Again she can't finish.

"I don't understand. Why don't you just take it to her?"

"I have somewhere—something to do."

"What?"

"It's for Danny."

"Carey."

She usually told her older brother everything. He was her Irish twin, born in January, ten months before she was. Their father had insisted the boy be named Jonah because he said Serenity grew as big as a whale while carrying him. Pregnant again six weeks later, Serenity decided her new child, boy or girl, would be named Carey.

Jonah had been Carey's rock when she left Detroit and Bledsoe behind and returned with baby Danny to Bleak Harbor, where she would eventually learn that her parents wanted little to do with her afflicted youngster.

He had picked her up at the Amtrak station in Kalamazoo that night. It was raining, and Carey cried at the sight of her brother while Danny twitched in his fevered sleep. Jonah took him from her, and immediately he settled down. She drove while Danny slept in Jonah's arms.

When Carey decided to leave Bleak Harbor again, Jonah loaned her enough money to set herself up in Chicago, and he came to visit weekend after weekend. He'd take Danny in his stroller up and down the city blocks while Carey went shopping or got her hair cut or just stayed in her apartment, reading and napping. He accompanied her on many of the doctor appointments when it was beginning to become clear that there was something different about Danny. "Different is not wrong," Jonah told her over and over. "Different can be better."

He taught Danny backgammon when he was six. Soon Danny was doing the schooling. Jonah marveled at how the boy's eyes darted back and forth, from one die to the other, as he calculated the possibilities before a hand emerged from his lap and he slid the stones around the board with the decisiveness of a croupier, his eyes never leaving the board until he looked up at Jonah and said, "You."

Jonah took Danny to the Chicago museums, the art institute, the music festivals, Wrigley Field. There were Friday evenings when the two of them would make the long walk to Millennium Park and sit in the pavilion, listening to the symphony orchestra. It was on one of those evenings that Jonah introduced Danny to the book of poems that would become his favorite, *The Palm at the End of the Mind*.

Carey gets off the table. "It's almost eleven," she says. "Malone is expecting this stuff."

"Chief said the ransom deadline is 11:46 tonight. Isn't that about when Danny was born?"

Carey remembers calling her brother from the recovery room at Henry Ford Hospital, downtown Detroit. He was at her bedside the next morning.

"Exactly when Danny was born," she says. "I have to go."

"Carey, why don't you just come back with me now?"

"We don't have time. Just take that and go."

She starts toward her car, hears Jonah call out. As she's getting into the car, she turns and shouts at him, "Do not follow me. I love you."

18

Pete shoehorns his SUV into the last remaining spot in the subterranean lot of Johnny's Ice House. He slides his window down halfway and listens for the click and scrape of skate blades carving the ice surface on the floor above him. Oly O'Nally won't be off the ice until 11:50. Pete doesn't mind waiting. The garage feels safe. Nobody knows he's here.

He's been driving aimlessly for the past two hours, avoiding festival roadblocks, listening to the radio for news, trying to work up the courage to make a certain phone call. He's also tried Dulcy a few times to let her know the store is closed for the day, but she isn't answering, and her voice mail box is full.

"All right," he says. He taps a number into his phone. He hears one ring, quits the call, drops the phone into his lap. He has no idea what he's going to say. Part of him is praying that Jeffrey Bledsoe or somebody else, anybody else, took Danny. But he knows that it's more likely that the kidnapper is the man Pete does not want to call.

He picks up the phone, dials again. Slim answers, as always, just as the fourth ring is ending, before the call bounces to voice mail. It's a code Slim has insisted upon, ostensibly so Pete will know he hasn't mistakenly called someone else before saying something that could get Slim in trouble. "Trouble for me is trouble for you," Pete has heard him say more than once.

"Yessir," Slim says, his standard greeting. As always, his voice gives Pete a small jolt of fright.

"It's me."

On the trading floor Pete had the ability to set his fear aside to get done what needed to get done. Not with Slim.

"Got the money yet?"

Pete doesn't know Slim's last name. He has never met the man and has no particular desire to. He pictures Slim as a mass of brown sinew, with a shaved head and a T-shirt that looks painted on, a character he has seen on a TV cop show, a dangerous black man running dope for a dangerous white man.

Slim has mentioned his boss only once, the first time he contacted Pete. Mr. V, as Slim referred to him, is the reputed head of a midwestern pot-growing syndicate that for decades has supplied illegal marijuana dealers from the Mackinac Bridge south into Ohio, Indiana, and Illinois. The weed is supposedly grown in vast underground greenhouses beneath the dense forest of Michigan's Upper Peninsula.

Mr. V's operation has slowly taken hold of the state's legal marijuana business while the legislators and regulators argue over how to spend all the new tax income they expect to reap from medical pot. The marijuana Slim delivers is truly killer, with at least the punch and staying power of any of the legal stuff. And it's cheaper. The politicians set price minimums for legal dope so high and tacked on so many taxes and fees that the illicit suppliers could undercut the legals and still make almost as much profit as before. If you didn't stock the contraband, your customers would find a state-licensed shop that did. Like that one in New Buffalo.

The first time Slim called him cold, introduced himself, said he could save Pete's business with Mr. V's "primo" product. "Same stuff your competitor down the road's kicking your ass with." Pete told him thanks, he'd go it on his own. Slim provided a number, just in case. A week of slow days later, Pete convinced himself he could go in with the guy just long enough to dig AMP Botanicals out of this start-up hole. Then he'd go street legal again.

Next came midnight deliveries of primo and drop-offs of cash-filled piggy banks in dumpsters behind Burger Kings. Things for AMP Botanicals improved. Customers liked the new stuff, liked the lower prices. Pete started paying down his debts.

Then Slim disappeared. Stopped answering calls. AMP Botanical's inventory of primo was down to a few ounces when he finally showed up on Pete's phone one evening. He said Mr. V was sorry for the delay, but he was experiencing "regulatory issues," and while he would never raise prices, he would need an up-front payment for "security" purposes.

Your security or mine? Pete thought.

The next call came after Pete didn't pay by the specified deadline because he didn't have the cash. Slim informed him the security advance would now be $12,000, going up $3,000 each week Pete failed to pay. Pete said he couldn't afford that; sales weren't going up that fast. What if they just ended their relationship amicably? "You have that option," Slim replied. "But I will require a personal visit to tie up loose ends, if you know what I mean."

Pete wanted no loose ends with Slim. He could imagine the guy waiting for him behind the shop some night, tire iron in hand. He accepted a new shipment of primo, paid for that and half the security advance. Slim wasn't happy about half. He said he'd do what he could for Pete, but he couldn't guarantee that Mr. V wouldn't take "more decisive action."

That was two days ago. Then Pete started getting the texts from that weird area code threatening his family.

Then Danny was gone.

His chest feels like it might explode.

He hears a grinding whine—maybe a machine?—in the background on the other end of the call. Slim must be outside somewhere. It makes Pete think of a car trunk, a body duct-taped hand and foot inside, wheezing in the heat, a welt on the forehead.

"Slim," he says. "I will get the money. I promise. Just give me a day. But this—you can't do this. You can't . . . this is, this is . . ." He can't get the words out he's breathing so hard.

"I can't what?"

"You can't do this."

"What the—speak up, pussy. I can't hear you."

"I do not have five million dollars. I will never have it."

"Shitfuck. Hold on a second."

The whining sound is muffled for a moment, but Pete hears Slim yelling, "Can you shut that thing down for a minute?" The sound grows louder again, and Slim addresses Pete.

"Fucking idiots. So you"—he pauses—"so you got the money or not?"

"You sent me texts."

"What? Goddamn it, speak up, man."

"Don't lie," Pete says, then lies himself. "The police know."

"Police? Are you out of your fucking mind?"

"I'll get you the rest of your twelve thousand, I promise, but give our son—"

"I can't hear a damn thing. I suggest you get us our money, pussy. You don't want to deal with Mr. V—trust me."

Slim hangs up. Pete stares at the phone, thinking, *Something's not right—there's something different about this guy.* When he was yelling at somebody to shut off the noise, it was Slim's voice. But it wasn't. Pete replays what he heard in his head. As Slim was shouting, his voice sounded different. And when he came back on with Pete, he sounded different until he stopped and repeated himself.

Pussy, Slim said. It propels Pete back to December, Boz's bar, a Monday night, the Packers killing the Lions on TV, Carey still driving back from a weekend in Chicago with Danny. The Packers were lining up for an extra point when Pete's gaze wandered, and he was startled to see a stranger staring at him in the mirror behind the bar. He had an almond-shaped head that craned forward from a long neck, giving him the look of an ostrich. Pete couldn't tell whether the bluish swirls along his neck were veins or old tattoos. Behind him, the red nose on a plastic reindeer's head blinked.

Pete tried to act casual as the guy hung a thin-lipped grin over his longneck Bud. Pete glanced down the bar, and the guy's eyes slid sideways to meet Pete's. He raised his bottle in a toast. Pete nodded and drank, then slipped off his stool for the men's room, where he locked the door.

When he emerged, the stranger was gone, and so was Pete's Sam Adams Octoberfest. In its place stood a fresh Bud and a note scrawled in ballpoint on a damp napkin:

"Get real beer. Pussy."

It kept Pete up that night and the next. He avoided Boz's for a time. But the guy never showed his face again.

Pussy, Pete thinks again.

It's four minutes after noon. Oly O'Nally is probably in his dressing room by now. Pete will go up in a minute. But first he summons Google on his phone and enters "jeffrey bledsoe." He wants to know what he doesn't want to know.

The top results are all for a man who oversees a global mining empire from Vancouver. Pete moves to the next page. Halfway down is a link to a six-year-old *Detroit Free Press* story. The headline says, "Man Linked to Drug Boss Sentenced for Vicious Assault." Pete clicks the link. The man in the story is Jeffrey Bledsoe. There's a black-and-white mug shot. Pete stares at it, then closes his eyes. The guy in the photo is the guy who leered at him in the mirror at Boz's, the guy standing in front of the blinking deer head.

Pete lets his head drop to the steering wheel.

Slim is Bledsoe, he thinks. *Bledsoe is Slim.*

How utterly stupid could he be, not just to fall for Slim but to think he could keep everything from the cops while Danny's life hung in the balance? The only consolation is that he did not know that Slim was actually Bledsoe. Idiotic, he knows, but he really didn't. How could he have known?

Now he knows. And now, though it could destroy his marriage and his business, maybe even land him in prison, he has to tell the cops about Slim and Mr. V, the illegal dope, the piggy banks, the demands for security payments. All of it.

Pete pulls out Malone's card and dials her cell as he climbs the stairs to the rink. He hears the sound of a Zamboni groaning its way around the ice. He doesn't really expect Oly to help. The old man fired Pete, after all—one more thing Pete didn't make clear to his wife. But Oly is a good man. He might take pity. And Pete promised Carey he'd try. So he will.

Malone's phone rings three times and goes to voice mail. "Leave a message" is all the recording says. Pete, feeling relieved, is about to end the call without leaving a message when he realizes she'll see he called anyway. "Officer, I'm sorry," he says, then wishes he hadn't. "It's Pete Peters. I have to . . . call me, please."

19

"Katya?"

Malone spins, phone to her ear, and sees Mayor Jonah Bleak on the sidewalk where they agreed to meet outside Nucci's Tavern. He's carrying a brown shopping bag. "Mayor," she says, holding up a finger for him to wait.

She had almost made the cemetery when the call came for her to meet the mayor, who was bringing Danny Peters's laptop. She considered going to see Louisa anyway, if only for a minute, but reluctantly turned her cruiser around and headed back into town.

Malone half turns away from Jonah and tells Will, "Gotta go— mayor's here, Danny Peters's uncle." The sweat trickling down the back of her neck makes her think of the boy taped to that chair. She wonders if he's hot too, if he's suffering, wherever he is.

"This Pérez woman who works for Peters?" Will says. "The only address I find for her is in Detroit."

"Detroit?"

"I'll run it down. Weird, though, she did not show up for work this morning."

"Maybe Peters told her the store was gonna be closed. Or maybe she saw the cops and got the hell out of there."

"Or maybe she never planned to show up at all."

"You tried the cell number Peters gave us?"

"No answer—voice mail's full. Sent a text."

"Stay on her. Anything more on Bledsoe?"

He tells her about the circumstances of Bledsoe's assault conviction. She listens, holding her grimace inside. Then Will says, "One thing I read connected him to a dealer in Detroit, guy named Vend. So both Bledsoe and Pérez have Detroit ties."

"Great. Let's hope it's a coincidence. What about his middle initial?"

"Far as I can see, he didn't have a middle name."

Malone's phone beeps with a call. She ignores it. "Stay on the parole officer too, OK? We have to find this Bledsoe."

She stows her phone and turns back to Jonah. He's a slim man, a head taller than Malone, in a white button-down shirt open at the collar, khaki shorts, rimless spectacles, a goatee the color of snow-flecked wheat. His shirt pocket is stuffed with a cell phone, pens, a folded-over Dragonfly Festival street map.

They're standing behind a face-painting station on Lily Street, flanked on both sides by arts-and-crafts booths. Malone smells popcorn and kielbasa, hears the canned merry-go-round calliope, the shrieks of kids on the Tilt-A-Whirl. An oversized plastic dragonfly, lime green and gold, totters from a light post behind Jonah. Across Lily stands a tent where out-of-town strangers have started quaffing crappy beer and dancing to Tom Petty covers.

"Mayor," she says. "I'm sorry about your nephew. We have officers from here, Allegan, Berrien, Cass, and Kalamazoo Counties looking everywhere, going door-to-door, searching the dunes. The FBI is on the way. Alerts have gone out all over the Midwest."

Jonah is nodding, trying to keep his composure. She's seen it before. "Chief filled me in," he says.

Many of Bleak Harbor's year-rounders wonder why Jonah Bleak ever bothered to run for mayor. He's long divorced, childless, a real estate broker who could do the same anywhere, no less estranged from his whacked-out mother than his sister, Carey, is, with no compelling need to stay in Bleak Harbor. There were rumors that his father wanted a Bleak babysitting things, if not actually running them—that was

Jack Bleak's job—and that Jack Bleak had threatened to revoke Jonah's inheritance if he didn't step up.

Then Jack died, and his widow concocted the bizarre quid pro quo that the media labeled "Serenity's Gift." Jonah, who would get none of the gift himself, was left to wrestle with his counterparts at the county and township for his city's share of the loot.

He hands Malone the shopping bag and says, "Danny is a resilient young man. But I'm very . . ." He stops to collect himself. "I'm very worried about this person who may have taken him."

"Bledsoe? Do you—did you know him?"

Jonah briefly looks away. "Not much, but enough, unfortunately. He's a bad character. Really bad."

"He dated your sister a while back?"

"Not sure *dated* is the right word. What did he go to prison for?"

Malone thinks of Bledsoe's parking-block victim, jaw torn in bloody halves. "Assault," she says, leaving out the "aggravated" part.

"Carey told me he had a mean streak. And unpredictable as all get-out, just would snap at the slightest provocation. Which is what— I mean, I just keep thinking, if Danny doesn't—you know, he's not always, shall we say—"

"Don't," Malone says. "We're going to find him."

He takes a breath, then says, "And Pete was at the bar."

"Apparently so. Do you know him well?"

"Pete's Pete."

"Reminds me: Would you happen to know his employee? Name's Dulcinea Pérez."

"Dulcy. I've heard Carey complain about her, but I've never met her."

"Complain about what?"

"Nothing, just . . . coming in late, not being reliable. What about Bledsoe? Do you have any idea where he is?"

"Not yet, but we will. We're trying to reach his parole officer, who should at least—Jesus."

Both their heads snap around at a sudden blast of guitar chords from the beer tent. A band is warming up with a song a lot older than Malone. "Sorry, the parole officer should have Bledsoe's address. We've left messages."

"The parole officer can't be the only one who knows."

"There's a duty guy at the parole office, but he can only give it out if Bledsoe is under official investigation, and—"

"He's not? Do I need to call the chief?"

"Mayor, listen. It's probably unlikely he'd take Danny to his listed address anyway. But we're on it—we will find him."

"I'm sorry. I know you're doing your job."

"Don't be sorry." Her phone keeps blurting with texts, probably from Will. "By the way, Chief heard from your mother's assistant. Spitler? He asked that we try to keep this quiet, no publicity."

"Of course." Jonah's cheeks flush. With anger, Malone decides. "What could be more important than the Bleak reputation?"

"It's all right." She glances inside the shopping bag, sees a laptop, a phone, a knot of electrical cords like rat snakes. "I thought your sister was going to bring this."

"She had—has other things to do."

Malone chooses not to ask, *Like what?* "I've been trying to call her."

"I think she's with our mother. We may need her help."

Malone has a feeling he doesn't know where his sister is. She lets it go for now.

He looks at his watch. "I can't believe I have to go meet some damn festival donor."

"Don't hesitate to check in with me or Chief."

"I won't. So what about you? What's it been now, a year?"

"Pretty close. Chief asked me back early for the festival."

"Well," he says. "I'm glad you're here."

"Don't be afraid, OK? We will bring Danny home safe."

Jonah hurries off. Already the street is more crowded than it was ten minutes ago. Malone waits a few seconds, then sets the bag down, takes out her phone. There's a voice mail from a number she doesn't know and two texts from Will:

chief talking to dep warden in Muskegon . . .

Good.

might have a bead on bledsoe

Better.

But still, Malone thinks as she starts walking toward the station. She breaks into a jog, squeezing left and right through the gathering throngs, recalling what Jonah just said about Bledsoe's mean streak, feeling a spoil in her gut, feeling afraid.

20

The fingernails on Quartz's left hand are gnawed to slivers. Carey noticed it the minute she sat across from him at the restaurant in Valparaiso. Her father, too, had been a nail-biter, chewing the ones on his right hand until they bled. For a long time it was his only visible flaw. The others were hidden, until they weren't.

"I already ordered," he says.

"Traffic," she says. "There was an accident on 94." She's lying. After leaving Jonah, she drove down the beach road a mile and pulled over to cry again.

"Do you want anything?" Quartz says. "Randall's buying."

"No," she says. "Do you work for the company?"

"I get paid by the company."

"What are you doing here, in Valparaiso?"

Carey has been wondering that about herself since she pulled into Valparaiso's main square. What is she doing here? Sitting at a high-top table in a recess of gaudy gold-and-burgundy tile, in a place called Xochimilco that's empty but for a table of four across the room, this stranger Quartz, and a waiter in a red vest and black bolo tie. Danny's not here, the police aren't here—what is she doing here?

As she was driving from Bleak Harbor, questions swirled around her brain, tightening like a tourniquet: What is Danny eating? Is he warm? Is he dry? Has he slept? Has the bruise on his cheek spread? Did the kidnapper ice it? Are there other bruises, other scars? Is Danny scared? Is he crying? Just the disruption in his daily routine has to be horribly upsetting. Is the kidnapper aware of Danny's condition? What about his meds? Oh God, does Danny wonder if he's going to die? Is he begging for his mommy? The last question made her eyes well, and she nearly sideswiped a panel truck.

"I generally like to work from home," Quartz says. A sheet of paper rests facedown beneath his left hand. He has a can of Tecate with lime. He's waiting on fish tacos. "Thank you for coming down."

"Do you have a first name?" Carey says.

"Quartz. Tell me about your son."

"Your name can't be Quartz."

"I'm going to find your son."

"Is Pressman going to pay the ransom?"

"I'm going to find Danny. I need your help."

Carey wraps her arms around herself. The air-conditioned relief from the heat outside is too much. "So you're not going to tell me."

"Tell me about your son."

Quartz is a wire of a man in a black button-down shirt. The shirt has two button-flap breast pockets and two below those, one low on the left side above his belt. Slight bulges in each. Black jeans. Black sneakers. He's in his mid to late thirties, going away hair wisping around a face pale as skim milk, a skimpy afterthought of a beard, green eyes not unlike Carey's. Or Danny's. Tiny scars curl from the corners of each eye. The scars appear identical, as if they'd come not from an accident but something purposeful, maybe surgery.

Carey unwraps her arms, takes a drink of water from a plastic cup. Jumpy, she sets the cup down hard enough that it splashes drops on Quartz's hands. He gives no indication of feeling it.

"Is Pressman going to pay?" Carey says.

"Have you looked online? People are talking about you."

"Already?"

"Are you kidding? It's been hours, not minutes."

"So?"

"Some people think maybe you and your husband—Pete, yes?—are faking the kidnapping to get your mother to pay the inheritance you're not supposed to get."

"That's it. You got us. But you forgot the part about where we beat Danny up before we faked his kidnapping."

"I didn't say I believed it."

"Who are you?" She half stands in her chair. "Am I here to amuse you and Pressman? I can get that federal agent on the phone in ten seconds if you and your boss would like."

"Sit. Please. I'm merely trying to eliminate possibilities and—"

"And you think that I could put my son through this?"

"Fair enough."

"Those people are disgusting."

Carey wanted to track down every single one of the vile gossips and smack them across their faceless faces at the same time that she wanted to hide inside her house for a year.

"I agree. There's one individual on Twitter who's really been going after you. Do you know anyone named Drew?"

"Drew who?"

"Not sure. It's a Twitter handle."

"So you don't know if it's his real name."

Quartz nods in agreement, takes a sip of beer, then says, "Here's a real name for you: Jeffrey Bledsoe."

Carey sits up straight, feeling the blood rush to her head.

"Your ex," Quartz says. "The guy who fathered your son."

"I know who he is."

"Then you know he got out of the state prison in Muskegon last December after serving a term for aggravated assault. He was emailing with Danny quite recently. Did you know that?"

"No," she lies. "How do you know?"

"Let's just say I'm good with computers."

"You're one of those hackers?"

"That is such a crude term."

"You hacked into my son's computer?"

"No. Bledsoe's computer."

"Already?"

"Seemed obvious. Did you bring Danny's hard drive?"

Carey reaches into the purse hanging on her chairback and pulls out the portable hard drive, sets it on her side of the table.

"You don't monitor your son's email?"

"You don't have children, do you, Quartz?"

"Danny is—what's the politically correct word, *special*—is that it?"

"He's on the autism spectrum. That's the label the doctors use. No label, insurance doesn't pay."

"So, does he have things that, you know, interest him in particular?"

"Because all autistic people have obsessions, right?"

"All *people* have obsessions, Ms. Peters; they just don't display them all the time."

"Yes, Danny has obsessions. The Chicago Cubs. Lake fish, especially perch. Dragonflies. This one Wallace Stevens poem."

"Wallace Stevens? In college we used to get high and read his stuff aloud. No idea what it meant. I remember something about a blue guitar. Is that the poem?"

"No."

"But just one, over and over, the same one?"

She pictures Danny sitting across from her on the deck, shaking his head no like a metronome. A whispering drizzle had claimed that late March afternoon. It was too cold and damp to be outside, but Danny had opened the umbrella on the picnic table and insisted. Carey, wrapped in a wool shawl, had agreed on the condition that he consider just one of the other Stevens poems. The poem he loved—or perhaps *loved* wasn't quite right; perhaps *clung to* was more accurate—was a beautifully elusive verse, but Carey wished her son would, as she put it, "expand" his view of the world.

"My view of the world is right here," Danny said, gesturing toward the lake, the water boiling with the rain. "That's enough."

Carey picked up the book from the table and paged to a poem she thought Danny would like. "This one, look; it's about ice cream," she said. "Let's just try it. Please?"

Danny took the book from her, looked at the page she'd opened it to. "Ice cream?" he said. "You are not serious."

"Danny. No."

He gripped the page at the top and tore it out, then balled it up and tossed it at his mother. She let it bounce off her shoulder. "I'm going in," she said.

"Yes," she tells Quartz now. "Just the one poem. What does it have to do with anything?"

"Probably nothing."

He slips a phone from one of his pockets and with a stylus scratches something onto the screen, then returns the phone to its pocket. "OK, so Danny is connected to money, your mother's money, or Bledsoe figures he is. So he gets out of prison and gets a bright idea, and here he is."

"That's what you think?"

"If you saw their emails, you might. Do you think this guy's smart enough to pull this off? Does he have the, I don't know, the guts, the will? If he gets caught, he's fucked."

The man in the bolo tie appears at the table and sets Quartz's plate in front of him. "Gracias," Quartz says.

Carey stares at the plate as Quartz drenches the tacos in hot sauce. "I don't know," she says, but she's recalling the blood, how it geysered up and out, spattering Bledsoe's face, when he shoved that punk's head through the car window.

"Have *you* heard from Bledsoe recently?"

"Not until the ransom note. If that's really him."

"Any idea where he might be?"

"How would I know?"

"How about the police?"

A stab of guilt punctures Carey just below her collarbone. She doesn't know what the police know, because she's here with this stranger and his pockets instead of in Bleak Harbor.

"I don't know."

Quartz swallows half a taco in one bite. When he finishes chewing, he says, "Do I assume correctly that you and Bledsoe didn't part on good terms?"

"Things weren't good between us," she tells Quartz. "But he disappeared from my life, which was fine with me."

Quartz points at the hard drive. "Can I have that?"

She pushes it to him. Quartz shoves it into a pocket, then flips the sheet of paper in front of him faceup and turns it so Carey can read it. "Recognize this guy?"

At the top of the page it says, "LOCKE, Allen Philip." A snapshot shows a man with smooth brown skin marred only by a scar like a thread stitched from below his left earlobe to the corner of his mouth. He's unsmiling, bald, perhaps in his fifties. His tinted glasses sit slightly askew, so that his face appears unbalanced, as if one eye is set lower than the other. Carey scans the guy's job history beneath the picture while Quartz forks rice into a taco.

"This is your contact, right?" he asks. "Your federal agent? The guy who wants those documents you have. Stolen, by the way."

"The people I hand them to won't give a damn how I got them."

"Ha, yeah," Quartz says. "They're not better than any of us, are they? I mean, look at your guy Locke here. He had quite a career. DEA, Customs, ATF, FBI. Apparently couldn't hold a job."

Carey looks up. Quartz is wearing half a grin. He plays it cool, she thinks, but inside he's wound up like a jack-in-the-box. And he's here for more than just Pressman. He has his own plan. She doesn't know what it is—she just knows in her gut that Quartz isn't in this for anyone but Quartz. She wonders if Pressman has surmised the same. Maybe not. Pressman doesn't think anyone can put anything over on him.

"What's your point?" she says.

"Reach your own conclusion. You want to trust this guy? Apparently none of his previous employers did. I'm told the DEA pushed him out after they found a baggie of coke in his pickup."

"Why didn't they put him in jail?"

"That would've cost him his pension, got the DEA a bunch of bad publicity. It's quite a club, federal law enforcement. They just moved him somewhere else."

"Pressman could have told me this."

"Randall keeps his own counsel. But he knows Allen Locke is greasy. Hell, the guy's been trying to take him down for years."

"Why?"

"Who knows? Wants to catch a big fish? A way to resuscitate his career? Locke almost got him on a mail-fraud thing last year. I made it go away."

"This isn't going away."

"It is if you want your boy back."

"How do I know you didn't kidnap my son?"

Quartz grins. "So you'd have something else to blackmail my boss with? Randall's impulsive and a little full of himself, but he's not stupid."

"A *little* full of himself? Just pay the ransom."

"Tell me," Quartz says. "How did you hook up with Locke anyway?"

Carey heard from a young woman at the company—another of Pressman's conquests; she'd worked late one night and wound up beneath him on his office sofa—that a federal agent had contacted her out of the blue. Without saying anything about her Valentine's Day encounter, Carey let the woman know that she too might like to speak with the agent, whose name was Locke.

That was two months ago. By then the digital files with the Asian stamps she had stolen were stowed in her computer at home. It took her most of a bottle of Shiraz to work up the courage to return Locke's first call.

She isn't about to tell Quartz any of this, though. "Just pay, get my boy back, and Pressman will be clear," she says.

"Maybe you're bluffing."

"Don't you dare fuck with me, Quartz. My son . . ." She feels the sob rising in her throat, stops to collect herself. "Fucking pay, and we'll all go our separate ways."

Quartz finishes his second taco, drinks the last of his beer, sets the can down. "Relax. Randall's going to pay most of the ransom."

Carey feels an urge to slap Quartz across his face. "Most?"

"Two million will be plenty—trust me. We just need to lure the kidnapper out into the open so we can get Danny. Has he said yet how you're supposed to pay?"

"Two million's not enough."

"When you know how he wants the money, let me know. We will dangle the two mil. I guarantee he'll take it. He's in no position to negotiate, especially if it's this Bledsoe."

"And what if it's not?"

"We'll worry about that then." He taps the pocket containing Danny's hard drive. "I have other work to do."

"Pressman's condo alone is worth five million dollars."

"Exactly which condo would that be, Carey?"

Her cheeks flush. "I don't care. I just want my son back."

Quartz shoves his plate aside, reaches into a pocket near his belt and pulls out a purple sticky note, hands it to her. She notices his bitten-down fingernails again.

"Call me at that number if you must," he says. "It's very difficult to trace." He gets out of his chair. Carey's phone is ringing inside her purse. "Do not contact Pressman. I'm your man now."

"Just find my son."

"I will. Gotta hit the head."

She watches him move along the bar toward the back of the restaurant. "Quartz," she calls out.

He stops and turns, standing across the bar from the bolo-tied barkeep.

"Do you think I'm weak, Quartz?"

Quartz exchanges a look with Bolo Tie, who smiles.

"Who the fuck are you?" Carey shouts at Bolo Tie. He stops smiling, picks up a rag, goes behind the bar into the kitchen.

"You think I'm weak, Quartz?" she repeats. "Is that what you think?"

"I doubt you're weak."

"Uh-huh. I better see that two million by"—she hesitates, choosing a deadline—"by five o'clock, or I'll be talking, if you know what I mean."

"I need more time. You know Pressman's finances are complicated. Give me till—"

"Six then." Carey slips the sticky note with his phone number into a jeans pocket. "You have about five hours."

"It will be better for everyone concerned," Quartz says, "if we find Bledsoe before the police do."

"Why do you say that?"

He starts walking away again. "I'll be in touch."

21

Jeffrey Bledsoe snaps the deadbolt shut on the restroom door. LaBelle's Family Diner is busy. Petunia will have to deal with it.

He chooses a photograph from his wallet and props it on the back of the bathroom sink, then stares at it as he sets his phone atop the paper towel dispenser, strips off his T-shirt, drops his jeans, and whacks off into the sink. His gaze alternates between the photo and the mirror over the sink as he dry pumps his cock. He likes to watch his pecs flexing. The joint was good for getting in shape.

He finishes, a guttural squeak squeezing from his throat just as his phone vibrates off the dispenser and clatters to the piss-spattered tiles. "Shit." The vibrating stops. Bledsoe picks up the phone, stuffs it in a pocket. He gives the sink a perfunctory swab with a wad of tissue, then takes a last look at the photo of the girl before returning it to his wallet. "Sweet Amelia," he says. She can't be more than thirteen but has the rack of a broad twice her age.

He steps out of the restroom and glances into the diner. Petunia is behind the bar, bobbing her head in that annoying fucking way of hers and scribbling on a green pad as a guy who has each of his butt cheeks on its own counter stool orders his daily breakfast. *Eight eggs over medium, links and patties, double hash browns, rye toast, a banana, a bacon patty melt with three kinds of cheese*, Bledsoe thinks. *Fucking pig thinks a banana will save his fat ass. I am so fucking out of here.*

His phone starts to hum again. He moves down a back corridor and through a door marked EMERGENCY EXIT. Pussy Pete Peters is calling.

After four vibrations, Bledsoe puts the phone to his ear and slips into the voice he reserves for guys like Peters, the dropped-two-octaves growl he'd taught himself growing up with the thugs and skanks, white and black and brown, in his Detroit neighborhood. His *triple-badass* voice. What else did a bony-assed white guy who drank faggy beer expect to hear from a dope dealer?

"Yessir."

"It's me," Peters says. At least that's what Bledsoe thinks he says. He can barely hear because of the caterwauling of a giant tree shredder working in a cemetery behind the diner.

"Got the money yet?"

"Slim," Peters says. Over the shredding, Bledsoe gets only bits of what Peters says next. "I will get . . . me a day . . . you can't."

"I can't what?"

Peters says something else inaudible.

"What the—speak up, pussy. I can't hear you. Shitfuck. Hold on a second."

Bledsoe stumbled onto AMP Botanicals while stalking his bitch ex, Carey, on the internet. He'd located her after paying a website $27.50 for a personal file. It wasn't long before he learned that her hubby was in the pot business in one of those fancy towns on the lake, not too far from where Bledsoe had taken up after leaving prison.

The discovery had tickled Bledsoe even as it had pissed him off. All these preppy motherfuckers thought they were just gonna waltz in and take business from guys like Mr. V who'd been hauling ass for years; sweating the cops, Colombians and Mexicans, ATF and DEA; dodging the border dicks and IRS pricks; scrapping with the assholes on the other side of town or the state or the country for every last corner they could make a few bucks on. Jesus, what these new fucking guys didn't know.

Bledsoe had sized Pete Peters up one night at Buzz's or Biff's or whatever that beach dive was with the knotty pine and shitty Christmas decorations. Seeing Peters's string-bean ass drinking his pansy beer convinced Bledsoe that he could do business, so long as the guy didn't know who Bledsoe really was.

A few phone calls and texts later, he was leaving pounds of primo pot and picking up piggy banks filled with cash. Pussy Pete, scared shitless of the faceless voice named Slim on the phone, was none the wiser. The best part was that "Slim" was also what Bledsoe called his pecker.

He pulls the phone away from his ear and takes a few steps toward the guys operating the shredder. "Hey," he yells. "Can you shut that thing down for a minute?"

One of the men glances in Bledsoe's direction and cups a hand behind an ear. "Fucking idiots," Bledsoe says. He speaks into the phone again. "So you—so you got the money or not?"

Peters starts talking, but the only thing Bledsoe hears is the word *police*, to which he says, "Police? Are you out of your fucking mind?" He can't hear the rest, and he doesn't want to talk inside because Petunia is the nosiest bitch he's banged since he got out of prison. He probably should have gone to his car out front, but he didn't want Petunia to see. The last thing he shouts at Peters before hanging up is, "You don't want to deal with Mr. V—trust me."

He tries the emergency exit, but it's locked. He gives the door a kick and the shredder an angry over-the-shoulder glance, then walks past an overflowing dumpster and around to the front entrance of LaBelle's. Things are fucked up. This was supposed to be an easy job: grab the kid, shut him up, drop him at the safe spot, collect the second chunk of the cash, get the hell out of Dodge. Nobody was supposed to be calling cops. Bledsoe can't afford cops.

He wants to call Quartz, but he must have dropped the goddamn disposable Quartz gave him rushing to get out of the kid's yard the day before. He hopes nobody found it, but what the hell were they gonna find anyway but a bunch of shit nobody but him and Quartz could understand? Real problem was, the only number he had for Quartz was in that lost disposable. He hadn't actually written it down.

Of course Petunia is waiting beyond the double-glass-door entrance. She has an overdone boob job and a mousy face that looks better with his cock stuck into it. She's been hot to trot ever since he let her in on this caper. He just wishes he hadn't done it on email. Really fucking stupid, but he was flying on Crown and Percocet, and Petunia was emailing how she wanted him to blast on her titties, and before he knew it, he'd hit "Send," and she was on the phone cooing about beaches in Rio and how this was all so cool like a TV miniseries. He told her to double delete those emails. He hopes she did.

"Is everything OK, baby?" she says as he steps into the diner. She looks concerned. Bledsoe ignores her for a moment and scans the place for cops and anyone else who might have nothing better to do than eavesdrop. The double-wide dude is using the patty melt like a trowel to shovel eggs into his face.

Bledsoe gives Petunia his phoniest grin. "Everything's fine, sweet stuff. Went out for a smoke and locked myself out."

"Silly boy," she says, her face brightening. Then she whispers, "The kid's OK?"

"He's fine. Yeah."

"So when do you think, you know, we can skedaddle?"

Her lipstick isn't right. Never is. Even with a wake-up hummer every day, Bledsoe knows he won't be able to stand Petunia for long. He doesn't want to take her, but he sure as hell can't leave her behind. "How about now? Blow this pop stand forever?"

She frowns, looks over a shoulder. "I can't just leave this minute. We're the only ones here."

"Putter's in the back. He can handle it."

"Honey, Putter couldn't microwave a pizza without burning the place to the ground."

Bledsoe thinks for a second. "All right, then how about—what time do you get off?"

"Four."

"OK. Meet me in Schoolcraft at four."

"Schoolcraft? Can't we make it my place?"

"You know it's gotta be Schoolcraft."

"All right, but can we make it five? Fiveish? I have to pack."

Petunia lives a mile from the diner. Bledsoe gave her address to his parole officer even though he's been sleeping most nights in a place in Schoolcraft that only his old cellmate knows about.

"Four on the dot," he says. He undoes the apron around his waist and hands it to Petunia. "Done with this, eh, babe?"

She licks her lips, and Bledsoe feels himself getting hard again. Maybe he'll have time for one more before he has to do what he has to do.

He's about to pull out of the LaBelle's lot when he remembers the police scanner. He reaches over and jerks it out of the glove box, plugs it into the cigarette lighter, sets the volume to high. Then he reaches beneath the passenger seat and pulls out a foot-long piece of rusted rebar hacked off and honed to a jagged point at one end. He sets it at his feet.

So he fucked up losing that phone, and Pussy Pete fucked up calling the cops, if he really did. Fuck it. Bledsoe has the $100,000 down payment from Quartz's boss, whoever that is. It won't be long before he'll be sipping a fruity cocktail somewhere warm, savoring the memory of fucking with his bitch ex. He pulls onto Marcellus Highway, driving with one hand, working his phone with the other. He has a couple of errands to run and a few texts to take care of.

22

"Glory be," Oly O'Nally says. He's in the locker room next to the Zamboni garage. "What in God's name are you doing here?"

"You heard," Pete says.

"Good lord, Andrew, come here."

Oly rises from his folding chair, naked from the waist up, gray hair a sweaty tangle, and takes Pete into his pale old arms. Oly is the only person in the world, besides Pete's mother, who calls him by his given name. When Oly fired him from O'Nally Bros., it was bizarre to hear him saying, "Andrew, you have to learn from this," as if it were some other person who was being canned and Pete just happened to be there, watching.

Oly sits again. "Heard it from one of the youngsters," he says, nodding toward the dressing room on the other side of the cinder-block wall. "Was on his phone."

"I'm sorry to bother you. I would've called, but—"

"It's OK. I'm glad you're here."

Like a lot of Chicagoans, O'Nally summers at a beach house not far from Bleak Harbor, directing his trading crews by landline from afar. He doesn't carry a cell phone or bother much with the internet. Although he is the genius behind the long success of O'Nally Bros., he now leaves much of the firm's management to his son. Declan O'Nally had taken the necessary steps to modernize the business, which in turn had helped precipitate Pete's demise.

Pete knows Oly plays pickup hockey Friday mornings with some local guys. Afterward, they convene at Boz's to argue over beers and Italian beefs about who had the best hour and fifteen minutes on the ice. Oly has enough money to have written a big check for the rink's construction, and most Fridays he picks up lunch too. In return, the younger guys let him have his own dressing room and, once in a while, the puck.

Oly's mold-mottled shin guards and elbow pads are scattered across the rubber-mat floor. White curls carpet his sagging chest. In his seventies, he's on his third wife, with a thirteen-year-old son named, like the rink he paid for, Johnny.

"You want to shower first?" Pete says.

"Nah, I'll catch up with the youngsters later." He bends and picks a skate off the floor, wipes a frayed rag down the length of its blade, stuffs them both into the red-and-black bag at his bare feet. "They'll wait for my credit card."

"I need your advice."

"I'm thinking more than advice, son."

He sits up straight, looking right into Pete's eyes. It sends Pete back to his biggest day in the soybean pit at the Chicago Board of Trade. He made O'Nally Bros. almost $470,000, and Oly himself came down to the pit to thank him. Pete had some good days after that. Never any close to that good. Then one day Declan plucked him from the pit and planted him at a desk.

"Listen up, son," Oly is saying now. "What happened between us before happened. It's just business. But as I said before, and I'll say again, we'll always be friends. Now sit down, will you?"

Pete sits in one of the steel cubbyholes lining the room's walls. The place reeks of tape and sour leather. He's not sure why he came. Maybe just because Carey told him to. He doesn't expect Oly to give him anything more than that hug. How the hell do you ask anyone—let alone someone who fired you—for five million bucks?

"Tell me what you know, son."

Pete gives up most of it, leaving out, for now, the stuff about his dealings with Slim. Oly listens while peeling off the rest of his hockey gear. Pete can hear the profane jawing and guffawing of the younger players next door. They probably have worries about jobs and girlfriends and kids and wives, but Pete thinks they really have no worries at all.

———

If only Pete hadn't lost his shit, he and Carey and Danny might never have moved to Bleak Harbor. They wouldn't be in the danger they are now. And maybe, he thinks, Carey would still love him as she once had. If she had.

They'd had a good life in Chicago. They had their fourth-floor condo with the rooftop deck in the West Loop. Carey went to early-morning Pilates classes. Pete and Danny could walk to Bulls games at the United Center. Carey took Danny to school most days, while Pete hopped a bus to the Board of Trade. Because he traded ags, mostly corn and beans, he was done early and able to collect Danny from school.

Pete did well at trading not because he was better than his pit rivals at divining the market's next wriggle or because he had a stronger stomach for riding out a wrong turn. He did well because he was tall. At six feet five, Pete could see across the pit more clearly than anyone else. He could make his hand signals seen and his voice heard. He could spot the creased eyebrows and bitten lips that signaled a trader in trouble. That was someone you wanted to do business with.

His edge vaporized when Oly's son yanked him from the pit and stuck him in front of a semicircle of computer screens in a storefront cubicle a few blocks from Wrigley Field. Other such trading boutiques had sprouted in lofts and warehouses and office towers all over Chicago, even in the suburbs. It was the new, less costly, more efficient way to trade, abetted by ever-changing algorithms fed into computers a thousand miles away and reached by T-1 lines leased for $10,000 a month.

At first Pete was just bored. Declan kept saying he was going to send another trader or two, but for weeks he was the only trader in the shop, his sole companions the blind, oscillating screens. He couldn't even entertain himself by watching passersby, because Declan insisted on keeping the shades drawn, lest someone spy on O'Nally trading strategies. As if algorithms had discernible strategies. Pete felt less and less like a trader and more like an automaton executing commands delivered by faceless, faraway masters.

Then he started to lose. He had one pretty bad day—lost $172,000—followed by a really bad one—$293,000—then another and another, the losses mounting to a million bucks, a million two, to the point where Pete thought the only way he could stop it was to stay home.

Bad days happened sometimes, even to the best traders. But Pete couldn't understand why they were happening to him. He was following instructions. He was making the trades the algorithms told him to make. Declan suggested he take some time off. He took two weeks and returned to work thinking his luck—what else could it be but luck?—had to change.

He didn't say much about it to Carey. He told her once that he was bored, and she shrugged and said, "Try logistics." She had her own problems at work and with Danny's increasing recalcitrance with his teachers and fellow pupils. They were running out of schools where he would be welcome.

On the day that Pete finally took his $6.99 Walgreens umbrella to his eight computer screens, he was down almost $200,000 by 10:30 a.m. His height did give him an advantage swinging the umbrella. Later he wouldn't remember much except that, for a while at least, it felt good. He'd recall the sight of his CPU suspended in midair as it flew from his hands and through the plate glass window; how he felt the urge to grab it back a second before it shattered the glass and crunched to the sidewalk; how the yuppies peered through the jagged hole in the window with are-you-fucking-crazy looks on their faces; how he stood there in his sweat-drenched T-shirt waving and grinning at their picture-snicking smartphones, waiting vaguely for a police siren that never came.

Declan wanted him gone, of course. Oly said he'd take care of it. He sat Pete down. Pete apologized only because he liked Oly. "Apology accepted," Oly said, then fired him. "Those damn computers. I don't get them either, but I don't have to."

He called the $25,000 check he gave Pete severance pay. Later Pete noticed that it had been written on Oly's personal account. Pete used it to pay the attorneys who helped him open AMP Botanicals.

———

"Tell me, Andrew," Oly says now. "Why dope?"

"It's therapeutic. Really."

"For guys with a Fritos deficiency."

"You have arthritis, right, Oly? It'll help."

"I'll pass, thanks. Andrew, I know you believe your troubles at O'Nally were mostly about luck."

"I really don't know what I think."

"Well, there's certainly a bit of luck involved in buying low and selling high. And yes, it didn't hurt that you're a tall drink of water out there on the floor. Maybe we should've just left you there as long as we could have. But what you're doing now, there's not a lot of luck there, son. You've got to do the work, stay with your plan, make your own luck."

Pete's thinking about Bledsoe now. "You're right."

"So. You and your boy. Danny. You have a good relationship?"

"I think so, yes."

"He gets along with his mother?"

"He loves her. Sometimes they fight."

"He's fifteen, right? Who doesn't fight with their mom at fifteen?"

"Shit." Pete looks around the room, down at the floor. "Shit."

"What is it, son?"

"Listen. I'm sorry."

"Just say it."

Pete tells him about "Slim" and Bledsoe. As he does, Oly cocks his head to one side. Pete has let him down yet again.

"Jesus, Mary, and Joseph," Oly finally says, slapping his knees. "I never should've let Declan take you out. But you can't fix what you can't fix. So you know what we need. We need a hedge."

"What do you mean?"

"Think, son. The police will do their very best to find Danny, I'm sure. But this isn't Chicago; it's Bleak Harbor."

"I know."

"You don't have much time. You need a hedge."

"The ransom."

"Right. In case you can't—in case things don't work out with the cops, you've got to pay. You've got to be ready to pay."

Pete laughs a pathetic little laugh. "I don't have five million bucks. I barely have five thousand."

"Have you spoken to your mother-in-law?"

"We don't really speak."

"What about your wife?"

"Carey's calling her today. We're not expecting much."

Oly twists his body away and rolls his long johns down his legs. He grabs a towel from his cubbyhole and knots it around his waist. "Boz has a landline, doesn't he?"

"Yeah," Pete says. Carey called him on it the day before. It reminds him of Boz saying he'd seen Danny on the beach that day, sometime before he disappeared. They had talked. It probably meant nothing. But Pete had to ask about it. Or tell the cops.

"I'm gonna call your mother-in-law. Serenity. Her guy there—what's his name?"

"Spitler?"

"He's been trying to get me to come out publicly in favor of her little plan. So she's going to take my call. You got a pen?"

Pete feels around in his pockets. "Uh."

"Never mind." Oly takes a toilet kit from his bag, zips it open, digs in it for a ballpoint, hands it to Pete. "Find something to write on. Put down your bank account number, and stick it in one of my shoes."

"Jesus, Oly. My bank account?"

"You know," Oly says, "I had a Daniel too."

Army ranger Daniel B. "Boomer" O'Nally was killed by sniper fire in Mosul. No trading was allowed at O'Nally Bros. each year on the anniversary of his death. On what came to be known as D-Day, Oly would rent out Tufano's, and the whole firm and their families would toast Boomer long into the evening.

"Of course."

Oly reaches for Pete's hand, shakes it, holds on. Pete sees a glisten in the old man's eyes. "We're going to get your boy back, Andrew."

Oly goes through the door to the shower room. Pete scratches his account number on the back of an expired car registration slip and tucks the scrap beneath a Velcro strap on the old man's right sneaker.

Pete lets himself feel a shred of relief as he descends the stairs to the garage. Until he takes out his phone and sees that Malone called him back. Now that Oly might bail him out, he wishes he hadn't left her that message after all.

23

Carey steps outside the restaurant into a wall of mushy heat. Across the avenue, people jog up and down the steps of the county courthouse, lugging briefcases and backpacks, going about their lives.

Her phone says it's 1:17. There are missed calls from Jonah and some reporter from Battle Creek. A text from Jonah says, Can't hold off cops much longer. She skips to the next text, from that area code she doesn't recognize.

Tacos in valpo??

An icy ripple of fear crosses her shoulders. Carey looks around, as if she might see whoever it is who knows where she is. Of course there's no one. She goes to the next text, gasps at a photograph of two black-faced dogs, their dark jaws open and drooling over a green high-top sneaker:

rotts hongry too. daisey and hoho likin danny boy

She closes her eyes, tries to collect herself. Thinks of old Pip, expertly trained Pip, huffing wetly in the back of her Ford Fiesta, the blood stink on his breath, his nails scratching on the vinyl seats.

There are more texts. She doesn't want to open them but reads:

Blackmailing yr boss huh . . . ill take that cash 2 . . . ransom now $7.388 mill . . . payment direx coming . . .

"No," Carey says.

danny boy safe fr 10 hrs 29 mins . . . or not . . . everyone gotta
pay . . .

"You can't do this."

She stumbles back against the door to the restaurant, palms her
belly, thinking she might be sick there on the sidewalk.

"God. God."

She pushes away, steadies herself, taps a reply:

JEffrey if it's you . . . you can't do this . . . or whoVer this is . . . we
will have 5 million . . . it's your son. Please stop pleaxe

She sends it. Waits. A reply appears almost immediately:

5373642445 is a landline #. Reply Y to send all TXT messages to
this # as voice messages for 0.25/msg + std msg fee.

24

Quartz shuts the door inside his apartment above the Mexican joint and raps out a text to Pressman:

Witness not telling whole truth. Got curves though.

Then a second:

must address rogue, yes?

He fishes Danny's hard drive out of his pocket and tosses it on the kitchen table, a mess of devices connected by a jumble of white and black wires winding over the table edge and converging into a single red cord plugged into a knee-high rectangular box.

He glances up at the wall beyond the table. It's covered with thirty-six black-and-orange bull's-eyes aligned in columns and rows, six by six. Each is perforated by tiny holes he made at a local shooting range with a pistol that is now resting in his nightstand drawer. Quartz had gone most of his life without even touching a firearm until deciding that, in his business, he'd feel better having a gun handy in certain situations. He recalls he has a shooting lesson scheduled for this evening. He isn't going to make that.

He starts biting the nails on his left hand as he watches for Pressman's reply text. He's wondering why Carey never asked to see the emails between Danny and Bledsoe. Quartz had seen them after hacking into Bledsoe's sieve of a laptop a while ago. He mentioned them to Carey partly to show her he was on the case, partly to see her reaction. No way she wouldn't ask for those emails unless she already knew about them.

She can't be trusted.

He can't trust Pressman either. Which is why he won't tell Pressman about Carey Peters's walking-out-the-door threat. If Pressman thinks the whole thing is going to blow up in his face, Quartz could easily be collateral damage.

Pressman's text appears:

proceed as nec

25

"Officer Malone."

"Carey. Where are you? I've been trying to call."

"My phone's acting up."

Bullshit, Malone thinks. She glances into the corridor outside the break room at the Bleak Harbor Police Department. The chief is there on the phone, his double-wide back to her, moving around like he's agitated. She hasn't seen Radovich this worked up since those shit-faced teenagers set fire to the Saint Wenceslaus rectory eight years ago.

A woman Malone has never seen before stands against a wall behind him, waiting. She's wearing a navy pantsuit and a look that says someone should have gotten her a coffee or a chair or something by now. Probably FBI.

"We're working every angle," Malone tells Carey. "Nothing much to report yet, sorry to say. Are you coming in? Your brother gave me Danny's laptop."

Malone turns to a Bleak County wall map dotted with red push-pins where firefighters, paramedics, and volunteers have searched without finding Danny, green ones where they have yet to look. Searchers have combed the dune bluffs, the beaches straddling the channel from Bleak Harbor Bay to the big lake, the woods along the bay's southern shore. The red pins have started to outnumber the greens. Two Bleak Harbor cops scouring the Peters place have been calling in. So far they've found nothing helpful. The place is filled with fingerprints, of course—Danny's and his mother's and stepfather's.

"Have you located Bledsoe?" Carey says.

Watching the chief on his phone, Malone wants to say, "Maybe soon." Instead she says, "We're on it. Where is your husband? He tried to call me, but now I can't raise him."

There's a pause on the line, then, "I'm sorry; I don't know. I'll be there soon. I'll find him."

"Have you heard again from the kidnapper?"

Malone listens as Carey tells her about the higher ransom demand, the menacing dogs, the message from the landline. She detects a tremor in Carey's voice. "You're doing great, Carey," Malone says, trying to reassure her, even as she wonders why Carey isn't sitting here with her. She cups a hand over her phone when she hears Radovich's shout echoing in the hallway: "You don't give a good goddamn if this kid dies? Is that what you're telling me?" She assumes he's trying to get someone to give him Bledsoe's address. He's swinging his girth this way and that, and now he waves at the suit, and she hands him a pen, and he leans into the wall across the hall and scratches something on a piece of paper just as the dispatcher squeezes past and leans into the break room.

"Katya," the dispatcher says.

She tells Carey, "Hold on one minute," presses the phone to her chest. "What?"

"You want to talk to Michele Higgins?"

"Michele who?"

"Reporter from the *Light*."

"About the festival?"

"The Peters boy."

"We have nothing to report at this time."

"We've had calls from TV in Grand Rapids and Kalamazoo too."

The dispatcher is a twentysomething who wears ear expanders that Malone finds painful to look at. "No for now, but keep them on the hook. We might need them later."

"Will do. You heard about the rides and stuff?"

"The what?"

"Festival's all kinds of messed up. Rides aren't working right; lights are going on and off. People are pissed."

"I don't care." She waits for the dispatcher to leave, puts her phone back to her ear. "Carey, I'm sorry. I need to ask you about that email."

"Go ahead."

"Was there a particular reason you printed that one out?"

"I wanted to make sure you saw it. It's new, from this morning."

Malone sits at a table in the middle of the room and reads yet again the printout of the 9:43 a.m. email that Carey left with Danny's laptop. It's peculiar that the email was sent not to Carey or Pete but to Danny. Jeremiah wouldn't have directed it there unless he knew one of the boy's parents would see it. He knows more than Malone is comfortable with. She wants to hear what Will has learned from the laptop and the email addresses and the phone and internet companies he was supposed to call.

"All right. I'm going to get back to work. When will you be here?"

"Soon," Carey says. "I have to take this other call."

Radovich is still pacing with his phone. Impatient, Malone picks a photo of Danny from a scatter on the table. He's sitting in a small boat with a fishing pole across his lap. He's smiling, but Malone doesn't know enough about him to say whether he's happy or posing. Still, she's drawn to the photo because it reminds her of Louisa. Louisa liked to fish and had agreed to go with Malone's ex on the day when, in truth, he was planning to steal her away. Or so Malone had believed.

With her other hand she pulls out a prison mug shot of Bledsoe. It's a grainy, colorless scan, but his face, with its hatchet-blade cheekbones and smirk of empty defiance, registers on one look: *He's gotta be the one who took Danny.*

But if he isn't?

Goddamn it, Chief. She looks out at Radovich again. His face is tomato red. She picks up her phone, puts it down. She could try Pete

Peters once more, but she doesn't want him panicking. He knows something he's not telling, may have wanted to come clean when Malone missed his earlier call. Other officers are searching AMP Botanicals, so far to no avail.

Will steps into the room, closes the door. He has some paper in one hand. "Volunteer got hurt searching the Helliker place. Chunk of ceiling fell on his head. Just stitches, luckily."

"Who's Chief talking to?" Malone says.

"The warden at Muskegon."

"What about Danny?"

"I've run down every 'Jeremiah' within a fifty-mile radius. Not a lot, but a sex offender in Fennville. I let Allegan County know."

"A sex offender's not going to demand ransom."

"I also found four Jeremiahs in the Bleak family, all long dead."

"Any kidnapped?"

"Not that I can tell."

"What about the domain name?"

Will shakes his head. "Jeb.com is registered to one Morton Needelman," he says.

"Who's where?"

"In the ground. Since 1968. He apparently was once a prosecutor for the county."

"Great. How exactly does a dead man register a domain name?"

"I think somebody else took that liberty. Trying to track that, but so far I'm getting nowhere."

"What about the burner phone we found?"

"A single incoming text: '1ovrEZ@5.'"

"Huh?"

"Could've been a butt dial."

"Can you trace it?"

"How?" Will says. "No."

"What about the thing on Carey Peters's phone, the landline message?"

"That's not a landline; it's a ruse. Anybody could have cut and pasted that message in there."

"Can the phone companies help us?"

"They need a wiretap order."

"Right. Don't tell me—the judge is out of town. Or he's in the goddamn beer tent. Fuck. What about Peters's computer, from the pot shop?"

"Working on it. Obviously hacked. But hackers generally try not to leave trails."

"Damn it. I should've taken Carey Peters's phone when I had the chance."

"Maybe so."

"Jesus. What about"—Malone knows she's reaching now—"Jeb or Jeremiah or jeb.com as an anagram. Anything there?"

Will spends his lunches on a website fiddling with anagrams. He hasn't solved any crimes with them yet, but he's made Malone laugh, and cringe, a few times.

"You must be desperate," he says. "No, nothing yet. I gotta tell you, though: I'm worried about the kid's drugs." He nods at a bench behind Malone that holds two clear plastic bags. One contains Danny's green high-top. In the other are three drugstore vials, the boy's medications. "I don't know about autism, but I lost my epilepsy meds once on a bike trip, and it wasn't good. Had a seizure." He holds up his arm to show a scar zigzagged down the back of his elbow. "That's how I got this."

"And Danny's electronics?"

"Here," Will says, brandishing the papers in his hand. "Looks like he may have emailed with Bledsoe."

"No."

"Afraid so."

Will sets two printouts in front of Malone. Reading them, she feels torn between wanting Bledsoe to be the culprit and not wanting to see Danny unwittingly setting himself up. Oddly, the emails include only Bledsoe's end. The first, from April, suggests he and Danny were having a conversation. The second, from the night before Danny was taken, says only, "Y not, Danny boy?" Maybe Bledsoe was trying to arrange a meeting. Maybe Danny resisted. Maybe he eventually relented.

"Where's the rest of the chain?"

"That's it."

"So Bledsoe initiated this?"

"Hard to believe the kid—"

"Please call him by his name."

"Sorry. I doubt Danny would've known where to find Bledsoe. But it's impossible to know based on what we have so far. The kid's—I mean, Danny's phone looks cleaner than most kids'. Either it's new, or he was just anal about deleting stuff."

"Not was, *is*. He *is*."

"Yes. Is."

There's a sharp knock at the door. It opens, and the woman in the suit steps in. She's taller than Malone by half a head and carries herself with the stiffness of a steel girder. "Officer Malone?" she says. "Stefanie Hamilton, FBI." On her head a pair of sunglasses looks stapled into the tight, dark curls of her hair. Malone wonders if she wears them to bed.

Malone stands and gestures. "This is Will. You're in from Chicago?"

"Indeed," Hamilton says. She glances at the wall map dotted with pushpins, shakes her head. "Chief gave me the basics. You're looking for a felon named Bledsoe. But you don't even know where the boy's parents are at the moment? Is that correct?"

"I just talked to Carey Peters. She's on her way. Take a look at these." She hands the emails to Hamilton, who takes them without looking at her.

"Any skeletons in their closet?" the agent says.

"Not much, at least officially. An indecent exposure."

Hamilton looks up, hands the emails to Will. "Details?"

"Apparently they had sex on that big Ferris wheel in Chicago," Will says. "Eight years ago, before they were married. Peters got arrested; they let Carey go."

"How in the world do you have sex on a Ferris wheel?" Not expecting an answer, Hamilton looks again at the pushpin map, then at Will. "I'm sorry," she says, "are you an officer?"

"He's not," Malone says. "But he's the best we have at rooting around in computers."

"Agent Hamilton," Will says, "we think we can connect Peters to a Detroit drug dealer."

Hamilton turns to him. "Which Peters?"

"Pete."

"And?"

Malone reaches back to the table for a photo and hands it to the agent. "This is Peters's only employee. Dulcinea Pérez. Twenty-three. Moved here last year from a Hispanic neighborhood near the bridge to Canada in Detroit. She's been in and out of juvy and jail: petty theft, pot, cocaine, obstruction of justice. Used to work for a dealer named Vend."

"Might still, for all we know," Will says.

"We think Bledsoe worked for Vend too."

"Vend is Vendrowska," Hamilton says. "Jarek Vendrowska. Criminal right out of the womb. Certified shithead. I had the pleasure of dealing with him on a tour in Detroit a while back. He's mostly drugs, predominantly pot and coke, but also strip clubs, money laundering, politician greasing."

"Never convicted?"

"Oh, no."

"Pérez got an associate's in computer science three years ago from Henry Ford Community College. Then spent a year in code school."

"Computer code?"

"Yes."

Hamilton knits her brows, thinking, then says, "Christ. Petruglia."

"Who?" Malone says.

"Vincent Petruglia. Old-school mob boss in Detroit," Hamilton says. "He and Vend got into it over territory now and then. Vend—or one of his crew, maybe this Pérez—hacked into Petruglia's computers, got all sorts of stuff Petruglia wouldn't want law enforcement to see."

"They blackmailed him?"

"Looked that way. We knew about it—hell, Vend teased us with it—but could never prove anything. He and Petruglia settled up somehow. Nobody got killed, at least not over that."

"But Pérez could've been in the middle of it, helping with the hack," Will says. "There's definitely some hacking going on here."

Malone looks at the photo of Pérez again. In it, she appears younger than twenty-three. Peters said she knew Danny "a little," saw him at the pot shop a few times. Maybe she knew him enough to lure him into a trap. "Maybe it's just a coincidence," she says.

"And maybe it's a coincidence that Peters's employee is connected to the same Detroit dealer that Vend is, huh?" Hamilton says. Malone doesn't appreciate her sarcasm but can see her point. "I don't suppose you've picked Pérez up yet?"

"The only address we have is an abandoned house in Detroit," Will says.

"Wonderful. Maybe Peters knows. But you don't know where he is either, am I right?"

You're right, Malone thinks. *So help us, or fuck off.* "We will bring him in. What about Vend? Should we try him?"

"The only cops he talks to are on his payroll," Hamilton says. "Loves the press, though. He's a so-called colorful character, so they kiss his ass."

"You know," Will says, "when I was looking up Vend, I ran across some articles by that *Light* reporter. She used to work in Detroit."

"Michele something?" Malone asks.

"What's the *Light*?" Hamilton says.

"Local paper, online. And yeah, Michele Higgins."

Damn it, Malone thinks, and Louisa's face, dark bangs on her forehead, appears unbidden in her mind. "I'll give her a call after this," she says. "Maybe she knows him. And we ought to—"

The door to the room swings open, and the chief leans his bulk in, waggling a slip of paper. "Bledsoe's in Bridgman," he says. "Got an address. State police and Berrien County are on the way."

Hamilton steps up and snatches the paper from the chief. "Nice work," she says. "I'm on my way."

"I'm going," Malone says.

"You have jurisdiction there?" Hamilton asks.

Radovich gives her a look. "Far as I'm concerned, Agent, she does."

Hamilton turns from the chief to Malone and back again. She shrugs. "Fine," she says. "Officer Malone, let's get this Bledsoe."

The hell with Bledsoe, Malone thinks as she follows Hamilton out. *Let's get Danny.*

26

The officer sounds anxious.

"Now we're off the record," Malone tells Michele Higgins.

"No. Why?"

She'd called as Michele was walking back to the *Light* after shooting photos at the festival. Malone had confirmed that Danny Peters had been kidnapped for a ransom of more than $5 million.

"I just helped you on the record, Michele. Now we're off, or I'm hanging up."

"Go ahead."

"Do you know Jarek Vend?"

Vend. A reptilian coil of muscle that holds still and calm until it snaps free and dangerous. "I did once."

"We need you to get in touch with him."

"I can give you his number."

"No. We need you to call him."

Michele is half a block from the Victorian that houses the *Light*. An unmarked panel truck is parked in the side drive. A man is standing on the front porch, swiping his phone.

"You can call him yourself. Or ask the Detroit cops—"

"He's not going to respond to a cop in Bumfuck. I hear he likes you."

"Trust me—he doesn't. He really doesn't like anyone."

"Michele, you're going to call him the minute you get off this phone—do you hear me?"

"Why? Do you think he has something to do with the Peters boy?"

Vend is many despicable things, but Michele has difficulty seeing him as an abductor of autistic children. Not worth the trouble.

Then again, Vend is in essentially the same business as Pete Peters. She's seen the cop message boards speculating that illegal dealers are exploiting their no-tax, no-fee advantage over the neophytes selling legal stuff. Maybe Peters crossed Vend somehow. That would have been a mistake.

"Tell him we have one of his employees in custody."

"What employee?" Michele says. "Give me a name."

"Just tell Vend, and have him call me."

"I'm not sure I'm comfortable—"

"Don't even pull that shit." Malone's voice rises a pitch. "A boy's life is at stake." Then she's gone.

Michele isn't in the habit of helping cops do their jobs. But she's not so sanctimonious about her barely breathing profession that she's going to ignore Malone. She scrolls through the contacts on her phone, stops at "JV." She starts to call, then changes her mind and thumbs a text:

Cannot believe you'd kidnap an autistic boy.

Vend will respond. He's always had a thing for Michele. Michele never had a thing for him. Meanwhile, she has to post her first story on the kidnapping of Danny Peters. She feels remiss; even the local radio mopes have already picked up on it. But her boss, the ever-texting Gatti, has had Michele hopping on festival stuff.

The man on the porch is a good twenty years younger than Michele, his head enrobed in a green wool cap that puts her in mind of a grasshopper.

"You here for the air-conditioning?"

He looks up from his phone and sizes her up, top to bottom, lingering briefly on her breasts. She doesn't begrudge him that because her boobs are still pretty great, but the glance at her naked ring finger feels creepy.

"You're Michele Higgins? The reporter?"

"Did you fix the AC?"

"I don't have the right part yet."

"Then what are you doing here?" She bounds up the porch steps past him. "Come back when you have the part."

She hears him from over her shoulder. "Think I got a scoop for you."

———

Her computer screen is blinking blue and black and red again, as it was when she'd left earlier. Michele sets her phone aside and clicks her mouse. The blinking stops.

The screen goes gray, then black, before unfurling the image of a boy in a hard-backed chair. "Holy shit," Michele says. It's Danny Peters, blindfolded and wearing a single high-top sneaker. His legs are secured to the legs of the chair. There's a shadow on his cheek.

"Fuckin' A," comes the voice from behind Michele. She spins to see the Grasshopper looking over her shoulder.

"That the kidnapped kid?" he says.

"What are you doing? Get out."

"That's goddamn cool."

"Do I need to call the police?"

"They're pretty busy. But I might have something you'd be interested in." Canting his head, he gives Michele a smile that probably works on the bimbos he chases at Tuesday night happy hours. "About that kid on your computer."

"Uh-huh," Michele says. "Wait outside. We'll talk in a minute."

He leaves, and she returns to the computer. Danny has vanished from the screen. Another image, a rectangle of white and black and gray, is slowly coming clear, a ghost emerging from shadow. As it sharpens,

Michele thinks it could be something scanned from the files at the city library.

Centered at the top of the rectangle is the familiar *Light* logo. Beneath that is the date: Friday, May 18, 1945. The lead story on the page concerns two local soldiers returning from France after V-E Day. The story that catches her eye runs down the right side of the page in a single column:

Inquiry Concludes Drowning of Young Bleak Accidental

Teenager's 'Eccentric' Character May Have Contributed to Death

What is going on? she thinks.

Her phone buzzes. There's a new text from Gatti:

how bout a pic of someone in a d-fly hat on home page?

Michele ignores it and returns to the 1945 *Light* story: A fifteen-year-old boy, a great-grandson of the town's founder, died that May 1 in a sailboat on Lake Michigan. His name was Jeremiah Estes Bleak.

The story describes him as "ornery, unpredictable, and barely manageable from the day he was born." He was on the boat with his father, James Estes Bleak, and his brother, Jonathan Estes Bleak, known as Jack. The Jack who'd been married to Serenity until he died last Thanksgiving.

Something about the story feels familiar. She can't come up with it just yet. She reads on.

A squall rose up out of nowhere on that May afternoon. "As the waves crashed like thunder and the boat tossed about, young Jeremiah, who had inexplicably doffed his life jacket, pitched into the swirling waters," the article says. "His father, Mr. Bleak, almost drowned as he heroically tried to save his son." In the penultimate paragraph, an unnamed law enforcement official suggests the boy may have intention-ally thrown himself into the lake. "Nevertheless," the story's final line says, "police were unable to definitively conclude that it was suicide."

Nevertheless. Definitively. To Michele, they're winks and nods that would nudge readers to the suspicion that the "unmanageable" boy had in fact flung himself to his death. It strikes her as gratuitous, unless the police hoped to absolve the boy's father—and by extension, the Bleak family—of any blame in the tragedy.

Her phone goes off. Gatti again:

WTF is on home pg?!!!

Leave me alone, Michele thinks. She's guessing Gatti doesn't like the photo of disgruntled festivalgoers standing in a too-long line for beer because the coolers shut down. Whatever.

She clicks the icon for the *Light* home page. It takes a minute to open. There is no photo of a beer line, no festival stories, not even the current *Light* masthead. That day's page is gone. In its place is the 1945 page with the stories about the returning soldiers and the drowning of Jeremiah Bleak.

"What the—oh, shit," Michele says. Not knowing what else to do, she grabs the mouse and starts clicking. Nothing happens. If Gatti is seeing this decades-old page, then anybody looking at the website is seeing it too. She texts her boss back:

not me can you ask techs? Looks like a hack.

She goes into her email and calls up the message that arrived at 6:45 that morning. The signature at the bottom explains what nagged her when she was reading the old story: Jeremiah.

Is it coincidence? Or did the kidnapper intentionally take the name of that drowned boy? And if so, why? This kidnapper is not your run-of-the-mill bad guy. She clicks out of email back to the *Light*. The 1945 front page is still there. Gatti is buzzing Michele's phone again.

She calls out to the porch, "Hey, you."

The Grasshopper returns. Michele gets out of her chair. "Whatever you have better be good."

He actually laughs. "Yes, ma'am. You know the kid's house?" He gestures at the window facing the bay. "That big fence? I put that up."

"You're an HVAC guy."

"I freelance other stuff."

"And?"

He grins. "What are the odds of us meeting at the beer tent later on?"

She wants to say, *Are you fucking kidding me? Get out, and don't show your invertebrate face here again.* But she wants to hear whatever he knows more. "We'll see. What about the fence?"

"You know," he says, "that family ain't exactly the Brady Bunch. No wonder the kid's a retard."

"He's not a retard, asshole."

"I thought he was autistic or something?"

"What's your name?"

"Nathan."

"Last name?"

"Barringer."

"If you know something about Danny Peters and you don't tell me and he gets hurt, I guarantee that 'Nathan Barringer' will be in the paper and your skinny ass in the county jail."

"Skinny ass?"

"Spit it out, Nathan."

"Chill, eh? So, one day, it started raining like hell, so I knocked off early. Then a couple hours later I remembered I left some tools over there I needed, so I went back to get them." He yanks his hat off, and a thatch of carrot-colored wires springs free. Maybe that's why he wears the thing. "He had this sort of girlfriend."

"'Sort of' girlfriend?"

"Looked Hispanic, a little chunky, definitely older than the kid."

"And?"

He shrugs, grins again. "They were screwing."

Michele recalls the woman she'd seen through her binoculars on Danny's deck that one afternoon. She was wearing a Detroit Tigers hoodie.

"How do you know this?"

"I could hear them. Or, at least, her. I kinda envied that kid."

"That's disgusting."

"It was accidental, honest. I left my tools under a tarp along the side of the house where the kid's bedroom happened to be."

"So you heard, but how did you see?"

"Curtains were open a little. I thought maybe someone was getting hurt in there."

"Did you recognize the woman?"

"I happen to buy pot from her."

"At the shop in town?"

"Yep. She works for the kid's old man. Name's Dulcy."

Michele makes the connections in her head: the Tigers, Detroit, the Hispanic enclave beneath the Ambassador Bridge, the Jarek Vend Community and Health Center on Vernor Avenue. Vend threw a lot of charity cash at that neighborhood and hired a lot of its young people. Like maybe the one Malone is looking for.

"So Danny was having sex with a woman who works for his father."

"Yeah. That help?"

"Dulcy? What's her last name?"

"Not sure."

Her phone again. It's a text. From Vend.

"Why did you say what you said about the Brady Bunch?"

"Well, his parents, they don't seem to like each other much. They sure didn't agree about the fence. I was a little worried they wouldn't pay me. She wanted it more than he did, and he would tell her she was paranoid, what did she care what people think?"

"But you never saw any physical stuff?"

"You mean like abuse? No. Nothing like that."

"Why didn't you go to the police?"

The Grasshopper looks sheepish as he pulls his hat back on. "I don't always get along so well there. Besides, you were here."

Right. The beer tent later. "Have you told anyone else?"

"Maybe a couple of buddies, but they were drunk—they won't remember. So, am I gonna see you tonight?"

"How late's the tent open?"

"Officially, eleven. But I know a guy."

"I'll bet." She gives him enough of a smile to keep him loyal for now. "I better get back to work so I can finish up in time."

———

As he leaves, Michele grabs a notebook and writes down everything he told her. Then she looks at the text from Vend:

> ahh michelle my bell . . . long time . . . sorry no idea what you talk about

She starts to reply, decides to let him wait, returns to her keyboard. She clicks out of the screwed-up *Light* home page, opens Wordpress, and taps out the story she should've written hours ago:

Bleak Descendant Kidnapped for $5 Million Ransom

By Michele Higgins

Fifteen-year-old Daniel Peters, youngest member of Bleak Harbor's founding family, was taken from his parents' cottage on Bleak Harbor Bay yesterday and is being held for a ransom of $5.145 million, local police confirmed.

The abduction is all the more tragic because the boy, known as Danny, has reportedly been diagnosed on the autism spectrum. His mother, Carey Bleak Peters, daughter of Serenity Meredith Maas Bleak, declined to comment.

The boy left home on his own in April and was found hours later in an abandoned home next door to the cottage where he lives with his mother and stepfather, Andrew "Pete" Peters, at 39878 South Bay Drive. Peters is the owner of the new medical marijuana shop in town, AMP Botanicals.

Anyone with information on Danny Peters should call the Bleak Harbor Police Department, 269-551-4060.

Michele sits back in her chair, thinking about what Malone told her, then about Vend, then about Danny having sex with the woman from the pot shop. She wants to talk to this woman. The cops have commandeered Peters's pot shop; she doesn't know where else to find Dulcy.

For the first time since leaving Detroit, she can feel that thing she used to feel when she was in the *Free Press* newsroom after making her cop rounds, long after last call at the Anchor Bar, alone at her desk, the newsroom silent but for the burps and screeches of the police scanner, staring out the window at Lafayette Street, wondering how she was going to get the story she wasn't supposed to get, knowing that eventually she would. It wasn't about the byline or the money, which was shitty anyway, or even the editors telling her how great she was. It was really just about the chasing and the catching.

A name pops into her head: *Lengel.*

She picks up her phone and texts Vend back:

your friend Dulcy says hello

Michele opens her contacts, scrolls to Lengel.

Vend's reply appears:

hm poor dulcy if you see her tell her to call I miss her

She can't remember the last time she spoke with Lengel, but it won't matter. She competed against him when she was at the *Free Press* and he was covering federal courts for the *Detroit Times*. He kicked her ass on a story or two, maybe three; she kicked his on a few others. They became friendly, and he took on the distinction of being the only single male reporter who never once hit on her.

Lengel also is amazingly gifted at finding hard-to-find people. Michele texts him with their standard greeting: **Big deal.** Seconds later comes his standard reply:

Bigger than you think.

27

The old Bleak steel mill squats in a field of waist-high weeds a few miles south of the Indiana-Michigan border. Carey had passed it without noticing on the way to Valparaiso. But coming from the other direction, it's impossible to miss the FUCK BLEAK someone slopped in black over the faded Matsunaka logo on one of the idle smokestacks. Carey really can't blame the vandals. If she wasn't on her current mission, she might stop and take a picture, post it online with a smart-ass comment.

Her phone has been zizzing with texts from the kidnapper: A photo of Danny's shoe blotched with dark stains. Audio of a dog's growls and snorts. An accusation: u quit on people its in yr blood. She has read and tried to push each one from her mind, focused on the road and the deadline she gave Quartz.

Now the phone rings. She picks it up and says, "Jonah."

"Carey," he says. He sounds excited. "The police think they've found Bledsoe. They're going after him."

"Is Danny there?"

"We'll know soon. Let's hope. Where are you?"

"On my way back. Where are the cops going?"

"Chief wouldn't say; he doesn't want a screwup. But he gave me a heads-up that they got a break."

"Good. I just—" She has to stop for a moment. "I just want to hold him in my arms again."

"You will."

She knows it troubles Jonah that Danny doesn't know his grand-parents better. He had tried on several occasions to make peace between Carey and their parents. It was as much his nature to seek appeasement as it was Carey's to stiffen her neck and turn away. She knew Jonah meant well. But she had decided long ago that her mother and father were not the best for her or Danny.

Jonah knows all about her disillusions with her marriage and her daily frustrations with Danny. But Carey hasn't told him anything about her attempt to blackmail Pressman. Jonah would have tried to talk her out of it. She would have gone ahead, and she wouldn't have wanted her brother connected in any way, in case the authorities found her out. If she had to go to prison, she would feel all right leaving Danny in Jonah's care.

Now he asks again, "Where are you?"

"I just passed the old plant," she tells her brother. "I can't believe it's still there."

Their great-great-grandfather built it in the 1880s. Carey was eight, Jonah nine, when her father sold it to the Japanese company that would close it only two years later. It would take another two years of litigation for the unions to discover that the worker pensions had been dissolved.

"Why the hell are you in Indiana?" Jonah says.

"I told you, for Danny. Do not tell the cops—do you hear me?"

"Damn it, Carey, all right, I won't, but just tell me."

"We'll talk about it later."

Jonah sighs. "Come right to the police station, OK?"

She drops the phone in her lap and peers into the rearview mirror at what was once J. E. B. Steel. The receding vision beckons a memory Carey wishes she did not possess.

———

The dinner table at the Bleak Harbor mansion was an expanse of var-nished mahogany set along a wall of French doors rising to the high ceiling. On a clear day, the blurry trapezoid of the Chicago skyline was visible on the horizon across Lake Michigan.

Carey's father sat at one end of the table, seven or eight feet to her right, her mother the same distance to her left, Jonah directly across. Roland Spitler stood at one end of the room, near a double door that led to the kitchen, wordlessly awaiting orders.

Carey was twelve, a seventh-grader home from Cranbrook for fall break. The dining room windows were closed to shut out the megaphone catcalls of the protesters from the street below.

Jack Bleak didn't look at his daughter when she asked him why the workers' pensions hadn't been secured before he sold the mill to Matsunaka. Reaching for the scalloped potatoes, he said, "You know dinner is not the time for this, young lady."

"Carey, please," Serenity said.

Carey sneaked a look at Jonah, who gave her the slightest of nods. She put her fork down. She hated pork roast anyway.

"When is it time?" she said.

Her father ignored her.

"Tell me, Father. Did the pension money really have anything to do with the improvements at the marina?"

He stabbed a slice of meat, keeping his eyes lowered, giving no indication that he would answer.

"Did your bookkeeper really—"

"Controller," her father said. "He was the controller. He was supposed to have full control of the finances." He looked up from his plate. He didn't look angry or exasperated. He looked as sure of himself as if he was observing that the glazed carrots were overdone. "Unfortunately, he did not have full control. He's been dealt with. And that is all I will say on this topic at the dinner table."

"So one guy made a mistake, and all those people out there"—she waved an arm toward the windows—"they just have to lump it? What about the marina? Is that how you, I mean we"—she glanced at Jonah, who was pretending to be focused on his food—"paid for the new boat lift?"

Serenity addressed her husband. "She's been reading the Chicago papers, which I blame on that history professor, Krier. I don't know why we spend so much on that school."

"Sociology."

"I truly do not care, dear." Serenity did in fact look exasperated, as she often did with her adolescent children. "This isn't some classroom exercise."

"No, it's not. It's people's lives."

"What do you know about people's lives?" her mother said. "You don't know anything, little girl."

"Don't call me that."

"All right—why must you be such a bitch all the time? Is that language preferable to you?"

Carey felt her insides coil, hoping it didn't show on the outside. Her mother could have been her ally against her father. He wasn't worth it anymore. Carey's rants against her father's greed just complicated life for Serenity, who desired nothing more than to curl up alone in her noiseless vodka cocoon.

"Right back at you, Mother."

"Enough, all right? We pay for your book learning; please do not bring it into our home, if that's quite all right."

"It's not quite all right." Carey got out of her chair. "It's not all right at all."

"Sit down," her father ordered. "I'm trying to have my dinner. Goddamn it, can't we have five goddamn minutes of peace around here?"

Carey turned to her father. "You hurt those people. You knew the pensions weren't paid up. You knew that Matsushita company—"

"Matsunaka."

"—Matsu-whatever, you knew they were just going to shut the plant down so they could raise prices."

"So you're a business expert now? Sit. Or leave."

Carey started to sit, then recalled that morning, watching from her turret bedroom as the police wielding dark batons herded the demonstrators away from the house. "No," she told her father. "You shit all over those people."

"Watch your language."

Carey spun on Serenity. "And you're no better, living off of it."

"Miss Carey?" It was Spitler. He had stepped closer to the table. "Shall I bring your dinner up to your room?"

"It's fine, Roland," Serenity said. "This is none of your business anyway."

Spitler flinched as he stepped backward and then turned and disappeared into the kitchen. Carey's father set his utensils on his plate with a loud clink, snatched his napkin from his lap, and stood. That's when Jonah finally spoke up.

"Jeez, Dad," he said. He wore the weary, cocked smile of a thirteen-year-old who knew more than he should have. "Maybe you oughta stick with fucking women instead of fucking over your employees."

Jonah's father held his son's gaze for a second before shifting his glare down the table at Serenity. "Are you happy now?" He pointed Carey toward the kitchen. "Excuse yourself, young lady."

Carey took the kitchen elevator down and slipped out to the boathouse. She sat on the stern of one of the Chris-Crafts, knees beneath her chin, watching the cumulus tumble across the late-afternoon sky, hearing the angry shouts of the protesters on the other side of the mansion, her eyes hot with furious tears.

———

A few minutes after crossing the border into Michigan, Carey dials her mother's assistant, Roland Spitler.

Over the past few hours, her phone has filled with texts and voice mails from colleagues who've seen the news of Danny on social media. Carey hasn't bothered with them. And she has ignored the reporters promising that their outlet can help her find her son.

"Miss Carey," Spitler answers. "May I return your call in fifteen minutes?"

"No. I need to see my mother."

"I'm sorry, Miss Carey, but Miss Serenity isn't feeling well. Could you please call me—"

"Roland, I have my mother's cell number."

Spitler pauses before responding. "Please let me get off this other call."

Carey recalls the email Spitler had sent after Jack Bleak's death expressing "sincere regret" that Serenity "lacks the liquidity in her current portfolio" to assist with private school tuition for Danny. Carey had replied, "My mother doesn't know the meaning of *regret*." To which Spitler wrote simply, "Yes, Miss Carey."

She waits. At the click that announces Spitler's return, Carey says, "I don't have time for this. I need to see my mother, or if you can't arrange that, then I need her help with this ransom."

"Of course, Miss Carey."

"Which is it?"

"Tell me again what the ransom is."

She gives him the new one.

"That is a peculiar number."

"Serenity can handle it."

"I'm afraid it's not quite as simple as that, what with Miss Serenity's bequest."

"Explain, please?"

"Your mother's liquid assets are in an escrow account, as a demonstration of good faith to the various qualifying entities."

"I've been at every meeting about her money, and I haven't heard anything about escrow accounts."

"Correct me if I'm wrong, Miss Carey, but I don't believe you attended yesterday's city council meeting."

"Pete did. He didn't say anything about an escrow."

"It was briefly discussed. Perhaps Mr. Peters left early?"

That was entirely possible. "So what? Are you saying you can't violate some stupid escrow to save my son's life?"

"Miss Carey, the escrow was established at the behest of—"

"I will see Serenity, Roland."

"Of course, but you realize you haven't called your mother in at least six months. She hasn't—"

"I will see my mother this afternoon. You will call me with a time. If I don't hear from you in fifteen minutes, I'll be on the phone to the city attorney to ask about this escrow account."

"Please, Miss Carey."

"Fifteen minutes."

28

A ragged circle of officers, some in blue-and-gold and some in brown-and-mustard uniforms, surrounds the clapboard house on Beechnut Street in Bridgman. Something isn't right. The officers aren't crouching or moving in a way that suggests danger is imminent. Their guns are holstered. They're standing around talking.

"Shit," Hamilton says.

She's out of the car almost before she puts it in park, walking toward the house. Malone follows a step behind, scanning the yard. The grass is spotty with dust patches, the bowed hydrangeas a crackling brown. Whoever lives here doesn't give a damn.

A cinder block standing on end props the front door open. She can see cops moving around inside. Maybe Bledsoe is dead. That would be fine. But what about Danny?

She starts to jog and overtakes Hamilton, who calls out, "Hey, where you going?" A hatless state cop emerges onto the front porch with a phone to an ear. "Delacroix," the officer is saying as Malone stops at the porch steps. "Petunia? What about the landlord?"

"Danny Peters," Malone says. "Is he here? Is he alive?"

The state cop holds up a hand to quiet Malone. She's nodding at whatever she's hearing on her phone. "All right. One of their people just got here—I'll let her know."

Malone's heart sinks. "They're not here."

The trooper drops her phone to her side. "Afraid not. This Bledsoe either bolted or never was here."

"Wrong address?"

"Yes and no. It's definitely the address Bledsoe gave his parole officer. But the only trace of him is a pair of socks that might or might not be his and a used condom under a bed. The actual renter here is one Petunia Delacroix."

"And we're running her down?"

"Her landlord says she works at the diner in town. Berrien County has two officers there now. If Petunia knows Bledsoe, and I'm betting she does, we'll find him."

Malone checks her watch. A little more than nine hours remain to the ransom deadline. "Can I help?"

"I'd get back to your station and hope we get a break soon."

"This Bledsoe is a bad guy."

"Ten-four, Officer. Got a fifteen-year-old at home myself. She can sure be a handful, but I'd do anything for her."

An image of Louisa running on the beach, arms pumping, ponytail bobbing, feet leaving tracks in the sand, materializes in Malone's mind. She lets it go.

She walks around the back of the house, looking for Hamilton, invisible to the officers poking around in the bushes. She looks at her watch again. What if Bledsoe isn't anywhere nearby? What if he really is running a vile errand for that Detroit dealer? What if this Dulcinea Pérez somehow got to Danny? What does Peters know about it?

She moves away from the house and makes a call. "Chief," she says, "have you heard from Peters yet? No? Screw him then, eh?"

She finishes with the chief and circles to the front of the house, telling herself that Petunia at the diner will lead them to Danny. She keeps walking, circles the house, the yard. She can't find Hamilton. She turns to the street. The FBI agent's car is gone.

"Are you kidding me?" she says aloud.

"Looking for Agent Hamilton?"

Malone turns to see a dark-skinned stranger in a gray mock turtle-neck and a black leather jacket. He has a crescent scar on his left cheek, and his tinted glasses are askew.

"Special Agent Allen Locke. Indianapolis."

"Katya Malone, Bleak Harbor Police."

"Need a ride?"

———

"Don't feel bad about Hamilton leaving you like that," Locke says reas-suringly. "She doesn't play well with others."

"What's her problem?"

Locke is a cautious driver. He hits the turn signal whenever he changes lanes. He never looks over at Malone as he speaks.

"I don't know her that well, but supposedly she got a pretty big head after that Hayek kidnapping a few years ago. She's now the FBI abduction queen. Wants those cases all to herself."

"Hayek," Malone repeats. "Where was that?"

"Saint Louis. You probably saw it on the tube because it involved a rich guy."

"Ah, right, the pesticide exec."

"Hell hath no fury like a GMO activist. Anyway, Hamilton was the one who talked that idiot out of dropping the guy from the top of a building. And then there was the straight-to-DVD movie."

"No."

"Yeah."

"Why are you here all the way from Indy?"

"Ma'am," he says. "I could tell you my bosses sent me, which wouldn't be the whole truth. The whole truth is, I don't like people who mess with children."

Malone watches the trees flying past, wishing they were back at the station already. She wants to do something but doesn't know what.

"Can I ask you something?" Locke says.

"Go ahead."

"The mother—Carey Peters, right?—doesn't she work for that Pressman gentleman in Chicago?"

The randy Randall Pressman, Malone thinks. "Yes," she says. "Pressman Logistics."

"Have you checked in with him?"

"With Pressman himself? Why would we?"

"I've had reason to cross paths with him. He's involved in some unsavory activities."

Malone's phone goes off. "At a logistics company?"

"Contraband has to get somewhere somehow."

"It's Chief." She answers her phone. "Yeah?"

"This frigging guy," Radovich tells her. "Now we got him."

"Where?"

"Schoolcraft. He gave his parole officer his girlfriend's address while he was holing up at his old cellmate's place."

"The cellmate gave him up?"

"Yes, he did. How far are you?"

Malone points the phone at Locke. "Stop the car."

"Why?"

"We got Bledsoe. Pull over."

Malone's seat belt digs into her shoulders as Locke's tires scatter the shoulder gravel.

"Kalamazoo County's going," Radovich says. "Where are you?"

"On our way. Keep this off the scanner. Bledsoe might know we were in Bridgman."

"You gonna be OK?"

Malone knows what he's getting at. "I'm fine. Talk later." She undoes her seat belt and jumps out of the car.

"What are you doing?" Locke says.

"Switch seats. I know a shortcut."

Sliding behind the wheel, Malone maps the route to Schoolcraft in her head, seeing again the elbow bend where Louisa was sitting in the pickup next to her father as Malone gave chase. She closes her eyes but sees for the hundred thousandth time the tailgate fishtailing left and right before the truck skids sideways and lurches over the shoulder into the unyielding oak.

She slams the accelerator down and screeches out onto the road, her heart breaking a thousand different ways as she thinks, *Danny, please, just be there, alive.*

29

Bledsoe's trying to keep cool. He can't afford to get pulled over for speeding, but he's got to push it as fast as he can. He exited I-94 the minute he heard the scanner croak the order for Berrien County deputies to get to 1626 Beechnut in Bridgman. Petunia's place.

They're coming for him.

He kept the speedometer just below the 45 limit on Flowerfield and tapped it up a few miles per hour after turning north onto 131. He slows entering downtown Schoolcraft. Passing Bud's Bar, he wishes he could while away the hot evening with a bucket of cold ones, but he has to get out of here, out of Michigan, out of the country. Fuck the kid and his asshole parents. Fuck the rotts. Bledsoe is outta here.

He turns right on Clay, sees the gray box of his apartment building three blocks away. Corrigan, his Muskegon cellmate, had told him he could rent apartment 302 from a sister-in-law for fifty dollars a week. He wound up paying her in other ways she seemed to prefer and he didn't mind much either.

He sees no police cars in the lot but circles the block just to be safe. He swings behind his building and parks next to a dumpster just as an email from Petunia dings on his phone. That's not right. She's a texter, not an emailer. The subject line is empty. He clicks on a link to her Facebook page, and a wave of dread washes over him.

"Are you fucking kidding me?" he says. He looks around to see if anyone is watching or listening. "Dumb fucking cunt."

He has seen the photo before. Petunia in a too-tight yellow bikini. He took it on the sand at Warren Dunes. That's not the problem. The problem is that she pasted it into some kind of postcard graphic that shows her sitting on a different beach beneath a palm tree. "Ola!" the caption reads. "Time for a new adventure!!"

It's already been "liked" twenty-eight times.

Bledsoe looks at the dashboard clock. Petunia could be on her way to this very spot, with the cops on her rear bumper. He hopes like hell she didn't stop at her place first. Brainless bitch.

He skulks into the building's rear entrance, rushes up the stairs. Inside 302, he secures both deadbolts and goes directly to the laptop sitting open on the kitchen table. He has to clean out a few items he neglected to wipe the night before.

He signs on and slides the cursor to a folder labeled "bitch." It contains an email exchange from seven months earlier, a week after Bledsoe had left prison and bought that file on Carey:

C,

how u? got a minute for an old pal coming to chicago? give a shout

Jeff B

He'd looked at her blunt reply once every few days, more if he'd had a lot to drink. At first it had just pissed him off. Lately he's begun to regard it as a source of inspiration:

Jeffrey,

If you contact me again, I will call the police. I
assume you don't need any more trouble.

Good Bye.

Bledsoe hadn't forgotten the night he was sure he'd knocked Carey
up. Halloween damp seeped through the cracked-paint window frame
above Carey's bed. Bledsoe wore a flannel nightshirt, a fresh condom in
the pocket. She was the one who wouldn't stop. She was the one who'd
guzzled the white Russians at the Elwood. She was the one who had
raked her nails across his skin and shook her head when he offered to
pull the balloon on. "Don't stop fucking me don't stop fucking me."
Bledsoe had merely done what he did so well.

He reads her latest words one more time. The bitch couldn't even
sign her name. She had to drag out the goodbye, using two words,
like she got off telling him to stay out of her precious life. He had told
himself to let it go. Of course he couldn't. He couldn't let anything go.
Sometimes that was a good thing, in the way rich guys liked to say they
never gave up and that's how they got rich. Sometimes it wasn't, like
when you pushed too hard on a guy in the joint who didn't give a shit
if you lived or died or if he did.

Bledsoe deletes the emails, erases the files, goes to the trash bin,
deletes them all again.

He'd never thought of trying to contact his son until Petunia
pointed out the online article about the runaway kid named Danny
in Bleak Harbor. "Looks like his mama might've been knocking him
around," she said. That was all Bledsoe needed to hear.

One night, after four beers and a Vicodin, he found Danny on
Facebook. The kid had all of four friends. One was his bitch mother.
The others were members of some dweeby Cubs fan club, one of

them in a foreign country Bledsoe hadn't heard of. No wonder Danny responded right away. Bledsoe had emailed him with the subject line "YOU." What fifteen-year-old wouldn't bang on that?

Champ,

This is your real daddy. Sorry about what's goin on. Glad u are OK . . .

Danny had replied:

I am glad too.

Did you know that the dragonfly is one of the most vicious killers in the animal kingdom?

Bledsoe had not known that. He wondered why a teenaged kid would bring that up, then reminded himself that Danny wasn't right in the head. And yet, for a kid who was supposedly messed up, he turned out to be a hell of a lot smarter than Petunia. After they started texting instead of emailing, Danny listened to Bledsoe bitch about hauling paint buckets of grease in his trunk to the dump, creeping low in the night because LaBelle's owner wouldn't pay to have the stuff disposed of properly. Bledsoe listened to Danny gripe about his stepdad spending more time at that bar than with Danny. He started thinking, *Shit, this kid ain't retarded or agnostic or nothing. He's just shy and lonely and ignored. Goddamned if he isn't me.*

Now he double deletes the Danny emails and wishes he'd taken a last look at Petunia's computer. Too late now. He's about to shut the laptop when he decides to check his Sent email folder, just in case the cops happen to catch up with him. Which they won't.

He leans into the screen, squinting at the sent email four down from the top. It went to Danny's Gmail address. It contains the subject line "Re: YOU." But Bledsoe hasn't sent an email to Danny in weeks. It's been all texts since. The date on the email says he sent it two nights before. *No fucking way*, he thinks. He opens it:

Y not, Danny boy?

"Danny boy?" he says. "I didn't—what the fuck?" He wonders if Petunia was in his email. He thinks back to the last time she was in Schoolcraft. Sunday. Five days ago. Too stupid to be her.

He hears two knocks at the door, thinks, *Petunia already? She must have left work early.*

He goes back to his main email page, then to the trash bin, then back to the sent folder. He thinks back to Wednesday night. He was watching porn. He can remember the white-haired guy going down on the hairless kid with the skin like wax paper. But he can't recall sending a single email, certainly not to Danny.

He hears three more knocks, rapid and hard.

He remembers the text from Quartz—1ovrEZ@5—that sent him from the diner to collect the boy.

Wishing now that he had ignored it.

He gets up and tiptoes to the locked bedroom door. You could hear a mosquito breathing through the shitty particleboard. Bledsoe hears the twin rottweilers huffing and snarling and scraping their nails on the other side of the door. His nose tells him they've shit all over the floor. He's not about to clean it up now. The cops will find what they find.

He looks into the kitchen. From the window it's three floors to the ground. Too far to jump, but maybe there's a car or a trash can down there to break his fall.

There's another knock. Bledsoe edges sideways toward that door. It has no peephole. "Baby?" he says.

He pulls up short when no answer comes, takes a step back, glances over his shoulder at the kitchen window. He waits. Hearing nothing, he leans into the door again. Without touching it, he sniffs the air as quietly as he can. He wants to smell Petunia's perfume. At the diner he could smell it even over sizzling onions.

Now all he gets is sweat. He takes another backward step, then another, and reaches behind him for the doorknob to the room where the dogs wait.

"Petunia?" he says. "Who the fuck's out there?

30

Pete downs the double vodka tonic in one languid guzzle. He doesn't care about tasting it—he just wants to feel it, to drown himself in it for half a minute before resurfacing. The last drops trickle off the back of his tongue, bitter. He sets the glass down.

"Another?" Boz says.

Yessir, Pete thinks. And another and another. He pushes the glass across the bar. "Diet Coke."

"Sure?"

"Yeah. Needed that, though."

"I can imagine."

Pete left Oly at the rink and drove into downtown Bleak Harbor to check on his office. He couldn't get close because of traffic and pedestrians and blocked-off streets, but he really didn't want to get close anyway. He'd pulled into a pay lot three blocks up the rise on Lily and slumped low in the driver's seat, blasting the AC, as festivalgoers in "Anisoptera Always" T-shirts streamed past. Some of them paused on the sidewalk to peer into the building that housed AMP Botanicals. Police tape ringed the semicircular glass entrance, and sheriff's deputies were hauling boxes out to a police van parked in the middle of the street. Pete made a quick inventory in his mind. He'd been careful about packaging the illegal dope in the same vials and cellophane baggies as the legal stuff. He couldn't think of anything that would get him in trouble. *I'm not the criminal here*, he thought. *Why aren't they out finding Bledsoe? Why aren't they out finding Danny?*

He thought of Danny standing in their kitchen, wrapping the salami-and-cheese sandwiches in wax paper, how careful he was to make the wrap tight, the creases sharp. And then Pete started to cry. At first he tried to slump lower in his seat so the passersby wouldn't notice, but then he didn't care—he let the sobs shake him, let the tears drip off his chin. "Oh God," he said aloud. "My man, my man, my little man. Come home, Danny. Please come home."

Boz sets a tumbler of ice and Diet Coke in front of him. Pete says, "Traffic is a pain in the ass today."

"And will be until Monday."

"Listen, Boz, gotta ask you something, then I gotta get to the police station."

"They were here, you know. A couple hours ago."

"The police were here?" he says.

"Sheriff's deputies. Routine stop. Did I see the boy yesterday, see anything unusual at your house?"

"You did see Danny. You told me."

"Yeah. He was outside."

Pete waits, expecting more, but Boz moves down the bar to the sink without saying anything. "And?"

Boz shrugs. "Like I told the deputies, not much. I mean, I was in the dead spot between lunch and happy hour. He walks by every now and then; we talk."

"What'd you talk about yesterday?"

"Not much. The storm that's coming tomorrow. My new boat. Kid likes that boat. And we did some bitching about the festival, of course."

"Danny loves the festival."

"Huh." Boz takes his cell phone off the back bar, punches something in, sets it down again. "What do I know about kids?"

Pete picks up his own phone, considers trying Carey again, instead hits the app for their bank, types in the username and password. The numbers pop up again. He swipes to make them bigger. He has to look at the pending total three times before he believes it: $5,150,122.98. *Thank God for Oly*, he thinks as he sends Carey a text:

Oly came thru w5 mill+!!

He wants to show the bank entry to Boz, show him he's doing something for Danny. Instead he clicks out of the bank app, looks up, and says, "What do your ex-cop instincts tell you?"

"They have any leads?"

"Looks like it might be Danny's real father." Pete glances down the bar at the stool where Bledsoe stood mocking him months before. The reindeer decoration is still on the wall. "Guy just got out of prison."

"They have a bead on him?"

"I guess they're working on it."

"You guess?"

"Like I said, I gotta get over there."

"Right."

Boz busies himself at the cash register. The air in the room has shifted like it does when Pete and Danny are out fishing and a squall comes up. Pete looks over his shoulder through the picture windows at the empty beach, the bay lying still and silver in the humid afternoon. Down the beach, yellow tape is looped along the deck railings at his house. He presses his eyes shut, wishing it all away, seeing Danny strolling out to the dock with a fishing pole and minnow bucket, bobbing his head to a tune only he can hear.

Just find him.

When he opens his eyes, Boz's face is screwed up with what looks like emotion, maybe regret. Pete hears a door opening somewhere behind the bar, then footsteps, two people.

Boz leans forward and grips the bar hard with both hands.

"Something wrong?"

"Jesus," Boz says. "I'm sorry, man."

"Sorry for what?"

They both turn to see a woman and a man in Bleak County Sheriff's uniforms. Pete feels a little surge of hope.

"Oh my God, did you find Danny?"

The male deputy stays behind, standing stiff with his arms folded beneath the reindeer head, while the woman steps forward and says, "Andrew Michael Peters?"

Pete turns to Boz. "What's going on?"

"Sorry, buddy."

Pete smiles in his confusion. He turns back to the woman. "Yes," he tells her, then looks back at Boz. "Once a cop, always a cop, eh?"

The handcuffs pinch Pete's wrists. He feels guilt leach through him as the officer ushers him out the back door.

31

Boz watches through a window in his kitchen as the sheriff's cruiser pulls out of his lot, siren wailing. *For Christ's sake*, he thinks, *you don't need the damn siren.*

He likes Pete, and not just because he's a regular. The guy knows his Chicago sports, leaves a decent tip, agrees with Boz about most of the political bullshit that rules this town.

But the guy's in over his head. Way over. Boz saw guys like him all the time in his years on the Chicago force, retired cops especially, thinking they could do what they couldn't. Dreaming of that one big strike, getting themselves in trouble. As the cop flashers disappear around a bend in the bay road, Boz half smiles at himself. After all, he's doing the same thing, isn't he? The big strike is at hand for him now.

Pete will understand one day, if he ever finds out.

Boz walks back into the bar. Two regulars are waiting at a high top inside, three more at a picnic table on the beach deck. They've probably seen Pete Peters before, but Boz doesn't think any of them know him. They're going to ask about the deputies, and Boz is going to smile and zip his lips like he did when he wore a badge, tell them he's going to close the deck pretty soon—everyone come inside; first round's on him.

His phone is waiting where he left it on the back bar beneath the Schlitz sign. He leaves it there, opens a cabinet beneath the back bar, and takes out a disposable phone.

"Parched over here, Mr. Boz," a high-top customer calls out.

Boz waves at the customers, says, "One sec," then taps out a text:

pete in cuffs coast clear cops know nothin

32

Danny listens.

The echoing drums, the church bells, the tinny calliope.

He imagines the tack of cotton candy on his lips. Hears a rock song, something about Montreaux, Frank Zappa, a flare gun. The singer flat, the cymbals hissing, the bass too loud.

Hears Pete.

That one's a keeper, Danny. Do you think your mom still loves me? We'll sneak out to the big lake one of these nights. Do you think she ever did?

Hears Carey.

No lumps, my baby, eat your breakfast. Early meeting. The goddamn traffic. This goddamn place. I'm so sorry we brought you here. But soon, someday, someday soon, I will take you away.

Maybe she thought he couldn't understand. Entirely.

Does not hear the wet chuff and growl of the rotts.

Hears Paddle. Paddle barking at the dragonflies. Jumping and yapping at the end of the dock.

I'm sorry, honey—there is nothing we can do.

Paddle wheezing. The dragonfly wings aflutter. The veterinarian's perfect children will learn one day that a cure is not a realistic possibility.

There is nothing we can do, son.

Paddle hushed.

There was nothing we could do.

Did they think he wouldn't understand?

The dragonflies hover.

We will get a new dog, a new Paddle. I promise, honey. As soon as we're out of here.

Danny sees the face of Jeremiah, the one the newspaper used back then, not on the front page, inside the paper, black-and-white, the longing stare, the head canted ever so slightly.

Imagines him speaking:

The time is near. The perch are rushing to the hooks. You see, Danny, the summer is ours. This place is ours. The dragonflies are here, jaws agape with blood and fire.

33

"Where's the kid?"

"One thing at a time, Randall. Our immediate problem is solved."

"That was our guys?"

"Our guys."

"In broad daylight?"

"Inside an apartment building. It had to be done."

"What about the cops?"

"They'll think it's the Detroit dealer."

"How do you know that?"

Quartz doesn't. "Relax."

"I'll relax when we know where the fucking kid is."

"Working on it."

Quartz hunches over a table in the kitchen of his apartment above the Mexican café in Valparaiso. He has emptied his many pockets, and the table is strewn with laptops, Danny's hard drive, and other boxy black devices. Quartz speaks to Pressman through a Bluetooth earpiece as he works a mouse and a keyboard.

"I suggest you work harder," Pressman says. "Do you realize how many different ways we're screwed if we don't find that kid?"

Let's see, Quartz thinks, *the hundred grand to Bledsoe is long gone, and you promised two million dollars to Carey Bleak*. If the cops stumble onto what's really going on, Pressman could go down for conspiracy and kidnapping and murder.

Quartz will have disappeared by then, possibly with that two million bucks in one of his overseas bank accounts. He has considered leaving immediately but has been digging up things in his current digital excavations that are keeping him here for now. At this instant he's prowling the servers of the *Bleak Harbor Light*, trying to figure out how that 1945 page wound up on the website and what the hell it means.

"Let's focus on the positives, shall we?" he tells Pressman. The sweat beading at the backs of Quartz's ears itches. He tried to open a window, but it got stuck in congealed paint. "Bledsoe is dead. Nobody has a clue we're involved."

"Can't they trace what we paid Bledsoe?"

"I made sure that trail leads nowhere."

"Have we given Carey Peters any money yet?"

"I set up a timed transfer for close of business. But that could easily be explained as a magnanimous boss helping out an employee." Quartz stops typing to gnaw on a fingernail. The blood hasn't come yet.

"I don't like it."

"You don't like what?"

"All of it. Like, Jesus, why the hell did they have to kill dogs?"

Quartz looks up at the bull's-eyes arrayed on the wall across the room. He thinks about the .22-caliber pistol in the drawer next to his bed.

He hopes he doesn't have to use it.

"Forget the dogs, Randall," he says. "I'm actually getting somewhere."

34

The woman is sobbing so hard that Malone can't make out what she's trying to say.

"Why . . . ?" she keeps saying. "Why did they . . . ?" But each time her wailing swallows the rest of her words. Blood splotches the frills along the low scoop of her blouse. Her perfume smells as sickly sweet as dying flowers, with an incongruous hint of bacon.

Her driver's license identifies her as Petunia Marie Delacroix, age thirty-seven, of Bridgman. She's standing with Malone and Agent Allen Locke in the parking lot of an apartment building in Schoolcraft. Four Kalamazoo County sheriff's deputies are inside, service weapons drawn. Two others patrol the grounds. A pair of ambulances waits by the building's rear entrance. Locals gawk from a weedy playground next door.

"Ms. Delacroix," Locke says. "Would you like to wait in my car?"

Petunia shakes her head. Rivulets of mascara bleed into the lipstick smears along one of her cheeks.

"Is Jeffrey dead?" she says.

"We don't have confirm—"

"Yes, he is dead," Malone says. "How did you know him, Petunia?"

Locke takes a tissue from a back pocket and hands it to Petunia, who balls it up on her face and says, "Who killed him?"

The first officers to arrive found Petunia slumped against the wall outside Bledsoe's open apartment, a splat of vomit on the floor near her high-heeled feet. Bledsoe had three bullets in his head, two in his back.

"We don't know yet," Malone says. "Was Jeffrey Bledsoe your boyfriend?"

She gazes past Malone and Locke at the building. "We had some good times. He's—he was—"

"He gave your address in Bridgman as his, ma'am," Locke says.

"He did?"

Malone steps closer. "Why did you come here, Petunia? You need to tell us. We're running out of time."

Her face scrunches up as if she's going to start crying again. "I understand."

"Do you understand that a boy's life is on the line? Was he here? Did Bledsoe have a boy with him?"

"Maybe I should get a lawyer."

"Officer Malone?"

Malone turns and recognizes the sheriff of Kalamazoo County, a man named Krasean. She tells Petunia, "Stay where you are."

She and Locke and Krasean move a few steps away. The sheriff speaks softly. "There's no sign of the Peters boy."

"Nothing?"

"So far. The techs will be here any minute."

"No signs that he might have escaped?"

"I think we'd have heard by now," Krasean says. "We've checked every public area in the building, and now we're going door-to-door." He looks over his shoulder at the building. "I have to say, it looks like a professional job. These people didn't fool around. And the deceased was one disturbed person."

"How so?"

"You'll see. Bunch of snapshots on the wall in the bathroom, all around the sink mirror."

"Snapshots of what?"

"Girls. Young. Boys. Black. White. Brown. Mostly naked."

221

"So our number-one suspect was a pervert," Locke tells Malone. "And now he's dead. Could someone have killed him and taken the Peters boy? This guy in Detroit? Or what?"

Or we were all dead wrong about Bledsoe, Malone thinks. *Or the kidnapper is someone we haven't imagined, a depraved stranger toying with us while he gets ready to*—she forces the thought from her mind, hears Petunia blubbering again.

"I'd like to slap her," she says.

"Please don't," Krasean says.

"I want to ask her something," Locke says.

Petunia is shaking with sobs again as she dumps pills from a plastic vial into one of her hands. She jams them into her mouth, still crying, and tosses her head back to swallow.

"Ms. Delacroix."

She starts to gag, pitching forward, hands going to her mouth. Locke continues: "Did your boyfriend ever say anything about a man named Pressman?"

The pills are burbling out through her lips now. Malone catches one, the saliva slimy in her hand, starts to drop it, then squeezes it, opens her palm, stares at the gooey blue thing.

"Wait," she says. She remembers Will worrying about Danny's meds. She turns to the sheriff, points toward the building. "Did you find any sort of prescription pills in there? Anything that would have been Danny's?"

"Some Percocets, I believe, but we assume those were the deceased's."

"Nothing else? Nothing marked for Danny Peters?"

"Negative."

"OK, Sheriff, can you do me a favor and get Agent Locke back to Bleak Harbor?"

"Pardon me?" Locke says.

"Of course. Agent, do you want to take a look inside? We're also searching the deceased's car, in back."

"Yes, he does," Malone says, then tells Locke, "I'm taking your car. I have to get back now."

Locke looks from Malone to Petunia and back. "Should I bring her?"

"She's useless, but whatever."

Malone heads toward Locke's car, looks at her watch, starts running, hears Petunia bawling again. "Why?" she's wailing. "Why did they have to shoot the dogs?"

35

Carey flings the door to Radovich's office open and flips her phone onto the chief's desk.

"You arrested my husband?" she says. "Are you fucking kidding me?" She scans the room, heads swiveling in her direction: Chief, Jonah, Will, an official-looking woman she's never seen before. "Where is Officer Malone?"

"Ms. Peters."

"You're all fuckups. It's not Bledsoe, is it? What the fuck are you all doing?"

She knows she's out of line. She knows they've been waiting on her, trying to reach her. She'd planned to come in as calm and polite as she could be under the circumstances. Then the video had appeared on her phone, courtesy of Jeremiah. She had pulled into a rest area to watch it. It took her a while to settle down enough to drive again.

"We understand you're upset, ma'am," the woman says.

"You understand shit," Carey tells the woman, then looks at the chief, sitting at his desk. "For all you know, Danny's riding the merry-go-round with a box of popcorn."

"Ma'am—"

"And the ransom, incidentally, is now up to seven million something, according to this goddamn Jeremiah." She doesn't mention Oly O'Nally's contribution; the cops don't need to be bothering the only person who has helped so far.

"We'll need to see that phone."

"Who the hell are you?"

"FBI. Stefanie Hamilton." She offers her hand. Carey ignores it. "We've been trying to reach you."

"Watch the video," Carey says, nodding at her phone.

Will takes it from the desk.

Jonah comes over and joins Radovich and the FBI agent leaning over Will's shoulder. Carey knows the video by heart by now. It was black-and-white and slightly out of focus. There was no sound.

It opened on what looked like a living room, with a television on a stand near an open doorway. Discarded cans of energy drink littered the floor. The arm of a man, limp in front of the doorway, jutted into the bottom of the frame. The middle halves of two men in dark garb moved in and out of the scene. Neither acknowledged the camera, as if they had no idea it was there.

The arm twisted one way, then turned over and pushed the upper half of its body up from the floor. The head and shoulders of a man lurched into the picture. His face was turned away, but Carey recognized the tattoo on his neck.

He dragged himself toward the doorway. The barrel of a gun appeared at his back. There was a small flash of light. Bledsoe collapsed, black liquid pooling around his head.

Two more flashes followed. The dark-clad men left the room. At fifty-seven seconds, the screen went black. A timer at the bottom of the screen said twenty-three seconds remained. The black turned to blue, then gray. The gray began to peel back from the left side of the screen, revealing a backdrop of white and then, gradually, in the middle of the screen, Danny's thin, anguished face, in color.

The camera pulled back until Danny's shoulders and chest came into view. He was awake. He no longer wore a blindfold. The shadow remained beneath his left eye. He appeared to be sitting, his arms pinned behind him. He looked offscreen, then nodded.

His lips began to move. He was speaking, but there still was no sound. It took Carey a few views to read his lips. He wasn't saying much. Just three words, spaced about a second apart: "Mom. Pete. Why."

Then Danny bowed his head briefly before raising it to say, "What are you doing?"

The image flickered before engulfing Danny in black.

Now Jonah and the others move away from Will, who taps the phone screen, watching again. Carey is fighting tears. She feels Jonah's fingers on her elbow. He's whispering: "Calm now. Calm." She closes her eyes as she would when she was a child, Jonah's hand on her shoulder, her mother and father down at the deck overlooking the big lake, their choked-off shouting and cursing audible but blessedly unintelligible.

"Bledsoe's computer must be fitted with a miniature video camera," Will says. "Probably for women he brought back. Or—never mind."

"But Bledsoe didn't make this video of him getting shot," Hamilton says.

"No. It looks like someone accessed the cam remotely."

"A hacker."

"Is Danny in the same room as Bledsoe?" Jonah says.

"Doesn't look like it," Hamilton says.

Carey remains silent. Her brother speaks up again. "How do we know those men didn't take Danny with them?"

"We don't."

"Damn," Will says, working his own phone now. "This thing's all over the web. This guy—@drewthenobody—tweeted it like ten times."

Mom. Pete. Why.

"Are you going to bring Pete out here?" Jonah asks.

The chief turns to Hamilton, who says, "We need to ask Ms. Peters a few questions first." She gives Carey a practiced look that's probably intended to comfort. Carey takes her in: Early forties. Tai chi classes. No wedding band. "Ms. Peters—"

"Carey, please."

"Carey. As we understand it, you last heard from Jeffrey Bledsoe late last year—is that correct?"

"Yes. I told him to go away."

"Understood," Hamilton says. "Now, are you aware of any recent contacts between Bledsoe and your husband?"

The question slams Carey like a forearm to the breastbone. She repeats it once in her mind, then again, catching her breath. She knows the answer—no, she is not aware of any contacts—but the answer isn't the problem; the question is the problem.

"No," she says. "He—no, that can't be."

"Afraid it is," Hamilton says.

"Can you please get to the point?" Jonah says.

Hamilton says, "Mr. Peters was buying illegally grown marijuana from Bledsoe and reselling it in his shop."

"Oh, holy bullshit," Jonah says.

"That's ridiculous," Carey says, more because she doesn't want to believe it than that she can't.

"Mr. Peters has admitted as much to us," Hamilton says. "Our preliminary inquiries indicate that Bledsoe may have had similar relationships with other legal dealers in the region. And, as you may or may not know, Bledsoe is—or was—affiliated with a dangerous criminal in Detroit."

"Who may have had him killed."

"Your husband insists he didn't know he was doing business with Bledsoe. Everything was done by phone and text and anonymous drops involving piggy banks."

"Piggy banks? This is beyond silly."

"Mr. Peters says he was not aware precisely whom he was dealing with until very recently."

It hits Carey then that her husband may be responsible, however indirectly, for her son's disappearance. "I want to see him."

"What about Dulcinea Pérez?" Hamilton says. "Know her?"

Carey thinks of Dulcy's wide-set eyes, the stretchy V-neck sweater accentuating her cleavage. "She's a lazy do-nothing who couldn't get to work on time. Pete was supposed to fire her yesterday."

"Ah," Hamilton says. "Do you happen to know if Pérez was aware that she was about to be canned?"

"How would I? Why does it matter?"

"We think she works for the same Detroit dealer Bledsoe did, probably sent here to keep an eye on your husband." Hamilton waits a beat. "She also may have had communications with your son."

"No way. She came to the house once, and Danny probably saw her at the shop a couple of times, but that's all."

"Mr. Peters told us he would regularly send Pérez to check on Danny if he was busy at the shop. Usually late afternoons."

"So," Jonah says, "she could have seen the inside of the house, gotten an idea of Danny's routine?"

"He was taken in late afternoon."

When Pete was at the damn bar, Carey thinks. "So what are you saying? This person in Detroit took Danny? Or his guys did? Or that Dulcy bitch did?" She feels tears starting to come, pinches them back. "We're fucked. Danny's . . . oh my God."

Radovich comes around the desk, lays a gentle hand on Carey's shoulder. "We don't know that," he tells her. "We are looking for Pérez. The Detroit police are also on the case." He nods at Will. "Can you please go find Malone?"

As Will slips past her, Carey feels Jonah touch the small of her back. She feels woozy, closes her eyes against the sudden spinning of the room. She tries to picture herself on the beach deck with Danny on a bright afternoon, glasses of lemonade sweating on the arms of the adirondack chairs. She and Danny would be debating, yet again, his favorite poem. And he would tell her that the palm in the opening line, the one Carey mistook for a hand instead of the tree it was, "is forever out of reach."

She always heard his declaration as defeatist, as if Danny had given up on whatever dreams swirled in his mind. It crushed her. Now his observation strikes her as realistic, mature, even liberating. Danny wasn't saying people couldn't have what they yearned for. He was saying that the yearning would never cease, no matter what was gained or gathered. It was enough to embrace the yearning, then let it go. She wishes she'd listened harder.

"Carey?" It's the chief. "Do you happen to know where Danny's laptop was purchased?"

She thinks for a second. "Pete got it online, I think. Before we moved here for good. It was kind of a bribe."

"When was that? A year ago?"

"A little longer."

Radovich turns to Hamilton. "Will says the one in our possession seems newer."

Will comes back into the office, followed by another man. A thread of scar curls from the man's left cheekbone to his mouth. Carey thinks she has seen this face before.

"Dispatch is hunting Malone down," Will says. "No luck yet."

"Agent Locke," Radovich says.

Carey feels her shoulder blades contract around her spine.

"Locke?" Hamilton says. The look on her face is not approving. "We weren't aware you were assigned to this case."

Without so much as a glance at Carey, Locke holds up a small clear plastic bag half filled with a powdery white substance. "We found this in the tire well in the trunk of Jeffrey Bledsoe's car." Then he addresses Hamilton. "Missed you in Schoolcraft, Agent. Not polite to leave your riders behind, you know. Reflects poorly on the bureau."

Locke finally turns to Carey. His sepia-tinted glasses are crooked at an angle. "Special Agent Allen Locke," he says, moving the baggie closer to her. "Do you recognize this, Ms. Peters?"

"How do you know who I am?"

"I assumed. Sorry if I offended."

Fuck you, Carey thinks.

"Do you happen to know what this is?"

Carey wishes she didn't. She takes a breath. She sees Danny asleep on the leather sofa, the Cubs on the tube, Paddle snuggled into his supine body, the dog holding his head upright, eyes still open, watching over his slumbering friend.

"It looks like Paddle's ashes. Danny's dog. We had to put him down. Danny kept some of his ashes in his wallet."

Then Carey sees those jaws again, the ones on her phone.

"Could be cocaine in there, for all we know," Hamilton says. "Can we get it analyzed pronto?"

"We will," Radovich says. "But we probably should assume it's evidence that Danny was, well, I think you follow."

Locke nods. "Agent Hamilton is right. It could be something else. It could be a ruse, planted by someone who knew about the ashes."

"On it," Will says, taking the baggie from Locke and leaving the office. Jonah wraps an arm around his sister.

"Thank you, Chief," Locke says. "If nobody minds, I would like to speak with Ms. Peters in private for a moment."

"For what?" Hamilton says.

"For a moment," he says, looking at Carey. "Please."

She glares at Locke, refusing to flinch, instead lying: "I don't know you, Agent."

Locke nods and says, "All right," slipping a sheet of paper from inside his sport jacket. "I need to ask you about someone."

Pressman, she thinks.

"He calls himself Quartz," Locke says.

230

That throws her. How would Locke know about Quartz? How would anybody, unless they had followed her to Valparaiso?

"Like the many-faceted stone. Are you familiar with that name?"

She feels Jonah and everyone else looking at her. The longer she hesitates, the more suspicious they'll be.

"Quartz is not his real name, Ms. Peters. But it's what he told you, isn't it?"

Locke steps closer. "Carey?"

"What does this have to do with my son?"

"Good question," Hamilton says.

Locke unfolds the paper in his hand and holds it up in front of Carey. It's a printout of the Jeremiah email from Danny's laptop. "Mr. Northwood kindly provided this."

"No," Carey says, "I kindly provided the police with that. And there's nothing about any Quartz in there."

"But there is this." Locke reads aloud: "'Maybe hit up randy bossman.' I believe Randall Pressman is the head of the company where you work, is he not?"

"He is."

"And how well do you know him?"

"He's my boss." She stops herself from adding, "That's all."

"Do you have any idea why Jeremiah would refer to him in that way? The 'randy bossman'? Small *r*?"

Even with her brother at her side, Carey couldn't feel more alone. This man, Locke, is the one who's been harassing her with texts about her Valentine's Day tryst, demanding the documents she spirited out of Pressman's computers. Stalling, Carey says, "What does this have to do with anything?"

Locke withdraws the printout, backs away, looks around at the others. "Quartz works for Pressman. Off the books, as it were." He turns back to Carey. "But you already knew that, didn't you?"

Radovich speaks up. "Agent Locke, what does this have to—"

"I'll bet you've spoken with him, haven't you, Carey? Is that where you disappeared to today?"

He might be bluffing. But of course he's correct. *Fuck it*, she thinks. "I've made mistakes in my life, Agent Locke. Now's not the time to judge."

"Nobody's judging. I just don't want you to make decisions based on the assumption that Quartz is going to help you find your son. That would be a tragic mistake."

"Locke, would you care to fill the rest of us in on this Quartz?" Hamilton says. "Sounds like we ought to be looking for him."

Locke pushes his glasses up on his nose and addresses not Hamilton but Chief Radovich. "I'm not at liberty to say much, but Quartz— which is not his real name—is a fugitive from the law. He used to work for the federal government, and he compromised this country's security in serious ways."

"A spook."

"Yes. He does similar work for Pressman. Again, off the books."

"It's an anagram." Will bursts back into the office, waving his phone. "The Twitter guy's an anagram."

"One second, Will," the chief says.

Locke goes on. "Quartz may also have been in contact with Jeffrey Bledsoe."

He's just guessing, Carey thinks. But it's giving her a queasy feeling. She knows Quartz hacked into Bledsoe's laptop, which the police confiscated from the apartment in Schoolcraft. Maybe Locke knows it too.

"Have you considered the possibility," he asks Carey, "that your employer may be involved in this matter?"

I'm considering it now, she thinks, even if she suspects Locke is gunning not for the kidnapper but for Pressman. But if Pressman is involved, then he must know—and Quartz must know—where Danny is.

She's confused. Maybe, she thinks, she should tell them everything, from Valentine's Day to the blackmail. But what good would it do? Locke seems to know anyway. And if she reveals the blackmail, she could wind up in custody. She doesn't want to be sitting in a jail cell when Danny is found.

Or.

Carey doesn't know whom to trust. Radovich is clueless, Malone has vanished, she doesn't know the others. She hasn't heard from Quartz, with two and a half hours to her six o'clock deadline.

"For all I know, you took my son, Locke."

"Please," he says. "I'm not trying to upset you. But if you know where Quartz is, you should tell us."

"I'll keep that in mind."

"Look," Will speaks up. "I figured out this Jeremiah's phone number. And this Twitter handle, @drewthenobody, deciphers as 'the drowned boy,' like the kid in that story from 1945."

"Whose name also happens to be Jeremiah," Locke says.

"So we need to track this Twitter guy too," Hamilton says.

"And that number that's been texting Carey—5373642445? If you substitute letters for the keypad numbers, you get Jeremiah 45."

"Jesus," Hamilton says. "Chief, better get all this stuff to the Detroit cops. See if they can find a connection to Vend." Then she glances at Locke, reluctant. "The Quartz stuff too."

But they have no idea really, Carey thinks. Whoever this fucked-up individual is, he's smarter than all of them, leaving little trails of digital crumbs that might lead to Danny or not. She slips Jonah's grasp and shoves past Locke to the door.

Mom. Pete. What are you doing?

"Good luck," Carey says. "Jonah and I are going to see our mother now, because it's looking like we're going to need a lot of money." She reaches toward Will. "My phone, please."

"No way," Hamilton says. "We need that phone. You shouldn't have been allowed to keep it or your laptop. We'll also need any passcodes."

"I need the phone if this Jeremiah or Danny or Quartz or whoever it is tries to contact me."

"We'll pass on any messages. Meanwhile, get yourself a substitute. It doesn't look like this guy has any trouble finding you. Will?"

Will hesitates, looks to the chief, who nods for him to give the phone to Hamilton.

"What about Bledsoe?" Carey says. "Did you find anything on his phone?"

"Some, uh, unsavory texts between him and Ms. Delacroix from last night," Will says. "And this afternoon, one to his grandmother in Tampa and one to someone in the Detroit area we have yet to identify."

"We also have your husband's phone, Carey," the chief says. "We'll probably be releasing him soon."

"Fantastic."

"Ms. Peters," Locke says. He offers her a business card. She takes it without thinking. "Please think twice about trusting Quartz."

"I don't know what you're talking about, but it sounds like he could find my son before any of you do. Do not lose those ashes."

———

"Who is this Quartz person, Carey? Was he who you went to see in Indiana?"

"Don't worry about it," she tells Jonah. They're on the sidewalk outside Darlington's, the phone-and-computer store on Lily that used to be a TV-and-radio shop. Carey leans against an empty, rust-fringed *Bleak Harbor Light* vending machine near the door, focused on one of the two burner phones she just bought—one for her, one for Pete—for $49.95 each at Darlington's.

"Carey? Is that where you went?"

"Like Locke said," she says without looking up from the phone. "He works for Pressman. He finds things. He's damn good at it. Better than them."

"Did you tell—"

"Hold on, just hold on a goddamn—" She stops herself, squeezes her eyes shut, puts the phone facedown on a knee, looks up at her brother. "I'm sorry."

"It's OK. I'm just—I don't know what's going on."

"I don't mean to be such a bitch."

"I know. But, Carey."

They had left the police station through a rear door to avoid the reporters and cameras waiting out front, then squirmed shoulder-to-elbow through the sweat-slickened throngs of festivalgoers crawling along the sidewalks, the wings of their idiotic dragonfly hats flapping, their Nucci's go-cups sticky with vodka and cranberry juice. Most had come from elsewhere, but Carey could feel local eyes on her as she passed. *There's the witch who let her poor retarded son get kidnapped*, she imagined them thinking. *Fuck them*, she thought. *Every single fucking one.*

She comes up off the vending machine. "I know," she says. "Focus. I texted Malone with this phone number and emailed it to Spitler."

"What about the chief?"

"Fuck the chief."

She doesn't tell Jonah that she also sent a text to the number Quartz had given her, informing him of the new ransom amount.

"OK, but—"

"Where's your car?"

"This way."

They start down Lily toward Violet, the heart of the festival. As they walk, Jonah puts his arm around her and pulls her in close against the sideways glances. Lily is crammed with people tramping down the fake cobblestone. The beer-tent music blares. A voice on a megaphone says it's time for the blueberry-pie-eating contest. Carey keeps working her new phone. When she and Jonah reach the corner at Violet, she stops and breaks free of her brother.

"Shit," she says.

"What?"

"I'm just—maybe it's this phone."

"What is it?"

People bump and jostle them as they pass. Carey's punching numbers and letters on the phone keypad, trying to access the bank account she and Pete keep. "This isn't right," she says. "I know this password."

"What password?"

"This one."

She's squinting into the phone. She hasn't heard from Quartz and wants to see if Pressman has sent the money yet. She's worried that he won't, that he's just stringing her along, hoping the cops will do his work for him. And now the damn password won't work.

"Pete must have—shit."

Maybe Pete changed the password. Maybe because Oly helped out. She'd love to know, but Pete's sitting in jail, and she's not going back there, not while Locke is still inside. "He should have told me. And now here's an email from Spitler. He says we can see Mother at four thirty."

An email appears. A series of letters and numbers fills the To field. "What the hell?" Carey says, and clicks on it. "Oh Jesus. Oh God, Jonah, what the fuck."

"Now what?"

She pushes the phone up into Jonah's face:

wasting time with poh-lice? u want to find danny boy—or not find him—at bottom of the lake w me?

"Holy God," Jonah says.

Again Carey sees Bledsoe's limp body on the floor, the blood, the dark men, the empty room, the empty faces of the cops.

"This motherfucker," she says. "This—this—this motherfucking fucker."

Carey closes her eyes and squeezes the phone in both hands, wanting to crush it into a silvery powder, knowing people must be looking at her, thinking she's out of her mind. She takes a breath, eases her grip, and gazes upward, looking for something that makes even the smallest bit of sense. What she sees is an inflatable plastic dragonfly fluttering in the breeze over the building that houses Pete's pot shop. And then, in her mind, she sees again the sketch she saw that morning in Danny's bedroom, how vacant the insect's eyes looked as its jaws crushed its prey.

She turns to Jonah. "Where is my son?" she whispers. Then raises her voice. "Where is my son?" She could cry if she wasn't so angry. "Come on. Let's go crawl to the bitch."

36

Pete sits on a concrete slab. He looks down at his feet. He's wearing flip-flops. How the hell, he thinks, could he be wearing flip-flops on a day like this?

He stands and climbs onto the jail cell bed. On his tiptoes he's tall enough to see through the sliver of window carved into the wall. Through the silver wire crosshatched into the glass, he watches a Ferris wheel arcing through the sky over Bleak Harbor. The lights along the wheel spokes twinkle. He can't hear the fake calliope or the children squealing.

Reporters bristling with notebooks and TV cameras had bludgeoned him with questions as sheriff's deputies escorted him, handcuffed, into the police station. That was when he heard that Bledsoe was dead and Danny remained missing.

"Where were you when your son got taken?" he had heard a reporter ask. "Were you really in a bar?" Pete wanted to stop and tell them he was doing what he could, he really loved Danny, but the officers shoved him on. "Can you tell us whether you'll pay the ransom?" "What did you expect, bringing a business like that here?" "Do you think Serenity Bleak will help you?"

The Ferris wheel slows to a stop, hovering in Pete's field of vision, the early-evening sun throwing shadow trapezoids across the faces of the woman and the boy in the seat at one o'clock. The boy is kicking his legs, his head on a swivel, while the woman—his mother? his aunt?—frowns over the phone in her hands. Pete wants to call out to her, tell her everything he now knows.

In the interview room, he'd held nothing back from the chief and the FBI agent, Hamilton. He almost vomited when Hamilton told him, her eyes black bullets of barely disguised anger, about Dulcy Pérez and the hoodlum she worked for and how she might have been sent to keep tabs on Pete.

When they finished with him and ushered him down the hallway, the chief's hand a pincer inside his elbow, he was relieved to have unloaded his secrets, but as Radovich stuffed him in the cell and walked out, clanging the door shut without a word or a look of reassurance, he was frightened to think he was potentially connected to Danny's abduction. Even though he knew he'd had nothing to do with it. At least not intentionally.

He sat down and pondered the gray floor and feebly reminded himself that he'd gotten Oly to come through, and maybe that would save Danny.

The Ferris wheel starts up again. The boy and the woman cycle out of Pete's world. He's grateful for the hypnotic circling of the painted spokes, the swaying of the chairs. It's only a block away, but it seems as distant as the day Pete calls to mind.

———

He had met Carey on Chicago's Navy Pier after 5:00 p.m. It was a Tuesday in August, the sky gauzed with humidity, Lake Michigan a griddle sheen at the far end of the pier.

He was glad to see her sipping a margarita through a straw stuck in a red cup. She was standing at the outdoor bar at Harry Caray's in a summer dress that made him think of sunflowers. She didn't smile when she first spied him, so Pete started waving and clapping and mugging, and she began to smile around her straw, her eyes asking if he was nuts. When he leaned in for a kiss, she let him have a cheek. Grinning, though. Not disappointed at his lateness, just coy. Good.

"You're gonna want more than that," he said, "after you hear about my day."

She set her cup down. "Where have you been? You're sweating."

"I was running. Had a couple of beers with Oly."

"Beers with the boss?"

"Hell, yes. I had a day, girl."

"A day?"

"A great big fucking day."

"How big?"

"Guess."

She canted her head to the right, hair draping an eye. *God*, Pete thought. "Beat your record?" she said.

"Oh yeah."

"Three fifty?"

Pete jerked a thumb upward. "Higher."

"Four hundred?"

Carey picked her cup back up. "Four fifty?"

"Four hundred seventy-three thousand dollars."

Her big eyes went bigger. Pete felt himself swoon. He didn't care about the money, most of which would go to the O'Nallys; he just wanted to make Carey proud.

He knew he'd gotten lucky. A government report had suggested plains flooding would shrink the fall harvest. Corn prices zoomed up, soybeans followed, and Pete spied a trader on the edge of the pit who looked ready to off himself. The poor guy was sitting on a bunch of bets that prices would fall. Pete gladly took his business. It was especially gratifying because Pete had lost more than a hundred grand the day before. He hadn't mentioned that to Carey.

"Woo-hoo!" she said, high-fiving her boyfriend. "Not bad for a cow tipper from Wisconsin." She signaled the barmaid for another margarita. "I guess you can have one drink."

"Sorry I'm a little, uh, sloppy." He grinned and backed up a step, peering down the promenade. "Celebrate on the Ferris wheel?"

She squinted. "What about our drinks?"

"We'll take them for the line."

"Really? The Ferris wheel?"

"Yeah." Pete winked. "I heard things can get hot up there. Closer to the sun, you know."

"They can, huh? Oops—damn. Excuse me." Her phone was ringing on the bar. She grabbed it. "It's Kimi."

Pete's margarita arrived while Carey talked to the girlfriend who was babysitting her son. He took a sip, watching her face darken.

"All right," she said. "I'll be home for dinner."

"Everything OK?" Pete said.

"Nope." She dropped her phone on the bar. "He dumped all his pills again."

"The expensive ones?"

"They're all expensive. Only seven, but he knows what he's doing."

Pete offered her a hand. "It's going to be all right. Come on."

"We can't have dinner out."

"No worries. We'll eat with Danny."

The Ferris wheel line was short. Pete insisted they wait for cab number 11, partly for Carey's November 11 birthday, more because he saw no one in the cabs above or below it.

They sat on a plastic bench the color of a clown nose, facing the lake stretching beyond the pier and the locks along the skyline to the south, the skyscrapers backlit orange by the sun. A Stones' song floated up from the bar below, something about a kiss. Pete rested a long leg on the facing bench and took Carey's left leg and hooked it over his knee. As they rose from the platform, he slid his hand inside her dress.

"Pete."

She squirmed as he spread his fingers along the inside of her thigh. She almost pushed him away, but then she didn't. He bent to her neck as his forefinger slipped beneath her panties. "Goddamn it," she whispered.

He kissed her. Her tongue was silky with lime. "You're so beautiful," he said, and she gasped as he slid his fingers into her.

As they crested the arc, he drew his face away and said, "Look. Look at it, Carey. Everything is so beautiful," and he started to laugh. "It's ours. It's all ours. See the families playing Putt-Putt down there? It's all ours." He leaned back into the porcelain curve of her neck. "God, baby," he said. She was unzipping him. "I love you."

They were laughing as the cab descended to the ground, Pete hurrying to zip his jeans. "Uh-oh," he said. Two security guards in yellow-and-black vests were waiting.

"Pete, I have to get home to Danny," Carey said.

The people waiting in line were wearing goofy smiles, craning their necks to see. "I got this," Pete said. As he stepped off the ride, he shrugged at the guards. "I'd say I was sorry, but, you know."

Then he turned back to Carey. "You love me too?"

She smiled. "Sure."

———

"You can go for now."

The voice startles Pete from his reverie. The bittersweet thrill leaches away. Standing in the doorway is the young man he met that morning in his yard with Officer Malone. Pete wants to tell him he didn't mean for any of this to happen.

"I'm sorry. Any news on Danny?"

"Afraid not. Better get out of here before Chief changes his mind."

37

The woman in front of Malone turns and walks away, shaking her head. Malone steps up to the counter.

"Hello, Kris," she says.

Krissy Oliver is the pharmacist on duty at Strawman Drug. She's in a white smock with her name stitched in pink over the left breast, batting keys at a coffee-stained desktop computer and tugging the blonde hair out of her eyes. She looks perplexed to the point of annoyance.

Malone has to wonder if she's faking the distraction. Krissy can't want to see Malone any more than Malone wants to see her. Every six weeks or so, when Malone has to pick up one of her antidepression prescriptions, she calls ahead to make sure one of the other pharmacists is on duty.

"Oh," Krissy says. "Katya."

A lanyard marked with little red hearts and the words *LOVE LOVE LOVE* swings as she turns to Malone. The ID badge dangling at the lanyard's end has to be at least a year old, because it shows Krissy in the hairstyle she wore when she was sleeping with Malone's ex.

"Busy day?"

"Lately—oh, no, not again. Excuse me, sorry."

She turns and goes through a door marked **EMPLOYEES ONLY**.

Malone waits. Will had called her while she drove back from the murder scene in Schoolcraft to tell her Pete Peters was in custody.

Malone could believe that he wasn't aware he'd been dealing with Bledsoe, or that he didn't know that Dulcinea Pérez—an obvious plant—was connected to the dealer in Detroit. But she didn't believe Peters could harm Danny or intentionally put his stepson in harm's way. It wasn't that Peters was innocent. He was not innocent. But he was too defeated—best word she could think of—to be guilty. He was a loser, not a criminal.

Malone is a loser too, standing there in her cop's uniform, hat literally in hand, waiting on the woman who fucked the loser she had married, who had fathered her beautiful Louisa. Willowy Krissy Oliver, with the pouty mouth and exquisite teeth, was the "k" in the texts she'd found on his phone.

Malone has come to Strawman Drug on a hunch. If she's right, she might be able to find Danny. Otherwise, she doesn't know what to try. Maybe they can lure the abductor out with money.

Krissy returns and goes to the computer, taps a few keys. "I'm sorry, Katya. I'm afraid I might have to disappoint you like I did Mrs. Derdzinski and about—"

"I'm not here for a prescription."

"—a hundred other people. Our computer system caught some bug. It keeps sending these emails saying refills are ready when it's not time yet. At least for the people I know, and I know a lot."

"I'm not here for a prescription."

Krissy finally looks up. "How can I help you then?"

"You've heard about the Peters boy. Danny?"

"The kidnapping? I thought they—you—I thought you found the kidnapper. Isn't he dead?"

"We're not sure he had Danny."

"I'm so sorry. How is Carey holding up?"

"You know Carey?"

"I know of her."

"Is she the one who picks up Danny's prescriptions?"

"I'm sorry. I really can't divulge that. Privacy rules."

"Wherever Danny is, he doesn't have his meds."

"He doesn't?"

"No, and that's not good. Do you happen to know Danny's stepdad, Pete Peters?"

"I know who he is."

"Does he come in for Danny's prescriptions?"

Krissy tries to arrange her face into something stern. "Really, I just can't talk about that."

"You don't want to help find this boy, Krissy?"

"My hands are tied."

"I could get them untied with a warrant," Malone says, knowing she probably couldn't. "But by then Danny Peters might be dead."

"I can have you speak with—"

"Did you hear me?" Malone wishes she didn't have to say what she says next. "Do you really want another child's blood on your hands?"

The tears that appear in Krissy's eyes are angry. *Tough*, Malone thinks. *I won't ask you, Krissy Oliver, if you gave him permission to steal Louisa. You weren't driving the car I chased off the road into a tree. But I won't let you off the hook with Danny.*

"You know that's not fair," Krissy says.

"Can't help that. But you can help Danny."

Krissy wipes at an eye, glances over her shoulder. Malone sees the security camera pointing at them. Krissy hits some keys, waits, reads. "Danny's father was in here sixteen—I mean eighteen days ago to pick up prescriptions. He signed for them."

"His stepdad. How many prescriptions?"

"Three."

Malone takes out her notebook, where she had copied the numbers of the prescriptions off the vials at the police department. She tears out the page and hands it to Krissy.

"These?"

Krissy holds the paper up to the computer screen. Malone follows her eyes. "Yes."

"How long were they for?"

"Four weeks' worth."

"Were they automatic refills?"

"No, these are from Dr. Ringel. But they came with two automatic refills."

"Four weeks out and then eight weeks out?"

"Yes. All right?"

"Any activity since those were picked up?"

"There shouldn't be."

"Just check, please."

Krissy folds her arms across her smock. "I'm really not comfortable with this."

"You're already doing it. Any more activity?"

Krissy unfolds her arms, sighs, leans in to the monitor. "Hmm," she says. "Three more this week."

"Pickups? When?"

"Wednesday."

"What time?"

"Two forty-seven p.m."

"Same drugs?"

"Yes."

"Wouldn't your system have seen that and stopped it?"

"Normally, yes. But like I said, we've had this glitch. The computer suddenly thinks everybody's prescriptions are up for refills."

"Was it Peters who signed on Wednesday?"

Krissy clicks her mouse. "Yes, but . . ." She's shaking her head. "Here." She glances toward the front door while rotating the monitor so Malone can see. The signature reads "Pete Peters."

"I doubt he would've signed 'Pete,'" Malone says. "His real name is Andrew." She'd seen it on his driver's license that morning at his home. "And that handwriting looks girly. Were you here when these were picked up?"

"I was off. Lucia was here."

Krissy swivels the screen back, hits more keys, returns the monitor to Malone. "This is how Peters signed eighteen days ago. It's kind of hard to read, but that doesn't say *Pete* Peters."

"Would Lucia have let someone who wasn't actually Peters sign for a prescription? Someone with girly handwriting?"

"She's part-time. If it gets really busy, sometimes things fall through the cracks. Or if she knew the person and trusted her. I don't know."

"She speaks Spanish?"

"Yes."

An electronic jangle signals that the front door has opened. Malone turns to see a silver-haired woman walking toward her, leaning every other step on a cane. Malone looks back at Krissy. "What about video? That should show who signed."

"Unfortunately, that computer glitch killed our video too."

Pretty damn convenient, Malone thinks. "All right, then I'll need this Lucia's full name and contact information."

Krissy's eyes are darting between the approaching woman and Malone. "Please, I can't put her in that position."

"She put *you* in this position."

"Still—"

"I could give old man Strawman a call. I'm sure he'll be interested to know the whole story."

"Katya, please." Krissy averts her eyes, puts on a smile. "Sheila, how are you today?"

"Good afternoon, dear. Hello, Officer."

Malone nods at the woman. "Mrs. Dorset."

The woman says, "Have you found that poor youngster yet?"

Krissy slides a sticky note across the counter. Malone takes it while telling Mrs. Dorset, "Not yet, but we're hopeful."

"I'm praying for all of you."

"Thank you very much." She nods at Krissy. "If you think of anything else . . ."

———

Malone steps onto the sidewalk, oblivious to the crowd rivering past, the tourists streaming down Lily in their emerald-speckle dragonfly tees, the curly-headed girl crying over the scoop of chocolate chip ice cream melting at her feet, the AC/DC blaring from down the street. She stretches a hand out in front of her and starts to trot, bumping people as she goes, saying, "Police. Please. Let me through. Police."

She adds up what she thinks she knows: Danny gets snatched, but three vials of drugs remain behind, leaving the police to think the abductor neglected them. But three days ago, a woman pretending to be Pete Peters signed for refill prescriptions. Presumably, those are with Danny now, wherever he is. And there just happens to have been a computer glitch that helped the woman pick up the drugs.

Could the woman have been Bledsoe's girlfriend, Petunia? Malone doubts it. Bledsoe wasn't bright enough to have thought this through.

Could the woman have been picking up the prescriptions for Carey? Danny would have what he needed in captivity while she and Pete—or maybe Carey was acting on her own—distracted police with Bledsoe and the Detroit drug dealer, all part of a grand and lucrative deception. Serenity Meredith Maas Bleak would part with an ample enough sliver of her fortune. There would be a tearful reunion with Danny, the nonexistent kidnapper now supposedly vanished. The happy family would sorrowfully declare that they could no longer bear to stay in Bleak Harbor. Pete would dump his business, Carey would quit her job, and they would be gone.

But there's a problem with this scenario: Carey would have signed her own name. Or, if insurance required her husband's signature, she would have known to sign with her husband's proper name, Andrew.

There's one other possibility. It's one Malone has secretly hoped would not pan out. It makes her a little sick to her stomach. A little angry too. She's almost back to the station but calls anyway.

"Will," she says, out of breath.

"Katya. Where have you been?"

"We absolutely must find that Pérez woman. Now."

38

Carey's breath catches at the reek of cigarettes. "Good God," she says, turning to Roland Spitler, who just led her and Jonah into her mother's sitting room. "When's the last time you fumigated?"

"Please make yourselves comfortable," Spitler says.

Carey and Jonah waited downstairs for their 4:30 p.m. appointment for more than thirty minutes. Spitler said Serenity was just waking up from her afternoon nap and he didn't want to disturb her.

Now they're waiting again. Spitler is wearing his usual seersucker suit with a pink silk bow tie. Pink is everywhere at the Bleak Mansion, from the towering turrets to the polo shirts worn by the security guards at the compound's gated entrance. It wasn't always so. Serenity had had everything redone in pink a few years before, while Jack was on one of his extended trips. When Carey and Pete had moved into their cottage across the bay, the adirondack chairs on the deck happened to be pink; of course Carey immediately repainted them forest green.

"Where is Mother?" Carey says.

Spitler consults a digital tablet he'd brought as they ascended to the room, tapping on it to unlock doors along the way. Carey doesn't recall security being this tight when she visited last, but that was before Mother announced her "gift."

"I will be bringing her in shortly," Spitler says. "First, a couple of ground rules."

"Ground rules?"

"Your mother is not well. She can give you twenty minutes."

"No."

"Also, direct requests for money are not appropriate."

"Roland, we're not here to catch up on things," Jonah says. "We're here for money so we can get Danny back safe."

Except for a powdering of gray at his temples, Spitler looks exactly as he did when Carey was a little girl: short and slender, with a slight stoop, as if his body had been designed for subservience. Though Spitler was never subservient to anyone but Serenity, who had dismissed all of her husband's assistants and lawyers within twenty-four hours of his death.

"Please curtail the language when your mother is here. As you know in your capacity as mayor, Mr. Jonah, most of Miss Serenity's estate is currently in escrow."

"Shut up, Roland," Carey says. "Get Mother out here, or we'll go find her ourselves."

———

Carey and Jonah had come up the private road to the mansion, two lanes striped with pink lines repainted each year the week before Memorial Day. Pink plastic reflecting poles planted along both shoulders marked each tenth of a mile, forty-seven of them from the start of Mansion Way at the edge of Bleak Harbor to the mansion itself.

The drive needn't have been that long. As a gull flew, Serenity's estate was barely a mile from downtown. Once, long ago, there had been a road that curled directly around the southwesterly bend in the bay before climbing an incline to the house. Townspeople would drive and bike and walk up the road to picnic in the undulating dunes and swaying grass surrounding the mansion, spreading blankets on the sand. Sometimes Violet Bleak, Carey's great-grandmother, would stroll among the picnickers handing out caramel cubes and papery strips of candy buttons as if it were Halloween.

James Bleak, bastard son of Violet, husband to Catherine, grandfather to Jonah and Carey, had put an end to all of that. First he'd ordered the direct road blocked off in the late 1940s. He had stationed a security guard at a temporary barricade visible to puzzled tourists sunning on the downtown beaches. James himself had designed the road Carey and Jonah had just ascended.

James Bleak's lawyers had worked quietly in the background, filing papers that effectively partitioned the family property as a separate legal entity with its own zip code, protected by its own security force and fire department, as if it were a foreign country. Some citizens had organized a mild protest, but the officials elected with the help of Bleak dollars acquiesced to James's machinations on the condition that the family continue to pay an annual stipend to each of the surrounding municipalities.

Carey had never known the old road. But she had come to know and, for a time, love the new one on summer rides with her mother. After breakfast, three or four days a week, they would climb on their bikes—a sky-blue boys' Schwinn Typhoon for Carey, a crimson Hollywood for Serenity—and glide down the smooth asphalt switchbacks into town, hardly ever touching their pedals, laughing as they gathered speed, the pines rushing past in their peripheral vision. When the road flattened before curving onto Blossom Street, they'd both stand and pedal furiously in a race to the stop sign at Lily. Serenity made sure to come in first often enough that Carey wouldn't think she'd let her daughter win the other times.

They would park their Schwinns in front of the cake shop and sit at one of the sidewalk tables with coffee for Serenity and sweet tea for Carey. And they would talk. Sometimes till lunch. They would talk about the colors of that morning's sunrise, about Carey's future as a backstroke champion, about the boys who had begun to ogle her on the beach, about the books they were reading and movies they'd watched, about going to Chicago or Detroit to shop when Daddy took Jonah fishing in Canada.

One summer, their conversations revolved around the vacation they were supposed to take with Jonah and Daddy to Europe in August. Carey was eleven. Serenity attached a wicker basket to her handlebars to tote the travel guides she'd bought for London and Paris, Prague and Barcelona, Rome and Florence. They spread the guides on the little circular table, pretending they were at a café on the water in Nice, and discussed the cities one by one as Carey made a list of sights they had to see.

By the Fourth of July, the list was six pages long. One morning at breakfast, Carey showed it to her father. He glanced at the first two pages, smiled, and handed it back to her. "That is quite a list," he said. "Did your mother help you with that?" As he spoke, he gave Serenity a sideways look that Carey didn't understand. She turned to her mother, who, without looking at her husband, said, "We'll talk about it."

The four of them were supposed to leave for London on August 2. But Carey's father said he had too much business to attend to in London, so he would go over first, and they would join him a week later. The trip was postponed a second time, for similar reasons, then a third, before Jonah and Carey had to start school.

They never went. Carey threw her six-page list on a fire she and Jonah built on the beach one night. Her father stayed in Europe for many weeks. He sent postcards and gifts—an emerald necklace for Carey, a rugby shirt for Jonah—and spoke with their mother on Monday nights on the phone.

A few Mondays, Carey sneaked into the hallway outside her parents' bedroom to eavesdrop. Her mother spoke in hushed tones. Carey couldn't make out most of what she said. But one night Serenity raised her voice enough—in anger or fright, Carey couldn't be sure—that her words became briefly clear: "Then just stay there . . . never come home . . . no . . . no, bullshit, New York is not London, you're lying, Jack . . . just stay—don't ever come back."

Tuesday morning at breakfast, Carey asked her mother whether— not when, but whether—her father would be coming home. Serenity raised her eyes from the grapefruit half she had blanketed with sugar.

"Young lady," she said. "Have you been spying?"

Serenity's face gave Carey a start. She hadn't really noticed before, but her eyes were so bagged that their pools of blue were barely visible slits between her eyelids.

"Is Daddy coming home?"

Serenity stabbed a spoon into her grapefruit. Spitler moved in behind, placed a hand lightly on her shoulder. "Soon," Serenity said.

"How soon?"

"Who cares?" Jonah said, jamming a rolled-up slice of toast with peanut butter into his mouth. "I don't care if the fucker never comes back."

"Language, Jonah."

"Fuck Dad."

Carey felt her eyes welling. She looked from Jonah to Spitler to her mother. "What's going on?"

Serenity rose from her chair and without saying a word walked to the kitchen elevator, hitting the button for four. Spitler collected her dishes. "Time for school," he said.

Her father did return. It was late October. He moved immediately into a guest bedroom in the turret opposite the master. Serenity now spent hours every day locked in her bedroom. Spitler began ascending there several times a day, delivering glasses of what appeared to be iced tea. Carey and Jonah spoke with their mother at meals, if at all.

The Schwinns rusted in the garage.

Carey and Jonah sit next to each other in two straight-back chairs facing a slightly raised platform. In the middle of the platform sits a chair of snow-white satin in a wingback frame of gold flake.

The room is circular, like the turret in which it sits, the creamy-pinkish walls rising two stories into a dome ringed with arched windows. Long ago the room was a chapel where Violet Bleak, Carey and Jonah's great-grandmother, had prayed each morning.

Jack Bleak had it converted a year after Jonah was born. The lone remnant of the chapel is the outline of a crucifix that once hung on a wall. Painters over the years tried repeatedly to obliterate the shadow, without success.

Their father had used the room to meet vendors, customers, legislators, lobbyists. Carey imagines them sitting where she and Jonah wait, supplicants with hands folded on briefcases in their laps.

She feels as hapless as they must have.

Jonah is twisting in his chair, looking around the room. "You think anybody still uses the tunnels?"

Beneath the mansion are three concrete-walled tunnels. One leads to the mansion's private marina, one to the downtown bay shore, one to a boathouse secreted on the lakeshore a mile south. They were designed as security measures but had functioned mostly as means for Jack Bleak to spirit women into and out of the mansion.

Carey doesn't reply. She's staring at her hands.

"You look a little pale," Jonah says.

She reaches for his hand, squeezes it. "Thank you for being a good uncle to Danny."

He offers a weak smile. "You know, I plan to destroy him in backgammon this weekend."

"What about this escrow thing?"

"We asked Serenity's lawyers to put some of her estate in escrow as proof in good faith that she wasn't just messing with us. We have yet to see evidence that this account actually exists. Her two hundred lawyers keep telling us about it, though."

"How much money does she have?"

"Who knows? I've read three hundred, four hundred million. Spitler probably knows."

"Hell, Jack knows."

"Oh yeah." Jonah nods toward the wall behind the throne-like chair. "How about that, huh?"

Hanging there is a framed *Light* page. The banner headline reads:

City Father Bleak Dead of Heart Attack

A photograph of Jack Bleak as a younger man occupies a two-column space on the left side of the page. He's smiling in that beguiling way that left you wondering later whether he was laughing with or at you. Carey can see Danny in her father's arching eyebrows and cheekbones. She can see her son, too, in the inscrutable smile. She has told Jonah before that the resemblance unsettles her.

"Dashing," she says. "That's what the paper always called him."

"Dashing from woman to woman in city after city."

"He was a successful businessman—don't forget that."

"How could I forget that?" Jonah snorts. A door on the wall behind the platform opens. "Oh, there she is."

Serenity appears in a wheelchair being pushed by Spitler. She doesn't look up from the paperback she's reading as Spitler rolls her across the platform and locks the wheelchair in place next to the gilt-framed wingback.

Serenity raises a forefinger, still reading. Spitler steps away. Serenity turns a page.

"Mother," Carey says.

Serenity's hair, gray-turning-white, is swept into a bun secured with a pink-on-silver ribbon. Her book is open on an afghan striped in pink and gray on her lap. A tall glass, about half full, is seated in her left armrest. She sets her bookmark and looks up.

"How is Daniel?"

"Danny has been kidnapped, Mother."

"That I am aware of, dear. But I thought the police were close to finding him." Serenity turns to Spitler. "Mr. Spitler, were those church bells I heard all afternoon, or was that my imagination? Do they have Mass during the festival?"

"I'm sorry, Miss Serenity. Perhaps they were testing—"

"Damn it, Serenity." Jonah is hitched forward in his chair, elbows to knees. "We need your help."

His mother lifts her glass, sips. "And what of this article on the computer? Who would dredge up such trash?"

Carey and Jonah exchange looks. "The kidnapper calls himself Jeremiah," she says. "Like the boy who drowned in that story."

"Jack's older brother," Jonah says.

"He didn't like to speak of it," Serenity says.

"I'll bet."

"Miss Serenity," Spitler says, "I called the publisher's office. They had the article removed."

Serenity is staring at her daughter. "Don't be so hasty to judge," she says. "Did you know that your father kept a picture of his brother in his wallet?"

"No."

"He was buried with it."

"Didn't know."

"Now you do." She turns to Spitler. "Whoever put that newspaper story there chooses to disgrace our family in front of all of these strangers traipsing around our town."

"Yes, ma'am."

"I'd quite prefer that the situation with Daniel not become a national scandal."

Serenity's chest is heaving now, the exertion of two long sentences apparently exhausting. She starts to set her glass in its holder, reconsiders, and takes another swallow before addressing Carey again. "You look fraught, young lady."

"Maybe I am."

"You were always a fraught child. I expect you'd be fraught if you won the lottery."

Jonah interrupts. "Christ, Mother. What about Danny?"

"Language, Jonah."

"Oh, fuck that."

"Please," Carey says.

Serenity looks at her, gives her head a barely discernible shake. "Danny," she says. "He never liked me much, did he?"

"Or you him."

"Didn't you have one of those tests before you had him? We didn't have those tests when you and your brother came out."

"What tests, Mother?"

"Genetic tests. So you can, you know, avoid an unnecessary situation."

"I know you won't understand this, Mother, but Danny is the most necessary thing in my life."

Serenity pauses, searching Carey's face. "Granted," she says, "I was an awful mother. Terrible. You're no June Cleaver either, dear."

"What is that supposed to mean?"

"Oh, now," Serenity says, reaching again for her glass, "don't go putting words in my mouth. Don't think I believe the rumors. Roland keeps me informed on what's going around town. Those people are fools; you and I both know it. With nothing better to do than run their neighbors down. You wouldn't harm Daniel, no matter how difficult he gets."

"No, I wouldn't."

Serenity continues as if Carey never spoke. "It's not your style, dear. Better to simply, you know, abandon him—am I right? Abandon whatever isn't convenient to your life. Like your premed major? Or law school? Or your little bleeding-heart adventure in Detroit?"

Jonah stands. "I've had enough of this bullshit."

"I've done my best, Mother."

"Please sit, Mr. Jonah."

"Is our time up yet, Roland? What about Danny?"

"Thank you, Mr. Jonah."

He sits.

A wan smile appears on Serenity's lips, fading as quickly as it came. "Of course, that is the perfect alibi: 'I did my best.' Well, I did my best, dear, with no help from your worthless father, and as you know, it wasn't very good. I am well aware that it wasn't very good. Are you?"

Carey feels as if a sheath of unbreakable glass has materialized around her, and she is trapped inside it with her mother. Ten seconds pass that could be an hour. Serenity waits, smug frown frozen on her face. Carey imagines herself slamming the glass with the heel of her hand, cracks spidering out, speckled with her blood.

She tries to calm herself before speaking. "Are you going to let your only grandson die?"

Serenity smooths the afghan over her knees. She begins to rock back and forth, tapping her fingertips on her thighs. Without lifting her head, she says, "I am a dying woman."

Jonah starts to say something. Serenity stops him. "No." She turns in her wheelchair, cranes her neck at the framed *Light* page, gazes at it, turns back to her children.

"I should have left him. I should have left him a hundred times. I made excuses for him. I should have taken every penny and walked away. Or not taken every penny, just . . ."

She doesn't finish.

The words tear at Carey, not because of Jack or the newspaper sale or even her mother, but because of her, Carey. She had made the same devil's bargain when she said yes to Pete. All she could think of then was how she would provide for her blessed, yearning, troubled young son. Pete had provided, she had provided, but she had failed to find Danny the things she wanted most for him, things he needed most: friends, a school, a place in the wider world beyond the deck, the dock, and the boat. *Who is it?* he had asked her, speaking of himself. *Who is it?*

"You should have left him long before that," Carey says, knowing she could be speaking to herself.

"I should have—that's true. But I was afraid."

"Afraid of what?" Jonah says.

"Afraid of being poor. Afraid of being alone."

Carey thinks she sees tears in Serenity's eyes. She hasn't seen her mother cry in a long time, maybe not since Serenity's father's funeral, and even then, not much. Crying wasn't her way of coping. Instead she sucked her sadness and humiliation and fury into herself and, eventually, into her daily drinking regimen. She was well into that by the time Danny was born. She had never gotten to know her grandson.

That was Carey's fault too. It's something she's known for years but has never wanted to acknowledge. She had decided long ago, before Danny was even old enough to speak, that if her mother and father wouldn't accept her son as he was, then they wouldn't have a grandson at all. Jack and Serenity didn't seem to care.

Part of Carey wishes she could continue this don't-make-the-same-mistake-I-made conversation, find some middle ground. But there's no time for wistful epiphanies. She turns to Jonah, says, "I need that picture of Danny I sent you." He hands her his phone.

She stands, steps onto the platform, and approaches Serenity. "Miss Carey," Spitler says, stepping up behind her.

Carey holds the phone up in front of Serenity's face. She avoids looking at it, averting her gaze to her daughter instead.

"What is this, dear?"

"It's your grandson. Look."

Serenity's eyes focus on the screen. "Those are just feet."

"Danny's feet."

"Why doesn't he get up?"

Carey doesn't answer. She just pushes the phone closer to Serenity's face. Her mother recoils, leaning back into her chair as far as she can. "All right, take it away," she says. "That's enough."

Carey withdraws the phone and reaches across her mother's lap for her glass. She raises it to her lips and swallows the contents. It's mostly vodka, some sort of juice, maybe lemon. Her teeth crunch shrunken ice cubes. Then she raises the cup over her head and hurls it at the framed newspaper page on the wall. It clatters to the floor, a thin drip of backwash trickling down the wall.

"I'm not a dying woman, Mother," she says. "I need your help."

Serenity's lower lip is trembling.

"We're leaving now. Jonah."

Spitler walks them to the door. "Mr. Spitler," Serenity calls out, and they all stop and turn, seeing she has pushed her wheelchair to the edge of the platform. "Give them what they need."

"Of course, Miss Serenity."

———

Carey looks at her phone as the three of them descend the marble stairs. It's 5:58. Less than six hours till the ransom is due. She has two missed calls from Malone. Not a word from Quartz. In the front vestibule at the bottom of the stairs, she turns to Spitler. "What do you need from us? A bank account number?"

He tugs at his bow tie, looks at each of them. "I'm afraid it's not quite that simple, Miss Carey."

"Meaning?" Jonah says.

"Miss Serenity is not altogether aware—not aware at all—of how her finances work, especially as regards her new obligations."

"You heard her, Roland."

"Yes, but I cannot wave a magic wand and secure the funds that quickly. I need more time."

"Don't tell me it's because of those imaginary escrows."

Spitler gives them each a look as if to say, *Yes, it is.* Carey steps in close to him, lowers her voice.

"Don't you give a damn about my son, Roland? Are you just going to let him die?"

"I care very much about Danny."

"You heard my mother."

He bows his head. "I must attend to Miss Serenity. I will keep you apprised."

39

Dulcy Pérez crouches in a copse of birches twenty yards up the slope from Boz's Bayfront Bar and Grill.

Every few seconds, she looks at her phone, shielding its glow with a cupped hand. With each passing car, she squeezes herself into a ball against the ground.

Michele Higgins watches her from behind an oak across the bayside road. Pérez appears to be waiting for something, some cue to proceed with whatever she's about to do. The clinking of glass, the cackle of laughter roll up the hill from Boz's. Michele hears mostly the hammering in her chest.

Her instincts had been correct. Her pal Lengel's instructions on where to locate Pérez were on target. Michele had found her at a two-story, beige-brick apartment building in Watervliet.

The license plate on the sole vehicle parked behind the building, a black Ford Escape, was from Ohio. A rental, Michele thought. Probably charged to a credit card linked to one of Vend's shell companies.

Michele had parked down the street and walked back to the building. She was almost there when the Escape pulled out in front of her and swung into the street. She'd waited until the Escape was a few blocks away, then trotted back to her own car and followed. Soon the two vehicles were approaching Bleak Harbor from the north, skirting the bay.

Pérez's brake lights had flashed as she approached the Peters cottage. Michele had hit her own brakes, keeping her distance. She noticed the mailbox in front of the vacant house next to Danny's: **HELLIKER**.

A few more houses down, Pérez, without signaling, swerved up a sandy two-track and into the woods across the road from Boz's.

Michele drove past while keeping an eye on the side-view mirror, hoping Pérez hadn't noticed her following. When she saw the lights blink out on the Escape, Michele hit the gas, sped around a curve, then spun a U-turn and parked on the shoulder beyond the bend, where Pérez couldn't see her.

She grabbed her phone and a notebook and scrambled up into the woods for a place to hide. As she scuttled sideways along the hill, she saw Pérez run across the road toward Boz's and take up her crouch in the birches.

Where she still is.

She pictures Pérez nuzzling Danny Peters's milk-white neck, trying to imagine why Pérez would want sex with a teenager, let alone this teenager, and whether it was merely coincidental to the events of the past twenty-four hours.

Probably not, she decides.

———

Michele encountered Danny once in person. It was a few months back, before the night he ran away, before Carey Peters railed at Michele for writing about that night.

She had been perusing the zucchinis and squash at Sawyer's Farm Market when the boy appeared at her side. His narrow face was animated by bright-green eyes and framed by auburn curls that touched his shoulders. For a second she thought he might be a beautiful girl. She felt him next to her, giving her a once-over. She turned to him. His eyes locked on to hers.

"Why are you here?" he said.

It startled Michele. She had no idea who the boy was. "Looking for dinner," she said. "How about you?"

The boy's eyes wandered across the produce tables and past Michele, then back to the zucchinis and finally to her again. "You put those police officers in jail," he said.

"Excuse me?"

"At the *Detroit Free Press*. You were an exceptional journalist."

She chuckled.

"You were," he insisted, as if she shouldn't be surprised at all that he knew about her past.

"'Were'? Thank you, I guess. Who are you?"

"Always an excellent question," he said. She thought he was going to offer a handshake. Instead he stuffed his right hand into a pocket of his cargo shorts. He had something in his other hand. An orange.

"Danny," he said. "I live here."

"I see. You apparently know who I am."

"Yes." He opened the hand holding the orange and regarded it, as if he were surprised to find it there. "Do you know Wallace Stevens?"

"I don't think so. Does he live here too?"

"I thought you were a writer."

Who is this kid? Michele thought. Then it came to her. "Oh, that Wallace Stevens." The boy was staring away from her across the store again. "I read him in college."

"Poems."

"Yes, poems."

"Did you have a favorite?"

"Hmm. I can't say I really remember."

"Of course not. People only read him in college. Then they stop."

"Sorry about that."

"Not your fault. So why are you here?"

"I told you. Getting dinner."

"No," Danny said as Michele heard a man's voice calling the boy's name from the next aisle. "You don't really know."

He set the orange in the zucchini bin and walked away. On a whim, Michele took out her phone and googled *Wallace Stevens* and *orange*. It took her to a poem, "Sunday Morning," with a line about a late breakfast of oranges and coffee.

Michele looked up. Danny was gone. She thought, for no particular reason, that it would be easy to underestimate that kid. She didn't see him again until she began spying on him from afar through the window at the *Light*.

———

Now Pérez rises from her crouch in the birches. She's short, probably shorter than Danny, certainly thicker. She takes a step outside of her shadow cage, hesitates, then steps back inside, squats again. Michele imagines she can hear Pérez's heavy breathing. She must be afraid. She's doing something she isn't really ready to do.

On the deck that fronts the beach at Boz's bar, a white-haired guy with a belly sagging over his apron—Michele figures it must be Boz himself—limps around collecting pint glasses and bottles, lowering umbrellas at the tables. He goes inside the bar. The deck is empty.

Why are you here? Danny asked Michele that day at the market. As if Michele never asked herself the same question, as if she had no idea. She knows she ran from Detroit in shame and anger after the security guard walked her out of the *Free Press* building with her packing box of photographs and old press passes. She knows she found a hiding place in Bleak Harbor. She knows she doesn't belong. She knows this when she lies alone on her futon at night with the sheet and blanket scattered to the floor, hoping the sweat beading along her arms and legs is from the summer heat and not the stirrings of menopause.

I am here, at this moment, to find you, Danny Peters, she thinks, almost saying it out loud. *You are my last assignment. Then I'm getting the hell out of Bleak Harbor forever.*

A few more minutes pass. Michele is considering whether to edge nearer when Pérez scurries down to the rear wall of Boz's, where she dips her head and moves beneath the windows along the side of the building. Michele slips down her hill and crosses the empty road.

Pérez is on all fours now, creeping along the sand next to the outer deck. She stops at the far end of the deck, looks down the beach both ways, then crawls to the covered boat at the dock. Michele sidesteps down the bank into the trees where Pérez hid before. She stops and watches as Pérez unwinds the rope tethering the bow of the boat to the dock, then slides into the water along the starboard side, her wrist flicking upward as she undoes snaps on the tarpaulin.

No way, Michele thinks.

At the stern, Pérez undoes another rope, unsnaps another snap, and hoists herself onto the gunwale, the soaked lower half of her body disappearing beneath the tarp.

The bow of the boat swings away from the dock. Michele listens for the outboard to start as she crab walks through the sand closer to the shoreline. From there she can just barely see the water churning at the stern. The boat is now a good hundred yards from shore.

Pérez is stealing the goddamn boat.

What the hell for? Why would Vend have her steal a boat? Too public, too obvious, too easily traced.

The boat putters away, trailing almost no wake, Pérez staying low as she steers it into the channel to the big lake.

She's either working for Vend or against him; Michele can't tell which. It reminds her of what she thought that day in the market, that it would be easy to underestimate Danny Peters. And then she thinks, with a certainty that surprises her: *Pérez knows. She knows where Danny is.*

Michele spins around and crawls past the deck and back up the hill. She stops in the birch stand where Pérez had hidden and takes out her phone. She dials the Bleak Harbor Police, then kills the call and stands watching the boat recede, considering, deciding, then dials the cops again.

40

"So that Dulcy bitch was in our home?"

Carey and Pete sit elbows to knees on the balcony outside Jonah's fourth-floor condo, the festival cacophony floating around them. Indoors is a swelter. A blown fuse has killed the air-conditioning throughout the building.

Jonah made them sandwiches they barely touched; then they slept, fitfully, for an hour or so. Carey and Pete haven't spoken since she finished a short call with Malone twenty minutes ago. Pete asked about the call, and Carey had chosen not to say anything. Until now.

Pete looks up. "Is that what Malone told you?"

"Was Dulcy in our house or not?"

"She just looked in on Danny once in a—"

"She works for a drug dealer, Pete. A real fucking bad drug dealer."

"I didn't—"

"Stop."

"—know."

"Just stop lying."

"I swear, Carey, I did not know. Do you really think I would've done business with that guy if I had known?"

"Did you send Dulcy to pick up Danny's prescriptions?"

"What are you talking about?"

"Malone told me a Hispanic woman picked up Danny's prescriptions two days ago. Twenty-four hours before he was taken."

"How do you know it was Dulcy?"

"I just told you the police think it was."

"No, you didn't; you said—"

"Stop with the bullshit, Pete. You lied about Bledsoe, you lied—"

"I never saw him. I didn't know. I fucked up, all right? I'm sorry. I'm—Jesus—I wouldn't have done it if I knew."

"No, you chose not to know."

Pete looks away. She can tell he's about to say something he only partly believes. Then he says it: "Maybe I was feeling a little too much pressure to make the thing work."

Carey wants to grab him by the collar of his baggy T-shirt and fling him over the balcony railing. "You're not putting this on me. You made the decision to up and leave Chicago and pursue this stupidity. And now you've put Danny's life in danger."

"Calm down."

"Fuck you."

"Carey. Why would Dulcy get Danny's prescriptions? Huh? Malone's just guessing. All they've got is guesses. This whole Bledsoe thing could be just a sideshow to what's really going on. A coincidence."

"Sure it is," Carey says, but in her head she hears Locke again: *Have you considered the possibility that your employer may be involved in this matter?*

The thought's been trying to wriggle its way out of the back of her mind ever since. Maybe the men who killed Bledsoe don't work for the dealer in Detroit but for Randall Pressman. She recalls the catalytic converter thieves who were unlucky enough to encounter Pressman's men.

It had been Quartz who found them. *My hunting dog,* Pressman had called him. What if Quartz really was the criminal Locke said he was? Quartz, the scrawny dweeb with all the pockets, had compromised national security? Seriously?

She gets to her feet, goes to the balcony railing. Quartz still hasn't responded to her texts. His 6:00 p.m. deadline came and went more than two hours ago. She hasn't had any calls or emails from Spitler either.

What is she supposed to do?

She thinks of Quartz again and digs in her back pocket for the card Locke gave her. She warned Quartz before. He must not have taken her seriously. His mistake. Carey takes Locke's card, copies his cell number into her phone, writes him a text:

C peters here . . . quartz last seen mexican restaurant across from Valpo courthouse

Then she texts Quartz:

locke here, deadline up. goodbye

She lowers her phone and peers through the dark skeleton of the festival Ferris wheel half a block away, lifts her view to the bars along the beach, the misty glow of the phony streetlamps, then beyond to the bay and the haphazard silhouettes of the masts, the stray blinking cruisers and speedboats anchored there, their sloshed occupants making the last feeble noises of the festival's first day.

"Carey?" Pete says behind her.

She locates their house on the far shore. The yellow do-not-cross tape scissors the deck and front windows into jagged shards.

She pictures herself and Danny and Pete sitting on the deck on this very night, watching the festival fireworks. Danny liked the fireworks best when the explosions were spaced far apart. He would leave the deck and walk out to the end of the dock and try to count each of the starburst strands falling into the water. The fury of the finale brought cheers from the festivalgoers but frustrated Carey's beautiful son.

The question is out of her mouth before she knows she's asking: "Why the perch?"

"What?" Pete says.

"Why does Danny love the perch so much?"

"He's never really said. I always figured it's because they seem so gentle and, I don't know, helpless?"

"He loves the dragonflies too, and they don't seem helpless."

The glass door on the balcony slides open. Carey's and Pete's heads both snap around to Jonah. "Sorry, nothing new," he says. "But I was thinking maybe we should head back to the police station."

"A few more minutes," Carey says.

"Any instructions from the kidnapper yet?"

She shakes her head no. Jonah goes back inside. Pete leans on his knees again, drops his head into his hands. He is the handsomest man who ever loved Carey. She turns back to the town, wipes sweat from the skin along her collarbone, squints into the Ferris wheel.

———

On the Ferris wheel that night in Chicago, the air tasted of fried shrimp and mustard.

As Carey clambered into the red cab, number 11, with Pete, she was trying not to think of the expensive pills Danny had flushed down the toilet and how she would try, probably in vain, to talk the pharmacist into replacing them for nothing.

Pete was giddy and a little drunk after his best day ever on the trading floor. He had made almost half a million dollars for O'Nally Bros., an amount her parents would sneer at but that she could see, hard as she tried not to, as a kind of salvation for her and Danny. OK, so Pete didn't get the whole half a million. But even a fraction of it would go a long way toward paying for her son's needs.

She felt Pete's tongue wet on her neck, the tip just beneath her ear, his long slender fingers gliding along the inside of her thigh. She opened her eyes, saw the skyline swoop down beneath them as they rose, told him *no*, not meaning it, as he took her hand and pressed it against his firm crotch, gasped as his three fingers slid into her, Pete whispering into her ear, "You're so beautiful," Carey letting go of her son for a delicious second, then another, then one more.

Pete started to laugh. Carey wanted to laugh with him, but she was struggling to catch her breath.

"Everything is so beautiful," he said. "Look at it. It's ours."

She had him unzipped before they began the descent, and she was coming as they slid past the apex of the circle, her heart pounding, coming again, opening her eyes, seeing the lake stretching into the distance, a shimmer of green and then blue disappearing into the sky. Somewhere out there was Bleak Harbor, as safely distant and invisible as China.

She truly and sincerely liked Pete Peters. She liked his nickname, obvious as it was. She liked how he got out of bed before her alarm went off and took Danny down the street for coffee and turnovers. She liked the way he jabbered about his day on the trading floor over a glass of wine until Danny appeared at the dinner table, and he just shut it off, never brought it up again, as if it didn't matter as much as being there with her and Danny. She liked how he teased Jonah about Danny kicking his butt in backgammon. She liked how he taught Danny to fish at Diversey Harbor. She liked how he told her everything would be all right after Danny threw one of his fits.

Carey wanted to love Pete Peters. Truly and sincerely, she did. And she thought maybe she would, with enough time.

She was glad to be with him on the Ferris wheel. She had known then that it would never get better than that afternoon. She had known she should have ended it then, or that night, or the next morning. She had known it as they stepped off the ride and saw the waiting security guards, had known it as she took the taxi to collect Danny from Kimi's place, had known when Pete showed up at her apartment giggling after three hours at the precinct.

She had known it the next morning when she was trying to decide whether to return his emails. She had known it when he asked her three days later to marry him. Did it matter whether Carey loved him? She loved Danny, he loved Danny, and he could take care of Danny, and her.

Until he couldn't.

———

Everything is rushing back at Carey now as she stares through the black bones of the Ferris wheel, sluicing through her heart, rattling up her spine, tumbling into her head: everything she and Pete did and failed to do, every choice they made or didn't, every foolish, selfish, shortsighted decision that has trapped them on her brother's balcony above Bleak Harbor on this muggy, endless night.

She had told herself over and over she was doing it all for Danny. Only for him. She conjures a vision of his face, so calm and certain as he told her that the palm in his favorite poem "is forever out of reach."

Forever.

How ridiculous she was, she reminds herself now, to think that the palm was a hand she could grasp instead of a tree with a bird perched in its wind-rustled fronds, a bird that could fly away at any instant.

She turns and looks at Pete. He's too tall for the folding chair he's in, looks like he might tip it over. His head is in his hands. He might be dozing. The sandals she kicked off earlier are askew beneath his chair. For a second, she considers telling him she slept with her boss. Telling him it was just the once, and the once was horrible. Imagines Pete looking up, face pleading. At this point, he might even apologize. She thinks to reach out and touch him but can't bring herself to do it.

Then he actually says it. "I'm sorry."

Carey almost laughs. "Sorry for what?"

"I'm sorry I brought you back here."

"What difference does that make now?"

"Can I ask you something?"

Carey waits.

"Who do you think would be better off without the other?" Pete says. "On their own again?"

"What do you mean?"

"You know what I mean. You or me? Who?"

"Who cares?"

Pete's chuckle is sour. "Right. So now what?"

"Now what *what*?"

"Now what with our son?"

Our son, Carey thinks, knowing Pete loves Danny almost as much as she does. "What choice do we have? We pay this guy; we get Danny back."

"And then?"

"I don't know."

"Well. I'm thinking I love Danny, and I don't want to be without him. I'm thinking you and I gotta rethink things. Everything."

"Like how?"

"Maybe we can, you know, go back. Rewind."

"Go back to Chicago?"

"Yeah."

She looks at the balcony's concrete floor, unable to say this directly to Pete: "I guess we have to try."

"We'll just pay this jag-off. All that matters is we get Danny back."

"OK."

"You hear anything from Spitler?"

She shakes her head. "Not yet. Thank God for Oly."

"But we still need another two million? Before midnight?"

"Maybe Mother really will help."

"That reminds me," Pete says, pulling out the burner Carey had bought him. "I think Oly might have called me right before they put me in the cell."

The door bangs open. "Chief called," Jonah says. "They got Pérez. She stole a boat."

"A boat?"

"Trying to get away?"

"The Coast Guard grabbed her."

"Omigod, does she have Danny?"

"Don't know. We should get over there. Pete? You hearing this?"

Pete is leaning out over the balcony railing with a finger in one ear and his phone on the other, shaking his head.

"This makes no fucking sense," he says.

"Chief sounded pretty excited, Carey," Jonah said.

"Let's go. Come on, Pete. You can call him later."

"No, wait—listen to this. I couldn't get into my cell phone voice mail, but old-school Oly left a message at my office too."

He puts the phone on speaker and holds it up for them to hear: "Andrew," Oly's disembodied voice says. "I guess this is your answering machine. Son, what are you doing wiring me the money back? I wanted you to—unless—did something happen? Did you find your Daniel? I haven't heard anything on the news. If you can, call my secretary, Wanda—you know her. She'll find me. God bless."

"Wire the money back? What's he talking about?"

"Gimme a second."

"Do it on the way to the station."

"It's the ransom, Carey. Hold on a damn second."

He's punching keys, starting over, punching more. "This browser sucks," he says. He stops and waits, then stares into the phone, eyes widening as he brings it closer to his face. "No. Carey, what's our password again?"

"I thought you changed it."

"No. What is it?"

"*MommylovesDANNY*. Lowercase *mommyloves*, all-uppercase *Danny*."

Pete types, his face aglow in the phone light. "Not working. I'm gonna try 'Forgot Password.'"

"Did you type it in right? Here, give it to me."

Pete twists away. "I can't type if you're making me move. Security question. 'What's your favorite pet?' Paddle?"

"Yes."

"Our money's in here, Jeremiah's blood money." Pete types and waits, the changing light flickering on his skin. "OK, I changed the password to *carey11PETE11* for now. *Pete* all caps."

They wait.

"This can't be right."

"What?"

"Goddamn banks."

"Pete, come on," Jonah says.

"Fuck. The money. It's gone. It's fucking gone."

"What money?"

"Oly's money. Five-point-one million fucking dollars. It's not there."

"What do you mean it's—"

"It's gone. It was there before, I told you. What is happening?"

"Are you in the right account?"

"Yes I'm—fuck. I checked it earlier. It was all there."

"How much?"

Carey grabs the phone from Pete.

"Five million plus."

"It says two thousand three hundred fifty and eighty-one cents. Is that what was in here before Oly transferred his money?"

"No. We had like five grand."

"So what happened?"

Carey feels her phone vibrate. Another text.

"Maybe Oly changed his mind? I don't know."

"He said *you* sent him back the money, Pete." She looks at her phone. "Why would Oly leave two thousand three hundred whatever bucks behind?"

A text appears on Carey's phone. From Quartz. She opens it:

D found. meet rt 23 and s bay no cops no locke

She almost drops the phone. She looks up at Jonah. "Malone," she lies. "Let's get out of here."

Carey thinks fast as she follows Pete and Jonah out of the condo and into the elevator. She's wishing she could take back that text she sent Locke.

The elevator opens into a ground floor garage, where Jonah's Camry is parked. Pete's getting into the seat behind Jonah when Carey pulls up short. "My car's on the street," she says. "I don't want it getting towed because of the festival. We might need it."

"It's not going to get towed."

"I'll go with you," Pete says from inside the car. But Carey's already trotting, then running away, waving him off.

"No, go. I'm right behind you."

She doesn't know why, but as she gets into her car she has a fleeting feeling that she's never going to see Pete again. It makes her sad; then it's gone.

41

The text from Carey Bleak Peters shoots a needle of fright through Quartz:

> locke here, deadline up. goodbye

Locke hasn't been this close to Quartz since DC. And then, actually, it was Quartz who got close to Locke. The agent was speaking on a panel at an internet security conference at the National Press Club. Quartz sat near the back of the meeting room in a tattered winter coat he'd bought for $8.50 at an army surplus store. He wore a fake beard and tinted glasses beneath a Baltimore Orioles cap. When the session ended, Quartz crept behind Locke and his fellow panelists as they posed for a group photo. The next day, Quartz posted the picture of him photobombing Locke on Locke's LinkedIn page. He sent a link to the page to a *Washington Post* reporter. Then he fled DC for good.

That was four years ago. Now Quartz wishes he hadn't met Carey at the restaurant beneath his apartment. At least, he reassures himself, he hadn't let on that he was staying upstairs. Still, he'd been lazy. And cocky. To be fair, he was unaware then that Bledsoe had screwed up. And out of selfish curiosity, he'd wanted an up-close look at the woman Pressman had fucked and seemed bent on fucking over.

Quartz knows he should probably disappear now. The $2 million Pressman sent for the kid's ransom is parked in an account Quartz created for a shell company at a bank in Nevada. From there it will zigzag among other phantom accounts he has at other banks in other cities before it winds up safely overseas. Those transfers will never be traced—not to Pressman, certainly not to Quartz.

He could find work again. There are plenty of self-obsessed rich bastards who need a wraith like Quartz, the kind who can find almost anything almost anywhere and has no qualms about calling in men paid to punish the fools who dare to steal a self-obsessed rich bastard's things. Like those dunces who hijacked that Pressman semitrailer supposedly filled with catalytic converters—actually, Chinese carfentanil—and tried to make Canada via North Dakota.

Or Quartz could simply use the ransom cash to go totally dark, hide in some faraway place. He could hope that Locke—an FBI veteran of twenty-three years, not the hapless job-hopping bureaucrat Quartz had invented for Carey's sake—would give up after a few more years. Quartz would have to change his identity again, maybe have some more surgery. He could do it if he had to. Eventually he would be free to live his life as he saw fit.

He hopes.

He knows all of this, knows that Locke might at this very moment be on his way to Valparaiso. But Quartz stays at his table above the restaurant, bent over his devices, rattling his keyboards, chewing his nails. The blood has come. A strip of black electrical tape is twisted around the tip of Quartz's left forefinger. His ring finger is next. He pictures Locke pushing his speed on I-94, imagines the agent creeping down the hallway outside his apartment door.

But he stays. He hasn't left his kitchen table except to piss since leaving Carey at the restaurant downstairs. Because he's onto something he's having trouble believing.

———

He had spent a fruitless hour scouring the innards of Danny's hard drive. There were glittery close-up photos of dragonflies alight on dock pilings, slow-motion videos of dragonflies devouring mosquitoes. Word files filled with musings on a Wallace Stevens poem whose meaning escaped Quartz, PDFs from environmental websites about the spawning tendencies of yellow perch. And a drawing, presumably in the boy's hand, of a dachshund that appeared to be sleeping, or dead.

There were also photographs of Danny's mother. Quartz skimmed them quickly, then went back after noticing that they all seemed to have been taken without her being aware.

She was standing at the end of a dock, backlit by sunset, head bowed, arms enfolding her shoulders. She was on one knee in sand, smiling as she scratched the belly of the dachshund. She was leaning on a balcony railing in evening shadow, one hand holding a phone to an ear, the other covering her eyes. She was curled into a quilt in a chair on a balcony with a distant view of Chicago's silhouetted skyline.

Looking at the pictures, Quartz wondered if Carey knew that, whatever his mental state, her son loved her. Loved her a lot. It reminded Quartz of his last memory of his own mother, the fragrance of hairspray blanketing him as she bundled him into a minivan he'd never been in before. She'd taken him away to Valparaiso, where his grandparents had raised him. Locke undoubtedly knew that, undoubtedly had checked it out before, undoubtedly assumed that Quartz would never hide in such an obvious place.

Quartz thinks of his grandparents' twin gravestones at the Graceland Cemetery off State Road 2. He liked to go there once a week, around dawn, when their names, Patricia and Norbert, seemed to glow in the early sun. He realizes that he's probably been there for the last time.

Sitting at his kitchen table, he has plundered the emails and social media accounts of every individual and institution that he can imagine could be involved directly or indirectly in the taking of Danny Peters: Carey; stepfather Pete; the boy's now-dead father, Bledsoe; Mayor

Jonah; the *Light* reporter, Higgins; Officer Malone; Chief Radovich; an employee of Pete's named Dulcinea Pérez; the bartender Boz Flanagan. Some Detroit drug lord has surfaced here and there. The sleuthing hasn't been difficult because even police officers and coke dealers are ridiculously trusting of the online world.

Serenity Bleak apparently had no internet presence. Quartz succeeded in hacking the email of a man named Roland Spitler who spoke on her behalf on the rare occasion that she deigned to address the commoners of Bleak Harbor. Spitler's email account was barren, as if he deleted everything on a daily basis. It made Quartz wonder what he had to hide.

Wherever he went, Quartz kept stumbling over the digital footprints of another hacker. Each time Quartz squirmed through some back door in the computers that made these people's lives whole, he saw that the hacker already had been there. And not just minutes or hours before, but days before, even weeks. Whoever it was had been rooting around in servers like a raccoon in a garbage dump. And he—or maybe she?—wasn't just excavating but was manipulating, perpetrating. He'd been inside the computers at Pete Peters's sorry pot shop and invaded the porous servers of the *Light*, where he appeared to have posted the article of the 1945 drowning of the "eccentric" young Jeremiah Bleak.

This hacker had, in various guises, conversed with Carey and Pete and Bledsoe. He'd posted a gruesome video of Bledsoe's demise to Facebook, Tumblr, and Twitter. He'd prowled the servers at Bleak County on several occasions, accessing, for reasons unclear to Quartz, property tax records. For the hell of it, Quartz wormed his way into the servers at two local banks. He couldn't be sure, but it looked as if the hacker had penetrated one account at Bleak County Bank & Trust.

He or she had also been at play on Twitter under the handle @ drewthenobody, an account Quartz discovered was registered to one Morton Needelman. The name was strangely familiar. Quartz had flipped back to the 1945 story that popped up on the *Light* website.

And there was Morton Needelman, the Bleak County prosecutor who had declared the drowning of Jeremiah Bleak accidental. Quartz was still laughing when he noticed the date atop the *Light* page. "Holy shit," he said. The date was May 18, 1945. The boy, Jeremiah, had drowned seventeen days earlier. On May 1. The original ransom demand had been $5.145 million. As in 5/1/45.

———

Now an icon starts blinking yellow in the lower-right corner of Quartz's laptop screen. He shifts his mouse, clicks on the icon.

"Show me, T. rex," he says.

When he was Danny's age, Quartz obsessed over dinosaurs and an ancient world dominated not by women and men but by mindless meat-eating beasts who didn't waste a second of their short lives pretending they were anything but predators. He enrolled in Purdue University to become a paleontologist. Organic chemistry put an end to that. Video games nurtured his only intimate relationship, with computers.

In his ensuing fourteen years at the National Security Agency, Quartz thought of his work prowling in other people's digital lives as that of a paleontologist who could discern the size and shape of a forty-five-ton brachiosaur from a smattering of bones weighing no more than the chisels and awls used to dislodge them from prehistoric rock. It helped him rationalize the consequences of what he did for a living, which more and more he came to consider amoral.

When that hollow logic no longer helped him sleep, Quartz sought out a *POLITICO* reporter he mistakenly thought he could trust and gave her a thumb drive filled with classified files suggesting how his employer routinely spied on law-abiding American citizens. For her stories on the NSA's intrusions into private lives, she won a promotion and some prizes that Quartz assumed nobody but journalists cared about. By then, Quartz had changed his name and his looks and was discreetly hiring himself out to men like Pressman. "The bitch for the rich," Quartz told his mirror reflection each morning. At least most of the people he hurt in his new incarnation deserved it.

His phone pulses on the table. Quartz glances at it, sees it's Pressman again, ignores it again. A rectangle opens on his screen.

Quartz leans forward, squinting. "Aha," he says.

On a hunch, Quartz had ventured into the computers at the Bleak Harbor Police Department. Soon he had the make, model, and serial number of Danny's laptop. He'd spent fifteen minutes concocting a program he named "T. rex" that would search FedEx, UPS, and the postal service for that serial number. It took almost two hours to produce the date, time, place, and credit card attached to the purchase of the laptop Carey had given the cops—Danny's Lenovo ThinkPad X.

It had been ordered April 11 from a website called SalesAblaze. Two days later it appeared in a mailbox at a UPS store on Lily Street in Bleak Harbor. The price of $1,299.63 plus tax and shipping was charged to an American Express credit card held by the City of Bleak Harbor, specifically Jonah E. Bleak, mayor.

Quartz leans back into his computer, fingers hopping across the keyboard as he follows the hacker's trail into Jonah Bleak's city Amex account. "Come on, come on," Quartz says, urging speed on the computer. He bites the electrical tape off of his left forefinger. The mayor's most recent statement appears on his screen.

The card has been busy buying things for the past week: Two Champion portable power generators. A wireless router. Half a dozen disposable phones. A thirty-seven-inch-tall Vornado tower fan. A $499 pair of night-vision binoculars. A police scanner. Two goose-down pillows. A box of chocolate brownie Clif Bars. A case of Gatorade. And a small library of security software, the essential tools of a digital B-and-E artist: Spy Argus96, Metasploits, John the Ripper, Nmap, HellRazer666, CataLyst, MrKleen.

Impressive, Quartz thinks. Even he hasn't tried Spy Argus96.

He can't tell where the software wound up. But the generator, router, and other items were delivered to an apartment in Watervliet, not far from Bleak Harbor. Quartz finds a rental website that lists the building, calls the phone number, gets a recording in Spanish, then English. He hangs up and flips back to the Amex statement to see if he missed anything. On his third try, he sees that something new has appeared in the pending transactions column:

Nardella's Pizza. $12.31.

It makes Quartz laugh again. "Are you kidding me? A pizza? Dude, you are the man."

He googles the pizzeria on Haroldson Road, a mile north of Bleak Harbor, and punches the phone number into a disposable. A boy answers in a pubescent squawk.

"Nardella's. Can I help you?"

"Yeah, hey, sorry, didn't get my pizza."

"Pardon?"

"My pizza. It should be here by now."

"Oh. Uh, can you hold a second?"

The phone goes to a country song. Quartz considers what he'll say if the kid asks his name.

The kid comes back on. "When did you order, sir?"

"At least an hour ago."

"Name?"

"Jonah."

"Joe?"

"No. Jo-nah."

"Got it, Jo-nah. I don't have that here."

"No?"

"Nope."

Quartz has a notion that actually makes him a little giddy. "Oh, yeah, my brother ordered. Jeremiah."

"OK," the kid says.

Fucking A, Quartz thinks.

"We have it being delivered at 7:43. Cheese with ham and pine-apple. Left it on the front porch, as requested. Have you looked?"

"Yep. Nothing there."

"Yeah, we really don't like just leaving things, but . . . lemme just confirm, you're at 39874 South Bay Drive?"

Quartz pumps the address into the Google slot. A map pops up on his laptop.

"Sir?"

Quartz kills the call. He sits still for a second, staring at the map on the screen, light-headed at what he believes he has found. He fits a Bluetooth device into an ear and dials Pressman, who answers in the middle of the first ring.

"Why aren't you answering my calls?"

"Been busy working for you."

"Any luck on the kid?"

"Maybe."

"Time is running out."

No, Quartz thinks, *it really isn't.* But no sense letting Pressman know what he knows until he knows for sure.

"I'm getting calls from the Bleak Harbor Police," Pressman says.

"You haven't spoken with them, have you?"

"Hell, no. Why are they calling me?"

Quartz relishes the idea of Pressman having to answer other people's questions without getting paid in cash or sex or obsequiousness. "It's probably just routine," he says. "Although Agent Locke is in Bleak Harbor. Did I mention that?"

"Fuck me. Fuck. We're back at square fucking one. This was a stupid fucking plan, Quartz."

"Relax. As long as the kid comes back alive, you're fine. They're not going to bust you for screwing his mom. You get your two million back, and Locke has no case."

The phone goes silent. Quartz hears the squeak of Pressman's chair. He pictures him turning, as he often does when things aren't going his way, to look at the sole photograph on the wall, of a man holding a giant wrench. Pressman's father, Harold T. Pressman.

Quartz conjures a picture of a much younger Randall, home from Bloomington on spring break, going frantically from room to room in his father's bungalow in Hammond, finally, reluctantly, resignedly, going to the garage out back. The young man hearing the hum of the car engine as he lifts the garage door, coughing against the fumes.

Twenty years old and suddenly alone. Blaming not his feeble, embittered drunk of a father, Quartz now realizes, but the rich family in Michigan who had sold his father's plant and left Harold Pressman jobless, broke, and wallowing in Seagram's. Pressman had told Quartz about it late one night when he'd had a few too many Macallans himself.

When did that plant close? Quartz thinks. *What was the date?*

"Who's got the kid?" Pressman says.

"Hang on," Quartz says. "Gonna mute."

He's googling. He can't immediately bring to mind the Japanese company that bought Harold T. Pressman's steel mill. Matsuyama. Mayeda. Murakami. Something with an *M*. And then, there it is. Matsunaka. The company that bought the mill that Joseph Estes Bleak built in 1887 was sold by his great-grandson, Jonathan Estes "Jack" Bleak, on July 3, 1988.

Quartz unmutes his phone. "Back," he says.

"Where is the fucking kid?" Pressman says.

"His name is Danny."

"I don't give a flying fuck. Where is he?"

As Pressman continues to yell, Quartz works his mouse and keyboard, trying to find the hacker's jump box, the computer from which he's launching his attacks. It probably won't reveal much, but it's worth checking for clues to the hacker's identity.

"Maybe we wouldn't be in this position," Quartz says, "if you didn't have to bang every woman on your payroll."

"Excuse me?"

"I mean, really, why this Carey chick? I'll admit she's pretty hot. But she's married with a kid. Do you ever—"

"Do you think I can't find you, Quartz? Do you imagine that you're the only finder on my payroll?"

A site is loading on the laptop screen. "Listen, Randall. This afternoon, Carey was told the ransom is now seven-point-three-eight-eight million dollars."

"So I'm supposed to give her more money? Give me a fucking break."

"Doesn't that number strike you as odd? Seven-point-three-eight-eight million?"

"Get to the point, Quartz."

"It happens to correspond to the exact date that Bleak Holdings sold its steel mill to Matsunaka. The mill that employed your dad."

It takes a moment for this to register with Pressman. "Bullshit," he finally says. "Coincidence."

"That's the thing about this guy. He picks numbers that have some weird significance to him. There's a pattern. He's serious, Randall."

"I don't give a shit."

"But the authorities might give a shit. If things go sideways somehow, they might see something in that number. Like maybe motive."

Pressman goes quiet again. Quartz walks into his bedroom. The bed is made but rumpled because he rarely bothers to get under the covers.

"No," Pressman says. "I wouldn't do that."

"You wouldn't take revenge on the Bleaks?"

"No, I would not. Not for that."

"Please."

"It was just business. I wouldn't—this has nothing to do with that."

Quartz doesn't find that convincing. He slides the nightstand drawer open and removes the .22-caliber Luger. He holds the gun in both hands, pointing it away and down by the butt. Engraved into the grip are his grandfather's initials.

"Quartz, are you listening?"

"I'm sorry, Randall. What did you say?"

Quartz had taken the pistol from a locked cabinet in his grandfather's house two days after the old man died. Quartz hadn't any idea how to pick an actual lock. He finally used a hammer on the cabinet glass. He took the .22, a box of bullets, and a pair of handcuffs his grandfather had used as an MP in Korea. He signed up for shooting lessons. Turned out he wasn't bad at hitting targets. He started bringing his bull's-eyes home and pushpinning them to the kitchen wall.

"You heard me," Pressman is saying, his voice back to its usual tone of a man who knows he will get what he wants. "Jesus, Quartz. I don't even know your first name."

Quartz sits back down at his laptop. "You never cared."

"I care now."

The queue of files in the hacker's jump box—Jeremiah's jump box—is on the laptop screen.

"No point in telling you now, Randall. Best for both of us if we remain anonymous, don't you think?"

The names of Jeremiah's dozens of jump-box files are not words Quartz knows. They remind him of high school biology. He copies one at random—*pachydiplax*—then punches up Wikipedia and searches the word. *Pachydiplax longipennis* is the scientific name for the blue dasher, a dragonfly common to the United States.

"You think you're pretty damn smart, don't you, Quartz?"

He chooses another file name, *libellula*, and searches that. Another common dragonfly.

"Quartz, do you hear me?"

He gets out of the chair and goes to the window facing the street, peeks through the blinds. A Valparaiso police car is parked across the street, idling.

Time to go, Quartz thinks. *Back way.*

"I hear you, Randall."

"What are we gonna do here?"

"Well, you know what they say."

"What's that?"

"All's well that ends."

Quartz tosses the burner phone on the table. He looks at his watch. At this time of night, he can make Bleak Harbor in an hour, an hour fifteen. He briefly considers that he will miss those fish tacos downstairs. He picks the phone back up and types a text to Carey Bleak:

D found. meet rt 23 and s bay no cops no locke

Quartz takes his backpack into the bedroom and tosses in two pairs of underwear and socks, an extra pair of sneakers, some CVS sunglasses, his grandfather's handcuffs. He makes sure the Luger is at the top of the pile.

He returns to the kitchen and unplugs the laptop before stuffing it into the backpack, telling it, grinning, "You didn't count on me, did you, Jeremiah? Or, sorry—Danny."

42

Danny watches.

Across the bay, his mother and stepfather are silhouettes against the setting sun on the balcony of his uncle Jonah's condo.

They keep their distance.

Carey and Pete are autistics of a sort, albeit supposedly functioning ones. It's not pain that fills them at this particular moment but fear. They are afraid of the choices they have made and how those choices could now lead to the unbearable.

Danny lowers his night-vision binoculars and steps back from the gable vent in the attic of the Helliker place.

A sole pair of headlights gleams on South Bay Drive, approaching from downtown Bleak Harbor. Danny follows them from his dark hiding place. They bend one way and disappear behind trees, bend another and reemerge, winding past Boz's bar.

Danny has tried not to worry about the vehicles that have driven past since he left one of his green high-tops in a clump of grass near the bay road, crawled through the broken boards in the security fence, and climbed into his secret shelter the day before. The snapping turtle that surprised him in the weeds on the Helliker side of the fence met with the sharp, fatal end of a rock.

He watched with mild amusement as his long-gone father, Jeffrey Bledsoe, skulked around his parents' cottage, looking for him. He watched him move around the house, peeking into windows, looking over his shoulder, finally giving up and going to his car on the bay road shoulder and pulling away. *Milkshakes*, he thinks. He was supposedly going with his father for milkshakes.

He heard Carey and Pete searching downstairs that night until he triggered the alarms. He'd sent Pete a text from the phony 537 number—alarmed?—and later watched his stepfather lope down the beach toward his shop, where he would see on his pathetically unguarded computer the selfie Danny had taken of himself duct-taped into the chair, one green shoe missing, a smudge of charcoal on one cheek meant to look like a bruise.

Pete: *lukkytrayd72*. Profession, birthday, password. He didn't change it even after trayd upon trayd went unlucky.

Early the next morning, Danny pressed an ear to the floor as the fat guy who had come with the lady police officer walked around the ground floor, coughing and gagging, obviously allergic to the mildew in the walls and what furniture was left behind.

Later, Danny listened to the volunteer searchers giving the Helliker house a once-over. He heard a woman tell someone else she thought the kidnapping was a scam. "I don't trust these Bleaks," she sneered. "That Carey woman is probably trying to shake her mother down for money. They hate each other, you know." Her partner said, "You seen that movie *Fargo*?"

Danny allowed himself a grin at that.

He watched the cars and SUVs and pickups that slowed as they passed the house next door, his home since his parents had dragged him here from Chicago. What did the gawkers hope to see beyond the police tape?

They reminded him of a black-and-white photograph that had appeared on the front page of the *Bleak Harbor Light* in 1945. Men in Sunday suits and women in dresses were crowding the beaches to gape at the search-and-rescue boats out looking for Jeremiah.

They never did see Jeremiah.

And they would never see Danny.

Joseph Estes Bleak had come to Michigan from Boston in 1868. He had created a family and a town. He would have recognized neither today, either in structure or soul. He and Eudora Marie Randolph Bleak had had Blossom. Then had come Lily and, much later, Violet.

Typhoid had taken Blossom. A horse had flung Lily to her death. Violet had left the convent to care for her mother after her father died. It was 1902. Four years later, she had had a son, James Estes Bleak, out of wedlock.

James had married a woman named Polley. They had had two children, Jeremiah Estes, and five years later, Jonathan Estes, whom they called Jack. Both had been in the sloop with their father on Lake Michigan that day in 1945. It had been unseasonably warm and humid for May. The clouds had sunk lower and heavier as the afternoon had worn on.

Sitting alone at the microfilm machine at the Joseph E. Bleak Public Library, reading about what happened to Jeremiah, Danny always wondered if the clouds should have been a warning. James Estes Bleak was an expert sailor who competed each year in the Port Huron-to-Mackinac race, so he must have known the weather would be dangerous. Yet he still had gone out on the day Jeremiah would die.

Danny would try to visualize the storm clouds stacking up on the horizon. He'd imagine Jeremiah reaching out to sweep them away. As Danny himself would have. He'd imagine what happened on that dark afternoon, and it would become as true to Danny as if he'd read it, word for word, on the old *Light* page.

Jeremiah and Jack, fifteen and ten, wore life jackets. Jeremiah had refused to buckle his. He called it a straitjacket. He had glimpsed straitjackets in the hospital where his parents took him to see his special doctor. His father usually did not wear a life jacket on the sloop. Today, though, he did.

Danny would wonder if Jeremiah had noticed.

The storm boiled up from the north. A wave swamped the deck as the boat bottomed in a swell and keeled starboard. The mast snapped in two. The boat capsized. James Bleak and his sons bobbed orange in the water. They clung to the hull. Jeremiah's jacket dangled from an arm. "Jer," brother Jack called out. "Your jacket. Fix your jacket."

Jeremiah heard. He knew about his straitjacket. He saw his father's hand reaching across the hull. He looked up. The sky was a roil of smoke and feather, swaying to and fro. Jeremiah asked himself if that could be heaven. Or so Danny would imagine in the library, the vinegar tang of the microfilm in his nostrils.

Young Jeremiah's father and brother were yelling. Jeremiah reached for his father's hand. It was slick with the lake. Jeremiah turned toward Jack. "Hang on, Jer." Jack was draped over the bow end of the hull. Spray obliterated his face. He saw his brother trying to stretch an arm toward him. His father turned to Jack and screamed, "Hold on with both arms." But Jeremiah felt his hand slipping. Young Jack couldn't hold him. And his father merely watched.

"Your jacket," Jeremiah's father yelled. "What did I tell you?"

"My jacket," the boy gurgled. His father watched as Jeremiah slid off the boat slowly enough to look up one last time at the welcoming sky.

In Danny's mind, that's how it had been. Something terrible. No accident.

James Bleak "almost drowned as he heroically tried to save his son," the *Light* lied. Danny printed a copy of the page and sneaked the roll of microfilm out of the library. That was the day he told Zelda that she was a very beautiful woman. He had wanted her to know because he didn't think he'd ever see her again.

Danny unraveled the film from the microfilm roll and burned it on the beach as horseflies swooped through the coiling smoke. The Bleaks had abandoned their "eccentric" boy just as they would their timber mill and steel plant, just as they would abandon the town that was named after their family by isolating themselves on their wedge of land. Danny was sure that if Pete and Carey would abandon Paddle, then eventually they would abandon him. Like young Jeremiah, like the helpless perch, he was drowning too.

———

The headlights pass. Danny hangs back in the darkness. He reaches for the half-eaten slice of pizza in the box on the floor, the pieces of shattered chair resting nearby.

The pizza is cheese with ham and pineapple. Barely more than a day in the attic, and already Danny is sick of Clif Bars. The delivery boy left the pie on the Hellikers' front stoop. Danny counted to three hundred before snaking an arm through the front door to retrieve it. Risky, he knew.

It has all been risky since the day after Mother and Pete killed Paddle. They could have saved Danny's dog. It would have cost them $2,350.81. Danny saw the veterinarian's to-the-penny estimate in an email on Pete's laptop.

There is nothing we can do, son.

Pete's new casting rod (February, $439.77) + Carey's shoes (March, $228.14) + dinner at Carmine's (January, $321.00) + the security fence (April, $1,897.96) = Paddle gone.

Danny sees the dachshund wobbling along the shoreline in his final days. He knew the sand felt cool and soft on his sore pads.

Good boy, Paddle-daddle. Good boy.

That's when Danny put his plan into place. He would save his mother from Pressman, whose emails and texts he had read with disgust. He would save Pete from himself.

And Danny would save himself.

Now Pete and Carey have their $2,350.81. He left it in their account when he emptied it of all the other money that afternoon and returned Oly's to Oly.

Everyone must pay for their sins.

Gotta pay, in Bledsoe's imagined lingo.

Danny washes down the last of the cold pizza with a swallow of Gatorade. He has to crouch a little beneath the trusses to tip the bottle up over his head. Staying low, he moves to the folding table.

The table holds a small electric fan, his laptop, a box of kitchen matches, and three disposable phones. A police scanner rests atop the box of Clif Bars. Beneath the table, a generator powers the laptop, Danny's main source of light. Next to the generator stands a one-gallon can of gasoline he took from his parents' garage.

Danny leans his face toward the battery-powered fan. The tepid air blows across his cheeks and forehead. By now Dulcinea has dropped her own disposable into the lake. He heard the dispatches on the scanner. She is in custody.

Not optimal, Danny thinks. He quiets the apprehension pinging in his head by assuring himself that Dulcinea will tell the police nothing. One million of the dollars he would soon be snatching would guarantee her silence.

She had come to Danny on many afternoons. She said she liked him, then was falling in love with him. Danny knew she pitied him. He knew he would never find love. Pity would always come first. Even his parents pity him. They forget he's almost sixteen years old. They forget he's smart. Smarter than they are. Now they will know.

Dulcinea became integral to his plan. She used what she'd learned at coding school to help him infiltrate the digital lives of his family and the others who figured in his plan. He promised Dulcinea an escape from the people who enslaved her, in the form of $100,000. And she relieved him of his virginity, riding him as in his head he recited a verse from his favorite Stevens poem over and over to the accelerating rhythm, without feeling, without meaning.

The dragonfly is without feeling. Its exquisite senses of hearing and direction enable it to deduce precisely where its ignorant prey will be when the dragonfly is ready to strike and crush and mash and digest while veering immediately toward its next target.

Now, as Danny sits before his laptop, he lets the song his mother made up float through his head:

Pretty pretty dragonflies . . .

Danny has had the laptop since moving to Bleak Harbor a year ago. The police have in their possession another one that he bought a few weeks ago with his uncle Jonah's city credit card. Danny filled that computer with what the police and his parents expect to see, frivolous evidence of his various interests, what they and his doctors refer to as "obsessions," and he copied the same things to his external hard drive.

Danny sent the text Thursday night with the picture of the empty chair holding the roll of duct tape. He had photoshopped the images of the angry rottweilers, Daisey and Hoho—pictures and names he'd found in a Google search—and sent the phony audio of them drooling over his green sneaker.

He planted the glitch in the Strawman Pharmacy computers (password: *StrawFrm220lily*) that allowed Dulcinea to pick up an extra cache of his meds so he could leave his others behind. He rang the bells again and again at Saint Wenceslaus through the church's computer and shut down the generators that powered the festival rides. He made the tavern sound system blare that awful Eagles song Dulcy liked. He bounced that $5 million gift back to Oleson O'Nally. He taunted his mother's lecherous boss with the second ransom number that matched the date of the steel-plant sale. He even went to the trouble of telling the post office to send his uncle's credit card statements to Dulcinea's Watervliet address so Jonah wouldn't see them and notice any odd purchases.

Sometimes it was fun.

Danny had become Morton Needelman, owner of Twitter handle @ drewthenobody. He had posted on the *Light* site (password: *lightNOOZ*) the 1945 article about Jeremiah's death, with the headline that called his distant cousin "eccentric." The label pasted on Danny—autistic—hadn't yet become fashionable in the 1940s.

Danny sent the email to himself from Bledsoe's computer (password: *Jbl33dsoe*) that Carey saw Friday morning: *Y not, Danny boy?* He planted the spyware on Carey's phone that traced her to Valparaiso. He typed 5373642445 is a landline # into a text to his panicked mother.

He read the reckless emails between Bledsoe and Petunia Delacroix that funneled him into her Facebook account, where he posted the photo of her in a yellow bikini. He accessed the webcam on Bledsoe's laptop that recorded his father's demise.

The sudden appearance of the two men in Bledsoe's apartment had taken Danny aback. They had not been part of his plan. He'd had to remind himself that no scheme would play out perfectly, that there would be unexpected glitches. Even the dragonfly missed his quarry on rare occasions. This development, though unexpected, wasn't entirely unwelcome. Bledsoe had long ago chosen his perilous path. Danny's mother, and Pete, were finally free of him.

But now, on the laptop aglow in the attic gloom, there is something else he didn't expect.

Earlier Danny had noticed that someone or something from the outside appeared to be looking in. Someone or something that might actually know what to do, and how. There were digital fingerprints in Danny's jump box. Someone or something had looked at his files. Danny had hoped it was merely some anonymous hacker who had blindly stumbled in, maybe even a misdirected bot.

But his laptop makes a sound Danny has never heard before, a sharp retort like what he imagines a gunshot sounds like. An image materializes on the screen. Danny hits the "Esc" button to kill it, clicks his mouse, but it continues to take shape. It is a hand holding something he cannot yet make out.

He looks over his shoulder at the vent where he was standing a few minutes before. Diffuse light is bleeding in. Another vehicle on the bay road. Danny stays in his seat, watching the light brighten, then fade to dark. He imagines a clacking keyboard, chasing him. He closes his eyes, tries to slow his heartbeat. It can't be Pressman, not the police, not Locke. None is smart enough.

He looks back at the screen. A man's right hand displays a pistol in the palm. The hand is moon white, the pistol midnight black. The grip is engraved with letters of dull silver:

N A G

Danny whispers them to himself, reaches for his mouse. Before he can touch it, the screen goes dark. Danny's hand hovers over the mouse. The screen slowly turns the color of blood. A thin white line of words appears at the middle. Danny leans in a little, sees it:

hereSheis

Taunting Danny as Danny had Pete with *hereheis* on the computer in his office.

Danny lowers his hand and left-clicks. The words vanish. He knows what comes next. The red bleeds away. A shape begins to form at the bottom of the gray. Danny clicks again and bends his head to the screen. The image unfolds, two feet at the bottom of the screen, duct-taped to the legs of a chair. Danny watches the rest.

Mommy.

He picks up his phone. A noise, scratchy, barely audible, begins to emanate from the laptop. A song. Danny stands, leans an ear in.

Desperado, he hears.

He reaches under the table, drags out the can of gasoline. He taps a key on his phone.

"Bleak residence."

"Mr. Spitler," Danny says.

A pause, then, "I thought you weren't going to call."

"I'm going to need your help."

43

"I will handle this, Locke."

Hamilton steps pointedly in front of Locke, blocking the corridor two cell doors from where Dulcinea Pérez waits behind bars.

"I'll just be a fly on the wall, Agent," Locke says.

"Why are you here anyway?" She angles her head in a way that suggests she's not inclined to believe whatever he says. "Chicago didn't say anything about Indy working this."

"I don't work for Chicago."

"Excuse me," Malone says. She heard the exchange as she stepped into the hallway, her hand clutching Pete Peters's elbow. He had arrived a few minutes ago with Jonah Bleak but no Carey Peters. They said Carey was right behind them. But she isn't responding to calls or texts. Peters and Jonah swear they have no idea where she is.

Hamilton and Locke turn to Malone. "Hamilton and Chief are on the phone to Chicago now about Pressman. Let's go see Pérez," she says. "Mr. Peters has a few things to say to her."

"Pressman?" Pete says. "What about him?"

"Quiet, sir," Locke says. "You're in a lot of trouble."

"I told you I did not know that—"

"Just shut up."

"We really don't need a clusterfuck in there," Hamilton says. "Pérez will know we're grasping."

"I'll be a polite observer, agent," Locke says. "I'm not interested in headlines or book deals."

"Seriously? I heard you were a jag-off."

"This is my jail," Malone says, tugging Peters past them. "We have less than two hours. Both of you. Now."

———

Pérez slumps over her knees on the concrete bed, wrapped in a gray wool blanket. Her black hair still glistens with damp.

Hamilton takes a spot facing her. Locke backs up against a wall. Pete steps into the cell with Malone, who says, "I brought a friend."

Pérez looks up, sees Pete, swallows hard, looks back down.

"Dulcy," Pete says, his voice cracking. "We need your help with Danny."

The Coast Guard had picked her up in Lake Michigan off the beach at Van Buren State Park. She was close enough to shore, as if she had planned to tie up there, that she had tried to make a swim for it. Malone and Radovich had confronted her in the interview room. They told Pérez they'd seen communications between her and Danny, told her a witness had put her in Danny's bedroom, told her they could charge her with statutory rape.

She had stared at the table, hands folded in her lap, shaking her head no to each question, even about her name and address. She had no cell phone to inspect, probably lost it in the lake. Her soggy driver's license put her last address on Bagley Street in Detroit.

Now Malone nudges Pete closer to Pérez. "Dulcy," he says, "if you know where Danny is—"

"She knows," Hamilton says.

"—you need to tell us. He may be in danger."

Pérez says something, barely a whisper.

"What was that?" Malone says.

Pérez says it again, a little louder: "El niño va a estar bien."

Hamilton and Malone both look at Peters.

"She's always doing that with the Spanish," he says, then turns back to Pérez. "Dulcy. Goddamn it, I thought you liked Danny. Do you want him to get hurt?"

Hamilton squats down at Pérez's level.

"Dulcinea," she says. "You don't want to be an accessory to kidnapping. It's a federal felony. You could spend a lot of years in prison, with no parole or breaks for good behavior. Your boss's friends will have all those years to reward your disloyalty."

Pérez is shaking her head no again. "El niño va a estar bien."

Hamilton rises from her crouch. "You give me no choice, Dulcy. I'm going to take you out of here and into federal custody."

No, you're not, Malone thinks, but holds her tongue, looks over at Locke. He steps over, sits on the slab next to Pérez, and asks, "¿Alguna vez has oído hablar de un hombre llamado Quartz?"

"No. Es un nombre muy extraño."

"Agent Locke," Hamilton says. "We are trying to find a boy. Tell us what she's saying."

Locke ignores her and asks Pérez, "Nunca se ha oído hablar de Quartz?"

She shakes her head harder.

Locke looks up at Pete. "What about you? The name Quartz ring any bells?"

"Mr. Peters?"

Pete rubs his goose neck. "No," he says, then lowers himself to a knee in front of Pérez. "Dulcy, you don't want to end up in prison, do you? Isn't that why you came here in the first place, to get away from all that? Isn't that what you told me when you asked for a job?"

"Oh, she's not going to prison," Malone says. "Think about that for a second, Dulcinea. Excuse me."

Malone hurries down the corridor to where she's out of earshot. She returns the call she got earlier from Michele Higgins.

"Higgins."

"It's Malone."

"Did you find her?"

"Yes. Thanks for the tip. I know you didn't have to do that."

"What about Danny Peters?"

"So far, Pérez isn't talking. I need the name of Vend's lawyer."

"He has a lot of lawyers."

"How about one Pérez might recognize?"

"Hang on. I'll text it."

Malone waits.

"Done."

"Thank you."

"You gonna find the Peters boy?"

"I hope so."

———

As the cell door clicks shut behind her, Malone sees Locke and Hamilton having a whispered conversation against the back wall. They stop and separate, neither looking pleased.

Peters is sitting next to Pérez. His eyes are red. A snapshot rests on Pérez's knee. Malone sees it's a picture of a boy sitting on a balcony, a city skyline in the background. Maybe, finally, Peters has done something right.

"Dulcy," Malone says. "We're out of time."

Pérez looks up. She's been crying too. Malone says, "We have videotape of you picking up Danny's prescription on Tuesday."

"No," Pérez says. "You don't."

"Ah, now you speak English. Great. So you'll understand this. I was just returning a call from an attorney in Detroit." She waggles her phone in Pérez's face. "Henry Stokes. You know Mr. Stokes? He represents your old boss, Jarek Vend."

"Officer Malone, can we have a word?" It's Hamilton, with an incredulous look on her face. Behind her, Locke wears a faint, knowing smile.

"Not right now," Malone says, then addresses Pérez again. "Mr. Vend is concerned about you, Dulcinea. He doesn't want you in jail. Mr. Stokes called from Battle Creek, so he should be here soon."

"No."

"Yes. We will release you into his custody, and he can take it from there. I'm sure he and Mr. Vend will take very good care of you."

Pérez picks up the snapshot. She looks at Pete. He puts a hand on her shoulder.

"No más," she says.

"No más," Pete repeats.

"Danny is a good boy."

"What does that mean?" Malone says.

Pérez holds herself as she rocks back and forth. "He's in the house," she says.

Malone leans closer to her. "What house?"

Pérez nods at Pete. "Next door. Boarded up."

Pete sits up straight. "No way. We checked it."

"What is she talking about?" Hamilton says.

"Go ahead, Dulcy," Malone says.

It takes her a couple of minutes. As she speaks, Pete keeps saying, "Oh my God," again and again, louder and louder, while Malone thinks of the morning before, she and Will and Peters standing on the dewy lawn next to the supposedly abandoned house where Danny, poor Danny, poor autistic Danny, was probably watching them, maybe laughing to himself, the little bastard.

Malone turns and bolts the cell, rushing down the corridor. *The kid's going to pay*, she's thinking. *His mother, too, if she's in on it. Where the hell is she, anyway?*

She stops at the door to the main room, closes her eyes, steadying herself, her head spinning dizzily again as it did that afternoon she saw blessed, lovely, fragile Louisa's tiny body crushed between the pickup truck and the tree. Her cheating husband, who'd lost control of the car as Malone had given chase on those twisting two-lane roads, was unconscious behind the wheel, secured by a seat belt. Malone bent over her dead daughter, shrieking with grief that would calcify into permanent, irredeemable guilt.

"Malone." She feels Locke behind her. "You OK?"

She takes a breath, tells herself, *Do your job, Katya.*

"I'm fine."

The door opens. Radovich is standing there. "Did she give it up?" he says.

"It's the kid," Malone says. "It was him the whole time."

"What do you mean?"

"He bamboozled us."

"He frigging kidnapped himself?"

"Danny fucking Peters is in the boarded-up place next to his parents' house."

"The Helliker place? No way. We just sent fire there."

"Fire? Why?"

"That place'll be burned to the ground in ten minutes."

44

When Quartz undoes her blindfold, the first thing Carey thinks is that she has been here before.

The walls are corrugated steel, the floor concrete, the peaked ceiling high above her, the air sickly sweet with diesel. There isn't much light. She thinks she can see a stack of old tires standing in a corner. She's sitting in a metal folding chair. Duct tape fixes her ankles to the chair legs. Her wrists are handcuffed behind her. Two feet away, a phone faces her atop a tripod.

She hears the blurt of another phone's text alert, recognizes it as the burner she bought. She starts to recall what Quartz told her about Danny in the car when he appears in front of her, brandishing the phone.

"Text," he says, reading her the number. "Password?"

It comes to her. She's in a Pressman Logistics truck depot, seven or eight miles east of Bleak Harbor, one in a network that stretches from Spokane to the Twin Cities to Chicago and across Michigan to the East Coast and Canada. She came here once to pick up a package for Pressman. She had wondered why he hadn't had it delivered directly to his office, but never inquired about it.

"Undo my legs," she tells Quartz.

"The password, now, if you want to live to see your freaky genius of a son."

She had considered slapping the pistol from Quartz's hand when he had surprised her at their rendezvous on Route 23. But she knew from her time dealing with Detroit druggies that guns went off. She let Quartz lash her hands and feet with the plastic ties. He hid her car in some bushes on a dirt turnout.

"I'm losing circulation."

"Why do you have a disposable phone anyway?"

"Cops took my phone," she says.

"And who's this text from?"

"Sounds like Roland Spitler," she says. "My mother's personal assistant."

"Why would he be texting you at this hour?"

He would never be texting me, Carey thinks. Roland Spitler, pushing seventy, does not text. He calls. Sometimes he emails. He does not text. "You can find out when you undo my legs."

There was no kidnapper, Quartz told her, grinning over the front seat of his car. Danny had been hiding in the Helliker place since the day before. Watching. Eavesdropping. Manipulating. Torturing his mother and stepfather. "He ordered a pizza," Quartz said, laughing out loud. "A goddamn pizza with pineapple."

Her son. Her Danny.

"You and your hubby had no idea, huh? Right."

Carey remembers looking up at the nailed-shut attic with Pete the night before, the flaking paint, the parched odor of abandonment. Was Danny peering down at her through a crack in the ceiling? Laughing at her? Or cursing her? Was he playing, or was he punishing?

Her anger wants out. It wants to flow from her like smoking lava, to surge and burst from her veins. But where to send it? She should be angry at Quartz, at Pete, at her mother, at her late father. She should be angry at herself for not knowing what she did not know, what she should have known. She should be screaming and banging her head against the chairback, kicking her feet free, snapping her wrists from the tape, tearing Quartz to pieces. Instead she's telling herself to breathe, stay calm, listen, get away, get to Danny.

And she's thinking that Roland Spitler does not text, would not text, that's not Spitler on her phone. That's someone else.

Quartz collects the other phone from the tripod, his pale cheekbones aglow in the shadows. He puts that phone in one of his pockets and says, "I sent some nice pictures to our friend Jeremiah. A.k.a. Danny."

"What exactly do you want?"

"I want what your son wants, Carey. What he's been trying to get. I might even give you some of the money, if Danny plays."

"What are you talking about?"

"I think he'll play. Password?"

Carey thinks Danny will, too, though maybe not the way Quartz intends. She gives Quartz the password, watches him punch it in, sees his eyebrows pop up as he reads.

"So," he says, "this is a shakedown. Nice."

"What does it say?"

He leans into Carey, gloating, shaking the phone in her face. She can smell sweat, though, and it isn't hers.

"It says you have a husband with a money-losing pot shop and a nasty dealer breathing down his neck. And you, you're not going to see a cent of your daddy's money. So you get your mommy to pony up the ransom, and you bolt town. You cut in Roland, who might be the only one who can get at her money anyway—am I right? The old lady gets hurt, but so what; she's on her deathbed. And meantime, you job your fuck buddy Pressman for a few million more. Nice."

"You're delusional, Quartz."

"Call me cynical—that's how I see it. But here's what it actually says." He seems pleased with himself. "Something about a gold bird. How obvious can you get?"

It's obvious, all right, Carey thinks, *but not to you.*

"I'll bet your brother's in on it too. He's probably just as pissed off at Serenity for screwing him out of his inheritance."

"Probably."

"Danny boy is a smart kid. He just didn't figure on a smarter one showing up."

He's typing. Carey says, "What are you telling him?"

Quartz shows her:

what now?

"You know," he says, "I could blow your plan out of the water."

"But then there's Locke."

"Locke. Fuck him."

"Undo my feet, Quartz."

"What do you know about Locke, really?"

"I know he wants you." She's bluffing, a little. Guessing. "He doesn't really care about Pressman, does he? Pressman's just a way to get at you."

She hears the muffled ring of a phone. The one Quartz put in his pocket. "Quiet," he says. Carey can't tell whether he means her or the ringing. "Unknown caller," he says, then puts the phone to his ear. "Hello, Danny."

"Danny," Carey shouts, straining forward in the chair. "Honey, call the police—it'll be all right."

"Or do you prefer Jeremiah? I hope you liked those pictures."

Quartz cups the phone close and turns away. Carey hears him say, "My name is Quartz," but she can't make out what else he's saying.

She cranes forward again and shouts, "Let me talk to him. Quartz. Let me talk to my son."

He swivels back toward Carey, listening with his eyes closed, his other hand on the back of his neck. "We want the same thing, Danny," he says. "No, I can't—" A pause. Quartz's eyes open. "I—Daniel." Another pause, then he lowers the phone from his ear and stares at it, looking surprised, even embarrassed. He drops the phone to his side.

"He's telling you what you're going to do, isn't he?" Carey says. "Danny can be pushy."

Quartz shakes his head. "We'll see about that."

"You're no longer in charge, Quartz."

Carey recalls the hot afternoon on the sidewalk outside the Mexican place. Jeremiah—Danny—texted her then. He knew where she was. Or at least where her phone was.

"Danny knew I went to Valparaiso, Quartz," she says. "He tracked my phone."

"He can't track your burner, even if he knows the number."

"You can take a chance on that, Quartz," she says, bluffing. "But I'm telling you he knows where we are. Why don't you just let me go, and you can get out before Locke and the cops show up? Danny's probably telling them this minute."

Quartz is shaking his head. "No, he's not. That would mess up his plan." The phone beeps. He looks at it, holds it up for Carey. "What does this mean?"

The text says, proceed to the wedge of space.

It takes Carey a second. But it fits with the gold bird, from the poem. "The mansion," she says. "My mother's place."

"It's called 'the wedge of space'?"

"It's a joke."

"A joke? Your son wants us to go there."

"Why would he want that?"

"Maybe he's cutting me in on your not-so-little scam."

"I guess we should go then."

"I'm a sitting duck there, and you know it."

"Actually, no. Real cops haven't been allowed near the mansion in years. They won't even know you're there."

Quartz stares at the floor, considering.

"Tell me, Quartz," Carey says. "If you're so good with computers, why don't you just hack into Pressman's bank accounts? He has way more money than Serenity."

"Maybe I don't want to die."

"Good luck with that. Maybe Danny's the smarter kid here, huh?"

Quartz steps over and leans his face close to Carey's. Again she smells his sweat. He's afraid of something. He says, "Did I not find your son?"

"I don't know. Could be he found you."

Quartz steps back, reaches into one of his pockets, and produces the pistol. "Now we're all in this together. See?" Then he stows the gun, digs in another pocket, shows Carey a box-cutting knife.

"What the fuck?" she says.

"Relax. You're still going to get your money, and you're still going to screw your boss over. Isn't that what you wanted?"

"I want my son back."

"Right." Quartz squats and takes the box cutter to the duct tape on Carey's ankles. "You're going to take me to the wedge of space."

45

Michele Higgins tastes soot on the back of her tongue. The heat stings her cheeks and knuckles and nostrils. She has watched houses burn before while waiting for the smoldering corpses to be hauled out. She wishes she wasn't so accustomed to it.

"Malone," she says.

The officer is crouched on the lawn of the Helliker place, shielding her face with a hand as she squints at the flaming bones of the house. The firefighters appear to have kept it from spreading to the Peters cottage next door. Next to her a man Michele doesn't recognize stands holding a kerchief over his nose. He's wearing those clunky black shoes that detectives wear. Maybe FBI.

The second floor of the house has collapsed into the first, which convulses with coal-black billows and intermittent plumes of flame. Serpents of smoke slither up the surface of the security fence alongside the house. Silver spews of fire-truck water arc through the camera lights. The TV trucks rolled up a few minutes after Michele arrived, male anchors crouching into side-view mirrors to shape their gelled hair.

"Malone," Michele says again, louder, as she steps closer, waving her phone. "You need to see this."

The man turns and motions Michele away with his kerchief. "Police scene. You'll have to move back."

"Who are you?" Michele says.

"Move back now, please."

Malone turns and touches the man's elbow. "It's all right," she says. "Agent Locke, this is Michele Higgins, with the local paper. She helped us with Pérez."

"I'm sorry, Katya. I don't think we need—"

"Are you looking for someone named Quartz? Or something like that?" Michele says. Locke's face changes. "If so, you need to listen to this."

"Let me see," Malone says.

"Officer, can you tell us what's going on?" The voice comes from behind Michele's shoulder. She turns to see a TV reporter and a put-out-looking cameraman standing next to her.

"Move back to the road now," Malone tells them.

The reporter, a tall redhead named Portia something, says, "What about her? She shouldn't get—"

"Move now, or you're going to jail."

Portia gives Michele a look as she and her cameraman retreat. Michele doesn't care.

"What do you have there?" Locke says.

Michele taps her phone and waits for the *Light* mobile app to display the front page. Locke reaches for the phone; Michele yanks it away. "Hold on," she says. "Here."

She punches a headline that reads, "Festival Weathers Minor Glitches for Opening Day Success," and hands the phone to Malone. The headline gives way to a miniature video screen. A tiny dot at the bottom of the screen begins to slide to the right along a timing bar.

"I don't see anything," Malone says.

"It's audio. Listen."

An oscillating schematic in the middle of the screen comes to life with the echo of a man's voice:

Hello, Danny. Or do you prefer Jeremiah?

And then:

My name is Quartz.

314

A woman's voice in the background:

Let me talk to my son.

Michele watches Malone and Locke listen. She has listened to the two-minute-eight-second recording half a dozen times since it appeared in her email an hour ago.

A man who calls himself Quartz is speaking with what sounds like a boy, apparently over a phone. Quartz wants something and seems to think he has leverage. The boy, who doesn't seem at all fazed, hangs up on him.

"That's Danny Peters," Malone says.

"Play it again," Locke says.

"Wait," Michele says. "Danny's coming on again."

After a short silence, Danny's voice returns, clearer now, as if he's speaking directly into a recording device. "The festival is on," he says. "The dragonfly lives."

"What does that mean?"

The schematic melts away. A silhouette materializes in pale gray against a black background. As the gray gradually brightens to pink, Michele sees the shape she saw each morning hovering over downtown Bleak Harbor as she parked in front of the *Light*.

"Looks like the Bleak Mansion, doesn't it?" she says.

"What are you saying? Danny is there? Why aren't you there if you think he is?"

"Maybe I went. Maybe the gates were locked and the house was dark, so I gave up and went looking for you."

The screen goes blank again. Malone looks at Locke, then back at Michele. "Danny put that there?"

"Yeah. Like he put that old story on the page today."

"Like he fooled us with his meds," Malone says. "The kid's just been toying with us."

"Quartz too, it appears," Locke says. "The young man is not to be toyed with."

"That was Quartz's voice?" Malone asks Locke. "You sure?"

"I'm sure."

"Who is this Quartz?" Michele says.

Malone is on her phone ordering a roadblock on the road to the Bleak Mansion. Locke says, "Not his real name. He's wanted by the FBI on separate matters."

"And you're FBI?"

"I am." Locke nods past Michele. "And so is she."

Michele looks left and sees a woman trotting toward them.

"Let's get out of here, Malone," Locke says.

"I want to ride with you," Michele says.

"Not happening," Malone says. "But do us a favor. See this woman coming up the road with Chief? She's an FBI agent, and she's a bitch. Occupy her for a minute. You'll be the first reporter I call when I know what's what." She grabs Locke by the arm. "Let's get to the house."

———

Michele watches Malone gun the cruiser past the approaching FBI agent, who's waving her arms at them and yelling while the chief watches.

"Agent?" Michele says, waving a notebook at her. "Can I ask a few questions?"

Hamilton points back at Malone's cruiser receding around the bend. "Where are they going?"

"No clue."

"Get out of my way."

The clamor of the firefighters comes back to Michele as she walks around the TV trucks toward her car. She hears the crash of the cascading water, the boom and crack of the fire.

For some reason, she doubts Danny is at Serenity Meredith Maas Bleak's mansion. She doubts he's even in Bleak Harbor. She pictures again the lithe boy in her binoculars, swatting at the air from the end of his dock, so alone and so—no, not helpless, not helpless at all.

Hearing a TV reporter calling out for her, Michele walks faster. She feels everything falling away behind her—the dying house, the taped-off one next door, the cops and firefighters, the Peters family, the boy, the bay, Bleak Harbor.

Maybe Danny is safe now. Maybe he is in danger. He may be brilliant, he may be deranged, but he's responsible now for whatever happens to him.

Inside her car she takes her phone back out and calls up her email. The screen fills with the email with the link to the audio posted on the *Light* website. "You should look at this" was all the unknown sender had written.

Beneath that was a separate email that had been forwarded from Carey Peters's email at Pressman Logistics to her personal Gmail account and apparently purloined by whomever had sent it to Michele. Attached to it were eight PDFs. Michele had opened three. They appeared to be copies of bills of lading from Pressman Logistics. There were references to catalytic converters, lists of some large dollar figures, and stamps etched with what looked like Asian characters.

Michele doesn't know what it all means, but she plans to find out. Whatever it is, she figures it probably isn't good for the billionaire Pressman. But it might be good for what remains of her career.

As she pulls off the shoulder, she takes a last look at the Helliker place in her rearview mirror. It's almost gone. She steers toward town, slowing at the fork where the two-lane veers south toward the interstate and Chicago. She imagines that repairman, the Grasshopper, probably sipping from a Solo cup in the beer tent at this very moment, waiting for her. She smiles.

A canopy of trees shrouds the road to Bleak Harbor in darkness. Michele starts to take the right, then swerves left and punches the accelerator hard toward the freeway and Chicago.

46

The surface of the bay flashes and throbs with the glittery reflections of the festival rides. Beyond the town, security lamps bathe the Bleak Mansion turrets in a pinkish glow.

"My grandmother is in that tower," Danny says, pointing. "She is sedated, asleep. I locked her door so she can't get out and nobody can get in. The rest will be in the turret on the opposite side."

"Serenity's a little nuts, isn't she?" Boz says.

"Are you still holding a grudge about her interfering with your liquor license?"

"How do you—never mind."

"Actually, Mr. Flanagan, she is brilliant, in her way."

Danny sits at a high top at Boz's Bayfront Bar and Grill, Boz standing at his shoulder, both of them peering across the bay through the one window on which the blinds aren't drawn. Lifesaver rings festooned with the USS *Boz* and other fake boat names hang from the knotty pine paneling above their heads.

A laptop is open on the table in front of Danny. It's the one he took with him to the Helliker attic. The screen presents a checkerboard of static black-and-white images:

Two high-ceilinged corridors leading from opposite directions to a downward staircase. A wingback chair set on a platform in a circular room. A kitchen with an empty fireplace. A dock extending from a boathouse on the Lake Michigan shore. A brick plaza sloping down to twin iron gates. An upward swoop in a two-lane road. Another gate crossing that road, blocked by police cars, lights flashing, officers pacing.

"You're in her security system?" Boz says.

Danny doesn't reply.

"I suppose you spent some time in that place."

"I can count the times on one hand."

"She is your grandmother, right?"

Danny recalls one of his earliest memories. He was sitting on the floor in a room with ceilings that stretched far over his head. A man the adults referred to as Mr. Spitler crouched before him, offering a spatula. There were no real toys at the mansion; spatulas and whisks were the main entertainments. "Grandma?" Danny said to the man, who shook his head. "Grandma is tired," the man said. "She is very tired."

"Technically," Danny tells Boz, "she is my grandmother. But she is too inebriated and too wounded and too alone to be much of anything to anyone. Unfortunately."

"Like I said, nuts—whoa, what the hell's that?"

Danny clicks on one of the image boxes. It expands to fill the screen. Two shadows inch along the boathouse deck, each with an arm extended frontward.

"Those guys got guns," Boz says.

"My mother's boss sent them."

"Sent them for what?"

"For someone he no longer needs."

"This was supposed to go down without any trouble."

"There will be no trouble for you, Mr. Flanagan."

"I thought that damn fire was gonna burn down this whole side of the lake."

"You will have your money. You can go wherever you like. You can buy yourself a nice new boat."

Boz points at the screen. "They don't look like good guys."

"They are not my concern or yours." This is partly an untruth, but Danny can't have Boz losing faith at this juncture. "My mother should be gone by the time they do anything."

"How did they even know to go there?"

Danny taps a finger on one of the three disposable phones resting next to his laptop. "My mother's boss knows."

"You told him?"

Yes, Danny thinks, *but Pressman has no idea.* Nor does he suspect how badly this will go for him. Danny doesn't tell Boz any of this, instead asking, "What did you do with the title?"

"The title?"

"The title to the boat."

"Ah, right. I put it in the name of my asshole ex-sergeant."

"And where is he?"

"Retired in northern Minnesota, last I heard."

"So by the time the police locate the title, then locate him, you will be long gone."

"Let's hope. Shitbags, kid."

"Everything is under control. You should get yourself a drink."

"Good idea."

"Could I please have a Coke too? Without a cherry, thanks."

Danny closes his eyes and listens as Boz walks away, his bottle-shaped body and bullet-shot leg syncopating the rhythm of his steps.

———

"What happened to your leg?"

Danny posed the question to Boz Flanagan on a May afternoon. They were standing on the beach deck outside Boz's bar. The sky was dull with prickly gray mist. Danny had taken to stopping at Boz's on afternoons when Pete was peddling pot and his mother was away. Now he intended to persuade the white-haired man to participate in his birthday plan.

Boz looked down at his leg self-consciously. "Why?" he said, looking back up with a grin. "Does it show?"

"You walk funny."

Danny knew he could say this without offending. His condition gave him a tacit license to say almost anything to people who might in fact be offended but would be too filled with pity to respond with anything but that.

"All barkeeps walk funny, son."

"Pete said someone shot you with a gun."

"Uh-huh. You want to come in where it's dry?"

Danny had gone inside and taken a stool at a high-top table along the windows facing the beach. He noticed the Bleak Mansion across the stirred-up bay, framed in one of the knotty pine rectangles. Behind him a mop leaned against the bar into an aluminum bucket. Danny smelled soap and old beer. He scanned the back of the bar, three TVs hung around a pair of ceramic starfish. One TV was tuned without sound to *Jeopardy!*

Boz brought him a glass of 7UP with crushed ice and a maraschino cherry. He set a plastic sport bottle on the high top and sat across from Danny.

"So what did your old man tell you?"

Danny plucked the cherry from the glass and dangled it in front of his face before setting it on the table. "He said you were off duty. You intervened in a fight at a bar."

"Something like that," Boz said. "That's pretty much it."

"Actually, no."

"No?"

"Pete didn't tell me. He didn't know. I know."

321

"You know what, kid?"

"I know you were undercover, not off duty. I know about the man you shot in the back." Danny patted the back of his left shoulder. "I know about the department investigation. I know you didn't really need or want to retire. I know your superiors didn't back you up."

Boz had been a cop for too long to show surprise. But the grin he offered Danny then wasn't its usual shape. "That's some juicy stuff, kid. You make that up all by yourself?"

As Boz spoke, he tapped the bottom of his cup on the tabletop.

"I can print out the file and bring it to you."

"What file?"

"Your file. Robert John Flanagan Jr., CPD02-126674D."

Boz took a drink, then swished his cup around, trying to look undisturbed. "How could some kid get a file?"

"Computer. It's not that hard if you know what you're doing."

"Shitbags," he said. "Gonna get a refill."

Boz went behind the bar. Danny looked across the bay. The mist shrouded the mansion's pink turrets. Danny imagined his grandmother sitting at one of the windows, looking across the water at him without knowing it.

Boz came back with his cup. "Computers, huh? That one of your, like, you know, things?"

Danny knew he meant obsessions. "Computers are useful," he said. "I like dragonflies better."

They sat in silence for a moment, Boz staring at his hands folded around his cup. Then he looked up and said, "That guy was a gangbanger, you know."

"OK."

"They paid that scumbag's family ten times what they paid me when they kicked me out the door."

"Yes."

"And, by the way, he wasn't 'running away,'" Boz said, curling his forefingers to signify quotation marks. "He was chasing another guy he was going to shoot through the fucking head."

"I did not see that in the file."

"Ha, fuck no, you didn't. They're not that stupid."

"No."

"So." Boz pointed a finger at Danny. "Now you know it all."

"I can help you, Mr. Flanagan."

"Too late for that, kid."

"You hate this place, and you want to get out, go spend your days fishing somewhere sunny."

"That wouldn't suck."

"I can help."

"You know what, Danny? You are full of surprises."

"For someone like me."

"For—yeah, exactly. You said it."

Danny got out of his chair. He said, "Be sure to look at your bank account first thing in the morning. You will see a deposit for three hundred ninety-eight dollars and eighty-two cents from this afternoon."

"What are you talking about?"

"It's actually a transfer, executed"—Danny looked at the time on his phone—"one hour and nine minutes ago, from the Chicago Police Pension Fund."

"Kid."

"Computers."

"You can't be serious."

Danny picked up the cherry, put it in a pocket. "Thanks," he said. "I better get going before Pete gets here."

"You're going to get me in trouble."

"Nobody will be able to trace it until you're long gone." Danny had the door to the deck open, the breeze damp on his cheek. "I told you I want to help you."

"What does that mean? How?"

The door slapped shut behind him. Danny heard it squeak open as he stepped onto the beach.

"Danny," Boz called out. "What was that number again?"

Danny smiled. "Three-nine-eight-dot-eight-two."

"My address here?"

"We will talk."

———

Danny hears Boz clumping back to the table as he clicks into the grid on his laptop screen, maximizes another image box. It shows a small table set up in the circular room. Spitler has adjusted the security camera as Danny had instructed.

On the table stands a desktop computer, wires winding away from it across the floor. Spitler crosses in front of the table, then stops and gestures as Danny's mother and a scrawny man with a hand in one of his many jacket pockets move into the view, their backs to Danny.

"That's your mom, ain't it?" Boz says.

"Please do not transfer the bar over to Pete for a few weeks. Wait for this to run its course."

"I didn't like turning him in, kid."

"This place will be perfect for him." Danny almost smiles at the thought. "And I couldn't just leave him nothing."

"What's your mother going to think?"

"She has nothing to do with Pete."

Boz looks confused. "Don't you want to get them back together?"

"They were never apart."

Danny clicks his mouse, and the matrix of images reappears. He sees an apparent commotion involving Pete, Uncle Jonah, and some police officers at the entrance to the mansion road. Pete is pointing up the road and shouting at a cop who's trying to calm him.

In another square, Danny sees the two dark men inching down a second-floor corridor. He will manipulate door locks to direct them where he wants them when he wants them there. In another square, he sees the police officer, Malone, who'd come to his parents' house that morning after he disappeared. She's scaling one of the twin gates at the mansion entrance with a boost from a man wearing a jacket and slacks, no uniform.

Danny hits a combination of keys. The gate slowly opens. Malone climbs down.

"I assume you think this is about love," Danny tells Boz as he manipulates his mouse to zoom in on the face of the man with Malone. "Like all of this is going to make my parents realize how much they really love each other?"

"What's wrong with that, kid?"

"Nothing is about love."

"Nothing but money, eh? That's it?"

Danny zooms out from the man's face and punches a name into Google. It pops up on the LinkedIn page Danny had seen two weeks before: Allen P. Locke, special agent, FBI, Indianapolis. George Washington University.

Danny doesn't understand why this man would be here. But it doesn't matter now. *Calm*, Danny thinks. He picks up a phone and hits a single number followed by the pound sign. On the laptop, he sees Roland Spitler touch a finger to his left ear.

"Mr. Spitler."

Serenity Bleak's aide turns away from the others. "Yes."

"This function is going to be a bit bigger than we expected."

Spitler's words come in a harsh whisper. "Who is this man? Did you send this man here?"

"Quartz is going to help us."

"He has a gun, Daniel. This was not part of the bargain."

"He will not affect your cut."

"That has nothing to do with it. He kidnapped your mother and brought her here."

"She belongs there. You need to proceed with the plan, Mr. Spitler."

"We are in danger."

"I am prepared for everything. Remember, on my signal, direct my mother, get her out of there."

Spitler lets out a long breath. "Daniel."

"Or you can wait around and take your chances. I do not see them working in your favor."

Danny puts the phone down. Boz is rapping his cup on the table again. "Kid, what the hell you got me into?"

"Have you checked the account I set up for you?"

"Yeah, saw it." He gulps from his cup. "A hundred large. Jesus."

"With more to come. Just do your job, Mr. Flanagan, and everything will be all right."

"Someone's gonna catch me. You should have left me the speedboat."

"You will be better off in the fishing boat. No one will suspect anything. I programmed the locations into your phone."

"You got focus, kid. Pete had a word for it. Brain-blindness?"

"Mind-blindness," Danny says.

"Doesn't sound so good."

"Most people have blindness, period."

Boz points at the laptop screen. "Who's that guy?"

"It doesn't matter."

Danny looks out the window at the mansion. Today he will be sixteen years old. Danny has never cared much for birthdays, the song as inane as a revolving door, the pointless gifts, all the pretending that a particular day had more meaning than another. Although his uncle Jonah did give him the Wallace Stevens collection for his twelfth birthday—he was glad of that. Sometimes he wished he could remain one age forever. It would simplify things. It wouldn't even matter what age it was. Eighty-seven, sixty-four, forty-two, twenty-eight. Just one, all the time. Fifteen, sixteen. Any one.

But the moment of his birthday—his birthdate—was useful in his current endeavor. He had known it would engage his mother's emotions. He had known it would make the ruse believable, had known Pete would go for it, the police would go for it, everybody he needed to believe would believe. And they did.

His plan is going as he had plotted it in his head. Except for Dulcy's arrest; she was supposed to collect Danny's mother in Boz's speedboat. Dulcy: her eyes glittering onyx marbles until she closed them hard and leaned back and away from him, gasping, begging him in words he did not understand.

Danny will not see her again.

Then there are the dark men. And Malone and Locke. Danny had anticipated there would be complications. He was prepared to deal with them. *Mother will be fine*, he tells himself, steadying his breathing, instructing his heartbeat to slow. He had not expected a complication quite like Quartz, though Quartz could actually be useful.

"Quartz," Danny tells Boz, "is me."

"Meaning what? He's autistic?"

He feels Boz's breath on his neck, sees the fear on his face reflected in the laptop screen. He says, "I am not autism."

"Uh-huh. Kid, you got two bad guys with guns in the same house as your mom and grandma. What are you gonna do?"

Danny refocuses on the computer screen. "This is not your concern, Mr. Flanagan. You should get going."

Boz is looking around, rubbing his arms, more nervous by the second. "What about the storm?"

"That doesn't hit until midafternoon. You'll be safe by then. Your money will be safe."

"That's what it's about, huh?"

"On the other hand, if you renege on me, the money will evaporate, and the police will know all about you within one minute."

"I can't believe a damn kid is threatening me."

"You wanted out of Bleak Harbor. You wanted to sell your bar. It is sold. You are leaving. So leave."

Danny moves his mouse, and the gate that opened for Malone and the man with her swings shut. They're now crouched in the shadows of the mansion's enormous front vestibule, a spiral staircase before them. Danny has trapped the two dark men on a different stairway between the second and third floors.

Danny punches up Malone's cell number on his phone. After seeing her in his parents' yard, he'd copied her number from a supposedly private directory in the city computer system. He sends her a text:

house mine. follow me

He watches Malone squint into her phone before she shows the text to the man, who nods in apparent recognition. They both look around as if the texter might suddenly materialize out of the shadows. Danny texts again:

elevator in kitchen behind stairway. go. 4

Malone reads it, starts typing, shows the man. A text appears on Danny's phone:

Who are you?

Danny smiles as he texts:

jeremiah

328

He watches Malone and the man step alongside the staircase and vanish into the shadows behind it.

Danny adjusts the small video cam attached to the top of his laptop screen so that it points up at his face. He needs to focus. He needs Boz gone.

"Why aren't you up there, kid?"

"I am where I always am. Go now."

"What if I need to contact you?"

"You won't. Leave now. My mother will be waiting."

Danny watches Boz walk outside past the spot where he used to set out a bowl of water for Paddle.

He climbs into his fishing boat and yanks the cord on the outboard motor, once, twice, before it splutters to life. The boat chugs away toward the channel, Boz looking around anxiously as he vanishes in the gloom.

Danny checks the time: 10:54. Fifty-two minutes to go.

47

Carey gasps.

"Danny, my God, Danny."

Danny's face fills the desktop screen on the table where Spitler sits, his eyes peering downward, curls falling along his ears, the bruise on his cheek gone.

Carey leans over Spitler's shoulder as if she could gather her son out of the screen into her arms. "Danny, can you hear me?" she says. "Are you all right?"

"I can hear you." His voice issues from speakers on the desktop. "I am perfectly fine."

The background behind Danny is a blur of chalky white that Carey doesn't recognize, something shaped like a star beyond his left ear. "Where are you?" she says. "I thought you were coming here."

"Everything is going to be fine if we move quickly. Mr. Spitler?"

"Yes."

"Mr. Quartz, are you ready? Mother, you need to stand aside."

———

The kid's not here.

A hot flush of foolishness washes over Quartz. Danny is not here, in this room, in this house. Quartz looks around, his neck muscles taut and cracking as he turns. He shouldn't be in this room, in this town, with these people. He should be gone. He should be in his car racing the back roads up Michigan's little finger, across the big bridge and around the peninsula to Sault Sainte Marie.

Quartz really hadn't wanted all that much. Just enough to escape to somewhere warm and bright and green and far away. Somewhere nobody could find him—not Locke, not Pressman, not anyone. After two years, he'd had enough of running, had enough of serving vile masters like Pressman. He would be perfect alone.

Now there's a text on his phone. From Pressman:

U are dead Q

Quartz could have escaped with the $2 million in ransom. But then there was Jeremiah, there was Danny, the brilliant boy with the brilliant plan, the plan so impossible and diabolical that it was truly beautiful to someone like Quartz, who was, he had thought, not all that different from the boy.

But Danny is not here. He's an image on a computer screen, averting his eyes.

"Where are you, Danny?"

"I am where I belong, Mr. Spitler."

The room isn't quite dark, the window shades drawn. The smell of stale cigarette smoke is choking. Quartz doesn't like the decisions he's made in the last hour. He looks over at Carey, watches her watching him. She's breathing hard. He takes out his pistol.

"Put it away, Quartz," she says.

She punched him hard in the chest when they got out of the car at the iron gates outside. He had let her. Now he's wondering if she knew that her son would not be here.

"Where is he?" he says. "You lied to me."

"No." She turns to the screen. "Danny?"

"We have work to do, Mr. Quartz. And we don't have much time. It is in your interest to cooperate."

"You know, I could walk out of here now."

"No, you couldn't. Mr. Spitler, please let Mr. Quartz take your chair, and stand by. We are going to move some money around."

Spitler stands. Quartz sits and stares into the screen, into Danny's face. The boy's eyes are fixed downward. He's busy with something. *This kid*, he thinks. *What if the spooks at NSA knew about him?* Quartz hitches his chair forward, sets a hand on the mouse. *Maybe they will someday.*

———

Danny watches Quartz's eyes dart about. He knows the feeling. Every few seconds, he feels his hamstrings quivering against the chair seat. *Calm*, he tells himself.

On the checkerboard screen, the dark men, their faces shrouded in hoods, glide down a third-floor corridor to a door Danny has locked. He holds his breath as one of them slams a shoulder into the door, to no apparent effect. The other points his handgun at the doorknob, but the first one touches his arm, shaking his head.

Danny had not expected that someone might shoot out the locks.

Malone and Locke are in the elevator. Danny told them to go to 4 but then stopped it between 2 and 3. She texted him a moment ago: get us out now more police coming. She's talking on her phone now, and Locke looks like he's trying to jimmy the elevator doors. Danny hits some keys. Malone and Locke back away as the elevator rises to 3 and stops. Danny releases the doors and texts Malone:

follow corridor to stairway.

He cannot let them get to the turret room before the job is done. Same for the dark men.

Danny has never been in the turret. Spitler had provided him with a hand-drawn map indicating the location of the hidden wall panel that opens to a staircase spiraling down to the tunnels that once facilitated Jack Bleak's trysts. Danny uses his mouse to swivel a camera, scanning the room until he sees the spot that Spitler marked on his map.

He looks up from his laptop toward town. Between the shadow shapes of buildings, he sees the flash of police vehicles and ambulances speeding toward the mansion road. He hears the church bells clanging. He closes his eyes and thinks of Jeremiah flailing in the churning lake, the burn and resignation in his lungs as the water rushed in to devour him. He imagines the docile silver perch spinning and rising as they passed Jeremiah, both going to their deaths.

An overhead camera in the turret room captures his mother's face. Weariness pinches her eyes, sags her cheeks. Danny knows the look too well. He has seen it as she waits in doctors' offices, as she walks into the house after another three days in Chicago, as she sets her phone aside after an abortive conversation with her mother, as she listens to Pete expostulate after his fifth beer about expanding his marijuana business, as she toils on her laptop while the eleven o'clock news plays on the great-room TV, as she leans on a deck railing with a gin-and-tonic tumbler, staring at a sunset, dreading the next morning.

Danny has seen enough.

Soon this will all be over, he thinks. *Soon you will be saved. We will all be saved.*

———

Frozen behind Spitler and Quartz, Carey watches the downcast eyes of the boy on the computer screen. She doesn't know him. Not this boy, with his face bent to his mysterious task, issuing his blunt orders to Quartz.

But Danny knows her. Or at least knows her in ways Carey never would have wanted. He has prowled inside her email, her phone, her texts, her online explorations of new places to live. He knows about her fantasy of escaping from Pete and her revenge plot against Pressman.

She steps backward to a window and eases the shade over an inch. Downtown Bleak Harbor is ablaze now with the lights of what seems like a hundred police cars. Blockades are set up at both intersections leading to the interstate. Clusters of townspeople and tourists line the mansion road up to the point where the police have obstructed it. Carey sees Jonah and Pete standing in the road, looking helpless.

She lets the shade go. There will be no escaping. For anyone. Even Danny. He can't have gone far. The police will find him. And then what? Interrogations? Charges? A trial? Danny walking with a lawyer through a phalanx of shouting citizens and reporters? His face on TV screens and front pages of newspapers? She would have thought a few days ago that any of that would be too much for her Danny. But now, she has no idea.

An image appears, unbidden, in her mind. Danny is sitting at a table with her and Pete on a Saturday morning at the Palace Grill near their Chicago condo. The owner, a large, smiling man named George, is telling Pete a groaner of a joke. George always stopped at their table to say hello, and Danny liked him enough that he broke his daily CoCo Wheats routine to have blueberry pancakes and sausage. On this morning, while Pete laughs at George's joke, Carey reaches across the table and touches her son's free hand. He doesn't stop eating, doesn't even look up from his plate, but he doesn't pull his hand away—he lets Carey take it in her fingers and squeeze.

If only, she thinks now, *we could just go back and—*

"We have four accounts to access."

It's Danny voice, behind her, louder than before. Quartz must have turned up the speaker volume. Carey lets the shade go and walks back to the table, positioning herself just behind Quartz, where she can keep watch on the doors at either end of the room.

"Mr. Spitler has installed the correct links and software you will need," Danny is saying. "I have the passcodes. Mr. Spitler will provide his thumbprint."

"Really?" Quartz says.

"My grandmother signed over her power of attorney five months ago. The accounts held quite a bit more money then, didn't they, Mr. Spitler?"

"Roland," Carey says. "You stole from my mother?"

If Spitler regrets this, he doesn't show it. "Forgive me, Miss Carey," he says, "but I don't recall you or your brother ever being around to mop up her vomit."

"Mr. Quartz, do you see the icon in the top-right corner of your screen?"

"BCBT? Bleak County Bank & Trust?" Quartz says, recalling how the mystery hacker—Danny—invaded the bank's servers.

"Click on it, please."

"Why?"

"Proceed, Mr. Quartz. Our visitors will be arriving very soon."

"Danny, hurry," Carey says.

Quartz clicks on the icon, and a window filled with a list of twelve-digit numbers materializes. "We're going to access all of these?"

"No, just the first, the fourth, the tenth, and the thirteenth."

"Because?"

"Because I said so, Mr. Quartz."

Quartz clicks on the first number. "It wants a thumbprint," he says. "Mr. Spitler."

Spitler leans over and presses his left thumb onto a small biometric pad. The computer screen fills with columns of numbers blinking in green on black.

"Damn," Quartz says. "One hundred eighteen million? And there was more?"

"There is more. Deploy the software."

"This isn't going to work," Quartz says. "The bank's gonna notice if you start moving big sums of cash around."

"I have accounted for that," Danny says.

"Really? OK. So mine is here?"

"Your share? Do not worry. You will get yours, Mr. Quartz."

Quartz sits back from the table. "How much?"

"How much do you get? Let me think." Danny pauses. "One million, one hundred eleven thousand. Deploy, please."

"Why that number?"

Carey leans forward and slaps Quartz across the back of his head, shouting, "Do what he says, goddamn it." Quartz comes halfway out of his chair, but Spitler grabs him by a jacket pocket and shoves him back down.

"I don't have to fucking do this," Quartz says.

"Look at this, Mr. Quartz." Danny's face disappears from the screen and is replaced by a view from a camera of two dark men edging along a corridor wall. "Do they look familiar?"

"My God," Carey says. "They're in the house? Now?"

"Near the guest rooms in the south turret," Spitler says. "One floor below us."

"Fuck me."

"That is a perceptive analysis, Mr. Quartz," Danny says as he switches the image off. "I suggest you proceed if you want to leave that room alive."

48

"Now what?"

Malone and Locke crouch in darkness, weapons out, heads swiveling, at the top of the stairway to the fourth floor. A series of texts signed *jeremiah* guided them here. Malone suspects the corridor extending to her right leads to the turret they saw from the ground with the two dimly lit windows.

"The kid say anything else?" Locke says.

Past Locke through the windows on the front of the mansion, Malone sees fire trucks blinking at the Helliker ruins. "Goddamn it," she says.

"What?"

"He better be here."

"The boy? Where else would he be?"

"I don't—never mind." Malone peers into the corridor blackness, looking for a door. "Gonna call Chief."

"For what?"

She ignores Locke, dials Radovich. "We're on the top floor," she tells him. "It's dead quiet, no sign of anyone."

"You shouldn't have gone up yourself, Katya."

"Well, we're here now." Her phone beeps. "Hang on," she says, clicking on the new text from Jeremiah:

two men armed and dangerous in the house

She raises the phone briefly so Locke can read it, sees the glow of the text reflected in the lenses of his askew spectacles. "That's not good," he says.

Malone returns to Radovich. "Just got a new text from the kid. He says some bad guys are here somewhere."

"This is why—never mind. Just stay where you are then. I got backup coming, along with the FBI guys."

"Ten-four."

Another text beeps in.

"Just stay there, Malone. Hear me?"

She hangs up and reads the new text. "The kid says the door we want is down this hallway to the right. Chief said to wait."

"I don't like this."

"What?"

Locke is looking up and down the corridor, checking the ceiling, glancing back down the stairs. "Gonna wager those are the guys who killed Bledsoe," he says. "They don't work for a drug dealer. They work for Pressman."

"How do you know?"

"I know." Locke cranes his neck to squint around her at the corridor. "Setting aside their identical outfits, just make the connections: Quartz, who works for Pressman, all of a sudden has Carey Peters. I'm thinking Bledsoe was supposed to grab the boy, but he screwed it up."

"And you don't want those guys to get to Quartz before you, do you?" Malone takes a step back, reassessing Locke. "You don't give a shit about Danny or his mom. You're not here for them. You're here for Quartz."

Malone knew it before but didn't want to believe it. In her mind she sees her ex's lying face again, its smirk of willful ignorance, the wandering eye she once thought sexy.

"We're in this together, Katya. If you're right and the kid's not here, then he might be OK, but we've gotta get his mom out."

"You know, Locke, I can't explain why fucked-up people do the fucked-up things they do."

He gives her a sideways what-the-hell-does-that-mean look as he moves into the hallway and crosses to the far wall.

"You coming or not?"

"I'm here for the boy, Locke—got it?"

She turns then and bolts down the dark hallway, raising one leg high as if to kick in the door.

49

Danny watches Malone assault the door, sees her stumble backward, almost topple over.

He sucks a breath through his teeth and looks away from the laptop screen. He makes himself imagine Paddle asleep in his lap at the end of the dock, the dachshund's ear silky between his forefinger and thumb. Sometimes Paddle would snore, and then Danny knew the dog was happy. Danny was happy too.

Calm. Every ninety-third target evades the dragonfly, he reminds himself. *Only by luck: A sudden gust. Another blind, stupid bug disrupting the vector. And only every ninety-third.*

Calm.

He spent the last day and a half preparing for this, breathing mildew and seagull-poop fumes in the muggy rot of the Helliker attic, his fingers pink with cracking, wishing he had thought to order some Vaseline Intensive Care lotion, wishing he had had just a little more time, wishing Paddle would come trotting down the beach, ears flapping, snout swaying like a metronome over the sand.

Paddle never came, of course.

That drizzly spring afternoon on which Danny and Dulcinea had stumbled onto Spitler's ham-handed manipulations of Serenity's funds was one of the few happy moments Danny could recall from the days of Paddle's final sufferings. Dulcinea had wriggled out of her jeans and sat smiling on the edge of Danny's bed, beckoning him. "OK," Danny had said. "I guess that would be all right."

And it was.

Once Danny had hatched his plan and blackmailed—or, alternatively, incentivized—Spitler into cooperating, he could have simply used Spitler's credit card to buy the stand-in laptop and the extra prescription meds. But it was so much more amusing to tap into the City of Bleak Harbor's budget just as the bureaucrats and elected buffoons were plotting how to squander Serenity's gift.

Working overnight in the Helliker attic, Danny used his laptop and a batch of code improvised by Dulcinea to create a daisy chain of automatic bank transfers that would propel digital cash from account to account, each account accepting a fraction of the fortune that Serenity Meredith Maas Bleak had inherited and that her faithful servant Roland Spitler had tried, at least in part, to appropriate for himself. Danny scheduled the transfers, each different by a few cents, so that they would be staggered over the course of several weeks, preventing anyone from noticing how the four accounts he'd selected were slowly being drained. When the operation was complete, each account—he would leave Serenity plenty in the other accounts—would be left with a balance of $5,145, to match the date of the drowning of Jeremiah Estes Bleak.

Danny wishes he could sit in Quartz's chair to watch up close the shrinking sums flitting from one account to the next to the next like so many dragonflies darting from one unsuspecting mosquito to a hapless moth to an ignorant, fluttering butterfly. But he is where he belongs, at a distance. He had needed Mr. Spitler's thumbprint. Having the able Mr. Quartz to work the keyboard was fortuitous, although he might soon have to confront the ruthless men his employer had dispatched.

Quartz is nearly finished emptying the third of the four accounts when Danny switches back to the checkerboard screen on his laptop and sees that one of the squares—the one where he last saw the two men—has gone blank. Either the camera malfunctioned or the men found it and shot it out.

Danny hadn't expected that either.

The entire face of the mansion blinks with cop lights. Danny will turn sixteen in eighteen minutes. He should be done and gone by then. He hopes.

He checks on Malone and Locke again. Locke is rearing back to take his own shot at the door to the turret. The two men appear in another view in the hallway leading to the room from the opposite side.

"No," Danny says. "Stop."

His view of the men goes black. He hears a muffled explosion. The three heads in the turret room snap around. Another blast sounds, and the door to the left of the table where Quartz sits buckles inward, the knob bursting away in a spray of wood and metal splinters.

"Stop what?" Quartz says. "What the fuck?"

Danny holds his right palm up to the videocam. "Mr. Spitler, now," he shouts. "Mommy, it is within reach. It is within reach."

Malone crashes into the room behind Locke and dives to the floor, shouting, "Police, everyone down, police," as she hears the dull spatter of gunfire through silencers. She sees a man in a suit grab Carey Peters by the shoulders and haul her down and another man sitting at a table reaching frantically into a pocket and saying, "What the fuck what the fuck what the fuck?"

The lights go out; the room goes dark. Bullets thwap the wall and shatter windows behind Malone. She's shimmying along the floor, smelling old cigarette smoke and fear, when a single ceiling light flashes on across the room, shining on two men covered in black but for a thin slit exposing the widening whites of their eyes. Malone shoots one in the left collarbone. He screams and flails backward against the wall while his partner ducks out of the light.

"Police, drop your guns now," Malone is yelling. Her eyes have begun to adjust to the dark. She's looking around as fast as she can, looking for the other shooter, but mainly for the boy, for Danny Peters, when a knee cracks the back of her head. It's Locke, crab walking past her to the man at the table, who's now on the floor, fumbling with his jacket. Locke karate chops something out of the man's hands.

Quartz, she thinks. Locke grabs him by his collar and starts dragging him back toward Malone. She sees a shape sliding along the wall behind them and squeezes off two shots in that direction, yelling, "Locke, gun behind you." He doesn't seem to see or hear her—he's just hauling his man back to the door where they entered the room. "Locke, what are you doing?" she shouts again. A wall sconce blinks on over the head of one of the masked men dropping to a knee and extending his pistol toward her. *Danny*, she thinks as she twists around to fire, *where is goddamn Danny?*

———

Quartz sees the two strangers in black scurry into the room just as everything goes dark. Picturing their masked faces as a pair of black-and-orange bull's-eyes, he reaches into a pocket for his Luger, but it's the wrong pocket, no gun there; he reaches into another pocket, but he can't get his hand on the gun butt, maybe because he's shaking so hard, telling himself, "Fuck fuck fuck." Without the earplugs he wore on the range, he can't hear anything for the exploding guns and the cold silence of the intruders.

A bullet tears through the computer monitor in front of Quartz. "Oh God, oh God," he cries out, feeling bits of plastic and glass cut into his face. He falls to the floor, and just as he gets his Luger out, something hard smacks his hand, and the gun goes spinning away across the floor. Then he feels a hand rough against his ear, his jacket collar tighten around his neck. He's being pulled away.

Without even looking, Quartz knows it's Locke who has him in his grip. Locke is saving him from these men Pressman sent to kill him.

And while he's still scared shitless, he feels a certain relief. For all his years of running, Quartz, wanted by the FBI for half a dozen different crimes of espionage, would rather be taken by this clumsy, desperate agent than shot to death because of a boy who outsmarted him.

But then Locke stumbles, drops to a knee, loosens his grip. Quartz lifts his head and sees a police officer lying a few feet away, blasting as she yells, "What the fuck are you doing?" Locke is struggling to right himself when he lurches forward onto his face. "Hit," he gasps. Just beyond him, Quartz now sees Spitler stuffing Carey into a doorway Quartz hadn't noticed before. He rises to his hands and knees and begins to crawl away from Locke, bullets whizzing over him as he calls out, "Take me. Please."

———

It is within reach.

Carey sees Danny's palm on the screen. She hears the alien passion in his cry. She understands. She lets Spitler take her by the shoulders. "Miss Carey, follow me. Now."

They stoop low and move past Serenity's gold-flake chair across the platform to the wall beneath the framed *Light* page blaring the news of Jack Bleak's death. Behind her she hears two rapid gunshots, then another, then a male shriek of pain, a clatter and thud. She knows she should be afraid. Spitler's face is a rictus of fear. But Carey feels an odd, welcoming calm, as if she is bulletproof, as if she is untouchable, immortal. She understands now what Danny was telling her a moment ago:

It is within reach.

Spitler reaches up and thumps the wall with his fist three times fast, pauses, looks around, sweating, breathing hard, whacks the wall again twice. A door swings open into the wall. "Here," Spitler says, pulling Carey into a cramped, dark space smelling of must.

"Now, Miss Carey," Spitler says, but she turns back to the room, sees Quartz crawling toward her. "Take me," he's saying. "Please." Locke is behind him, struggling to raise himself from the floor, holding the back of his left leg. "I found your son," Quartz is saying.

She reaches out and takes his hand, hears Locke groan, "No." He's on an elbow, the heel of one of Quartz's shoes in his other hand. "You are aiding and . . ." His voice trails off. He collapses. Carey pulls Quartz away.

"Do not move," Malone says. She's lying on her side beyond Locke with her gun pointed in Carey's direction. "Stay where you are." Their eyes meet. Carey sees that Malone is in pain and for a fleeting instant wishes she didn't have to disappoint the officer. But she knows now that she will finally be with Danny, only Danny, always Danny, forever.

There's another gunshot from the other masked man. A chandelier smashes on the floor next to Malone, and she rolls out of the way. "I'm sorry," Carey says. Spitler pulls the door shut, slams two deadlocks into place, and takes Carey hard by her wrist.

"Hurry."

They move a few steps in one direction, Quartz following, the floor uneven with screwheads and warped boards. They swerve right, then left, and a light snaps on, a bare bulb overhead spilling a glow the color of puke down a wooden stairway corkscrewing into blackness. Carey hears Malone yelling after them, "We'll find you, Carey. We will find you."

Spitler stops—"Wait one second"—takes out a disposable phone, hits a few buttons. His hands are shaking. "Damn it, damn it," he says, hitting more buttons. "All right. Let's go. Hold on to me, go go go."

———

Officers in blue and brown, a few not in uniform, rush the mansion from every side. Danny undoes all the locks. On the laptop he hears

Malone's shouts, the splutter and bang of the guns, the thuds and screams.

The masked men might be dead. Locke and Malone have been shot. Danny's mother and Spitler are escaping. Quartz might be with them. That wasn't part of the plan. Nothing Danny can do about it.

With a ripple of keystrokes, he sends a neutron bomb of software to the computer in the turret, erasing all the steps that he and Quartz just took.

Then Danny picks up a phone, texts Boz: on their way

Boz replies: 10-4

Danny gets off his chair, steadies himself with two hands on the table's edge, takes some deep breaths. It's over. Quartz got to only three of the four accounts. That will do. Everyone will get paid: his mother, Dulcinea, Boz.

And the others Danny has in mind.

He walks outside, keeping his eyes on the mansion. Boaters have pulled up there to ogle the goings-on from the bay.

Danny crosses Boz's deck, the sand in front of it, then steps up to the dock. At the end of the dock, he takes a wallet from his back pocket and digs out a folded-up plastic baggie. Danny unfolds the baggie and shakes it.

Paddle's ashes float away.

Danny stands for a moment watching the white flecks disappear on the water. He wishes he hadn't had to have Dulcinea plant the other ashes in Bledsoe's trunk, but he'd wanted the ruse to be authentic.

He drops the baggie on the dock. Then he stares across the bay to the turret where his grandmother sleeps in a drugged haze. He closes his eyes, imagines the big lake beyond, stretching all the way to Chicago.

"Goodbye," he says.

He walks back into Boz's, gathers up his laptop and phones, and goes through the bar into the kitchen, where he stops, reconsidering.

He returns to the bar, finds an order pad and a ballpoint pen, tears a page out of the pad, and writes:

Pete,

I would not call it Pete's if I were you.

Good fishing. Go Cubs.

Danny

He folds the note over once and secures it beneath a bottle of vodka, then moves past the men's room through the kitchen to the screen door facing the bay road. He glances around, making sure no one is near before he walks to the SUV parked in the gravel driveway. A single key is in the ignition, where Boz left it. Danny climbs in and turns it. The dashboard clock lights up: 11:46. He's sixteen. He latches his safety belt and pulls out onto the bay road, heading north, away from Bleak Harbor.

LATER

50

"Locke."

Malone reaches out with her good arm to touch him, draws it back. He's on his back in a hospital bed, his left leg suspended over the bed, wrapped in bandage. He's been in a drugged stupor for three days.

"Locke. I know you're awake."

His eyes open, slowly focus. He gives Malone a once-over, inclines his head at the sling on her left shoulder. "What happened to you?"

"Shot through the arm. Pretty clean. Like on TV."

"What happened?"

"You don't remember?"

He stares at his leg. "We were in that room. There was shooting. Some screaming. I don't really know."

"You got shot in the butt."

"Hurts."

"Yep. Tough. I mean, it's good you're not dead. But tough."

Locke nods at that. He looks at the empty tray next to his bed, as if he might find something there. "Your head OK?"

"You probably don't remember that either."

"Remember what?"

"You kicked me."

"No, I didn't."

"Yes, you did. In your hurry to get Quartz."

Locke doesn't say anything.

"You really screwed with me, Locke. You better hope I forget."

This doesn't seem to register. Locke says, "Quartz got away."

"Yep," Malone says. "Your fellow agents are looking for him, but so far, they've got nothing. Just deserts, in my opinion. Had you done your job—"

"Excuse me, Officer, but—" Something, maybe pain, stops him, contorting his face.

Malone doesn't care.

"Excuse me, Agent Locke," she says, "but I was on my own in a shit fight with two assholes, and you were basically AWOL. And you haven't even asked about Danny Peters."

He's still catching his breath. "What assholes?"

"Just stop, Locke."

"They shot me. Where are they?"

"One's in ICU; the other's in the morgue."

"Good."

"You still haven't asked about the boy."

Locke shakes his head. "He's not the dangerous one. Quartz is the dangerous one. I told you."

"No. You told me shit."

"I told you, Quartz—"

"Really, Locke? Really?" Malone thinks about rapping a knuckle on his leg, decides no. "Danny Peters is gone. Nobody has a clue where he is. His mom and pop are lawyered up, not saying a word, probably because they don't have a clue either."

"Don't you wonder, though?"

"Wonder whether they were in on this somehow?" Malone recalls Carey Bleak Peters disappearing into that door in the wall. "The thought has crossed my mind. But as for evidence? We have nothing. We have a plastic baggie with the residue of a dead dog's ashes. We have some drawings of dragonflies and a bunch of computers and phones full of jack shit. Although there's some evidence that Carey may have been trying to blackmail her boss. Not that it really matters now."

"Hah," Locke says. The chuckle makes him grimace. "No shit."

"No shit what?"

Locke coughs, shifts himself in the bedding, coughs again. "She and Pressman had a little Valentine's Day date."

"Really?"

"Yes, ma'am. You don't want to mess with that woman. She went after him, stole a bunch of documents that could've gotten her boss in a lot of trouble. I'd have liked to get her to give me those."

"So you could squeeze Pressman for Quartz."

Locke shrugs.

"How the hell did you know all this anyway?" Malone says.

Locke leans his head back into his pillow, closes his eyes. "I don't know for sure, but I got a couple of emails out of nowhere."

"Of course. The boy."

"The boy."

"Damn. That kid." Through the window beyond Locke's bed Malone sees the festival Ferris wheel, partially disassembled. "How the hell did he invade all these people's private places without getting noticed?"

"Are you kidding?" Locke says. "You got Fortune 500 companies with people crawling around in their stuff for months, and they don't notice. These people are good, Malone."

"They're bad, Locke."

"Well, bad but good. What the boy did isn't all that big a deal, really."

"So far as we know," Malone says. "But fuck that kid. It's on you now to find him, Locke."

Locke shakes his head. "Officer," he says. "You don't know anything about me."

"You're right about that." Malone cradles her bad arm with her other. "Don't take this personally, Agent, but I hope our paths never cross again." She starts to leave, then stops and turns back to Locke. "On second thought," she says, "do take it personally."

———

Malone steers her car with one arm past the cemetery gates.

The road curves into a shallow rise. She parks at the crest and steps outside. Lake Michigan glistens in the sunny distance. The grave is a few steps away, beneath an oak. Malone kneels before the headstone lying flush with the trimmed grass:

LOUISA JOSEPHINE BRECHER

She starts to whisper her customary prayers—an Our Father, a Hail Mary, a Glory Be—but stops in the middle of the first at "Forgive us our trespasses as we forgive—"

She leans down and lays her hands flat on her daughter's headstone. A sob escapes her, then another. "LouLou," she says, barely a whisper. She hears the gentle surf washing up on the shore below. How Louisa loved to swim in the big lake.

"LouLou. Honey. Please forgive me. I've done—I'm doing—my best. Please, please forgive me."

51

Carey's phone is ringing again. She sees the number, turns the phone facedown on the café table.

"Hi."

She looks up. "Jonah," she says, accepting his over-the-shoulder hug. "Glad you came."

He nods at the phone. "Pete again?"

"Yeah. I don't want to talk to him just yet."

Jonah sits. "You heard about the bar."

"How the hell did that happen?"

"Who knows? Boz just up and disappears, and Pete suddenly owns a bar. The cops are all over it."

Carey says, "Just what Pete needs, huh? A liquor license. You gonna order something?"

"In a minute. I don't think I've ever been in a place that sells bikes *and* coffee."

"Very hipster."

"Give Bleak Harbor two years, we'll have one too."

"I'm sure."

"What is this neighborhood again? Lakeshore?"

"Lakeview. Even though you can't really see the lake."

"How long will you stay?"

"I got it online till the end of the month. Then we'll see."

"But you're glad to be back in Chicago."

Carey sighs and sips her tea. Jonah reaches across the table for her free hand. "You haven't heard from Danny?"

She pushes something across the table. Jonah picks it up. "A cherry stem?" he says.

"I found it stuck in his laptop last week. I don't know why; I just kept it."

"OK."

"He sent me a text this morning. He says he's all right."

"That's good. He hasn't called?"

"He keeps saying he will when the time is right. Whenever that is."

"Can't the police trace the texts?"

"Fuck the police."

Jonah lets that sit there for a few seconds, then says, "You've got to come back, Carey."

"Does anyone know you're here?"

"No."

"Nobody followed you?"

"The Bleak Harbor Police?"

"What about Hamilton?"

"Hamilton. As soon as the national media started calling it a fiasco, she disappeared. Reminds me, I did see the chief last night at a budget meeting. He said to tell you they're on it twenty-four seven."

"Well, now, that is a relief."

Carey pushes her teacup to the side and reaches into the purse hanging on the back of her chair. She pulls out another phone, looks to see if she missed anything. She didn't. "His texts come on these disposables," she says. "He FedExed me a box of them."

"No way."

"He thought of everything, Jonah."

"Was there a postmark?"

"Yeah." She chuckles sourly. "Hingham, Massachusetts."

"Hingham?"

"Think."

"Shit. The patriarch?"

"The esteemed birthplace of the esteemed Joseph Estes Bleak, founder of Bleak Harbor."

"You don't think he's really in Massachusetts, do you?"

Carey shakes her head. "I wish I knew. Speaking of the Bleaks, how is Serenity?"

"Hard to say. She hasn't returned my calls. I spoke briefly with one of her lawyers. There's apparently some problem with her finances. He wasn't too specific."

Carey's real phone starts ringing again. Jonah stands and says, "I'm gonna get a coffee. Want anything?"

"I'm good."

She turns the phone back over. The area code is 616. Probably not Pete. She answers. "Hello?"

"Mrs. Peters?"

She doesn't recognize the voice. It sounds like an older man's. "This is Carey Peters."

"I'm terribly sorry to bother you, Mrs. Peters."

"Carey, please. Who is this?"

"Carey, of course. My name is Brian Doyle. I teach literature at Kalamazoo College. In Michigan."

Carey turns to see Jonah waiting in line between two young women with baby strollers. "And?"

"Well, it's this. I happen to know your son a little, in a sort of side-long way, and I just wanted to call to say I'm so sorry—"

"Excuse me? You know Danny?"

"I do, I mean, not well, a little. We corresponded via email."

Carey sits upright, pressing the phone against her ear. "Do you know where he is? Have you heard from him?"

"No, no, I don't. I wish—no. I haven't heard from Daniel for at least a few weeks."

"Why didn't you come forward—I'm sorry, what was your name again?"

"Call me Doyle. I did try to call you last week, just after Danny was kidnap—that is, disappeared. There was no answer. Maybe I should have left a message."

Everything crashes over Carey again, as it does whenever her phone rings, she walks past a TV, she walks the beach on Lake Michigan. Danny tricked her, tricked Pete, tricked them all. But more than anything, Danny is gone, and she has no idea where.

"Carey?" Doyle says. "Are you there?"

"Yes," she says, swiping a damp cheek. "Why were you emailing with Danny? Forgive me, but it's weird."

"I understand. Please rest assured there was nothing untoward about it. Danny actually reached out to me. He is—"

"He reached out?"

"—such a smart and wonderful boy, Carey. Honestly, I had no idea until I saw the newspaper stories that he was autistic."

Autistics can be as smart and wonderful as anyone, Carey thinks, but she says, "Why did he contact you?"

Jonah sits across from Carey with a latte in a foam cup. He mouths, "Danny?"

Carey shakes him off.

"As I said, I teach literature," Doyle says. "Mostly poetry, and especially the poetry of Wallace Stevens."

"Danny emailed you about Wallace Stevens?"

Jonah leans in closer.

"Yes, several months ago. Daniel has such an enthusiasm for Stevens's poetry, and—"

"Danny. Nobody calls him Daniel."

"Oh, apologies. He never corrected me."

Carey looks at Jonah, seeking comfort. "Go on. Wallace Stevens. How did Danny even find you?"

"Google, I assume. One of my essays comes up quite prominently in searches for Stevens. I'm sure you knew of Daniel—Danny's appreciation of Stevens's verse."

"Yes. I did. But you said 'poems,' plural, not singular."

"Why, yes. He was especially fond of 'Sunday Morning.' Also 'The Man with the Blue Guitar.'"

Carey struggles to remember the name of the poem that had ice cream in it. She feels her heart breaking. "I see."

"For such a young man, your son has an unusually profound understanding of Stevens's work, if a little personal. But that's how we all read poetry, isn't it? The best poets don't have a fixed meaning in mind, they leave spaces for the readers' imagination. And Danny had quite—well, you know."

"Can you excuse me a moment?"

She presses the phone against her chest. She closes her eyes. She's remembering the text that Jeremiah sent her as she was driving back from Valparaiso. That actually came from Danny:

u quit on people its in yr blood.

"Carey?" Jonah says.

She shakes her head, gets back on the phone. "I'm sorry, Mr. Doyle, but I'm afraid I'm going to have to report this to the police. Please don't call me again. Goodbye."

"Who was that?" Jonah says.

"No one."

Carey tells herself she will not cry. She sets her phone down, picks up the disposable in both hands, and breaks it in half with a sharp crack. "What are you doing?" Jonah says. She unloops her purse from the chairback and stands.

"Sorry," she says.

"Sorry for what?"

"The palm."

"The palm?"

"The palm. The palm is a fucking tree," she says. "And it really is forever out of reach."

52

"I've been learning about snails."

"Snails?"

"The lake here is shaped like a snail."

"The lake where?"

"Snails can just crawl into their shell and hide for a while."

"Are there dragonflies?"

"Yes. Big ones."

"Where are you, honey?"

"Where are you, Mother?"

"Chicago. I have an appointment tomorrow with the police."

"You did nothing wrong."

"They want to talk about you."

"So I will not put you in the position of having to lie."

"What about your meds? You must need more."

"I am fine."

"I miss you."

"I have been avoiding the internet, but I did hear that your former boss is encountering some legal trouble."

"That reporter did a number on him in the *Trib*. I guess she got hold of some documents. You wouldn't know anything about that, would you, Danny?"

"She is an exceptional journalist."

"Uh-huh. I can't say I mind that Pressman is finally getting his."

"And Gordon Michael Baron got away."

"Who?"

"You know him as Quartz."

"That's his real name?"

"Nobody knows where he is, do they?"

"Just like you."

"Has he tried to contact you?"

"No. The last I saw of him, he was running into the woods off the beach where Boz picked Spitler and me up."

"I suppose he is the one who took over my Twitter account."

"Your what?"

"At drewthenobody."

"That was you?"

"That was Jeremiah. Now it is Quartz. So he is out there."

"Does that frighten you?"

"Not too much. Gordon Michael Baron liked me. What about the FBI agent?"

"Which one?"

"The one who was harassing you. Mr. Locke."

"One of Pressman's guys shot him in the mansion. I heard he woke up in the hospital screaming for Quartz."

"It really is a connected world."

"Excuse me?"

"You will see."

"When? Where are you? I won't tell anyone."

"Soon enough. I have to go now."

"No, Danny, wait. I have so much I—wait. Why in the world would you give Quartz that money?"

"He did not get any money."

"When we were up in the house, you said he was getting one million, one hundred, whatever it was."

"Yes. I lied. Apologies."

"Why that amount, though?

"Think, Mother. Eleven eleven."

"My birthday?"

"Obviously. Sometime in the near future, you will receive notification of a new bank account in your name. I would not tell the police about it just yet."

"Danny."

"What of Mr. Spitler?"

"Unemployed and spending a lot of time with lawyers."

"But he has not been charged with any crime?"

"I don't think the cops understand what happened, Danny. Do you?"

"I have to go."

"Not before you tell me why."

"Why what?"

"Why you did this. Why you kidnapped yourself and put me and Pete and everyone else through all this."

"Why did you kill Paddle?"

"Paddle? That is not fair."

"Why did they kill young Jeremiah?"

"This is ridiculous. You did all this because a dog died? Because somebody drowned half a century ago?"

"Why did they close the mills? Why did they abandon everybody who made that town what it was?"

"Danny. I never would abandon you. Never."

"It all could have been much worse."

"Never in a million years."

"But look: You will be OK. Pete will be OK."

"I will not be OK until I see you again, safe and sound."

"You will. In the meantime, you can let Pete go."

"He is still my husband. And your stepfather."

"That is not what this is about, Mother."

"What?"

"Did you think I was trying to get you two to be happy together? Would everything be all right if that was why I did what I did?"

"It's not all right."

"Correct. I have to go now. I have work to do."

"Honey."

"Remember: 'They flit about the sunny sky like flowers that can fly.'"

"Danny."

"I have a plan. I love you, Mommy."

"Danny, please—"

Feds Investigating Mysterious Bank Deposits

"Free Money" May Be Linked to Autistic Boy's Disappearance

By Michele Higgins of the *Chicago Tribune*

Federal bank and law enforcement authorities are investigating the sudden appearance of large, identical sums of money in the bank accounts of hundreds of residents of Bleak Harbor, Mich.

Deposits of $59,666.67 began mysteriously popping up in Bleak Harbor, Bleak Township and Bleak County checking accounts last week, said a federal official who spoke on the condition of anonymity. "Looks like free money to me," said Bleak Harbor mayor Jonah Bleak. He confirmed that he had received one of the deposits but declined to comment further.

Bleak Harbor is a popular summer retreat for Chicagoans. The deposits originated from bank accounts in Illinois and at least 13 other states. Officials were still getting reports of additional deposits late yesterday.

The common thread appears to be that recipients identified thus far all have lived in the Bleak Harbor area for at least 20 years, authorities said. Longtime local librarian Zelda Loiselle called it "a godsend for a single mom like me, with four kids." She said she had no idea who might have sent it.

Coincidentally or not, at least some recipients are former employees of Bleak Steelworks, which was sold decades ago to a Japanese conglomerate that later closed the factory in northwestern Indiana.

"I couldn't believe it," said Russell Brenner, 72 years old, of Saugatuck. He lost his job and pension in the sale. "It sure ain't all what I lost, but I'll take it."

Law enforcement sources said they're looking into whether the cash movements are related to the disappearance six weeks ago of 16-year-old Daniel Bleak Peters, sole grandchild of Serenity Meredith Maas Bleak, heiress to the Bleak fortune. The boy is believed to have faked his own

LOG IN OR SUBSCRIBE

ACKNOWLEDGMENTS

Thanks first to the readers of my earlier books for bugging me about the next one. I hope you liked it. Another one is coming soon. No, really, it is. Promise.

This book would have remained unseen in my laptop if it weren't for my agent, Meg Ruley (who obviously belongs with me, Gruley). My heartfelt gratitude to Meg, Amy Tannenbaum, Jessica Errera, and all their helpful colleagues at the Jane Rotrosen Agency. And thanks to Bob Dugoni for the introduction.

Liz Pearsons at Thomas & Mercer grew up in southwestern Michigan not far from my fictional town. She insists, however, that that wasn't the only thing that attracted her to the tale. I'm forever grateful to her and to Gracie Doyle, Alison Dasho, Sarah Shaw, and all the T&M folks for giving Danny, and me, a chance.

Caitlin Alexander made Danny's story better in countless ways. Headstrong writers are prone to recoil at editors who fill the margins with questions like, "Why do you say this here when you said the opposite four pages ago?" Caitlin delivered her incisive queries with gentle affection and made the rewriting invigorating and fun.

For their generous advice on hacking and hackers, thanks to my Bloomberg colleague Michael Riley; Tod Beardsley (who happens to look like Quartz) and Jen Ellis of Rapid7; Trey Ford of Salesforce.com; and my brilliantly geeky son-in-law, Andy Stoutenburgh. For cop stuff, thanks again to my sister, Kimi Crova, and my dear hockey pal, Detective John

Campbell of the Chicago Police Department. My sister-in-law Laura Nitsos helped with Spanish translations, and my old *Detroit News* colleague Bob Roach gave me some personal insight into autism. Any screwups with this material are mine and mine alone.

I had to be kicked in the ass a few times to make this book happen. Marcus Sakey embraced this duty with gusto over occasional boozy lunches, as did Jonathan Eig, Ali biographer extraordinaire. Thanks to those who read drafts and offered suggestions and encouragement: Joe Barrett; Tom Bonnel; John Brecher; Jim Casurella; Michael Harvey; Julie Jargon; David Kocieniewski; my beautiful daughter Danielle and her ex-trader hubby, Billy Leinemann (no, he's not in the medical marijuana business); Javier Ramirez; Sean Sherman; and especially Erin Malone Borba. I'm also grateful to the kind folks at Chicago's finest coffee shops—Heritage General Store, Nohea Café, and Osmium Coffee Bar—where I wrote big chunks of this book.

Nothing is possible without my family, the heart of which is my wife, Pam, who endures my bouts of insecurity and self-doubt with just enough impatience to make me think she's right—I probably ought to keep writing.

And so I will. Thank you for reading.

ABOUT THE AUTHOR

Photo © 2014 Graham Morrison, Bloomberg News

Bryan Gruley is the award-winning author of the Starvation Lake trilogy of novels. He is also a lifelong journalist who is proud to have shared in the Pulitzer Prize awarded to the staff of the *Wall Street Journal* for their coverage of the September 11 terrorist attacks. Gruley lives in Chicago with his wife, Pam. You can learn more by visiting his website at www.bryangruley.com.